HORROR ISLAND

WHERE NIGHTMARES BECOME REALITY

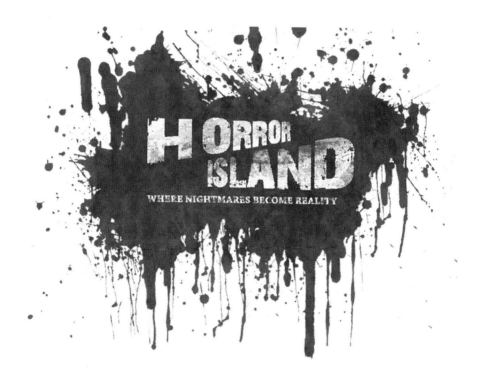

HORROR ISLAND

Where Nightmares Become Reality

Ben Hammott

ISBN: 9781980573593

Author can be contacted at: **benhammott@gmail.com**

www.benhammottbooks.com

Cover Design by Robert Ryminiecki

PREFACE

Extraterrestrial

The meteor approached Earth almost lazily at 25,000 miles per hour and entered its atmosphere at an angle of 42 degrees, which proved optimal for an object its size to survive the extreme heat peeling away its mass. The friction rapidly decreased its cosmic velocity and a few miles above the Earth's surface, it reached its retardation point. Just as the many thousands that fell to the Earth each year, the rock succumbed to gravity and arced to the ground at 200 miles per hour. Though the ocean below spread out for miles in all directions, the meteorite headed for a small patch of green and brown amongst the blue. It struck the side of a hill and threw up clods of earth and vegetation as it gouged a small trench down the slope until plopping into the stream at the bottom with a hiss of steam. The rapid change in temperature cracked the rock as it sunk to the streambed. For many years it laid dormant while the organism within fed on the nutrients the current washed over it.

Attracted by the tasty-looking, pale, worm-like tendrils waving enticingly in the water, the trout approached the algae-covered rock to which they were attached. A swish of its tail darted it forward with its mouth open to receive the food. Though the fish sensed danger when the tendrils twisted together into a single form and stretched towards it, it had no time to react. With lightning speed, the tendril worm released its attachment on the alien rock that had been its home for thousands of years and dived down its victim's throat. The fish struggled to eject the thing that squirmed inside it but failed and fell still while the alien parasite adapted to its new host. A few moments later, no longer in control of its own body, the fish swished its tail and swam away.

The male fox glanced disinterestedly at the bright moon reflected in the stream when it lowered its mouth and lapped up the cool liquid. When something leapt from the water and flopped on the grass beside it, it sprung back into a defensive stance and stared at the plump, wriggling fish. Pleased by the unexpected easy meal that would cut short its hunt, the fox pounced on the fish before it wriggled back into the water and ended its thrashing with one bite. With the meal clamped in its jaws, it headed into the undergrowth. After only a few steps, the fox convulsed, fell to the ground and lay still. A few moments later, it awoke, picked up the fish that now had a rip in its side, and headed for its den where the vixen and her newborn cubs anticipated its return.

The vixen stopped nuzzling her cubs, glanced along the dirt tunnel at the sounds of something entering her den and sniffed the air. Though at first reassured by the familiar scent of her mate, her keen sense of smell detected something else she couldn't identify. She placed herself between her cubs and whatever approached and waited for it to appear.

When the male fox rounded the bend in the passage and saw the vixen waiting with her claws extended and jaws formed into a vicious snarl, its host sensed the oncoming fight and the likely damage to the bodies it needed to make use of.

As the vixen prepared to battle her mate that was somehow different and that she sensed was a danger to her and her cubs, she crouched ready to spring. She watched her mate open his mouth wide, and before the fish he carried hit the ground, something long and pale shot from his mouth, slithered around her and squeezed. Her frantic struggles to be free from the constricting menace so she could protect her offspring were in vain, and she flopped to the ground.

The vixen's mate settled to the ground and observed the transformation that took a few minutes and ended with her barely resembling her original form. The part of him that was still vaguely conscious of what was happening, looked on in horror as the thing drew breath and roamed its evil eyes around the small den. The cubs would be next, and he was powerless to prevent it.

CHAPTER 1

Midnight Misadventure

The four passengers in the small motorboat emerged from the swirling mist cloaking the entrance to the large harbor and looked towards shore as the pilot idled down the engine and let momentum drift them towards the rickety jetty stretching out from the island. Though the trees and bushes had reclaimed much of the shoreline, hints and shapes of infrastructure were glimpsed amongst the gloom-shrouded overgrowth that the light from the full moon failed to penetrate.

When fingers of apprehension dampened Susan's enthusiasm for what they were about to do, she glanced back at the mist swirling around the gated entrance they had passed through. Her previous alcohol-inspired eagerness to visit the mysterious island they had all heard about was waning rapidly. 'An exciting adventure' the boys had called it, but she had the feeling they should never have left the large luxury cruiser moored one hundred yards away and where her parents were deep in slumber in their plush cabin.

Susan turned her worried gaze back upon the unwelcoming island. “Are you sure this is such a good idea?” she asked, hoping her friends would come to their senses and turn the small boat around.

“Yeah, it will be fun,” replied Gary. He leapt from the boat with the bowline and fended the boat off to prevent it from ramming the jetty that creaked in protest with his every movement.

Penny gripped the side of the boat that rocked violently from Gary's sloppy departure. “Don't back out on me now, Sue. I only came because you convinced me it would be fun.”

“Yeah, well, now I'm here, fun is far from what I'm thinking it will be. Maybe we should turn back or wait in the boat while the boys go exploring.”

“Oh, come on, Sue. You've come this far so you might as well go a little farther, then you can brag to your friends back at college that you've been on the island. If we get a signal, you can tweet a photo to make them all envious.” Ryan switched off the engine, threw Gary the stern line and smoothly stepped onto the jetty.

Still reluctant to step ashore, Susan gazed above the tree canopy and glimpsed ghostly shapes of the imaginative constructions born from the macabre and creative mind of their reclusive designer, Ezra Houghton.

Ryan held out a hand. “Well, are you two coming?”

Susan looked at Penny. “I'll go if you do, but if you want to wait here,” she said hopefully, “I'll stay as well.”

Penny's eyes swept the shoreline; it looked creepy as hell. "I suppose we could go a little way, and if we don't like it, run back to the boat as fast as our shapely legs can carry us."

"That sounds like a plan I can handle." Susan grabbed Ryan's hand and let him help her disembark. As soon as her feet touched the jetty, he pulled her close and pressed his lips to hers.

Penny rolled her eyes. "Don't worry about me. I'm fine climbing out on my own."

Gary rushed forward to help, but as usual, arrived when he was no longer needed. Penny wobbled from the creaking jetty put in motion by Gary's rushed enthusiasm and grabbed at his arm to stop from falling back into the boat.

"Sorry," apologized Gary, guiltily.

Penny released her grip and smiled warmly. "No harm done, and your intentions were good." She gazed along the jetty at the shore and sighed. "Let's get this done before Susan and I come to our senses."

Gary led them to the island.

Almost an hour later, Penny and Susan staggered through knee-deep undergrowth that seemed to wrap around their legs. Barbed vines reached out for them like monstrous tendrils, snagging their clothes and hair and scratching their skin. It was as if the island's vegetation was trying to prevent them from leaving. Acutely aware of the terrible consequences a fall would bring, both fought to stay upright when they stumbled on the uneven ground and rocks concealed beneath the thick vegetation.

Things, fast, heavy and vicious, crashed through the undergrowth behind them. Howls terrifying enough to instill fear into the bravest souls increased the girls' terror to the verge of panic.

During Susan's sprint across a clearing, she glimpsed moonlight reflecting off water through the trees. It had to be the shoreline. She glanced behind to check on Penny and wished she hadn't. It wasn't the look of abject terror on her friend's face mirroring her own, though that was reason enough, that prompted Susan her regret; the responsibility fell to the reason for their flight and fear. The word monster seemed to have been coined especially for the creature that leapt into the clearing and spurted for Penny with its jaw parted wide to receive her flesh. Before Susan's warning had formed on her lips, the monster was upon her friend and knocked her to the ground. Susan turned away when another of the monstrosities appeared and growled at her. She knew if she lived through this, Penny's terrified screams would haunt her for the rest of her life. There was nothing she could do for her friend now; she had her own life to save.

The beast's pounding footsteps drew nearer. Though her panic pleaded with Susan to take the most direct route to the water, she dodged amongst the trees in the hope it would slow the vicious pursuer. She now knew some of the rumors associated with the island were true and they should never have set foot on it, but hindsight wouldn't help her now. She aimed her mobile phone—as an essential part of her as a body part—behind her and clicked the take photograph icon in the desperate hope the bright light would affect the creature and slow it down.

Blinded by the sudden burst of bright light, the monster screeched and leapt to the side. It crashed into a tree and tumbled to the ground. When it regained its footing and its sight, it howled at its fleeing victim.

The glimpse of a wooden hut covered in moss and creepers gave Susan hope she might survive; it was one of the buildings they had passed earlier when they had first stepped ashore. She pictured the sign they had all read fixed between two buildings, WELCOME TO HORROR ISLAND, and underneath, a little smaller: YOUR SURVIVAL IS NOT GUARANTEED. They had made light of it at the time and had laughed; they were not laughing now.

At first, though creepy, their exploration of some of the island's strange amusements were thrilling. Susan had begun to suspect the rumors of the deaths and missing people associated with the island had been exaggerated, if they had happened at all. That changed when Gary and Ryan had entered the gaping mouth of the monster that formed the entrance of the Ghost Train ride. Though Penny's and her own bravado had increased, it hadn't reached the point that it would coax them to enter the foreboding darkness of the tunnel. They had remained outside and watched the boys' flashlight beams grow distant before they disappeared. Their screams that shortly followed had startled them, but Susan had rolled her eyes at Penny. Both thought the boys were playing about and trying to scare them. However, when they had aimed their flashlights at the thumping footsteps echoing from the ghost train entrance and saw the glowing eyes of the monstrosities rushing along the tunnel, they knew the boys' screams had been real and both were probably dead. The blood dripping from the approaching jaws was all the confirmation they needed. They had fled.

A short dash past the hut brought Susan to the jetty and the boat a short distance away. If she could reach it, she would survive. As adrenaline powered her desperate sprint along the jetty, she worked out what she had to do to get the boat moving and escape the monster chasing her.

Untie the ropes.

Push boat away and jump in.

Switch on engine and full throttle it to safety.

She could do this.

She would tell her parents what had happened.

Dad would know what to do.

She reached the gnarled wooden post the stern-line was tied to. A yank of the hanging end released the knot. Thumps shook the jetty. Susan forced herself not to look at what was coming in fear she would panic. If she panicked, she would die. The bowline wouldn't release like the first. Gary had tied a different knot. She didn't waste what little time she had untying it but slipped it off the post. The thumping footsteps grew louder, nearer. Susan silently screamed at her senses to remain calm as she gripped the side of the boat, shoved away hard and jumped in. She almost tripped on landing when the boat tipped and rolled from her clumsy boarding. Grabbing the back of the pilot seat kept her upright. She turned the key as she sat in the chair. The engine started. Thumping footsteps shaking the jetty were almost upon her. She slammed the throttle forward to its limit. The bow rose as power spun the propeller and shot it away from the jetty. The footsteps ceased. She had done it. She was safe.

The boat lurched and rocked fiercely when something heavy landed behind her. Susan sobbed and shook uncontrollably when something behind her snarled. With quivering lips and terror masking her pretty features, Susan slowly turned her head. Teeth-lined jaws filled her vision. She screamed.

CHAPTER 2

Dracula Reborn

Almost six months later...

Waylon Darcy Winslow stepped from his car he had parked in the small area set aside for visitors, stretched out the aches collected during his long drive from London and shivered from a gust of chilled, early evening air that swirled around him. His gaze drifted to his destination situated on the peak of the tree-covered hill that rose before him. Silhouetted by the setting sun, the chimney-adorned rooftops of the ancient castle stood out starkly from the tall trees it nestled amongst.

The neighing of a horse and the clip-clop of hooves redirected Winslow's gaze at the horse-drawn carriage he had been told to expect, heading down the track towards him. Except for the castle owner's car, motorized vehicles were forbidden to drive on the precarious track that wound around the hill up to the castle.

The driver perched on the front of the carriage turned the Victorian conveyance in a circle to face the track and pulled on the reins to halt the two horses under his control. He turned his head to observe the well-dressed man. The stranger looked so out of place, he had to be the person he had been tasked to bring to the castle.

"You gonna stand there all-day gorping like a townie, or yer gonna climb aboard. 'Cause if it's the former, I ain't waiting. I 'ave other things to do."

Enjoying the whole experience and glad to be out of the city for a day or two, Winslow smiled at the driver. "I have a suitcase in the car."

The carriage driver glanced at the Mercedes Benz he could never afford and back at the man wearing the hand-tailored grey suit also far beyond his means. "Yer had better grab it then, 'cause with me back the way it is, I ain't shifting me arse from this seat, however uncomfortable it is, until journey's end, or the horses bolt on the hill and drive us over the edge to our deaths."

Winslow grinned. The driver was like a character out of one of the old black and white horror movies he loved to watch. As he turned to retrieve his suitcase from the backseat, his eyes swept the top of the hill again. A self-confirmed vintage movie buff, especially horror movies, Winslow was aware the castle mostly hidden from sight was one of the settings used for the 1979 Dracula movie, and he would be spending the night there. It was the reason he had travelled so far. Normally, he would have remained in his plush London office and invited the man he had an appointment with to come to him, but he couldn't resist the opportunity of visiting the castle.

Winslow grabbed his briefcase and suitcase, beeped the doors locked and approached the carriage. He looked at the driver and nodded at his suitcase. "What shall I do with this?"

The driver glanced disinterestedly at the man's posh luggage. "Throw it off the cliff for all I care. Now 'urry up and climb aboard, or you'll find yerself alone and 'aving to walk up to me master's castle." His gaze drifted to the early evening sky. "And I warns yer, it ain't someink yer wanna be doing at night."

Winslow positively beamed. It was like he had stepped back in time. *Wonderful.*

No sooner had he climbed inside and shut the door when the carriage lurched forward, throwing him onto a seat. He left his suitcase on the floor where it had slipped from his grasp and gazed around the carriage interior. Red velvet lined almost every surface, including the ceiling. The two generously padded bench seats that lessened the jolts from the carriage's hard wheels bumping over the uneven track were upholstered in a cream-and-red-patterned material. An unlit oil lamp swung from a brass bracket in the center of the ceiling.

Winslow shifted along the seat to the window, pulled it down and peered out at the passing landscape. As the carriage wound around the ever-rising track, the drop became alarmingly steeper. He glanced worriedly at the wheels barely half an arm's length from the edge of the unguarded track and pulled his head back inside. Though concerned the driver might lose control of the horses and they would be dragged to their doom, he was determined to let nothing spoil the experience. The journey reminded him of that taken by Jonathan Harker when he went to visit Count Dracula.

Winslow's thought drifted to the reason for his journey. Though the man he would shortly meet at the castle was as much a stranger to him as the carriage driver, he did know of him. Zane Baloc was a successful author. Though the horror stories Baloc penned were a little graphic for Winslow's tastes, he recognized their appeal in today's demanding market where, it seemed, little was taboo anymore. Just like modern horror movies, graphic violence and gory scenes were now what many people demanded for their entertainment. Zane's huge fanbase, which kept him constantly on the bestseller charts, was testament to that.

Sensing they were nearing the top of the hill, Winslow poked his head out of the window again and gazed past the horses. The chill night air infused with damp mist washed over his excited features. The castle's gated entrance came into view when they rounded the track's final curve. Thick mist drifted around the gates' wrought iron scrollwork. Wide open to receive the carriage, they were supported by two brick pillars. When they drew nearer, the swirling fog disturbed by the Victorian conveyance parted to reveal the gargoyles perched like evil sentinels on the top of each brick post. Winslow tilted his head to gaze at the one on his side as they passed through the entrance. Though its stone-carved eyes lacked sight, they seemed to be staring straight at him. He turned his head to keep the gargoyle in view until the fog shrouded it from sight. Trees lining the dark, clinker-compacted driveway drove his head back inside the carriage in fear of an overhanging branch whipping his face.

The horses slowed and were steered in a shallow curve towards the building's front entrance and reined to a halt. With his face close to the window, Winslow ran his eyes over the castle's impressive sandstone facade. It was obvious the once fortified gothic-inspired castle had undergone some changes during its three-hundred-year history to turn it into a suitable home. On the front and back opposing corners, two circular towers with sharply pointed slate roofs gave it a French château appearance. The arched entrance of the porch led to a sturdy wooden door covered in strips of metal highlighted by a single dim bulb that was the only light emitted from the building. With the feeling he was being watched, Winslow swept his gaze over the dark windows, but he saw no sign of life in any.

"Yer getting out? 'Cause if yer ain't noticed, we are 'ere," called out the driver, impatiently. "And yer can leave your luggage as I'll take it ter yer room."

Winslow grabbed his briefcase, opened the door and climbed out. He looked at the closed entrance door and then questioningly at the driver.

The driver rolled his eyes. "Turn the 'andle an it'll open. The master's inside waitin'." He clucked the horses into movement and drove around the side of the castle.

Winslow shivered when a damp-laden breeze embraced him. Hoping he would receive a more hospitable welcome within, he headed for the front door. The large iron handle he turned was cold to the touch. The door creaked open atmospherically when he released his grip. His eyes swept over the entrance hall that was dimly lit by flickering electric lightbulbs fashioned to mimic candle flames. He cautiously stepped inside and glanced back at the door he expected to slam shut of its own accord. When it failed to do so, he closed it. The booming chime of an antique grandfather clock startled him when it announced the hour and echoed through the house. When the dongs faded, the ominous tick of its pendulum sounded like the castle's heartbeat.

Winslow's raised his eyes to the ceiling when footsteps creaked the floorboards above. His apprehensive gaze followed them to the top of the stairs positioned on the left side of the hall. Slowly, menacingly, the footsteps began their climb down the staircase.

The glow of a candle, its flame dancing erratically, hailed the appearance of a tall figure, who, except for a white shirt, was dressed in black. Winslow stared at the shadow-cloaked figure whose features the flame failed to shed light on.

When the figure had descended farther, he raised the candle slightly to highlight his face, smiled at his guest and held out an arm theatrically. "I am...Baloc!"

Winslow smiled on recognizing the scene and slightly altered line delivered in the exact same manner in Bela Lugosi's 1931 Dracula movie, when the count first met Jonathan Harker in a similar setting as they were in now.

Playing along, Winslow assumed the role of Jonathan Harker, and acting nervous, he recited Harker's lines. "Oh, it's really good to see you. I don't know what happened to the driver and my luggage, and well" —he raised his arms to indicate his surroundings—"with all this, I thought I was in the wrong place."

Baloc descended the stairs, placed the candle on a small table set to one side and smiled at his guest. "I bid you...welcome." He turned away with a flick of his cloak and headed for a nearby door, which creaked loudly when he pushed it open. A wave of his arm bade his visitor to enter.

Winslow halted mid-step when wolves bayed loudly, as if they were in the room. His eyes flicked to the small Bluetooth speaker beside a tall cupboard to the left of the entrance. Though inwardly smiling, he contrived an outward anxious appearance when he turned back to his host expectantly.

Baloc didn't disappoint. Keeping in the role of Lugosi's Dracula, he stared at Winslow. "Listen to them…Children of the night…What music they make."

Enjoying himself immensely, Winslow refrained from clapping his hands and shouting out, bravo! Baloc's impression of Lugosi's Dracula was flawless. He instead feigned Jonathan Harker's nervousness and entered the room.

For a moment, the unlit room fell to darkness when his host closed the door, shutting out the candlelight spilling in from the hall. Winslow squinted when lights sprung to life around the room.

Baloc crossed to a sideboard adorned with drink decanters. "You were very good," praised Baloc, shedding his Lugosi impression.

"As were you," complimented Winslow. "Your inflection, tone and mannerisms were faultless. It was as if Lugosi's Dracula had been resurrected."

Baloc swept his cloak theatrically when he bowed. "Thank you. It's a role I had always wanted to recreate. When I learnt that you were a vintage horror buff and a fan of the old Dracula movies especially, I couldn't resist. I also believed you would appreciate it."

Winslow beamed. "I did, immensely, and thank you for going to the trouble. Your castle is a perfect setting to recreate Dracula's iconic first words. And, of course, this castle was one of the settings in the 1979 production of Dracula."

"It was indeed," Baloc confirmed. "An ideal home for a horror writer, don't you think?" He held up the decanter from which he had just poured himself a drink. "Whisky?"

Winslow nodded. "Please, and yes, perfect I should imagine."

Baloc poured a second drink for his visitor. "Did you also appreciate your driver?"

Winslow's eyebrows rose. "That was also a set up?"

"He was." With a wave of his hand, Baloc indicated one of the four armchairs in the room. "Please, sit." Baloc handed his guest a glass and sat in the chair opposite the chair chosen by his guest. "As well as a good friend who is willing to suffer my little whims, Henry is also my gardener and odd jobs man. I inherited him with the castle." He swept an arm around the room. "An ancient building like this needs constant maintenance; I'd be lost without him. Henry is also an accomplished cook, as you will soon find out as he is preparing our dinner."

"I thought Henry was wonderful, very authentic. You must tell him he played his part extremely well."

Baloc dismissed the thought with a wave of his hand. "He'll only get bigheaded if I do." He looked at his guest with a serious gaze. "So, Mr. Winslow, I am hoping you bring me the good news I have longed to hear, that Ezra has finally decided to sell me his island."

Winslow took a sip of his drink before placing it on the coffee table between them. "Please, call me Darcy."

"Then you must call me Zane."

"As you wish, Zane. Before I explain my reason for arranging this meeting, I assume by your question that, like most people, you are unaware of Ezra's passing."

Baloc leaned forward. "Ezra's dead! Though I'm not sure why that surprises me, but it does. He must have been in his nineties."

"Ninety-six, actually. He died three months ago. The funeral was a quiet affair held at the family estate."

"If Ezra's dead, why are you here? Please let it be because the island is for sale?"

"The island is definitely *not* for sale."

Baloc's face dropped, his dream of owning Ezra's infamous island dashed.

Winslow opened his briefcase and pulled out some papers. He sorted through them and handed a stapled bundle to Baloc. "The island is not for sale, because it's yours; Ezra left it to you in his will."

Slightly dumbfounded, Baloc gazed at Ezra's lawyer. "Why would he do that after refusing to sell it to me on many occasions?"

"As I am sure you are aware, Ezra had no shortage of money, so that was never a consideration when he refused your offers. The reason he kept hold of it was that the island had claimed too many lives for him to take the risk of letting anyone else set foot on it again. However, with the recent deaths of the four teenagers, he knew something had to be done to prevent the island claiming any more casualties. He was working on this problem when he fell ill, a heart attack that he never fully recovered from."

"That doesn't explain why he bequeathed it to me."

"Though the island is legally yours, it comes with certain conditions."

Baloc looked at the man suspiciously. "And these conditions are?"

Winslow pointed at the documents Baloc held but had yet to read. "Everything is set out in that document, which if you agree to the terms, you will have to sign to take ownership of the island.

I'll run through the main points, but first, did you know Ezra was a fan of your work?"

Surprised by the revelation, Baloc replied, "I had no idea."

"He read all your books and watched the movie adaptions, but I digress. One of the conditions of the ownership documents is that you agree to engage the services of professional hunters to go to the island and hunt down the monsters responsible for the deaths that have occurred there."

Baloc's eyebrows rose higher than they had ever done previously. "Monsters?"

Winslow nodded. "Yes, Ezra was adamant there are monsters on the island, or at the very least, a new species of apex predator unique to the island."

"That's crazy," scoffed Baloc. "I can believe dangerous animals are on the island—big cats, bears, wolves or such—but not monsters."

"I wouldn't be so quick to dismiss the possibility." Winslow handed Baloc a photograph. "This was on one of the teenager's phones found in the drifting dinghy."

Baloc stared at the image. Though out of focus, starkly lit and blurred by movement, there was no mistaking the predator eyes and the rows of sharp teeth. He turned it this way and that, trying to make sense of the details, but it was impossible to tell what species of animal it might be. "I agree it doesn't look like any animal I recognize, but the quality is so bad it could be anything and most likely not the image of a monster."

Winslow shrugged. "That's as may be, but it falls to you to interpret the image as you see fit. I am here to inform you of Ezra's wishes."

Baloc held out the photo.

"Keep it, it's yours. Another condition of the will is that you must write a book about what you find on the island."

"A book?"

"Yes, one of your horror novels. As I mentioned, Ezra was a fan of your stories and would like you to write one about what you find on the island and what he built there."

Baloc smiled and shook his head. "That's the reason I wanted to buy the island, to write a horror story about it."

"Then both of your wishes will come true," stated Winslow. "That is about it concerning the conditions, but I recommend you have your lawyers read through it before signing..."

He stopped at the sound of pen scrawling on paper. Baloc was flicking through the document signing each page.

"   or not."

"I've waited too long to gain possession of Ezra's island to risk my lawyers ruining it for me with legal mumbo jumbo." He handed the signed document to Winslow. "Is that it? The island's mine now?"

Winslow nodded, "For better or worse, it is. I have the island's blueprints and other paperwork back at the office, which I will send to you on my return."

Baloc held out his hand. "I had a good feeling about you when you made the appointment, Darcy, and I'm glad to say you haven't let me down. If I can return the favour, you only have to ask."

Winslow clasped Baloc's hand and shook. "There is one more condition I haven't mentioned, and to tell you the truth, something I persuaded Ezra to add."

Baloc sat back in his seat. "Well, what is it, my friend?"

"I am to accompany you to the island to ensure Ezra's wishes are carried out."

Baloc grinned. "I have the feeling someone is yearning for an adventure. Of course, if you aren't worried about Ezra's monster, you are most welcome."

"I wouldn't say the thought doesn't cause me some concern, but for years I have been dying to see what Ezra built on that island and this is likely to be my only chance. Apparently, it's a whole range of different movie sets he constructed, at great expense, for the movies he never made. From what I have seen on the blueprints, they should be quite spectacular."

"Glad to have you onboard, Darcy. You never know, you might end up being a character in my book featuring Ezra's mysterious island."

Winslow smiled. "As long as I survive past the epilogue."

Baloc smiled a little evilly for effect, and again mimicking Lugosi's Dracula, said, "My friend, the world is full of monsters. The trick is to know those that are illusory from those that should be feared."

Baloc glanced at the clock on the mantelpiece.

"Dinner will shortly be served, so let's relocate to the dining room before Henry comes looking for us, and afterwards I'll give you a tour of my humble abode."

"Thank you, I'd like that very much." Winslow followed Baloc from the room.

CHAPTER 3

A Job Proposal

Wendy Monroe slipped through the subway train's doors and pulled her coattail clear just before they thudded together. She let out a relieved sigh and glanced both ways along the carriage. Pleased to see she had beaten the rush-hour sardine-packed crowd, she crossed to one of the many empty seats on offer. After ensuring the seat was free of gum and any staining substance, she sat as the train lurched into movement. She slipped the phone from her handbag and checked for any new messages and emails. Pleased to discover nothing needed her urgent attention, she returned the phone to her bag and swept her eyes around the almost empty carriage. Her gaze ended on the bold headline of the newspaper discarded on the seat across the aisle. Intrigued enough to read more, she stretched across for it. Careful to avoid getting newsprint on her white coat, she held the newspaper out as she read the story:

NEW OWNER FOR HORROR ISLAND

Zane Baloc, the bestselling novelist famous for his horror stories based on actual events and the successful spinoff movies, is the new owner of the infamous Horror Island situated over one hundred miles west of Costa Rica.

When asked about his obsession for buying the Island associated with many deaths and strange disappearances, the author joked it would make a perfect holiday home for a horror writer. When pressed, Baloc revealed the island would be the basis for his next novel, and he was considering staying there while he wrote it to soak up the atmosphere.

Controversy surrounds the island purchased fifty-eight years ago by failed film director, Ezra Houghton. Ezra believed the secluded island was the perfect setting for a series of creepy horror-themed movie spectaculars he planned on filming. He is quoted as saying, '*...they will astound and shock the world and will be the greatest horror films ever recorded on celluloid and would both scare and thrill cinemagoers.*'

To realize his directing dream, it is rumoured Ezra spared no expense in constructing movie sets for his actors to play out their roles. So encompassing were Ezra's ideas for his movies, it took him almost seven years to complete. The closing days of construction were plagued with delays, injuries, and two deaths, which caused workers and contractors to vacate the island in fear of their lives. His workforce returned only when a team of armed specialists were hired to protect the workers and bonuses were offered. It seemed none of them wanted to stay on the island longer than necessary, however good the wages, and Ezra's grand schemes were completed ahead of schedule.

On October 31st 1965, the actors, actresses, technicians and staff, which included makeup artists, cameramen, sound engineers and the small army of specialists Ezra had hired to star in and make his movie extravaganzas, were shipped out to the island. During the special first-night Halloween horror spectacular Ezra had laid on to welcome his chosen professionals, five people died under horrific circumstances. The survivors fled from the island on the ship that had brought them there a few hours before. The only two bodies recovered had, it seemed, injuries that could only have been caused by wild animals. The coroner's report held bears or large cats responsible as he was at a loss what other species could have inflicted such savage wounds.

To save his movie dreams, Houghton sent seven hunters to the island to track and kill the beasts responsible, but only one managed to get off the island alive. He was so traumatized by what he had witnessed, he never spoke again except for the word, MONSTERS. He was later committed to an insane asylum. When no one in the movie business would set foot on the island after the horrific Halloween events, Houghton had no choice but to abandon his movie director dreams and his island and suffer his losses.

Since its abandonment, the island has become infamous with rumours of bizarre creatures, strange events and disappearances. The latest fatalities assigned to Horror Island legend happened almost six months ago, when four teenagers cruising aboard a luxury yacht owned by one of their parents, John Frobisher, had moored near the island for the night. The teenagers, who no doubt thought exploring the island would be a fun adventure, snuck off in a dinghy when their guardians were asleep. When the adults aboard the boat discovered the teenagers' absence, a search ensued. The missing dinghy was discovered near the shore, and when retrieved, it was found spotted with blood that was later identified as belonging to Susan Frobisher.

When authorities carried out a brief search of the island, the nervous officials were wary of travelling too far away from the shore and spending too much time there. According to the investigating authorities, traces of blood that were later confirmed as that of the other missing teenagers, was evidence they had suffered wounds serious enough to bring about their demise. The search, much to the protests of the parents, was abandoned and no bodies were ever recovered.

Refusing to accept the death of their children on such flimsy evidence, the parents hired a small team of professionals to investigate the island, but they were never seen again, forcing the parents to accept their children's fate.

Houghton, who had become a recluse, died of natural causes three months ago. He bequeathed the island to Zane Baloc, who had apparently contacted Ezra on many occasions with offers to purchase his Horror Island, offers that had always been refused.

It remains to be seen if the famous author becomes another casualty to add to the list when he visits the infamous Horror Island.

Wendy stared at the image of Baloc included with the story. Dark receding hair that seemed to have been styled to accentuate his large forehead, dark bushy eyebrows and small, piercing eyes that gave the effect they could peer into your soul and discover all your secrets and fears fit perfectly with his narrow face, slightly too large nose, wide mouth and cleft chin. Though he would never be labelled as handsome, his dark, smouldering, almost creepy appearance ideally suited his chosen profession as a horror writer.

Wendy placed the newspaper on the empty seat beside her and wondered how much Zane Baloc had offered for the island he eventually got for free. She imagined, even with the controversy surrounding it, it must have been a million or more. She sighed. She couldn't even afford to get her old banger of a car repaired—the reason why she was on the subway.

She vaguely remembered reading one of Baloc's books. Something about a family haunted by the entity of a past resident of the house they had recently moved into. Though it might have been loosely based on fact, from what she remembered reading, the author must have embellished it out of all proportion as she was certain the events in the book couldn't have taken place as described. Still, true or not, Baloc's fans lapped up what he wrote.

Maybe I should become an author. Wendy smiled at the thought. *What would I write about? My work? Yeah, a book about* structural *engineering would really sell millions of copies.*

She sighed again as the train began to slow when it approached her stop.

As if to rub it in, when she stepped onto the platform she was confronted by a large poster with the smirking Zane Baloc displaying a copy of his latest book, *Sarcophagus*. As she passed, his dark penetrating stare seemed to follow her. She stuck out her tongue at him and turned away.

*****

Zane Baloc ran his eyes over the large blueprints spread out on a table and occasionally shook his head in fascination of what Ezra Houghton had designed and constructed on his infamous island. *With his twisted imagination, if the man had ever turned his hand to writing fiction, he could have written spine-tingling horror.*

Like many others, Baloc had always wondered what exactly Ezra had spent so many years building on the island. Although rumours had surfaced, the workforce and the few visitors who had experienced it firsthand were unable to confirm or elaborate on them, as all had signed ironclad nondisclosure agreements with crippling financial penalty clauses for those who broke it. He strolled along the line of blueprints laid out on the tables. Each detailed a construction of Ezra's movie sets, or *horror experiences* as the man often referred to them. Some rose into the sky and others stretched below ground. This, though, wasn't everything. As Houghton's lawyer, Winslow, had explained, Ezra added and altered things on the go without always recording his impromptu alterations on the plans. Winslow also revealed Ezra had set aside a group of workers on a secret construction that no one else had seen, which increased Baloc's craving to find out what had been done. Excited to visit the island that was now his, Baloc glanced at his watch; his visitor should arrive shortly.

Five minutes later, his personal assistant knocked on the door and entered. "Miss Monroe has arrived."

"Thanks, Karen, please show her in."

Karen opened the door wide and admitted the visitor, who stopped as if in shock at seeing the man before her.

Baloc smiled when he crossed to the door. “Hello, Miss Monroe, please come in, I don’t bite.” He was always surprised by the effect his notoriety had on fans and people in general, though to be fair to Miss Monroe, she hadn’t been notified her appointment would be with him.

“What? No, of course you don’t bite,” said Wendy, flustered by the unexpected encounter with the well-known author who had been so recently in her thoughts.

She shook his offered hand before being led over to the tables and gazed at the blueprints Baloc halted by.

“Are these of Ezra’s island?” she asked.

Baloc nodded. “Amazing, aren’t they? Please, feel free to examine them. That is why you are here, after all.”

Creases crinkled Wendy’s brow in puzzlement. “I don’t understand.”

Baloc smiled. “Before I explain, would you like tea, coffee, fruit juice or water?”

Wendy shook her head. “I’m not thirsty, thanks.”

Baloc glanced at his assistant in the doorway. “That’s all for now, Karen.”

Karen closed the door on her way out.

Baloc crossed to the table where Wendy examined one of the blueprints. “As you recognized the nature of the plans so quickly, I assume you’re aware I am the island’s new owner, and along with it, Ezra’s horror-themed movie sets.”

“Not until a few minutes ago, when I read about it in a newspaper on my way here, which stretches the bounds of coincidence further than I’m used to. But why am I here?”

"I need a structural engineer who specializes in the island's constructions to survey the sites and tell me if they are safe or about to collapse. It's been abandoned since 1965 and satellite photos indicate Mother Nature hasn't wasted her time reclaiming some of the land and buildings."

Wendy shook her head. "That's not possible, Mr. Baloc. It doesn't matter how detailed these plans or the satellite photos are, there's no way I or anyone can evaluate their true condition from them."

"I wouldn't expect you to. That's why I want you to join me and my small team on the island."

It took a few moments for Wendy to recover from the shock. "You want me to go to Ezra's island?"

"I do. I'll pay you well for your time, of course."

Wendy strolled past the tables examining the blueprints. "I don't know, Mr. Baloc..."

"Please, Wendy, call me Zane."

Wendy continued, "All of this is very unusual and a bit outside my or anyone's realm of expertise. You would be better off contacting the original foreman in charge."

"Alas, I can't. He's dead. Ezra oversaw every stage of the construction personally to ensure everything was built to his exact requirements. What I understand from his lawyer and the papers I received, separate groups of workers only worked on one particular part to speed up construction."

"As I'm sure you know, or I wouldn't be here, I am a structural engineer and safety inspector specializing in tourist attractions and public buildings." Her hand swept over the blueprints. "This might look like a theme park, but it's no Disneyland. Proper tourist attractions must adhere to certain associated building standards and strict codes of practice to protect the visitors who engage in the activities on offer. Ezra, on the other hand, was far from prying eyes and had no one looking over his shoulder to ensure he followed correct construction procedures. He could have done what he liked, how he liked, cutting corners left, right and center to get the job done."

"Yes, that is possible, which is why I want you to come and check it out for me. We go there, you have a wander around, poke about a bit and report on your findings. When you are done, you fly back home with a nice fat fee in your bank account. So, Wendy, what do you say? Are you in?"

"I'm still not sure I'm the person best qualified for the task. You should try Hank Peterman. He's the best in the business."

"I already did. He's not interested."

Wendy looked at Baloc suspiciously. "Henry Jones is a good second best."

Baloc shook his head. "He also declined."

Wendy narrowed her eyes at Baloc.

"Rodney Carter."

Zane shook his head.

"Tim Kingsman, Jane Fredricks, Louis Granger."

Baloc's head continued shaking.

Wendy glared at Baloc. "I have the suspicious feeling that I was nowhere near the top of your preferred list of structural engineers."

Baloc smiled guiltily. "To be fair, it wasn't me that made the list and I'm sure the order of names is in no particular preference. Yours could have easily been at the top."

Wendy didn't believe him. "Out of interest, in just what position did I appear?"

Baloc walked to his desk, picked up a piece of paper and glanced at it. “You were quite near the top, actually.”

Wendy snatched the list from his hand, examined it and huffed. “The only way my name would be anywhere near the top is if I turned the list upside-down. I can’t believe you put me below Robert Peters. He barely passed his exams.”

“Please, Wendy, as I said, the list was random. That’s why your name wasn’t near the top—”

“Come on, second from the bottom is not exactly a confidence booster, is it?”

“I suppose not, but you’re here now. Let’s forget about the list.” He tugged it from her grip, screwed it up and threw it in the wastepaper basket.

“Out of interest, why did the others decline?”

“Various reasons, work, family commitments, didn’t want to travel so far and”— Baloc studied Wendy to gauge her reaction— “some were worried about what had happened on the island before.”

“Yeah, well, it’s a concern of mine also. People have died or gone missing on that island, some only a short time ago. What assurances do you have, *if* I decide to go, the same thing won’t happen to me or the other members of your team?”

“I assure you, Wendy, I have studied the deaths attributed to the island, and though some were proved to have happened, it’s not as many as people believe. I have also talked to a couple of the surviving members of the original batch of workers Ezra sent to the island and who fled after... seeing things.”

Wendy paused her flitting from blueprint to blueprint and looked at Zane. “What sort of things?”

Baloc shrugged. "There's the rub. The creatures appeared mostly at night. No one who wasn't killed got a good look at them, only shadows moving through the darkness. The only descriptions are evil eyes, big teeth, long sharp claws, big as a bear, fast as a tiger and the size of a wolf. Extrapolating from this information and allowing for fear to cloud witnesses' judgment, I, and the experts I consulted, concluded there are either bears, wolves or big cats, or all three species, on the island. Furthermore, it seems they weren't afraid of humans and looked upon them as food. This was probably due to the limited amount of food sources on the island, given its size—six miles at its longest point and half that wide.

"However, there is a problem with this theory as the experts believe it's doubtful wolves would be able to survive on such a small piece of land cut off from the mainland. They are pack animals and carnivores, meaning their prey would soon be diminished. A single mating pair of bears might be able to exist because their diet consists mainly of vegetation, leaves, roots, berries, etc., and the occasional animal they caught, though there is a problem with this also, which I'll explain in a minute. The big cat theory, though possible if confined to a single mating pair and game, like deer, rabbits, rats and other similar sized fast-breeding mammals were in plentiful supply, the experts thought it unlikely. With no diverse gene pool to mate from, problems would soon arise, which would include low fertility, deformities and genetic diseases. This would also apply to the bear theory and even the wolves."

"If the experts told you there couldn't be bears, wolves or big cats on the island, then what's doing the killing?" asked Wendy.

"It could still be one or more of these species, if they were introduced to the island around the time Ezra's building work got underway."

"That doesn't make sense. Who would take those kinds of animals to the island? It couldn't have been Ezra as he wouldn't risk them killing the workers or his actors."

"It's impossible to say what Ezra did or didn't do as he wasn't an avid record keeper and much of what he did on the island is still a mystery. That's one of the reasons I am so keen to visit. However, I don't think it matters how or when they got there, only that they might be. Whatever species is responsible for the killings can be hunted and killed. To this end, as we speak, professional hunters, who came highly recommended, are heading to the island to begin stalking and killing the animals responsible."

"Didn't Ezra hire a group of hunters to do the very same thing and only one of them survived, and he went mad?"

"He did, but Ezra went to the nearest town on the mainland, walked into a bar and offered five hundred dollars, a huge amount in those days, for every dangerous creature killed on the island. I doubt any of them were professional hunters."

"That's as may be, but it's still a concern. I could be risking my life stepping foot on that island."

"Life is a risk, Wendy, but we won't go until the hunters give us the all clear. Also, if you decide to come and at any time you want to back out, I will have you taken back to the mainland and you'll still get paid."

Wendy studied Zane as she pondered his proposal. She could certainly use the money. "How much are you offering?"

Baloc picked up a piece of paper from his desk and handed it to her. "I think you'll find it very generous."

Suppressing her surprise at the high figure she would get if she accepted the job, Wendy looked at Zane. "Anytime I don't feel safe, I can leave. No arguments."

Baloc put a hand to his heart. "I promise."

"I want half up front before we go," Wendy demanded. Her tone clearly stated it wasn't negotiable.

"Leave your bank details with Karen on your way out, and I'll have the money transferred today." Baloc held out his hand and smiled. "Welcome aboard, Miss Monroe."

Wendy held back sealing the deal when she realized the opportunity before her. "One last thing. I am a keen amateur photographer and quite good if I say so myself. Ezra's island is infamous and no doubt many people across the world would like to see what Ezra built on the island, so how about I photograph what we find there for a book and you have your publisher publish it?"

Baloc lowered his hand as he considered Wendy's proposal. "That's actually a good idea, but we'll have to time its release around the novel I plan to write. I'll tell you what I'll do. I'll have a word with my agent to sort out the legalities and what percentage each of us will make from the book, so bring your camera and take lots of pics and we'll talk about it later."

"That's agreeable to me," said Wendy.

"Does that mean you're coming?"

Ignoring the sense that she might come to regret her decision, Wendy held out her hand and sealed the deal. "When do we leave?"

"Everything is arranged, including the essential supplies we'll need for our stay delivered by helicopter to the island. So as soon as I receive the all clear from the hunters, our adventure will begin. To ensure no time is wasted, we will all be heading to Costa Rica tomorrow and then traveling to the small island of Isla Isabela, where we'll be staying in a four-star hotel until we hear from the hunters."

"Tomorrow! That's rather short notice."

"You are a late addition to the team. If you had declined, I would have gone without a structural engineer. Is it a problem?"

"More of an inconvenience, but I suppose after I've rearranged a few things I can make it."

Baloc beamed. "Splendid. On your way out, my secretary will furnish you with the forms to sign, the traveling details and anything else you need to know."

"Who else will be joining us on your island?"

"Apart from you, me and the hunters, there will be Ezra's lawyer, Winslow, and Mannix Hardy, the film director who is responsible for turning some of my books into movies. He wants to scout out the locations in preparation for turning the book I will write about the island into a movie."

"A horror, I assume," said Wendy.

Baloc smiled. "Of course. A cameraman, Quincy Jones, who will film the locations for future reference, will accompany Mannix. We are also toying with the idea of making a documentary about the island, so some of the film footage might be included in that. I have also arranged for an electrical engineer to join us in the hope he can get the generator working, so we'll have power. That's everyone, apart from a small security team as an added safety precaution to protect us against any surprises the island may throw at us."

Wendy was impressed. "It seems you have all the bases covered."

"Unless you have any questions, I think that's it. As we'll be leaving on the morning flight, I suggest you rush home, do what needs to be done and pack for your adventure of a lifetime."

"Though it was a shock at first, I am looking forward to it. I could do with some excitement in my mundane life."

Baloc smiled. "That's the spirit, Wendy. From the little I've learnt about Ezra, I'm certain his island will provide us all with a few thrills."

After Baloc had shown Wendy out, he returned to his office, glanced at the clock on the wall and calculated the time zone in Costa Rica. The hunters he had hired to take care of the island's predators should be on the island now. Hopefully they would make short work of tracking and killing the animals, whatever species they might be, because he was chomping at the bit to get there.

CHAPTER 4

Fear Fair

The three passengers glanced out the side windows of the helicopter as they flew over the ring of mist surrounding the island. Mountains and high hills covered in vegetation almost completely surrounded the island's flatter middle where Ezra Houghton had constructed his bizarre, horror-themed movie-land.

Ray and Laura Chase were, perhaps due to their television hunting documentary series, blog and books, the most famous and influential hunters of the modern world. When Baloc had approached them to ask if they would be willing to go to the island and hunt down its vicious animal inhabitants, they were at first disinterested. However, when Baloc had shown them the photograph of what might be an unrecorded apex predator, the couple couldn't resist the prestige of being among the first to hunt it.

Excited by the forthcoming hunt, Laura drew her eyes away from the time-dilapidated fairground they flew over and looked at her husband. "This isn't going to be like any hunt we've been on before."

Ray kept his gaze fixed on the strange landscape below. Though, like his wife he was excited at hunting a new species of predator, he was also apprehensive now that he had seen the creature's stalking grounds.

"The island might be small, but it's full of dark places for the creature to hide and set up an ambush. We also don't know if it's alone or its hunting method."

Laura, a twinkle in her eye, squeezed her husband's arm. "That's what makes it so exciting. This is a once in a lifetime opportunity." She glanced back out the window as they swooped over a crumbling mansion. "It's a shame Zane wouldn't let us bring our camera crew. It would have made for a spectacular episode of our TV show."

Ray glanced at the large African opposite when he snorted loudly. "Something wrong?"

Unmasked contempt marred Jabari Kwanza's face when he slowly turned his head and glared at Ray. "Yes, there is. *Celebrity hunters.*" He returned to gazing out the window.

Ray, unaffected by the insult, smiled. Kwanza's reputation as a skilled tracker and hunter was well known and well deserved. He might be the only man alive who had hunted and killed every species of *Africa's Big 5*: lion, leopard, buffalo, rhino and elephant.

"So, Jabari, I assume we won't be joining forces once we are on the ground."

"You do your thing and I'll do mine."

"That suits us just fine," said Laura. Though as a fellow professional she respected Kwanza's prowess as a hunter, she had taken an instant dislike to the brutish man.

"Then I guess we're all happy," stated Kwanza, shooting them a glance absent any joy.

The helicopter swooped in a circle and slowed when it flew over the village.

"We're here," stated the pilot.

Kwanza peered down at the deserted village. The long main street was edged with old buildings and intersected by a smaller street set at ninety degrees out from a square towards one end, forming a cross with a long tail. As far as he could tell, the village was positioned in the middle of the island. He directed his gaze at the celebrity duo.

"To avoid getting in each other's way, we need to coordinate our search patterns. I suggest you two search north of the village's main street and I hunt the area south."

Ray recognized the sense of Kwanza's self-proclaimed decision, which he had delivered more as an order than a suggestion. North or south made no difference to him.

"Makes sense and you have the satellite phone Zane supplied us with if you need our help."

He smiled at the glare the South African aimed at him.

The co-pilot, Emilio, pulled his headset mic nearer his mouth as he turned to the passengers. "We'll drop the supplies off and then land in the square. It'll seem a little hairy as there isn't much room to maneuver."

The pilot, Mathias, focused on the square below where they had already dropped off one pallet of supplies the day before.

Abandoned for years, there was no telling what state the buildings were in and the powerful downwash could easily rip bits off. He lined up the helicopter above the street between the buildings and coaxed the helicopter towards the clear area the crossroads of streets led from.

When the helicopter hovered above the square, Emilio moved into the back and slid open the passenger door. The deafening roar of the engine invaded the interior. He peered down at the cargo swinging below. It was right on target. “Hold it there, Mathias.”

Battered by the rotors backwash bouncing off the buildings, Mathias fought the controls to keep the helicopter steady. He glanced at the nearby rooftops as the rotors vortex stripped moss from them and swirled it around the square. He hoped the roof tiles were well fixed.

Emilio opened the winch control cover and pressed the button to feed out the cable from the winch attached to the undercarriage. When the cargo gently touched ground beside the previous delivered pallet, he opened the small hydraulic clamp that tethered them together. The ring attached to the four ends of the cables secured to the pallet clanked to the ground.

Mathias compensated for the release of the cumbersome weight that had dragged the copter down and edged the helicopter backwards. When he had reached the middle of the square, he checked the spinning rotors wouldn’t snag on anything and gently landed.

As the rotors slowed to an idle, Kwanza pulled off his headset, released his seat harness and climbed out. Even aware the helicopter’s loud engine would have scared away any creatures in the vicinity, his hunter’s eyes swept the surroundings and the sides of the canal that passed beneath the square. Though far from an architectural expert, the buildings lining the crossroad of streets seemed medieval in design and gave the impression he had stepped back in time. His scan of the area revealed shops, blacksmiths and even an inn. He moved aside when his fellow passengers disembarked.

"Quaint," commented Laura, glancing at the cute dwellings. "According to Baloc, all the houses are, or were, fully functional." She nodded at the cargo pallets across the square. "We have everything we need to make our stay comfortable, including food, water, cooking equipment, bedding and mattresses for the beds in the houses."

Kwanza humpfed. "You celebrities might be treating this as a holiday, but I won't be doing much cooking or sleeping." He grabbed his weapon bag from the helicopter and strode south along the side street.

"Not exactly a conversationalist, is he," commented Emilio, staring after the ill-mannered hunter.

"Maybe not, but he is good at what he does. A lot of hunters are loners, especially on a job like this where distraction might get you killed."

Ray took the weapon bag the co-pilot handed him and handed it to his wife. The second bag was his.

"Good luck," said Emilio.

Ray nodded. "Thanks for the ride."

"You're welcome." Emilio glanced at the creepy mansion in the distance. "I think you are mad staying on the island with no way of getting off, but I've caught a couple of your shows, so I'm sure you'll do okay."

Ray grinned. "Thanks for the vote of confidence." He stepped back when the man slid the door shut, and joined his wife, who gazed through one of the house's grimy windows.

Laura turned on hearing the helicopter rev up and watched it take off. She waved to the pilot who gave them a thumb-up sign for good luck.

Laura and Ray picked a dwelling a few doors down from the square and entered. Though a bit musty with a film of dust covering everything, it was dry and in a reasonably habitable condition.

Ray raised a cloud of dust when he dropped his bag on the two-seater couch. "I suggest we collect what gear we need from outside and then consult the map of the island Zane supplied us with to find out what's in our search area."

Laura placed her bag on the table. "Sounds good to me, darling. Maybe we can look around the immediate area to see what's what and search for any tracks that might give us a clue to what species of animal we are hunting."

"Good idea." Ray glanced at his watch. "That's about all we'll have time for today. It'll be dark in a few hours."

After they had collected some food, bottles of water, bedding and everything else they would need for their stay on the island from the supplies the helicopter dropped off, Ray spread out the map of the island on the kitchen table. He used a red marker pen to draw a line down the center of the main street and studied the north side and ran his gaze over the small village they were currently in. One end of the main street contained the industrial units Houghton required to create his movies. They included workrooms, a maintenance and machine shop, sound stage, camera, film and cinematography equipment storeroom. An editing suite and small cinema viewing room. Props, costumes and makeup and lighting departments. A large kitchen with attached dining room and dry and cold food stores. It seemed Houghton had thought of everything.

Laura joined him in looking at their search area. "It's small compared to our usual hunting grounds."

Ray, deep in thought while his eyes explored north of the village, replied, "It's not the size of the search area that concerns me, but the many places our prey can hide. The chances are, if it attacks, we won't see it coming."

"Then we'll just have to take extra care." Laura placed her arm around her husband's waist. "We make a good team and have never failed in a hunt yet."

Ray leaned in and gave her a kiss. "I know, but this hunt is like no other we have been involved with. We don't even know what species we are hunting."

Laura brushed her husband's concerns aside. They were in the top ten of the best hunters currently alive. Whatever species they hunted, they had the experience and professionalism to see it killed. "Aren't you excited by the prospect of hunting what might turn out to be a new apex predator?"

"Of course, it's a once in a lifetime opportunity. It's the unknown that worries me. But it's going to make a great episode for our TV show. The GoPro cameras we smuggled on the island to record our hunt are high definition, so we should get some fantastic footage, including, hopefully, the first film of this new predator."

Zane had forbidden any cameras except for what his own team would bring. Like Ezra, Zane didn't want information about what was on the island getting out until the time was right. He understandably wanted to save the publicity for when he had finished his Horror Island novel, but Laura and Ray had both realized the unique opportunity they had been given. When they had learned of what might be on the island, they hadn't charged Baloc for their services; they would have gladly paid him for the chance of hunting down a new predator species, so a few minutes film seemed a good exchange. Their lawyers could work out the legality of their deceit later.

"If it turns out to be a new species, I'm thinking we might get a special out of it." Laura broke her hold on her husband when he didn't comment. She knew he was committing the search area to memory. "Fancy a coffee, hon, before we set off?"

Ray dragged his eyes away from the Dollmaker's Cabin near the swamp outlined on the map and where the mud might offer the best chance of finding animal tracks. He smiled at his wife. "That would be lovely."

Laura crossed to the kitchen area and plucked a couple of cups from a cupboard. To rinse out the collected dust and the dried husk of a long-dead spider, she moved to the sink and turned a tap. She wasn't surprised when water failed to pour out. The island would be without power until Zane and his team arrived, and that was if they could get the generator working, which she doubted after so many years. She grabbed a bottle of water, filled the kettle and placed it on the small portable cooking ring fed by a connected bottle of gas, and lit it. While she cleaned the cups with bottled water in the sink, she turned to her husband, who was unwrapping one of his weapons.

"What do you think Kwanza, our friendly neighborhood hunter, will do first?"

Ray shrugged without turning around. "Whatever he damn well wants, I should think."

*****

Unlike the Chases, Kwanza wasted no time starting his hunt. He chose a house, stowed his gear inside and cleaned the weapons he would take with him on his first foray of the island. He was keen to make the first kill before the lovebird celebrities. Not that he foresaw any problems with that. He had checked them out when he heard they would be joining the hunt. Begrudgingly, he admired their hunting record, but like many who had embraced the arms of fame, they had fallen into the trap of pandering to their audience rather than the masterful skill of the hunt. Camera shots became more important than rifle shots. He shook his head in dismay. How the hell could they hunt when accompanied by a camera crew? No, he was better off alone, the way he liked it. Only him and his prey. He checked his ammo, sidearm and knife, slung his customized Mannlicher-Schonauer hunting rifle over his shoulder, and shutting the door behind him, headed south.

It wasn't long before Kwanza found a set of tracks distinct enough to follow. He passed through a forest and glanced at the faded title of the attraction he approached, WELCOME TO THE FEAR FAIR, and halted at the tall wrought iron gateway the animal trail had led him to. His eyes scanned the abandoned rides that hadn't seen activity for many years and likely never would again. His eyes flicked to the large, rusty Ferris wheel when it screamed a piercing metallic scream-like squeal when a wind gust forced it to turn slightly. He cast his gaze over the other dilapidated rides that seemed to have suffered from their long dormant state and damp weather. However, based on what he had learnt from his brief reconnaissance of the island, he suspected their decayed appearance could also be intentional, at least in part.

With his rifle held ready for action, Kwanza passed through the open gates and continued along the animal trail. The tracks, though obvious enough to indicate animals had made them, were too indistinct for him to work out the species. If he had to guess, by their size he would say wolves or large cats were responsible, but the droppings he had come across belonged to neither. The fact that he was unable to determine what species had deposited them worried him. Certain that he had the necessary firepower to kill whatever species, and however large, was responsible for the tracks, he continued with his hunt confident of the outcome.

His gaze constantly swept his surroundings, roaming over the abandoned stalls and attractions displaying their now rotten and moldy wares, and decayed prizes no one now would wish to win. The stuffed toy prizes on show at the rifle range attraction were not the cute and cuddly teddy bears and sweet dolls commonly viewed at normal funfairs in the outside world, but grotesque stuffed devils, demons, vampires, zombies and other horror-inspired facsimiles. Particularly disturbing were the similarly horror-themed ventriloquist dummy dolls, whose eyes seemed to be watching and following Kwanza when he passed. They presented the impression they might be capable of movement and evil mayhem. The mildew and creeping strands of rot covering them augmented their abhorrent appearance.

About halfway through the macabre Fear Fair, Kwanza halted at a row of carts fashioned into the heads of skulls, demons, the Grim Reaper and other nightmare inspired ghouls. They were parked near a dark opening formed by the wide-open jaws of a ferocious mythical monster that looked like it could snap shut at any moment. The rusty rails the ride carts rested upon and the animal trail he followed, led beneath the double-doors set a short distance back from the uninviting entrance. Kwanza switched on the flashlight attached to his rifle and approached the doors. He knelt before them and ran his fingers over the worn edges of the join caused by the frequent passage of animals pushing through. He plucked off the dark tuff of hair caught in a splinter of wood and rolled it between his fingers; it was coarse, bearlike. He sniffed it; musty, earthy and damp grass mingled with the stench of carrion. Whatever animal it belonged to was an omnivore, which probably explained how it could survive on such a small island where perhaps meat alone wouldn't sustain it. He tucked the hair in a pocket for later analysis and pushed the squeaky spring-loaded doors open. He stepped through, let the doors swing shut behind him and followed the cart rails that disappeared into the gloom.

Apart from giving the skeletons and monsters displayed along the sides of the track a brief inspection to check nothing waited to leap out at him, Kwanza ignored the ghoulish theatrical exhibits. When he rounded a sharp bend he almost fell into the sudden drop-off the rail dived down. He aimed his flashlight into the hole and imagined the fright of the carts' passengers when they unexpectedly nose-dived down the almost vertical drop. The air rising from the void, tainted with the acrid reek of feces, urine and rotted flesh, labeled it as the unmistakable stench of an animal's lair. He almost smiled. The hunt could be over sooner than expected.

The flare Kwanza lit fizzed into bright red fiery light, bathing the horror-themed surroundings in an appropriate bloody glow. Particularly spooky was the large devil gripping a pitchfork it thrust out, which the carts' passengers would narrowly have avoided when they plunged into the pit. He dropped the flare and watched it roll down the gradual curve at the bottom and out of sight. His search for a way down revealed the maintenance ladder set to one side. Kwanza stared into the pit as he weighed his options. Aware anything could be waiting for him below, he returned to the entrance, collected a ride cart from outside and pushed it along the rail. Abruptly awoken from their long dormancy, rusty wheels squealed in protest when they were again forced to turn. Kwanza crashed the cart through the doors and along the track. A shove sent it diving into the hole. The cart's frantic rattling of wheels on the track grew fainter until they ceased altogether. Kwanza cocked an ear and listened for sounds of any creatures the cart might have disturbed. After a few minutes of inactivity, he shouldered his rifle and climbed down.

*****

The swampy area Ray and Laura paused at was thankfully, but bizarrely, absent the mosquitos that should have thrived in this environment. The dank air was filled with the dominant stench of rotting vegetation. Their eyes roamed over the ruins of the seven wooden huts partly submerged at sloping angles in the swamp water and the thick mud surrounding it. Wooden roof tiles, warped and decaying, were covered in dark green moss and the odd growth of vegetation. The dark, eyelike window openings of some of the ramshackle dwellings peeked above the foul swamp and presented an oppressive aura.

Laura turned to her husband. "This might be the remains of the leper colony Zane mentioned?"

Ray shrugged and pointed his weapon at the nearest hut. "I doubt they would have lasted from the seventeenth century. They are probably another of Ezra's movie sets or something."

"Well, they certainly establish an ambience of despair and abandonment, which I imagine is what the unfortunate people suffering from leprosy felt when they were banished to this island."

Her eyes followed the line of bubbles that emerged from one of the hut's doorways and moved across the stagnant swamp into the tall grass at its edge, an indication something lived below the surface.

Ray's eyes and his customized M77 Ruger rifle loaded with .416 Rigby ammo swept the far sides of the swamp. A nod of his head to the left indicated his preferred route to his wife.

Laura glanced at the overgrown and uneven path of flagstones that led around the marsh towards the trees on the far side. Spying nothing to challenge her husband's choice, she followed a few steps behind. Both would need room to defend themselves if they were attacked.

With eyes and weapons constantly searching the environment, they moved through the wood and halted at the edge of a clearing and observed the small, single story cabin thirty yards distance. A warped veranda and patches of moss and lichen on its clapboard walls and sagging roof indicated time had taken its toll on the simple wooden structure that offered up an uninviting aura. They had arrived at the Dollmaker's Cabin.

The couple's eyes scanned the grassy area that stretched from the forest to the hut. Strewn with wild flowers and bushes adorned with purple berries, it was surprisingly tranquil. If there was any wildlife about, it held its breath. The L-shaped wooden cabin had a small two-story stone tower with a single opening facing the small forest they had just passed through.

Focused on the partly open door of the Dollmaker's Cottage, Laura spoke softly, "I guess we had better check it out."

Ray was of a similar mind and headed for the cabin.

Laura moved a few steps to his side and turned to protect their flank.

The steps up to the veranda that stretched the full width of the cabin's longer side creaked alarmingly when Ray climbed them, but they proved solid enough to support his weight. While Laura guarded his back a short distance from the base of the steps, Ray stood to one side of the door and pushed it fully open with his foot. Rusty hinges screeched and announced their presence to anything inside. Ray cocked an ear for any sound that would betray the movement of something alive within. He heard only the natural creaking of the ramshackle wooden structure. He switched on the bright LED tactical flashlight attached to the rifle and stepped inside.

Laura moved swiftly up the steps and guarded the entrance, her eyes skimming the growing darkness beneath the trees encircling the clearing.

Ray's gaze followed the light around the room. A table set for one with a meal never eaten stood to one side. Two of the four chairs lay overturned on the wide-planked floor. A single mildewed armchair had suffered rodent activity, leaving rips from which stuffing protruded like pale fungus. A small kitchen in the adjoining room boasted a wood-burning stove and a chipped and stained enamel sink. A corridor ran level with the front wall and at its end, a dark opening stared at him, beckoning him to enter.

Laura backed into the cabin on hearing her husband's whispered whistle, peered past him at the far doorway his rifle pointed at and nodded.

Even though they stepped softly, each footstep on the old boards emitted the creak of strained timber, almost as if it had been designed to do so. Keeping her gaze and weapon focused on the main door, Laura backed along the corridor in time with her husband's steps along the corridor.

The faint scent of feces greeted Ray when he poked his head into the small room. It came from the piles on the floor surrounding the open trapdoor. He moved nearer and poked one of the lumps with a foot. It was hard and dry, old. He cautiously leaned over the opening and shone his light into the darkness below. Wooden steps led down to another room, a basement. He stared at the scratches on the wooden treads and around the opening—claw marks. Whatever made them, it was a large predator and most likely the killer creature they sought. He knelt to see what lay in the lower room, but apart from the area around the base of the steps, the rest remained a mystery. His finger stroked one of the deep gashes in the timber floor; they didn't seem to have been made recently. He stepped away from the hole and over to his wife who had remained in the hall and quickly explained what he had discovered.

Laura glanced at the open trapdoor. "Even though there's no sign of fresh activity, we'll have to check it out sometime, so it might as well be now."

Ray nodded. "I'll go down while you remain at the top." He crossed to the opening and started his descent.

*****

The flare Kwanza lobbed along the tunnel painted the scene in a red hellish glow, a perfect highlight for the devilish scenes of tortured souls artistically painted on the walls. His light and rifle swept the tunnel as he edged forward until he stopped and aimed them at the small side passage the pungent animal scents wafted from. He approached cautiously and peered through the open door at its end. The stench, almost overpowering now, indicated the lair was close. His gaze took in the room. Shelves loaded with small pieces of machinery, spare light bulbs in rotted cardboard boxes, and other assorted maintenance items lined one side. The animal bones scattered across the floor were covered in teeth marks. His eyes focused on the door set in the far wall, and he headed for it. The powerful acrid stench stung and watered his eyes as they took in the piles of urine sodden grass spread around the room. If this was their only lair, it was small and a good indication if there was more than one, it was a small pack. Kwanza gazed around the room. *Where were they?*

Although Kwanza sensed danger, the room was empty of life. He shot a glance behind to check nothing crept up on him and was relieved to see it absent any menace. A shuffling sound lifted his gaze to the ceiling. Fear momentarily replaced his shocked expression. The ceiling was alive with movement, the numbers hard to distinguish. One of the creatures unfurled its head, snarled and bared sharp teeth before it dropped. Two bullets fired in quick succession erupted from Kwanza's rifle before the creature knocked him to the floor. A screech indicated his bullet had hit one of the creatures he feared were about to feast on his flesh, his bones to be added to the pile in the adjoining room.

The thumps of the other monstrosities landing on the floor spurred Kwanza into action. He angled the rifle at the monster straddling him, but before he could get off a shot, the foul creature ripped it from his grasp and flung it across the room. The flashlight broke when it struck the wall, bringing darkness back to the room. Kwanza held back the pained scream brought forth when the claws of the monster's large paw pinning his left arm to the ground dug into flesh. Glowing eyes and wicked teeth moved in for the kill. He inhaled the reek of the monster's fetid breath when it sniffed his face. He had a pistol and a knife, but pinned to the ground, both were beyond his reach. His free hand scrambled for his pocket, snatched out the single remaining flare and ignited it with his thumb. The bright glow revealed the open jaws above his face and the spasms of the monster's head as if it was regurgitating food. When Kwanza glimpsed the pale tendril creeping up the monster's throat, he thrust the flare at the side of its head. Its coarse, wiry hair singed. The monster roared, dodged the second blow of the burning light and snarled when it leapt away, crashing into another of its kind and spilling both to the floor.

Doubting he would have time to kill them all with the revolver before one was upon him, and aware the flare wouldn't last long, Kwanza climbed to his feet. Ignoring the pain from his wounded arm, he waved the flare from side to side while he backed through the doorway and across the bone room. His attempt to shut the door to prevent the monsters slinking towards him from following, failed when it jammed on the years of dried feces littering the floorboards. He turned, fled along the passage and entered the ghost train tunnel. Kwanza shot a glance both ways. *Left or right?* Doubting he would be able to climb the ladder before the monsters were upon him, Kwanza ran in the opposite direction.

The creatures sprung from the room and gave chase.

Kwanza rounded a corner and saw the cart he had pushed down ahead and the flare he held growing dim. He threw the spluttering flare at the creatures, whose cautious chase would increase now the fire no longer held them at bay. He gripped the cart and shoved it into motion. When it had gained momentum, he climbed inside and glanced behind. The monsters gained rapidly.

They were fast. The cart tipped forward when it dived down a steep slope and sped down. Wondering if he would live through this, Kwanza looked ahead at the darkness. It was certainly the scariest ride he had ever experienced. The cart shuddered when it crashed into something. Daylight flooded the tunnel and briefly blinded him. He glanced behind at the doors swinging closed behind him and hoped the creatures had a similar disability to vampires and avoided sunlight. He smiled at his stupidity; vampires weren't real. This island was getting inside his head.

The doors opened violently. Four of the creatures rushed out. Almost spilled from the cart when it unexpectedly tipped to the side, Kwanza gripped the safety rail and stared at the long drop he leaned over. A glance along the track revealed the twist in the rail that carried on along the underside of a large rock overhang. He was about to be turned upside-down and carried out over the void. A growl too close to inspire confidence of a long life ahead of him followed the lurch of the cart. Kwanza spun towards his unwelcome passenger and glimpsed the claw swiping at his face. He leapt from the cart and plummeted.

*****

Ray checked the room as he descended the creaking steps. Boxes, an old bike missing a wheel, glass jars, discarded toys, a flat football, old newspapers and books spilled from a damp, rotted cardboard box, but there was no sign of anything alive. Not even a rat or woodlice. He stepped off the staircase onto an earthen floor. Satisfied no creatures were in the vicinity, he knelt to examine the tracks preserved in the soft earth. Wrinkles furrowed his creased brow at failing to recognize the animal that had formed them. He placed a hand over one for comparison. Disconcertingly, the paw print was almost the size of his hand. Uneasy, he rose slowly to his feet and swept his gaze around the dark room. A soft breeze on the back of his neck spun him. Nothing. The breeze washed over his face again. It came from the gaps between the stair treads. He edged along the side of the stair wall and aimed his light down a second set of wooden steps, banishing a small area of the uninviting darkness below. Wide-open plains, jungle, rocky hills and tundra seemed awfully inviting now.

He pressed the talk button on the walkie-talkie fixed to his jacket's chest pocket. "I've found another set of steps leading deeper. I'm going down to check it out."

"Okay, hon, take care," replied Laura. "And leave your mic open."

Cautiously, Ray began his descent. When he stepped onto the second tread, a click spun him towards the sound. A door, fashioned as part of the wall, creaked open. Ray aimed his weapon at the pale figure that emerged from the shadows into his light beam and let out a surprised gasp when he saw what it was.

Laura's voice, edged with concern, crackled over the radio, "You all right, hon?"

"Yeah, I'm fine. I must have activated a pressure switch that triggered one of Houghton's scary movie props. A creepy clown just appeared out of the wall."

"That's not good, dear, you hate clowns."

Ray stared at the evil, deathly pale face with its bulbous red nose, slanted eyes exaggerated by black makeup, and its grotesque, red-lipped smile filled with yellow pointed teeth.

"I hate them even more now."

He relaxed his finger on the trigger and turned his back on the scary clown. He felt the clown's eyes like daggers in his back all the way down the stairs, and he had to force himself not to turn to see if it followed.

The left-hand direction of the passage he arrived at led to a glass-fronted cupboard containing shelves filled with spooky doll heads. Each one had been expertly transformed from cuteness into the shockingly bizarre with horror-themed makeup and attachments, and all stared at him with lifeless, malevolent eyes. Ray repositioned the light to avoid the shadows it cast imbuing the heads with movement and aimed it in the opposite direction. A brick-formed tunnel led into darkness. On the right side were what seemed to be cages with fronts constructed from wood and chicken wire. About halfway along the passage, a line of child size dolls hugged the left-hand brick wall, a queue of freaky imagination. One of the dolls had its head turned back along the passage, as if it had heard a noise and was checking it out. Though its original form lacked the grotesque alterations of the cupboard dolls, the look of fear on its pale, childlike face, caused a cold shiver to claw its way down Ray's spine. He turned his gaze upon the dark red splashes on the walls and floor, which seemed to be dried blood spilt a long time ago, though it could be another of Houghton's fear-inducing theatrical effects. He glanced up the stairs. The glowing face of the evil clown stared at him. It had to be painted with some type of light absorbing paint to provide such a creepy effect.

He aimed his mouth at the radio. "I'm in an underground passage where there might be signs of dried blood."

"You want me to join you?" Laura asked.

"What's it like up there?"

"Quiet, dead quiet, and creepy."

Ray stared along the passage again where he knew anything could be hiding. He was at a distinct disadvantage hemmed in the narrow space. Two collective sets of senses would be advantageous. “Yes, come down. The second set of stairs is beneath the first flight and watch out for the clown.”

Footsteps drifted down from the floor above and climbed down the top flight of steps.

“Bloody hell, that is too damn creepy,” stated Laura, appearing at the top of the stairs and looking at the spine-chilling clown.

“I think it’s on a spring-catch I released when I trod on the second step,” Ray explained.

To avoid activating another of Houghton’s horrors, Laura avoided treading on the second step when she climbed down. “Ezra Houghton certainly had a vivid imagination.”

Ray nodded his head at the doll head cupboard. “Take a look over there.”

Laura gazed disapprovingly at the horror heads, a mockery to their intended purpose of bringing joy and comfort to little girls. “Ewwww, that’s just wrong.”

“We can see why it’s named *The Dollmaker’s Cabin* now.” Ray faced the long passage. “And I am sure more of Houghton’s surprises await us along there.”

He led his wife forward.

*****

After leaping from the ride cart, Kwanza straightened his body, held his arms tight to his sides and worriedly looked down at the white frothy waves breaking over the rocks. With luck, he would miss them altogether and land safely in the sea; if not, a painful bone-breaking death awaited him. A worried glance up revealed the monster hanging onto the upside-down cart as it headed beneath the large outcrop of rock protruding over the ocean. As cold water gripped him, Kwanza saw the monster drop. As soon as his downward momentum slowed, he clawed his way to the surface and sucked in air. Pounding waves and lashing spray was deafening all around him. He glanced around for the monster but saw no sign of it. Hoping it had struck the rocks and died, he swam level with the shore until he found a place where he could climb out.

Vegetation and tree roots aided his climb up the steep, rocky slope. A screech rang out as he neared the top. A glance down revealed the monster climbing speedily after him. He scrambled up the last few yards, drew his pistol and rolled onto his back as the monster appeared over the edge and leapt at him. Two shots rang out. Both struck their target. Kwanza dodged the creature when it flopped to the ground. A few deep breaths calmed his rapidly beating heart while he stared at the creature sliding over the edge; it was neither wolf nor big cat, yet had features of both with another unidentifiable species mixed in. He judged its size as that of a typical tiger and its claws were certainly a match for a big cat's. Its long, wolf-like, but wider snout, was lined with long curved teeth designed for tearing flesh. Kwanza could only imagine something had gone seriously haywire on this island to produce such a monstrosity. He holstered his pistol as he climbed to his feet and headed back to the village to re-arm from his stash of weapons and tend to his wounds. Though he regretted the loss of his faithful Mannlicher-Schonauer rifle his father had given him, he had others he could use until he reclaimed it. First, he would kill the strange creatures. Now he knew what he was dealing with and where they lived, he would continue the hunt forewarned and better prepared.

*****

Ray and Laura arrived at the first cage along the tunnel and pierced the darkness within with their flashlights. Their lights and shocked gazes roamed the horrifying details of the spooky diorama manifested in all its chilling details.

The scene pictured a small boy's bedroom, complete with bed, wardrobe, small chest of drawers and toys on shelves from the era when it was conceived. There the normality ended. The small boy that lay huddled under his sheets, whose terrified face was exposed by the blanket lifted by the clawed hand of the ghoulish doll leaning over the bed, didn't look like a doll. The figure was so human, so lifelike, Laura had to fight her maternal instincts that encouraged her to rush in and save him.

A scary face peered out through the gap of the partly open wardrobe door, and the pale-faced, dark holes for eyes, doll-adapted monster under the bed, was the vision of small children's nightmares. If that wasn't frightening enough, a yard-tall little girl doll with the face of an evil clown and holding a bloodied axe, stood at the bottom of the bed, poised to do its evil, bloody mayhem.

With his childhood fears rising to the surface, Ray stared at the scary clown doll. He took in its striped blue dress, white ankle socks and pink shoes, all splashed with blood, the straggly ginger hair bunched either side of its head and perched on top, a hat with a pink ribbon that matched the shade of its blood-stained shoes. He raised the gun and fired. The doll clown's face exploded.

Laura had noticed her husband aim the rifle and guessed his intentions. She knew his irrational fear of clowns came from an early age. A trip to a circus was responsible. He had become separated from his mother in the crowd and had wandered near the caravan homes of the circus performers. Angry shouting had bidden him to hide and observe a clown thrashing a young boy who, from what he could gather from the clowns furious berating, had spilled the clown's drink. The clowns around him laughed and egged him to beat the brat harder. When he was reunited with his mum, Ray had pleaded with her to take him home, but she had already purchased the tickets and told him to stop being silly and dragged him inside. He had been fine until the clown performance started. Though most of the audience laughed at their funny antics, he saw them as objects of fear and cruelty.

Laura studied her husband's face and saw his normally calm and controlled demeanor return. "Feeling better?"

Ray nodded. "I know it's illogical, but I really hate clowns."

"I know, hon." She gazed along the passage where anything lying in wait would now be notified of their presence. "Hopefully, that will be the last one."

Ray loaded a fresh bullet into the empty chamber. "Amen to that."

They cautiously moved on.

Halting at the queue of small dolls, they studied their fear-filled expressions—wide eyes and drawn back lips that gave the impression if they were real they would be quivering. Some of the dolls, both boys and girls, were frozen in the act of crying, glass tears in their eyes and on their cheeks. Their clothing, soiled and ragged, added to their collective ambience of suffering and fear.

"I know they are only dolls," said Laura, "but I'm finding it all too easy to picture them as real children."

Ray turned his eyes away from the depressing queue.

"I assume that was Houghton's intention." He gazed at the next cage a short distance away, where the sad doll queue ended. Though he felt no desire to view what Houghton's twisted mind had created, he led Laura forward.

It was worse than they could possibly have imagined.

"That is just sick," stated Laura.

The scene was of a classroom with small desks and chairs occupied by student dolls dressed in white, bloodstained doctor coats. Some studied, dissected or prodded the gruesome organs on their desks, and one, with a satisfied expression and bloody lips, held a heart missing a chunk edged by a bite mark. The teacher, dressed all in black, including a hooded cloak that gave him a Grim Reaper appearance, faced the large blackboard fixed to the wall and aimed a scythe-like pointer at one of the many lumps of blood-fresh organs pinned to the board.

A dissecting table stood in one corner of the classroom and nearby a selection of blood-covered medical instruments. Beside the table, a doll student held a bloody bone-saw in one hand and the top of a doll child's head in his other. A cruel smile played on its lips as it stared at the scream-frozen doll child standing on the table, where the student doll's accomplice was frozen in the act of lifting the brain from the freshly severed skull. Other *'dead'* child dolls lay in a heap, their discarded, dismembered and mutilated bodies missing limbs and emptied of various organs. All had pain etched on their porcelain faces.

Ray glanced at his wife, who had turned away from the horrible diorama. "I can't imagine what Houghton's intended audience would have thought of all this when cinema was perhaps still in its infancy. I know it's only dolls, but it implies children are suffering. It's sickening to us and we are somewhat acclimatized to gory horror films. Way back then, they had no such preparation."

"After witnessing this appalling monstrosity, I'm glad he never got to finish his films. The man must have been a complete sicko."

Eager to leave this place, Ray glanced ahead. Though he doubted any animals were down here, he'd rather make certain while they were here as he wouldn't be keen to return. "This place can't go on for much farther, so let's check out what's ahead and then call it a day."

"I'm right behind you, hon."

They avoided highlighting the next two cages they passed; neither of them wanted more of Ezra's nightmare scenes implanted in their thoughts.

A sharp turn brought them to a set of double doors stretching the width of the passage, one of which was partly open. Ray shone his light through the gap before entering. The couple scanned the large room that predominantly smelt of old glue and paint. Grey flagstones covered the floor and a long and wide wooden workbench in the middle of the room was cluttered with objects. Woodworking and sculpting tools, doll part molds, small pots of paint, jars of artist brushes, glue pots, rags and thick candle stubs.

A long floor-to-ceiling cupboard along one wall was portioned into cubbyholes filled with a myriad of objects that included jars of unknown substances, paint pots, bottles and rolled up parchments, but most of the sections contained different doll parts, limbs, hands, feet, heads and torsos, all waiting for the Dollmaker to imbue them with his horrifying metamorphoses. More cupboards and shelves around the room contained other objects, tools and materials the Dollmaker required to carry out his profession. One of the two alcoves in the room contained a sewing machine and bolts of mildewed cloth, the other a kiln for baking clay doll parts. A soot-blackened kettle hung in the hearth of the stone fireplace in the far corner of the room. Small, spooky dolls hung from rows of string stretched the width of the room like macabre Christmas decorations.

When Ray's gaze picked out two doors set in the wall beside the fireplace, he glanced at his wife. "Wait here while I check them out."

Laura nodded and watched her husband move through the room.

Ray skirted the workbench and ducked under the lines of hanging dolls. He grimaced disapprovingly at one of the Dollmaker's hanging creations, an eight-legged abomination. The spider-doll had an expertly rendered spider body and legs, complete with a bulging lumpy abdomen that seemed it might burst to free the hundreds of young he imagined within. Attached to the front of the spider body by the waist was a naked female doll. One talon-tipped hand cupped one of its bare breasts, the other was raised menacingly. Dark brown hair framed the pretty face disfigured by a vicious snarl.

Moving on, Ray's eyes flittered over what seemed to be the Dollmaker's latest ghoulish creations displayed, proudly it seemed, on a deep set of wooden shelves set into the wall. The evil, brown skeletons included one with lumps of flesh hanging from its bones, another climbing from a small stone sarcophagus was partially covered in cloth wrappings, like a badly wrapped Egyptian mummy. All gave off an aura of malicious, murderous intentions.

Ray turned away, halted at the first door and pushed it open. The ominous squeals emitted by the hinges came as no surprise; it seemed Houghton had designed most things that moved on his island to emit a theatrical creak, groan or squeal. When he stepped cautiously through the door, he almost gagged at the horrific sight his eyes were forced to witness.

"What is it?" called out Laura, crossing the room.

Ray turned at hearing her footsteps on the dusty flagstones. "Nothing, stay there. Believe me, Loz, it's nothing you want to see."

When Ray turned away to pull the door closed and shut out the horrific vision, he noticed something odd. He entered and ran his unwilling eyes over the human skins of men, women and children stretched taut on drying frames, something he was familiar with from trophy animals he had shot and skinned, and the heap of skinned corpses in one corner. If they were real corpses they would have rotted and perhaps left the lingering stench of decay in the closed room. They looked fresh, too fresh, and at odds with the years of accumulated dust that covered them. He approached the rack of skins beside the dissecting table awash with dried blood and ran his fingers over a human male skin. It felt something like rubber covered in a greasy, oily film to preserve it and keep it supple. He calmed on discovering the skins were another batch of Houghton's theatrical props and crossed to the pile of skinned corpses. A brief examination revealed the lifelike creations to be detailed sculpted models.

His gaze around the horrifying film set alighted on the metal bars at the far end of the room. Ray ducked under two rows of skin-laden drying racks, avoiding staring at the blank eyeholes that stared at him, and approached the two cages. His flashlight picked out the occupants of one cell. Though he knew the captives were another manifestation of Houghton's sick mind, they were so lifelike he experienced sorrow at their plight. It was with dismay that he saw most of the captives were small children, ideal doll size for the Dollmaker's alterations, Ray assumed. He looked at the children huddled at the back of the cell being consoled by women he thought might be their mothers. Three men gathered at the front of the cell, wore scared but determined expressions. One had his mouth open, as if shouting or screaming. Another gripped the cage door, as if he shook it violently. With the open bars they couldn't help but witness the terrible skinning carried out in the room while they waited their turn.

Wondering why Houghton had chosen to use dummies rather than live actors, Ray moved along the front of the cage and noticed cables running out from the trouser leg of the man holding the bars and into a hole in the floor. They were animatronic. They could move. He stared at the face of the man so skillfully designed it was difficult to tell it wasn't a real person. On camera and with atmospheric lighting, even with its limited movement, it would be impossible to discern it wasn't a real actor. Baloc had told him Houghton had intended to turn the island into a movie horror theme park, so those who wanted to experience the thrills and scares of the characters in his horror films could do so for themselves—all for a price, of course. The animatronic figures Houghton had skillfully designed wouldn't need paying, feeding or have sick days. It was a shrewd business move on Ezra's part.

Ray moved to the second cage and peered through the open door of the empty cage, which he assumed live actors would have occupied during filming.

"You okay in there, hon?" called out Laura.

Ray headed back to the workshop and closed the door. "I'm fine, just one more door to check and then we can leave."

"Sooner the better!" stated Laura. "This place gives me the creeps."

"It's freaking me out, too," agreed Ray, opening the next door.

This time, forewarned, he was more surprised than shocked by what the room contained. He turned and gazed across the workshop at his wife. "You have got to come and look at this."

"Nothing too scary, I hope," said Laura, heading for the room.

They both roamed their lights over what seemed to be the Dollmaker's climatic masterpieces and the reason for the skinning operation in the nearby room.

Laura focused her attention on the giant four-yard tall doll of a little girl. Her sweet pink dress, white shoes and socks, and dainty blue ribbon in her blond hair, were an abusive contrast to the cruel expression on her freckled face and the pointed stick she poked into the large ornate birdcage she held in one hand. In the cage, five lifelike human doll children dodged the sharp end of the stick the girl tried to skewer them with. The two dead and bloodied child corpses at the bottom of the cage revealed her first two victims. Even though it was a horrible act to witness, it was so credible, Laura would not have been surprised if the giant doll started moving, poking the caged children while she laughed in glee at their screams and painful yells when she landed a successful stab.

Ray moved on and aimed his gaze at the man stretched out in an X by his hands and feet tied to four rings in the floor and ceiling. He could almost hear the man's frozen painful scream as the sharp-toothed doll-headed rats climbed his body, biting and ripping off bits of his flesh, eating him alive. One rat-doll had burrowed into the man's stomach and poked its bloody head out like an inquisitive meerkat at the entrance to its burrow.

They wandered deeper into the room and stared at the naked female hung by her ankles. The female human doll was partly covered in webs spun by a group of the palm-size half-human spider-dolls Ray had first set eyes upon in the Dollmaker's workshop. Both could easily imagine that the bulges in her skin pulsating and contained the hatching offspring of the parent spiders currently crawling over her body. One of the protuberant egg sacks in the woman's cheek had hatched, emitting hundreds of tiny versions of their parent. They swarmed over her terrified, screaming face. Some entered her mouth and others her nostrils and ears.

Laura shivered and turned her eyes away.

Remembering the GoPro camera fixed to his shoulder filming everything he saw, Ray moved through the room to record the Dollmaker's fear-inspiring creations. Though unsure how much they would be allowed, if any, to air on their popular hunting show, which would unquestionably be a special now if they managed to track and kill the island's mysterious beast, he would film as much as he could if for no other reason than no one would believe it if they couldn't see the evidence to back up his story.

Once he had filmed everything in the room, he crossed to Laura who waited by the door.

"There's no sign of the creature down here, hon, so let's get out of this horrible place."

Ray took a last look at the nightmare scenes and nodded his agreement.

They backtracked to the stairway and were about to climb the lower set of stairs when Ray held up a hand, halting his wife. The creak of floorboards from the top floor drifted down to them. Someone or something was in the cottage.

With their eyes and weapons trained up the stairs, and Ray barely suppressing the urge to shoot the creepy clown staring down at them, they listened to the padding footsteps disturbing the creaky floorboards on the top floor and then creep down the upper staircase. Their eyes followed the bowing treads of the groaning staircase caused by the weight of whatever climbed down them. Though unsure if it was man or beast, both doubted Kwanza who, as far as they were aware was the only other person on the island, would have crossed to their hunting ground, but they couldn't shoot without knowing for certain. The footsteps, slow and menacing, skulked along the side of the staircase wall and approached the top of the stairs their attention now focused on.

Though confident either one of their hunting rifles could kill whatever was about to appear at the top of the staircase, fear began to invade Laura's senses. Her heart raced, pounding her chest. Sweat formed on her brow, and she desperately wanted to pee.

Ray, who tried to avoid locking eyes with the disturbing clown staring mockingly at him, though anxious, was more controlled. Though they had no escape route, whatever animal was about to appear had to come down the stairs and directly into their line of fire to reach them. The high caliber bullets loaded in their powerful weapons could easily kill any creature of a size to fit through the cabin doorway.

When the footsteps neared the top of the stairs and stopped, Laura's and Ray's fingers moved to rest on their triggers.

Their eyes stared at the right side of the stair wall where something waited out of sight, sniffing the air and their scent. When a deep rumbling growl broke the silence, the hunters knew it came from nothing human. A few breathless moments passed before the footsteps started up again and backtracked to the upper stairs.

When Ray noticed his wife's anxious expression, he smiled reassuringly, pointed at the bottom of the stairs the creature was about to climb and whispered, "I'll shoot it when it's on the stairs."

Keeping her weapon trained up the stairs in case the animal returned, Laura nodded.

Ray focused his rifle on the bottom of the stair treads when the creature placed its weight on them. Assuming it had similar physiology to big cats, he would attempt to shoot it in the chest and hopefully its heart. He waited until all its four limbs were on the treads before aiming just short of the tread its front limb had just depressed. The sound of the gunshot echoed through the cabin.

A deep, throaty screech made by no animal the hunters recognized sent a chill running down Laura's spine. Dust dislodged by the creature's hurried leaps up the stairs drifted into their light beams. A second shot rang out as Ray tried again to kill the creature before it escaped. The footsteps thumping across the floorboards of the upper floor were evidence he had missed.

Laura let out the breath she had unconsciously been holding and looked at her husband. "That was rather more intense than I'm used to."

"Yeah, great, isn't it? Let's go see if I wounded it."

They found splashes of blood on the top staircase, but not enough to indicate a serious injury. Both knew a wounded animal was a far more dangerous foe. Its pain and anger would cause it to act out of character and take risks it normally shied away from.

They cautiously climbed the steps and entered the trapdoor room.

Ray pointed at the spatter of fresh blood on the floorboards. “Hopefully, it has left a trail we can follow.”

Laura glanced worryingly at the twilight glow penetrating the two grimy windows along the corridor. “Are you sure hunting an animal we know nothing about and with night drawing in is a wise decision?”

Ray considered their options. They were hunting an unknown wounded creature that was most likely pissed off in a locality they had yet to fully explore. He mustn’t let the excitement of the hunt make him act rashly. He would never forgive himself if Laura was harmed.

“You’re right, of course, dear. It’s too risky given the circumstances. We’ll head back to base and hopefully pick up its trail in the morning.”

Grateful for her husband’s grasp of the danger, she followed him along the corridor. Though she was certain it would make an unwelcome reappearance in her nightmares, Laura was eager to leave the Dollmaker’s creepy dwelling behind. Her eyes flicked to the shadow that had just blocked the light from the window her husband passed. She reeled back in shock and stumbled to the floor when something crashed through the glass. As if in slow motion, she watched glass shards twist and turn as they sprayed the corridor and a dark monstrous head between outstretched claws dive though the opening. Sprinkled with glass, her husband reacted instinctively to the threat and dropped to a crouch. A claw lashed out, ripping his sleeve and skin. As the creature slammed into the wall above her husband, Ray dived onto his shoulder, rolled and sprung to his feet. He turned to bring his weapon to bear on the creature recovering from its fall. The creature sprung from its powerful rear limbs. A power-laden paw knocked the barrel pointed at its head aside. The gunshot that exploded beside its head deafened its hearing on that side. Ray released his grip on the rifle that was useless in such close quarters and reached for the magnum pistol holstered at his side. A sharp tug on the weapon freed the quick release strap. The creature smashed into him, sending them both to the floor. One of the creature's front paws landed on his gun arm, pinning it to the floor. The creature growled at the victim now at its mercy.

The gunshot brought Laura to her senses. She climbed to her feet and aimed her rifle at the creature's head.

When the creature erratically shook its head to try and relieve the ringing in its ear, Ray poked two fingers in the wound his bullet through the staircase had made in its side. It squealed in agony and leapt away.

The gunshot from Laura's weapon filled the corridor. The bullet grazed the top of the creature's head before striking the wall, sending out splinters when it penetrated the old wood. The creature glanced back at the new threat before it bounded along the corridor and out through the cabin's main door.

Laura rushed to the broken window as she reloaded and aimed her rifle at the fleeing creature, but it was surprisingly fast and was amongst the trees before she could get off a shot. She crossed to her husband, took in his torn sleeve and the deep scratches on his upper arm and knelt beside him. "You're hurt."

Ray sat up on his elbows. "It's nothing, really." He smiled. "Only a flesh wound, as they say in the movies."

"Nevertheless, it needs cleaning and covering." She helped him to his feet.

Ray glanced through the broken window into the darkness beneath the trees. “Whatever that damn thing was, it wasn’t a big cat, bear or wolf.” He looked at his wife with excitement in his eyes. “It’s as we hoped, a new species of predator.”

“As thrilling as that is”—her brow creased with worry, Laura gazed out at the gloomy forest—“that creature is out there somewhere and between us and the village.”

“It’s probably weary of us now it’s hurt and aware we aren’t the easy prey it expected.” He laid a reassuring hand on her arm. “We’ll be fine.”

He holstered his pistol, picked up his rifle and together they headed outside.

*****

After attending to his shoulder wound, Kwanza dressed in a fresh set of dry clothing. Loaded with everything he needed to kill the vicious animals he had encountered, he headed back to the Fear Fair.

He raised his eyes to the early evening sky. Dark, ominous clouds hinted rain might accompany the night rapidly approaching. He paused, turned and stared towards the distant, muffled shots. It seemed the TV celebrities were also on the hunt, or, he scoffed, more likely having some target practice. He wiped them from his thoughts; they were no competition. He would soon have the island’s threat neutralized and claim the prestige of having the first kill of a new predatory species in as many years as he could remember. Not that it was something he sought, but if it took the celebrity husband-and-wife-hunting duo down a peg or two, he would welcome it. Maybe he would be offered his own hunting show, or Hollywood would make a movie about his hunting prowess. Surely there was money in such things. He smiled at the thought as he wondered what actor would play him. Certainly not some namby-pamby white man.

The forest surrounding the Fear Fair he passed through a second time was even creepier in the low light of evening, and it was easy to imagine things in the darkness observing him. When he entered the Fear Fair, he discovered that it had also increased in creepiness. The strengthening breeze gave motion to anything it caressed. The Ferris wheel's metallic screech bayed for dominance over the myriad of sounds lower to the ground. Stalls creaked, ragged materials fluttered, cables thrummed, and the creepy dolls and stuffed toys chaffed against each other, as if they stirred from a deep slumber and nudged each other to attack the stranger trespassing in their domain.

Kwanza focused his attention on the unwelcoming gaping mouth that formed the entrance to the creepy ghost train. Aware of what dwelled inside, he wasn't keen on entering again, but if necessary he would do so to get the job done. He couldn't risk the dynamic duo claiming the first kill. Sensing eyes upon him, he halted, flicked the night vision goggles (NVG) attached to a hands-free strap around his head, over his eyes and turned 360. His ghostly, greenlit gaze swept the surroundings. Though the light-enhancing technology all but destroyed his depth of vision, they were perfect for picking out anything using darkness as concealment. Though he detected nothing in the immediate area, Kwanza wasn't going to ignore his honed senses that told him something was there, watching and waiting. It was a distinct possibility the creatures had left their lair and now hunted him. He raised the NVGs and studied the ghost train entrance while he pondered his next move. If he entered and some of the creatures waited inside for him while others snuck in behind, he doubted he would survive the ambush. He changed his plan.

His eyes searched the Fear Fair for a suitable defensive position. The top of the Helter-Skelter would give him an ideal raised elevation to observe the grounds without fear of being ambushed. Kwanza unhooked two smoke grenades from his extensively stocked ammo belt and approached the ghost train entrance. He nudged the door ajar with a shoulder, activated the grenades and hurled them deep inside. With his weapon raised, ready to repel the suspected attack, he hurried to the Helter-Skelter and climbed the rusty, creaking staircase and crossed the small walkway to the top of the slide.

He slipped off his rucksack, positioned spare ammo within easy reach and rested his shotgun against the rail, ready to ward off any creatures who got too close. Satisfied he had everything covered, he flipped down his NVGs and aimed his rifle at the ghost train entrance. The smoke that curled from beneath the doors was a good sign it was filtering through the tunnel. If it didn't force out any creatures inside to seek fresh air, he would have no choice other than to enter.

Just as Kwanza began to doubt the smoke would do what he wished of it, the twin doors crashed open and three creatures rushed out. Kwanza's first shot rang out a split-second later. It entered the lead creature's skull above its left eye and exploded out the back of its head, showering the following creatures in blood and brain matter. As the lifeless body collapsed to the ground, the following creatures leapt over its fallen comrade. One landed awkwardly and buckled onto its front limbs. Kwanza took aim on the fallen creature struggling to its feet and fired as the other creature bounded off behind a candy floss stall and into darkness.

The creature's erratic movements saved its life. Leaving a trail of smoking flesh in its wake, the bullet slid along the side of its thick skull and ripped off its left ear before embedding in the cheek of the ghoulish mouth entrance. Kwanza adjusted his aim, but before he could fire, the creature fled and disappeared.

His search for the monsters found one a few concessions stands away, staring out from behind the hotdog stall shaped into an evil hog's head. The cooking area was in the pigs open mouth, and its tongue the serving counter. By the time Kwanza brought the rifle to bear on the creature, it ducked back out of sight. A fleeting glimpse of movement from the other side of the stall altered the hunter's gaze. The creature was moving position. A second movement revealed the creature missing an ear had rejoined its comrade behind another stall, which was, appropriately, Kwanza thought, the rifle range. His eyes flicked from one side of the stall to the other as he waited for one of them to appear.

When the platform swayed slightly, he spun. The creature he believed had somehow crept up on him wasn't there. The ride swayed again. Though again slight, it was enough to put him on high alert. He checked the metal staircase; it was clear. He shifted position and stared down the Helter-Skelter slide. Convinced one of the creatures was climbing up the covered tube, Kwanza raised his NVGs, pulled a flare from his pocket, struck it into flame and tossed it down the slide. When the expected squeal didn't come, he glanced over the side. The flare lay on the ground at the base of the slide. He checked the rusty steps again, but it was still free of any menace. When the ride continued to sway, he gazed around for another way something might be able to reach him. His eyes fell on the small door set in the inner side of the slide tower. He turned the catch, pulled it open and peered inside. Two creatures climbed the framework inside the tower.

Clever, thought Kwanza. They had more intelligence than he had credited them with.

The nearest creature snarled at him when it leapt. Kwanza dodged back out of its reach, dropped his rifle and snatched up the shotgun. The creature gripped the edge of the small opening and hauled itself through, bending back the flimsy metal forced apart to accommodate its bulk.

Surprised by the creature's speed, Kwanza aimed the shotgun in its direction and pulled the trigger. The first blast stripped the flesh from the side of its face, revealing skull, gums and teeth, but it still came at him. It dropped onto the small platform and growled menacingly. When Kwanza pulled the trigger for a second shot aimed at the creature's gut, it sprung at him. The powerful blast shot the creature to the side. The railing it smashed against gave way, and both fell to the ground.

Expecting the second creature to appear through the access hatch at any second, Kwanza poked the shotgun barrel in the opening and pulled the trigger three times. Something heavy thudded on the base of the Helter-Skelter. Believing he had hit the creature, he was about to check when the platform he stood on vibrated violently. A glance over the edge revealed the one-eared creature rushing up the staircase. After firing a shot in its general direction, Kwanza grabbed his rifle and gear and feet first slid down the chute. A screech from below signaled he would have company when he reached the bottom. The chaotic tilts and drops of the slide threw Kwanza from side to side, almost smashing his head against the curved wall. *And kids call this fun.*

He glimpsed flare-produced shadows moving below when he neared the bottom. Something waited for him, and he didn't need any guesses to know what. He exited from the snake's mouth and was confronted by a creature with shotgun damage to its side, the second creature that had climbed the inside of the tower. Bathed in the red glow of the spluttering flare, it was easy to mistake it as a demon that had crawled from the depths of hell. It was in pain, angry, and thirsting for revenge. Cluttered by the rucksack on his lap, Kwanza dug his heels into the snake's forked tongue that would have deposited him at the jaws of the creature. His momentum stood him up and shot him at the creature. He slammed the rucksack onto the creature's head as he sailed over, knocking it off balance. Landing on its back, Kwanza rode it to the ground. He released his grip on the rifle, rammed the barrel of the shotgun in its back and pulled the trigger. The creature's spine and ribs exploded, spraying him and the surrounding ground with blood and bone.

Panting from the adrenalin rush, Kwanza totaled up the creatures he had killed— one on the cliff and four just now, making five. Though unsure how many he had seen in their lair, he thought there were about six, possibly seven, but no more. That left one or two to dispose of. A screech from above rolled him away from the dead creature. One Ear leapt from the top of the Helter-Skelter. Kwanza aimed the shotgun and fired. It clicked on empty. He cursed his stupid mistake; he should have reloaded. He grabbed the pistol from his side, aimed and fired shots in quick succession before rolling away to avoid the creature landing on him.

Some of the wounded creature's bones snapped when it struck the ground awkwardly, but still it wasn't dead. It turned its head at Kwanza as it tried to climb onto its broken limbs. The grinding and splintering of bones was terrible to hear. The growl it aimed at Kwanza gurgled with blood.

Surprised the creature was still alive after the punishment it had received, Kwanza climbed to his feet and shot two bullets into its brain. The creature flopped to the ground.

"Six." Kwanza smiled.

When a quick search of the area revealed no sign of any more creatures, Kwanza conceded he had killed them all. Like the wolves some of their amalgamated features were similar with, they were pack animals. If there were any more, they would be with the pack. Especially when hunting. He had disposed of the creatures before the celebrity couple had even begun their hunt. He hoped they would be mightily pissed. He reloaded and holstered the pistol, and then reloaded the shotgun.

Before he set about photographing the dead creatures and then skinning one as evidence of the new species he had made extinct, he wanted to retrieve his treasured rifle from the ghost train tunnel. As he headed towards it, he celebrated the thought that no one else would be able to hunt these creatures. To ensure he got the credit, he took the satellite phone Zane had supplied both hunting parties with from his pack and pressed the auto dial button programmed with the famous horror writer's sat-phone number. He listened to the clicks and whirrs as the connection was made miles above the earth.

When Zane answered with a simple hello, Kwanza informed him of his success. "It's Jabari. The threat has been neutralized...Yes, I'm sure. I flushed them from their lair." Kwanza glanced back at the dead creatures. "It doesn't have a name, it's a new species...I can't, there's no phone signal here to send a photo, but you'll see it when you get here...Okay, I'll return on the boat you arrive on. Before you go, Zane, does the five thousand bonus you offered count for every creature I killed that was a threat?...Good, because there were six, so you owe me an extra thirty thousand...make sure you do."

Kwanza broke the connection.

He had one more call to make. He dialed and when Ray answered, said, "Don't bother unpacking, I've killed them all."

He promptly hung up and smiled at the disappointment he imagined the love-struck hunters must now be experiencing. He pushed through the swing doors of the ghost train and headed along the tunnel.

*****

Ray and Laura approached the forest surrounding the cottage with their senses strained for sight or sound of the creature that might be waiting to ambush them. Ray glanced at a splash of creature's blood on the edge of the path and roamed his flashlight around the forest. After detecting no sign of the creature, he led Laura through the gloom-shrouded trees that offered the perfect environment for a surprise attack.

Laura couldn't remember when she had last felt so anxious on a hunt with her husband. She looked upon him as her protector and knew if it was within his means he wouldn't let any harm befall her—just as she wouldn't let any befall him if she could prevent it—but this place, this island, was different. It didn't play by the rules. She sensed the island was a place where anything could happen and very likely would. Their hunting rifles, which they had adapted to suit their needs, were some of the best on the market but wouldn't necessarily save them from harm, or worse, death. She pushed her concerns aside. She needed to concentrate fully on their surroundings or perhaps suffer the consequences. As if sensing her worries, her husband glanced behind and flashed her a reassuring smile.

Ray, though ill at ease with their current predicament because the creature could come at them from any angle, was confident they would make it through the small forest safely. The ground beneath the trees was littered with dead leaves, twigs and fallen branches that would announce its approach. His reaction time was so instinctive he could shoot the creature before it was upon them, unless—he glanced up at the tree canopy that formed a tunnel over the path—it came from above.

A gust of wind wove its way through the forest. Rustling leaves and creaking branches shifted the anxious hunters' gazes to each new sound. Thankfully, it wasn't long before they emerged from the dark forest into moonlight casting everything in its monochrome pallet. Glad to be free of the trees, Laura walked backward with her weapon aimed at the forest edge to guard against an attack and turned forward when they were a safe distance away.

Both halted when distant gunshots invaded the hushed atmosphere that seemed to be prevalent on the island, as if everything here held its breath to see if the strangers would survive. After a brief pause, the shots that halted them were followed by different gunshots."

"That's a shotgun," stated Laura.

Ray looked towards the sounds of gunfire and at the tip of the moonlit Ferris wheel, the only part visible due to the dip it rested in. Bright flashes erupted in tune with the gunshots. "It seems Kwanza is having his own problems with the island's wildlife."

"A close combat weapon might mean he's in trouble." Laura glanced around to check nothing crept up on them and turned back to the distant flashes. "Should we go and help him?"

"I doubt he's the kind of guy who would appreciate our interference." Ray took the sat-phone from his pocket to check it was switched on. "If he needs our help, he'll contact us." He returned the phone to his pocket. "Let's keep moving."

Unaware there were more than one, when the shots ended Laura wondered if Kwanza had killed the creature that had attacked them a little while ago, or it had killed him. She received her answer when the sat-phone rang a few moments later.

Ray answered the call and held it between them, so Laura could hear.

Kwanza's message was brief and clear. "Don't bother unpacking, I've killed them all." The line went dead when Kwanza promptly ended the call.

"He's not what I'd call a chatty, but he did say *them*, indicating there were more than one, so how can he be so confident he's killed them all?" queried Laura.

Ray sighed. "I guess we'll find out in the morning, but if he's telling the truth, then our hunt is over barely before it's begun." His disappointment was obvious.

After her recent experiences, Laura wasn't as despondent as she thought she might be. Something wasn't right on this island and the sooner they were both off it the better she would feel. "I know you wanted to claim first kill, hon, but it can't be helped. If Kwanza has killed them all, including the one that attacked us, we can still film the corpses and maybe Kwanza will let us interview him for the show."

Realizing he was being selfish, Ray placed an arm around his wife and gave her a gentle hug. "There's always a silver lining with you."

Laura kissed him. "Of course, now let's get back to the village. I am famished, and I don't mean just for food." She winked at her husband coyly.

Ray grinned. "The hunt always did turn you on."

They skirted the edge of the swamp and headed for the village.

CHAPTER 5

The Island

Baloc stared at the satellite phone. Though surprised the task had been carried out so swiftly, he was pleased Kwanza had neutralized the island's vicious inhabitants, and he was welcome to his bonus. After getting the island for free he could afford to splash out a bit. He wasted no time in finalizing the last few details of the expedition that was waiting to be put into motion. His gathered team were all housed at the four-star Villa Tuanis Jacó hotel on the small island of Isla Isabela, Costa Rica. At one hundred and ten miles from Costa Rica and forty-eight miles from Ezra's Horror island, it was the closest inhabited landmass for them to reach the island the quickest. The ship he had chartered was ready to sail and the majority of stores and equipment needed to sustain them for the length of their visit had already been ferried by helicopter to the island.

He went to inform the others they would be leaving at dawn.

While the team boarded the boat the following morning as first light lit the horizon, Zane used the sat-phone to contact the hunters on the island to let them know they were on their way. When he failed to connect with Kwanza, he dialed the Chases' sat-phone. It was answered after a few rings.

"Hi, Zane," said Ray, sleepily.

"Morning, Ray. Sorry to wake you so early, but I want to let you know we will be with you in a few hours."

Ray, now more alert, rubbed sleep from his eyes. "Then I assume Kwanza informed you of his successful hunt?"

"He did. Have you seen his kills?" Baloc was curious to discover what type of creature had inhabited the island.

"Not yet. We were leaving it until daylight." Ray glanced out of the bedroom window. Dawn was beginning to break. "Which isn't far away now. If it's the same species as Kwanza killed, we had a run in with one last night. As Kwanza no doubt told you, it's a new species of predator of the like no one's seen before."

"Can you describe it?" asked Baloc.

"It's strange. It has characteristics of a big cat, maybe a jaguar, and a wolf, but is neither, and there's something else I can't identify, something alien. It's best you see it for yourself when you arrive, but I can only imagine that cut off here, it evolved independently into the creature that's been terrorizing the island."

"It sounds exciting, and I can't wait to see it. I tried contacting Kwanza but couldn't get through, so can you let him know we are on our way?"

"Will do. Zane, before you go, I'm concerned that Kwanza might be wrong and some of the predators are still alive. It's possible he killed off one pack and there are others. It might be better for you to postpone your visit until we are certain the danger is past."

"I'm sure Kwanza wouldn't have notified me if he wasn't certain. I've also been told by experts that such a small island would be unable to sustain a large predatory force, so the six Kwanza killed is probably all there are. Anyway, we have already set sail. I'll see you in a few hours."

Baloc ended the connection before Ray could voice more of his concerns. He had waited too long to have more delays and an approaching storm could see them stranded for days if they didn't leave now. He was also confident if Kwanza had single-handedly killed six of the creatures, the small, well-armed security team he had employed could handle any existing threat the island offered. They would be fine.

"Anything wrong?" asked Wendy, peering down from the ship's rail.

Baloc smiled up at her. "Everything's fine. If we are all set, let's drop anchor and get this adventure started."

*****

"Was that Zane?"

Ray looked at his wife sprawled out on the bed beside him. "Yes. He's on his way and will arrive in a few hours. Kwanza told him it was safe."

"You don't seem convinced, hon."

"You know me, I like to cross all the T's and dot all the I's. Zane should have let us check the island thoroughly before setting off."

"I assume you think there might be more of the animals we encountered last night that Kwanza hasn't killed?"

Ray shrugged. "We don't know what Kwanza has killed yet or even if it was the same species as the one that attacked us, so I've no idea. I suggest we get up, have a quick breakfast and go and find Kwanza to find out exactly what he has shot. Whatever the outcome, we'll still have a few hours to scout the island before Zane and his team arrive."

Laura threw back the cover, revealing her nakedness. "I fancy breakfast in bed this morning."

Ray roamed his eyes down her body and placed the sat-phone down. "That might not be a bad idea as I'm suddenly feeling a little peckish."

"*A little peckish?* You had better be damn ravenous the mood I'm in." She hooked a leg around his waist and pulled him on top of her.

CHAPTER 6

HUNTER HUNTED

When the head-scarred creature returned from its encounter with the humans in the swamp and found another had slaughtered its kin, it observed the large human responsible and licked the congealing blood around the wound in its side, a reminder of the human's loud weapons it had little defense against. Aware its normal method of attack would probably bring it more pain or death, it resisted its instinct to charge at the human and skulked into the shadows. Its savage eyes followed the large human when he moved to the entrance of its lair. When he had disappeared inside, Scarred Skull approached its dead brethren and sniffed their corpses. Thirsting for revenge, it turned its head to the ghost train entrance and drew back its lips in a snarl that revealed sharp, flesh-ripping teeth.

Although Kwanza was convinced he had wiped out the creatures, he moved through the ghost train tunnel with the shotgun ready to fire. He halted at the pit, shone his flashlight below and cocked an ear. Satisfied the breeze blowing over him carried no sounds of any creatures, he climbed down the ladder and approached the storeroom. The acrid scent wafting out brought back memories of his previous foray inside.

He entered the storeroom and after a quick glance around to check it was free of menace, he focused on the doorway opposite. A few strides took him to the entrance. His eyes followed the light he roamed around the room and the ceiling. It was empty, just as he knew it would be. When he crossed to retrieve his rifle, his boots squelched into the thick layers of urine-soaked grass and threw up foul bursts of harsh, eye-watering stench. A brief examination revealed the weapon to be undamaged; only the attached flashlight had suffered. He slung the strap over a shoulder and made his way to the exit.

Still on guard against the unexpected, Kwanza exited the ghost train and gazed around his surroundings as he crossed to his kills. Confident the area was clear, he dragged the creatures' corpses together and laid them in a line. He fished his camera from his pack and took some photos before switching to movie mode and filming a short segment. With his kills recorded, he drew his skinning knife and knelt before the creature with the least amount of damage. Stuffed, it would make a fine specimen to add to his collection. Then realizing the uniqueness of the situation, he decided he would skin two, as surely a suitable museum would be interested in buying one for their collection. Humming cheerily, he went to work.

Kwanza failed to notice the squirming bulges beneath the skin of the corpse behind him or that he was being stalked.

Scarred Skull's savage eyes observed the large human and watched him drag its dead brethren together. When the human turned his back, it stealthily crept nearer. Not a sound did its carefully placed paws make on the ground. Its breathing, shallow and silent, would not alert the human to its presence.

Kwanza split open the creature's belly and pulled out its stomach. Balking from the sickening stench when the innards slid out and slurped onto the ground, he turned his face away. He never got used to the smell. When he turned back, he noticed something moving beneath the creature's skin. The beast was unmistakably dead, so it couldn't be any of its organs responsible; most of them lay on the ground. Remembering the pale thing he had glimpsed in the creature's throat when he was attacked in their lair, he assumed it was a parasite of some kind, a worm perhaps. He gripped a flap of skin and folded it back. A long maggot-like worm squirmed as it uncoiled from around the spine. As if sensing it was being watched, it pointed its eyeless head at Kwanza. A circular mouth opened to emit a ring of fine wriggling tentacles that stretched towards him.

Fascinated by the foot-long parasite he thought must also be a new species, perhaps exclusive to the wolf-like beast it resided in, Kwanza failed to grasp the danger it presented until it coiled like a snake and sprung at him. He swiped an arm at the parasite clumsily as he fell back, knocking it to the ground. Kwanza watched the parasite wriggling towards him, its mouth tentacles squirming, reaching out for him and prepared to squash it with a foot when it was close enough.

When barely perceptive footsteps alerted Kwanza to a second threat, he tilted his head back. A snarling wolf creature rushed at him. He had made a mistake, he hadn't killed them all. The fresh bullet wounds across its skull and in its side, were not his doing. It seemed the celebrity duo had already encountered this species but had failed to kill it. *Damn amateurs. Probably wasted time taking pictures of it for their TV show.* He yanked his pistol from its holster as he stood and aimed at the formidable beast charging him. His first shot missed when the parasite leapt and attached itself to his neck. One hand grabbed the parasite and tried to tug it free, while his other hand fired at the swiftly approaching creature.

Scarred-Skull was fast. It dodged the bullets, but wary of the pain the weapon brought, it changed course and headed around behind the human.

Kwanza turned to keep it in view but held off firing. He only had so many bullets, and he doubted—however fast he was—that reloading was an option. Worried he would rip off a chunk of his flesh before the firmly attached parasite released its grip, Kwanza placed the muzzle against its maggoty skin and pulled the trigger. The bullet ripped the parasite in half and splattered creamy pus over his face and shoulder. After a few spasms, the mouth released its hold and flopped to the ground.

With one ear deafened by the pistol's closeness, and a throbbing pain coming from the wound inflicted by the parasite, Kwanza's eyes flicked from the circling monster to his rifle and shotgun leaning against the Helter-Skelter a short distance away. If he could reach them, he should survive the encounter.

The creature glanced at what the human's eyes had flicked at and arrived at the opposite thought. To survive it mustn't let the human reach the more powerful weapons.

Both edged nearer the Helter-Skelter.

Kwanza reckoned he had about three bullets left. He wasn't certain that, even if he could hit the formidable beast, it was enough to kill the fast-reacting monster, but they might persuade it to retreat. His finger tightened on the trigger.

The parasites inside the dead creatures needed new hosts before they expired. Their bodies were cooling fast and weakening; it wouldn't be long before they succumbed. Sensing a new host nearby, the parasites detached their tentacles from their hosts' brainstems, unfurled from around their spines and chewed their way out.

The first parasite to emerge directed its snout at the suitable nearby host. With tentacles eager to claim a new victim, it coiled its body and sprung.

The shot Kwanza fired missed its target when the creature dodged away, a little farther. He was about to fire again when something struck his arm. He looked at the parasite responsible crawling caterpillar-like towards his face, grabbed it and flung it away. As soon as it struck the ground, it crawled back towards him. Kwanza was tempted to shoot it but couldn't afford the ammo. Checking the wolf creature wasn't about to attack, he stamped on the parasite. It exploded in a spray of pus. Movement turned his head to the dead creatures when more parasites erupted from some of them and sailed towards him. He'd had enough. He fired off his remaining two shots at Scarred-Skull and swiped the gun at the parasite aiming for his face, sending it flying. He holstered the empty pistol and sprinted for his weapons. Deciding the shotgun would be more advantageous in killing the creature, he slipped the hunting rifle strap over his shoulder and grabbed it. He needed to find a defensive position to pick off the remaining wolf creature and sprinted around the Helter-Skelter.

Scarred-Skull dodged the two bullets, ignored the parasite that jumped onto its back for a free ride and rushed to cut off the human's escape.

On reaching the far side of the Helter-Skelter, Kwanza headed for the rusty Ferris wheel. A glance back revealed the creature in pursuit, and he recognized it was too fast to outrun. Without stopping, he aimed the shotgun at it and fired to slow it down. The Hevi-Shot cartridge exploded its tightly packed pellets through the barrel and at its target.

The creature dodged to the side, but the unexpected spray of ammo peppered its face and side. Yelping painfully, it faltered briefly before recovering and veered away to a safer distance to continue the chase.

Kwanza reached the Ferris wheel and climbed the maintenance ladder welded to the inner rim of the large wheel. If he could reach a higher position he could pick off the creature with his rifle. Even if the monster climbed up after him he would be able to shoot it with the rifle or shotgun.

Fueled by pain and revenge, the creature rushed at the Ferris wheel. It jumped onto the flat roof of the ticket booth, leapt onto one of the wheel's cross struts and began climbing.

Kwanza glanced at the monster below. A blast from the shotgun ricocheted off the ironwork, releasing a rusty cloud and changing the creature's direction.

The parasite decided to take a more direct route to its new host and dropped onto the nearest strut.

Realizing he needed both hands if he was going to kill the nimble creature, Kwanza climbed inside one of the suspended carriages and sat on its cold, metal seat. It rocked, groaned and squealed alarmingly on its rusty, grease-congealed hinge. The door he kicked free clattered down the framework. He slid the rifle pressing uncomfortably into his back from his shoulder and laid it on the floor. The shotgun he aimed out the doorway, focused on its target and fired.

The creature had been watching its prey and was prepared for the shot. Its powerful legs propelled it higher up the framework as pellets pinged off the struts it no longer occupied. It ran along one of the long beams radiating out from the spindle to the outer ring the ride carriages were suspended from.

Kwanza's gaze followed the swift movements of the monster that seemed determined to reach him. It was clever. Moving above him, the carriage roof prevented him from getting off a clear shot. He leaned out and gazed up at the creature climbing down the outer ring. He waited until he had a clear shot and fired.

To avoid the blast, Scarred-Skull leapt onto the roof of a carriage two above Kwanza. The swaying carriage emitted a piercing metallic squeal when it was forced into frantic movement. Unable to stand the pressure, the rusty, corroded bolts attaching the hinge mechanism to the carriage snapped. Scarred-Skull dug its claws into the thin metal roof when its perch dropped and leapt back onto the solid framework when it crashed into the carriage below.

Kwanza ducked inside the precarious shelter to avoid the shower of rust and metal raining down. The crunching and squealing of tortured metal grew louder when the second carriage fixing broke. Kwanza was about to leap through the door when he glimpsed something pale and then felt a stinging pain on his cheek.

He staggered back and fell onto the seat. The roof buckled when the two loose carriages smashed into it. Thrown to the floor by the jolt, Kwanza felt the carriage roll farther than he suspected it was designed to do. Part of the roof ripped away when the fittings broke and sent him plummeting.

The parasite lunged at its new host's mouth. Its tiny tentacles squirmed between lips, forced jaws apart and dragged its putrid body inside. Gagging as it clawed its way swiftly down his throat, Kwanza dropped the shotgun and grabbed the parasite with both hands while he tumbled from side to side. Pain shot through his spine when the carriage struck the one below and jammed to a halt, stuck between the side of the carriage and the framework. Metal groaned in high pitch protest when the wreckage from above struck and bounced off. Kwanza yanked desperately at the creature. Its tentacles scraped his throat raw as they frantically grasped for purchase, but it was no match for the large man's strength and determination to dislodge it. As soon as it cleared his mouth, Kwanza drew in deep, hoarse breaths and slammed its writhing body against the side of the ride car until it split open. He threw the disgusting maggot out as his refuge began to shift and slide. Piecing shrieks of scraping and buckling metal accompanied the carriage's latest fall.

Kwanza hauled his aching body unsteadily to its feet as the framework slipped by and imagined the hard ground approaching fast. He leapt through the opening and wrapped his arms around a girder. Swinging precariously, he gazed at the falling carriage that crumpled and burst open on contact with the ground. The loss of weight on one section of the carefully balanced Ferris wheel, prompted it into movement with a protesting squeal.

As Kwanza was raised higher, he sought out Scarred-Skull above him. The two hunters locked eyes. It snarled murderously and leapt from the beam at him. To escape the claw that swiped savagely at his face, Kwanza let go. He groaned each time his body struck the framework. Hands grabbed at the beams, slowing but not halting his fall. The wooden roof of the ride operator's kiosk collapsed under his weight when he crashed into it. Kwanza groaned again when he struck the floor. His eyes, full of pain, peered through the destroyed roof at Scarred-Skull climbing down to him. He hauled his tired, battered body to its feet and winced from the pain in his leg. Blood seeped from the wound when he pulled the twisted metal shard from his thigh. His shoulder slammed against the door, breaking its lock and hinges and crashing it to the ground. When a quick glance amongst the wreckage failed to pick out his dropped rifle or shotgun, he ran.

CHAPTER 7

VOYAGE

To help pass the time on their voyage to the island and to inform his chosen team of what to expect when they reached their destination, Baloc had turned the galley into a temporary conference room. He began the meeting by pointing out the island's main buildings with a laser pointer on the large blueprint of the island hung across the galley kitchen's serving hatch.

The gathered group focused on the area Baloc circled with the pointer's blue dot.

"This is the village Ezra designed and built to house his actors, movie technicians and staff, and to later house his paying guests. Every house has electricity and running water, something which was still being connected in other more affluent countries."

Baloc moved the laser dot to the top end of the village.

"Ezra's movie workshops are located here. They include workrooms, maintenance and machine shop, sound stage, camera, film and cinematography equipment storerooms, an editing suite and small cinema viewing room. Props, costumes and makeup and lighting departments. A large kitchen with attached dining room and dry and cold food stores." He glanced at his audience. "Ezra had thought of everything to be totally self-sufficient from the outside world while he made his movies."

"Except for that new animal species that attacked and killed some of them on their first night party," added Winslow.

Baloc inwardly groaned. He had already explained his hired hunters had taken care of the island's predators. "*Was* responsible for the killings," he reiterated. "They have all been killed so the danger is past. However, as a precaution to ensure we come to no harm while we explore Ezra's fascinating island, let me introduce the security team I have hired to keep us safe."

Heads turned to look at the men by the entrance.

"Kurt Shaw, the man in charge of our safety, and his four men, Harvey, Thane, Ryker and Gunner."

After the introductions were over, Quincy, Mannix's cameraman, asked, "Going back to the creatures your hunter killed, what do they look like?"

"Let's not get sidetracked from our topic. You'll be able to see the animal when we arrive, but now we need to focus on the island's layout." Baloc turned back to the blueprint. "Perhaps the biggest single construction is the mansion that dominates the island and the first construction we'll explore." He directed the pointer at another detail. "South of the village on the far side of the small forest is the Fear Fair. It includes many attractions you'll recognize, such as the haunted house, merry-go-round, ghost train, and so forth, but all have received Ezra's unique blend of horrification, so as with all of Ezra's designs, expect the unexpected."

Baloc opened a folder, slipped out a small wad of photographs and handed them out. "These are copies of the only photographs taken by Ezra of his island. Though grainy and less sharp than we are used to nowadays with our high definition technology, they'll give you an idea of what to expect."

As the group examined and swopped photos between them, Baloc continued, "There is also an insane asylum, a subway—not a working one but a movie set—a swamp, the Dollmaker's Cabin, an abandoned mine, a Victorian street complex and a power room"—Baloc looked at Vince—"which will be our primary focus to get working when we reach the island."

"If that's still possible," added Vince.

Baloc smiled confidently. "You have come highly recommended, so with your skills and what we know of Ezra's fondness for throwing money at the best technology available at the time, I'm sure that won't be a problem."

Vince wasn't as convinced. "Obviously I'll give it my best, but you're talking about the best technology available *then*. It could be a seized-up lump of rusty metal by now."

"I think you'll be surprised when you see the power room. Ezra was way ahead of his time in most things, so I don't expect the generator crucial for making his movies would have deviated from that."

"I expect we'll find out soon," said Vince, "but if it's possible, I'll get the island powered up, make no mistake on that."

"Let's assume Vince gets the generators working—what's our next step?" asked Wendy.

"We explore Ezra Houghton's fantastical island, of course, to find out what he built and what condition it's in," replied Baloc.

Mannix stood to address the group. "To confirm what you have already been told, Quincy and I will be filming location shots for the forthcoming movie of the book Ezra will write about the island. It's my focus for this trip."

"If the structures are safe," Baloc glanced at Wendy, "I might stay on the island for an extended period to soak up the atmosphere while I write."

"As fond as I am of old horror movies, that sounds awfully creepy," said Winslow. "You wouldn't get me staying alone on an isolated island full of horror film sets for anything."

"They are only buildings, bricks, mortar, wood and plaster. It's the creepiness they extrude and the island's infamous reputation that will get my creative juices flowing to help me write a really scary novel. Another point of interest I've just remembered is that the island was a leper colony from 1749 to 1807."

"Is it safe?" asked Quincy, not relishing the idea of catching such a horrible infliction.

Baloc smiled. "I assure you, Quincy, the lepers are long gone and along with it the disease." He turned back to the blueprint. "I think that's about it for now. Once we are settled in the village"—he looked at his watch—"which will probably take us until midday, we'll have something to eat and then start exploring. While Vince checks out the generator, the rest of us can explore the mansion."

He smiled at his team excitedly. "It will be a couple of hours before we reach the island, so relax and enjoy the voyage."

CHAPTER 8

HOUSE OF HORROR

After discovering no sign of Kwanza at the village house where he had dumped his stuff, and no evidence he had spent the night there, Ray and Laura headed south to seek him out. They passed through a dark forest seeping a foreboding atmosphere. With their imaginations conjuring up thoughts of foul horrors skulking unseen through the shadows, watching, waiting, their eyes and weapons were driven to every rustle of leaves, sway of branch and crack of twig.

Glad to step into the sunlight again on its far side, they passed through the Fear Fair entrance and paused to gaze around at the macabre amusements and stalls.

"Remind me to never let our kids visit a fun fair," said Laura.

Ray looked at her in surprise. “Apart from this not being a typical fun fair, you’ve never mentioned you wanted kids before.”

Laura grinned at him. “Well, you’re not getting any younger, so I’m thinking we should start before you are past it.”

Ray laughed. “The way I performed this morning, you are probably already carrying triplets.”

Laura feigned shock. “I had better bloody well not be. Three babies at once, no thank you. One at a time at appropriate intervals is my plan.”

Ray raised his eyebrows. “You have a plan?”

“Of course, I’m a woman. I’ll fill you in on the details when we get back home, but first, we have to find our missing hunter.” Her eyes scanned the area.

Ray glanced at the top of the Ferris wheel at the back of the Fear Fair when it shrieked with movement.

“The flashes of gunfire we saw last night definitely came from around here somewhere. Even if there’s no sign of Kwanza, there should be evidence of the animals he killed, and we can see what species he was hunting.”

“Okay, lead on *Mister soon to be a daddy.*”

Grinning, Ray headed deeper into Ezra’s creepy Fear Fair.

When Laura noticed blood on one of the rides, she pointed it out to her husband.

They crossed to the Helter-Skelter and examined the bloodstains on the ground nearby. Whatever the copious amounts of blood had spilled from, it wasn’t there now.

Laura ran her gaze over the blood splatters on the snake wrapped around the tower. “This has to be where Kwanza encountered whatever he killed.”

Ray switched to defensive mode and trained his weapon around the area. "I agree, but where is he and where are the animals he obviously shot?"

"Maybe he moved them," suggested Laura. She noticed something on the ground and picked up the bloody object. "It's a skinning knife."

Ray glanced at the sharp blade. "That might explain the blood but not what happened to the carcasses." His eyes narrowed. "Something doesn't smell right."

Laura had been experiencing that very sensation shortly after they had started exploring the island. "Let's scout out the area. Maybe we'll find something that'll give us a clue to what happened here."

With weapons ready to defend against an attack, they cautiously moved around the Helter-Skelter and followed the trail of tracks that led to the Ferris Wheel. Their gazes took in the wrecked carriages strewn around the base of the wheel and the blood drips leading away.

Laura's eyes followed the blood trail. "Kwanza's or not, I guess we go see where it leads in case he's injured."

Ray's gaze scanned their surroundings. There were too many places of concealment for his liking. "Okay, stay sharp."

The gradually increasing wind flapped the skull-shaped bunting fixed around the top of the merry-go-round that looked anything but merry and nudged it into movement. Rusty bearings screeched as the ride turned. Laura and Ray glanced at the hellhound ride seats when they passed by. Some had wide-open jaws filled with sharp teeth, others had lips drawn back into vicious snarls. One had a baby—eyes wide and mouth frozen in a scream that would never end—clamped between its teeth, and another had two heads.

The blood trail led them to the entrance of another of Houghton's horror-themed rides. They both read the attraction's name written in blood-red paint complete with the effect of its letters dripping blood, HALLOWEEN HOUSE OF HORROR. The spooky façade was suitably decorated with ghouls, ghosts, skeletons and nightmare creatures.

Ray approached the warped wooden steps leading up to the ticket booth and beyond that the entrance to the scary house. The blood trail that continued up the steps had pooled on the top tread, as if whatever it had dripped from had paused before entering. He pointed out to Laura the partial smudge of a bloody boot print at the edge of the red stain. "It seems Kwanza is wounded, and he went inside."

"There's not much blood, so probably not life threatening." Laura cast her gaze around the attractions. "If I had to guess, I'd say he was being chased by something. Why else would he enter?"

"Maybe it was the creature that attacked us in the cabin after we drove it away?" Ray knelt and prodded a finger in the blood. It was dry, congealed. "He entered a few hours ago, probably not long after we heard his shots last night."

Laura looked at the entrance door apprehensively. "He wasn't at the village and we've seen no sign of him, so I assume he's still inside."

"If he was being chased, he might have holed up somewhere, or the creature chasing him caught and killed him. Either way we'll have to check."

Ray approached the door.

"You sure it's prudent to enter when there might be one of those vicious creatures inside?"

"It's a terrible idea, but Kwanza might be in trouble. Besides, if there is one of those creatures alive in there, possibly the last surviving member of its species, I want to be the one to kill it."

Laura took a deep breath. At that moment she couldn't think of anything less enticing than entering Ezra Houghton's Halloween house of horror, but if her husband was going inside, then so was she. "Let's get this over with before I come to my senses."

Ray smiled at his wife. "We'll be laughing about this later, you wait and see."

Hoping her husband was right, Laura followed him into the Horror House.

Before them, a hallway led to a closed door. The walls were adorned with old black and white photographs of spooky and ghostly scenes.

On the ceiling was an evil face formed by lumps and cracks in the plaster. It's open, grimacing lips displayed sharp teeth and two holes formed eyes with crack-wrinkles leading off from around them. Pale pupils in their centers stared at them unnervingly.

"I've been in more inviting houses," said Laura, attempting to make light of her anxiety.

"Yeah, I noticed the lack of any welcome mat." Ray nodded at the far door. "I'd be surprised if it doesn't take a turn for the worse through there."

"There's no need to sugarcoat it, hon, I'm with you all the way."

Ray grinned at his wife before heading for the door. The old, wide floorboards sagged and creaked beneath their weight. Though it could easily be attributed to the age of the long-abandoned building, both thought it was likely designed by Ezra to enhance the house's creepy atmosphere.

When Laura noticed something on the floor, she knelt, picked it up and turned the broken claw in her fingers.

As Ray neared the door, something clicked beneath his feet. He spun when Laura screamed and saw the floor dropping away taking Laura with it, fear in his wife's eyes as she looked at him. He rushed to her aid, but as soon as he took his weight off the board that had activated the trapdoor, a metal barrier slid from the ceiling and blocked the corridor.

He thumped on the barrier; it was solid. He knelt and tried to get his fingers underneath to raise it, but there was no gap. Frustrated, he banged on it again and called out his wife's name. He placed an ear to the metal but heard no reply. He stepped back and shouted, "I'm coming for you, Laura, and I promise I *will* find you."

Determined to find his wife, Ray crossed to the door and pushed it open. He ignored the rusty squeal of the swing door's hinges and stepped through, letting its spring catch slam it shut behind him.

*****

Laura gazed at her husband's feet when she heard the click, but before she could ponder its reason, the floor dropped out from beneath her and she fell. She slid down the hinged trapdoor when the front edge jolted to a stop on the lip of the metal chute that dipped steeply into darkness and heard it spring back into place behind her as she slid down the chute. She fumbled the rifle to point ahead, so the light fixed to it lit up what was coming. The chute curved into a gentle slope before depositing her out its end into nothingness. Her scream ended when she landed on something soft and bounced. As soon as she was able, she sat up and roamed the light around. Boards formed the four walls of the small chamber. On the sidewalls were two lightless-lamps long absent power. The high ceiling was timber-beamed with the bottom of the above room's floorboards resting on them. The end of the chute, too high for her to reach, meant even if it were possible to climb back up it, she couldn't.

Laura relaxed a little from her fright and drew in a deep breath of the stale, musty air. She was alive, uninjured and, for the moment, not in any danger. She had become a victim of one of Houghton's theatrical devices he would have no doubt used to heighten the fear in his movie and increase the thrills for the moviegoers. Splitting up those in peril to heighten tension had become a cliché movie plot device today. Assured her husband would be searching for her, all she had to do was make her way above ground and meet up with him. The only thing that might interfere with that would be the creature if it was still inside the house. Confident she would escape from Houghton's Horror House unharmed, Laura picked up the claw beside her and pocketed it, crawled off the large, thick mattress that had thankfully broken her fall, and approached the chamber's only viable exit. She took a deep breath to calm her nerves and pushed through the swing door.

*****

Ray aimed his light along the dark corridor's cracked plaster walls. In places the lime and horsehair plaster appeared to have fallen, revealing bare wooden slats. The lack of any debris on the floor hinted the dilapidated walls and ceiling had probably been designed this way. He ducked under the first ceiling lamp hanging at an angle on its electric cable as he moved along the corridor. When his light glinted off something behind the wall laths, he peered through the gaps. He almost reeled back involuntarily when his light reflected from the lifeless glass eyes of the spooky faces staring through the gaps. He had no doubts that when the haunted house was powered up the ghoulish figures would move and moan creepily. Ray turned away and pushed on.

When he rounded a sharp bend in the corridor, Ray was presented with two doors. A push of the nearest swung it open with the usual squeaky squeal. He backed away and aimed his weapon inside. A narrow wooden staircase led up—the opposite direction he needed to go. He moved to the second door and pushed it open. When nothing jumped out, he entered and shone his light around the windowless room. There was a fireplace, a matching three-seater settee and armchair, both torn and mildewed, a tattered rug, a lamp on a small table absent any chairs, and a bookcase crammed with dusty books. Ray strode towards the door that stood ajar to the left of the fireplace.

When he approached the armchair facing the door he was heading for and noticed someone, or something, sitting in it, he slowed and cautiously gave it as wide a berth as the objects in the room would allow. He almost gasped in fright at the cross-legged figure sat in the chair. Almost entirely covered in bandages, its head hung slightly to the side and rested on a shoulder. Its large wide-open eyes reflected the light he aimed at it and gave it the uncanny appearance of life. Its gaping mouth, stretched in an unnatural wide grin, almost clown-like, was filled with dirty teeth.

Curious to discover what it huddled in its arms, Ray took a few cautious steps nearer and immediately regretted his inquisitiveness when a shiver crawled down his spine. Thc baby in its arms was a smaller version of its mother and, though he found it hard to believe, it was twice as unsettling as its creepy parent. Even though Ray was well aware they weren't real, Houghton had created such a chilling atmosphere in his horror house it cast doubts on ones' beliefs and senses. A closer examination revealed the scary baby held a smaller facsimile doll of its mother, and it too held a tiny version of the baby.

Thankful he hadn't experienced the terrifying effect created when set into sound and motion by Ezra's theatrical wizardry, Ray scanned the figure with the Go-Pro camera to ensure all its chilling details were recorded. With that done, he crossed to the door and left mother and baby in solitude and darkness once more.

*****

Laura halted by the door she had stepped through and shone her light around the crypt. Most of the many stone niches formed in the walls contained coffins in various states of decay. A skeleton long stripped of flesh, lay half spilled from its decayed coffin. Large cobwebs she hoped were set decoration, hung from most surfaces. Laura brushed aside cobwebs that felt too real when she moved quickly through the room of the dead and climbed the short flight of twisting stone steps on the far side.

On hearing a sound ahead of her, Laura halted her nervous journey along the stone corridor and cocked an ear. Though she couldn't visualize what was making the click-clicking coming along the corridor, she thought it was a safe bet it wasn't anything she wanted to encounter, even armed with the powerful rifle, especially when the curve of the passage prevented her from getting off a shot until it was too close. She had seen how fast the monsters moved on this island and couldn't rely on killing it with one shot, which was probably all she would get. Erring on the side of caution, she retreated to the crypt and searched for a place to hide. When she discovered what was coming, she would decide her next move.

*****

Ray gazed around the large entrance hall of the horror house born from Ezra Houghton's macabre imagination. The main collapsed stairway prevented access to the upper floors. The large hole in the roof, the debris, dampness and the moss and patches of grass below it, indicated the collapse probably wasn't a design feature. A suit of time-tainted rusting armour stood against one wall and the largest grandfather clock he had ever seen against another; he could only imagine the loud ticking and thunderous chimes it would send echoing through the creepy house when it was working. The ghoulish carvings of skeletons, demons and foul creatures covering the wooden entrance and the large door in its center were both impressive and chilling.

Ray ignored the door. He doubted it was a real exit or even opened—probably put there to install false hope in those eager to escape the horror house—he wasn't ready to leave yet. Two of the five doors positioned around the hall opened onto brick walls. A third led to an unwelcoming corridor. When he opened the fourth and heard a click from inside the room, he dodged back to avoid whatever it was he had activated. When nothing happened, he peered inside and stared at the impressive spooky ghost before entering the short, narrow room and discovering the ghost was fixed to a rail in the floor. When powered up it would have shot forward when the opening of the door set it in motion and frightened the life out of the unfortunate person to have done so. He shut the door on the ghost and opened the last door. Pleased to see steps leading down, he quickly descended.

*****

The pitch blackness heightened Laura's senses when she climbed into one of the crypt's many alcoves and switched off the rifle light. Every creak of ancient casket, every flutter of web, were an imagined threat. Though almost an impossibility with the menacing clicks drawing ever nearer, she forced herself to remain calm and felt the rapid thumping of her heart against her chest settle slightly. If what was coming was out to harm her, she needed to defend against it. Aware the cramped space would make it difficult to use, she laid the rifle across her chest and un-holstered her revolver. When the ominous click-clicking on the stone floor entered the crypt, she peered through the gap between the wall and the end of the coffin she was concealed behind and waited for it to appear.

*****

The Queen was in a foul mood. One of the humans had all but wiped out her most powerful soldiers and her sole-surviving Ravager had strangely been disconnected from her thoughts. There was still a faint wisp of a connection, so she knew it wasn't dead, but something was wrong. Concerned it might be wounded, she had tracked it into the building to seek it out and offer aid if needed.

She entered the crypt to which the faint, but lingering scent of her Ravager had led her and wandered through the gloomy room where humans had once stored the corpses of their dead. Because the eyes of the form she had taken were useless in low light, she was forced to employ one of the human's light sources to search the room's dark recesses.

Laura stared through the web stretched across the gap and watched an orange glow move across the decaying coffins in the alcoves opposite. The light confused her as much as the clicks; animals don't use light.

When the oil lamp responsible for casting the orange light came into view, her fear wavered slightly when she noticed the hand holding it was human. Her fear rose swiftly when more of the creature stepped into view. Fighting back the shocked gasp that formed on her lips, Laura stared at the creature that in all that was holy should not exist. The human arm was attached to a slender female body, but what it was attached to at the waist was far from human. From below the waist the body was that of a giant spider. Its ugly, bulbous body was dotted with milky, semitransparent eggs with darker forms moving within. Each of the monstrosity's eight legs ended in single sharp claw. It was these that generated the clicks on the floor. Terror caused her body to tremble and her heart to race.

Forcing away the panic, Laura dragged her eyes away from the spider portion of the creature and studied the human part. Sharp talons tipped each human finger, and there were what seemed to be ridges of hard skin or bone along her arms, down her back and stomach. Her hair, if that was what it was, resembled multi-jointed spider legs. The medusa-effect tendrils wavered and clawed the air as if they searched for food or victims to ensnare.

Laura shrunk farther into the dark recess when the human-spider hybrid directed the lamp and its gaze in her direction, and she stared at the creature's face lit by the orange glow. Its eyes shone like cats' eyes caught in the headlights of a passing vehicle on a dark country lane. She was surprised by the face that looked familiar, as if she had gazed on it before, but it turned away before she could determine when and where.

Laura continued watching the creature when it moved past her position and shivered in revulsion at the hairy palm-size spiders crawling over its body tending the eggs. Because it looked like a larger scale version of the spider-dolls she had seen in the Dollmaker's Cabin, she briefly hoped it might be one of Houghton's movie creations, some type of clockwork animatronic robot or something, but she knew it wasn't. It was too real, too alive not to be flesh and blood. Whatever the human-spider hybrid was, it seemed to be looking for something or someone. Terrified it was her and she would be discovered and suffer an atrocious, painful fate, Laura tried to still her shaking limbs before they thumped on the coffin she was squeezed behind and revealed her presence. She gripped the gun in both hands ready to empty into the monstrosity if she was detected and focused on the creature's click-clicking footsteps heading for the far end of the crypt. The hinges of the chute room's door squealed eerily when the monster entered. Laura pondered making a dash for the stairs and running for her life, but the fresh squeak of hinges announcing the monster's return, belayed that thought.

With her eyes fixed on the orange glow moving nearer along the opposite wall, Laura clamped her lips together for fear she would scream when the creature appeared on her side of the room, less than a couple of arm lengths away. Her hand gripped the gun tighter, ready to use if the creature spotted her. When the creature's demeanor changed to one of alertness and it cocked its head, as if its senses had detected something, Laura imagined the worst and thought she had been found. Muffled gunshots echoed through the house and spurred the creature into action; it rushed for the exit.

It took Laura a few minutes to recover from the shock. Only when she was certain the creature had gone, did her trembling body and nerves begin to calm. She climbed out, switched on her rifle light and pulled the disgusting cobwebs from her hair. Her gaze went to the exit as she wondered who had fired the shots. Worried her husband might be in trouble, she fought back her fear and set off in the same direction taken by the horrific spider creature.

CHAPTER 8

Fog

A frown formed on Captain Rijas Santiago's brow when he glanced ahead at the fog bank his ship ploughed towards. He glanced at the radar and sighed; it was acting up again. A thump of his fist on the console brought it flickering back to life. Though it showed no indication of any obstacles in their path likely to damage the ship, he was hesitant to rely on the out-of-date equipment. Aware the island couldn't be far away, his worried gaze flicked back to the fog as his precautionary attitude bade him to reduce the old vessel's speed.

The island they would soon arrive at gave him the jitters. The sooner he dropped off his passengers and their supplies and departed, the better he would feel. If he wasn't being paid so handsomely, he wouldn't have accepted the job. His old boat desperately needed a new engine and updated equipment, and it was this that had persuaded him to accept the job, as the fee would go a long way to enable him to do both. Noticing activity on deck, the captain observed some of his passengers moving to the bow.

"Spooky," stated Quincy, gazing past the bow of the ship.

Wendy glanced at the cameraman. "It's only fog," she scoffed.

"That's as may be. However, it's not the fog that worries me, but what it might be hiding. I did some reading up on the island and something ain't right with it."

Mannix, the film director responsible for bringing some of Baloc's novels to the silver screen, joined them at the rail and flicked a cigarette butt into the water. "I think it will be great fun. Whatever's on the island, it sure doesn't include monsters, ghosts or any other form of unnatural or otherworldly entities. This is real life, not one of Baloc's scary novels."

"Then how do you explain all the deaths and some of those who have gone ashore never to be been again?" argued Vince. He too had researched the island and believed every word he had read on the Internet.

Mannix shrugged. "Stupid people doing stupid things I expect. Anyway, the hunters Zane sent to the island killed the beasts no doubt responsible for some of the alleged deaths, so we have nothing to worry about."

When the thick fog engulfed the ship, it brought with it an eerie atmosphere that coaxed the passengers to silence. The creaks and groans of the rusty vessel long past its prime, the lap of wash against the bow, the chugging of the antique diesel engine and the passengers' anxiety seemed amplified by the dense mist.

Slowly, dark shapes began to materialize when the thick mist thinned. When they emerged on the far side of the fog bank, they were greeted by a sight that startled and astounded them all.

Those on deck gazed at the amazing spectacle. The arm of a gigantic skeleton, whose intention seemed to be to snatch them and the ship from the water, reached down from the rocky cliff forming one side of the inlet. Though its skeletal chest and arm were covered by ragged material mimicking rotted clothing, its skull and hand were gruesomely displayed. The skull's dark sunken eye sockets stared at them evilly and its teeth-lined jaws grimaced with malicious intent. The gawping onlookers recovered from their surprise when they were thrown to the side by the ship's abrupt change of course.

The captain swore when the skeletal arm appeared from the mist as if to grab his vessel, and he looked apprehensively at the waves crashing over the rocks directly ahead. He spread his feet to secure his balance and spun the ship's wheel hard. The vessel responded immediately and swung around, sending out a wave that crashed against the rocky base of the towering cliff.

Gripping the rail to remain upright, those at the bow watched the skeletal fingers glide past high above them; the thing was massive.

Footsteps rushed to the bow as those below deck arrived to find out what was happening and joined the others staring in shocked fascination at the titanic skeleton.

The clicking of Wendy's camera broke the spell that had befallen the group.

"I think that is the most amazing thing I have ever seen," stated Mannix, smiling. He nudged his dumbfounded cameraman with an elbow to start recording. "And it's going to look fantastic on film."

Quincy placed the viewfinder of the professional high definition digital camera he used when scouting locations to his eye and recorded the spectacular creation he wouldn't have believed was real if he hadn't witnessed it with his own eyes.

"And this is only the entrance," beamed Baloc, wondering what other marvelous creations of Ezra Houghton's they were about to discover on the island.

Winslow gazed in amazement at the skeleton posed leaning over the cliff. So expertly had it been done, it seemed to have motion, which was reinforced by the tattered clothing that billowed and wavered in the wind. "The head alone must be six or seven yards from skullcap to chin."

Harvey, one of the four members of Baloc's security team, ran a hand over the back of his neck in an attempt to warm the chill that slithered down his spine. "How in hell's name was something like that even constructed?"

"Maybe it's the first hint why it took Ezra almost seven years to finish whatever he was doing here?" said Baloc, excited to start exploring. He turned to Wendy, who had stopped taking photographs and was gazing along the top of the cliff. "You're quiet."

"Sorry, was my having to continually make pointless conversation in the small print of the contract I signed?"

Baloc smiled at her abrasive but good-natured comment. "I'll have to check with my lawyers on that."

The captain steered his ship beneath the skeletal hand and piloted it through the narrow gap sided by tall cliffs of brown rock and towards the rusted metal entrance the skeleton guarded.

According to Baloc, this was the entrance to the only safe harbor the island offered.

The passengers gathered on the bow, ran their gazes up the steep cliffs that were only a few yards away from either side of the boat, and at the impressive wide-open gates that could be closed to ward off rough seas and keep prying eyes away from Ezra's secrets.

The ship glided through the entrance spanning the gap between the two rocky cliffs and entered the large natural harbor. The captain idled the engine as he aimed for the jetty, and the ship slowly drifted alongside. The wide gangplank thudded onto the jetty and two crewmen disembarked and tied off the bow and stern lines thrown to them. The crew shot nervous glances at the shore as they began unloading the supplies. Even though the captain and crew had been informed the island no longer presented a threat, they weren't inclined to take the risk and stay any longer than was necessary for them to fulfil their contract. None of them would remain near the island when night fell, whatever assurances the wealthy author gave them.

Armed with assault rifles and determination to protect Baloc and his team, the four members of Shaw's security team spread out along the jetty and roamed their eyes and weapons along the shore. Like the ship's crew, Shaw wasn't about to rely on the single phone call Zane had received that the island was now safe. He had been hired to ensure the safety of the exploration team against unforeseen circumstances and that was exactly what he would do.

CHAPTER 9

Blade Against Claw

Kwanza awoke to a throbbing horse-kick-to-the-head type pain in his skull and darkness all around him. Pushing through the fog that clouded his thoughts, he recalled how he had ended up here.

Kwanza had raced away from the monster climbing down the Ferris wheel and glanced back to see it leap to the ground. He checked his weapons, the pistol that needed reloading and the hunting knife, which he doubted he'd get close enough to land a killing blow with. He had no option other than to try and evade the monster. Fighting the pain from his wounded thigh that leaked blood down his leg, Kwanza dodged around rides and concession stands. When he arrived at the horror-themed house and debated whether he should enter, the monster's appearance drove him inside.

As he headed for the door at the far end of the short hall, Scarred Skull smashed through the door in a cloud of splintered wood and landed on the floor. To Kwanza's astonishment, the floor beneath the monster dropped away.

Scarred Skull reacted quickly and dived for the edge of the hole that had suddenly appeared. Its claws dug in, gouging splintered channels in the planks.

Before it had chance to pull itself up, Kwanza rushed forward and stamped on its claws, snapping one. The creature screeched, and as it dropped, lashed out at his leg with a claw, ripping Kwanza's trouser leg before he dodged away. Kwanza stumbled backwards through the swing door and spilled to the floor. He groaned when the swing door's return journey slammed into his leg wound. He was about to check the monster was really gone, when a metal door dropped from the ceiling. He glimpsed the trapdoor that had saved him spring back in position before the portcullis barrier fully closed.

Breathless from recent events, Kwanza adjusted the skew-whiff night vision goggles on his head and pulled them over his eyes. Wondering where the creature had fallen, and would it still be able to reach him, he climbed to his feet and checked the metal barrier. It was solid and firmly closed. He reloaded his pistol and returned through the swing door. The ghostly highlighted corridor he stared along was the opposite of welcoming. Eager to find a way out of the house and reclaim his weapons, he headed forward.

His search had taken him through a maze of corridors and rooms that led him below ground. When he had entered the room in which he currently resided, the monster that had lain in wait for him had attacked. He had lashed out with his pistol, catching the creature a hard blow to its head. The dazed monster had crashed into him, knocking him off his feet, and he just now awakened.

With no idea how long he had been unconscious, or why the creature hadn't killed him, his fingers gingerly probed the bloody swelling on the back of his head caused when he had struck the wall during his fall; it wasn't life threatening. However, whatever had just scraped on the floor too near for comfort might prove the opposite. His hands groped the floor for his pistol. Fingers brushed against something—his NVG. He hurriedly slipped them on and activated the power switch that must have been knocked off when they slipped from his head. He looked towards the increased scraping sounds and saw Scarred-Skull climbing to its feet and shaking its head. It too must have been unconscious.

Kwanza searched for his weapon and spied it a short distance away. A growl close enough to be life threatening spun his head. The creature's vicious snout was only inches away. Monster and man stared at each other. The creature shrieked. Kwanza raised a leg and slammed a foot into its shoulder. As the monster toppled to the side, Kwanza rolled towards the pistol.

When Scarred-Skull spotted the human's objective, it leapt at him and wrapped a claw around the wrist of the hand that snatched up the pistol. When bullets sped harmlessly past and peppered the ceiling, it dug talons deeper into flesh.

Kwanza gritted his teeth against the pain as the weapon slid from his grasp and slammed a fist into the side of the monster's head. Scarred-Skull curled back its lips, displaying wicked teeth in a vicious snarl. Aware he had mere seconds to act, Kwanza tugged his knife from its sheaf and plunged it into the creature's neck. It shrieked and leapt away. Kwanza climbed to his feet and brandished the bloodied knife at the creature. It was now claws against blade.

When Ray heard the gunshots coming from the floor below him, he knew they didn't come from any of Laura's weapons; he knew their sounds like he did his own. Kwanza must be responsible. He searched for a way down.

Worried about running into the spider creature, Laura's finger hovered near the trigger of the weapon aimed along the dark passage lit by her flashlight. She paused at the stairs at the end and listened for any sounds from above. Aware the wooden treads would creak and there was nothing she could do to prevent it, she began her climb.

CHAPTER 10

BALOC ARRIVES ON ISLAND

Concerned he hadn't been able to contact his hired hunters to let them know they had arrived, Baloc ended the hissing static and returned the sat-phone to his pocket. He glanced at the distant storm clouds intermittently lit with flashes of internal lightning he thought were responsible and joined the captain standing at the port rail overseeing the unloading of the cargo.

"Any chance your men can help us carry the supplies ashore?"

The captain glanced at Baloc disapprovingly. "Step foot on that island? Not a chance in hell. As soon as the last item is unloaded, we're leaving before the storm hits." The captain turned his attention to his disembarking passengers; he thought them all fools.

"I'll pay extra," tempted Baloc.

"No amount you offer will persuade me that staying on this island longer than necessary will be a wise thing to do. I'd rather face a raging hurricane than risk being stranded here for any longer if I can avoid it." His old eyes flicked to the heavens. "Storm's on its way and it will be night in a few hours. I don't aim to be anywhere near this damned island when either arrives."

"That's it, Captain," called out one of his crew, "all unloaded."

"About time," the Captain moaned. "Get everyone aboard that's coming and untie the lines." He turned to Baloc and held out a hand expectantly. "That's my side of the bargain completed."

Baloc pulled a fat envelope from his pocket and placed it in the captain's calloused palm. "You'll return in a week to pick us up as agreed?"

"I said I would, didn't I? Make sure you're ready as I won't be hanging around."

"We'll be waiting."

The captain scoffed. "That remains to be seen." Imagining things that shouldn't exist observing him, his eyes roamed the shadows amongst the trees hugging the shoreline. "I think you're all mad. You are messing with something you know nothing about. If you had any sense, you'd all get back aboard my ship and leave with me. It might be your only chance."

"I'm willing to take the risk," said Baloc, dismissing the captain's concerns as superstitious fears brought about by the islands' rumored past. Kwanza had killed the creatures, so as far as he was aware, the island was now safe.

The captain nodded at the disembarked passengers gathered on the jetty staring at the island. “You might be, but what about them?”

“They are not your concern, Captain. Like you, they have a job to do. I will see you in seven days. If I decide to stay longer, I will radio a list of any extra supplies I might need.” Baloc turned away, grabbed his rucksack and descended the gangplank that was raised as soon as his feet stepped onto the jetty.

The ship’s noisy engine belched dense grey smoke as it chugged hesitantly to life. Those ashore watched it turn and head back through the gate, leaving them stranded on Ezra Houghton’s mysterious island.

Baloc ran his eyes over his handpicked team and their last-minute supplies and equipment that included perishables he couldn’t have delivered sooner. “Okay, everyone, it’s time to explore the island. If everyone carries as much as they feel comfortable with, I’ll arrange for the rest to be fetched later.”

Vince finished loading his tools onto the sack truck and tested its weight. “I have room for another box.”

Mannix picked up a bag of potatoes and stuck it on top. “How’s that?”

“Fine,” said Vince.

Baloc turned to his head of security. “Kurt, are you and your men ready?”

Shaw checked his men were in position and alert for any threat. “We are.”

“Then what are we waiting for? Let’s go explore.”

Ryker, Harvey and Thane, led the group along the jetty to the shore. As soon as the armed men’s feet touched solid ground, they spread out and formed a defensive position. Their eyes and assault rifles constantly searched the surrounding foliage for any threat while the rest of the team explored the few buildings set a short distance back from the shore.

"Cheery greeting," said Wendy, framing the sign in her camera viewfinder.

The others looked at the sign arched over the path between the two buildings positioned either side of the stone path. WELCOME TO HORROR ISLAND – YOUR SURVIVAL IS NOT GUARANTEED.

Mannix grinned. "That's going to look fantastic on film and a great slogan for a movie poster." So far, the island was surpassing his expectations.

Winslow hoped the sign's ominous message was only something to set the scene for one of Ezra's movies or his visitors, and not an actual warning they should heed.

The simple but well-constructed wooden huts, though encroached with vegetation and evidence of rot, seemed in fair condition considering how long they had been abandoned to the elements.

"These were going to be the reception buildings where Ezra's visitors would have been received, booked in and allocated accommodation if his film-inspired theme park had ever got off the ground," explained Baloc. "This would have also been where they handed over their signed injury waiver and non-disclosure forms."

Mannix glanced at Quincy to check he was filming and then back at Zane. "So, just to confirm, Ezra was going to make a series of horror films that, in his words, '*would astound and shock moviegoers around the world*' and then turn his film sets into a theme park."

Baloc nodded. "That's the gist of it, but as we now know, a dangerous species of creature put an end to all that when it killed some of his actors and crew before filming had even begun."

"So, after spending many years, and god knows how many millions creating whatever it is we are about to encounter, it was all in vain?"

"Yes, unfortunately," answered Baloc. "However, his loss is our gain, and it's now up to us to reveal to the world Ezra Houghton's cinematic masterpieces. Another interesting fact, which Ezra may or may not have planned, was that his constructions took six years, six months and six days to complete."

"Six, six, six, the sign of the devil," said Winslow.

"That is so cool," said Mannix, "and fits in with the original name of Ezra's island when he purchased it—Isla Satana, *Satan's Island.*"

Keen to get moving, Baloc prompted the others into motion. "Let's move on as we've barely set foot on the island, and I'm certain we're all eager to see what lies ahead."

Mannix indicated to Quincy the short interview was over. It would all be information he could use later. He had a good feeling from what he had seen and learnt so far that Zane's book would be a best seller and the movie he would make a summer blockbuster.

Baloc nodded to Shaw to proceed.

Shaw pointed at Ryker and Gunner." You're with me at the front." He glanced at his remaining two men to check they had moved to the rear of the group, before heading along the overgrown path.

CHAPTER 11

Deathmatch

When the Queen passed through a large room, she glanced around at the strange devices that seemed to have been invented to cause pain and discomfort to the tortured human copies occupying most of them. She entered the adjoining room and flicked her gaze to the footsteps creaking the floorboards above. The shriek of her last surviving Ravager spurred her into action. She climbed a wall and walked upside down on the ceiling. She halted beneath where she sensed the human above stood and placed the point of one of her front limbs against the bottom of the floorboard. When a board bowed with a soft creak a short distance away, she altered the position of the sharp tip.

Kwanza and Scarred Skull locked stares as both waited for the other to make its move. Kwanza sensed the animal was stalling, waiting for something to happen. Perhaps there were more of its kind he hadn't killed, and they were on their way. If that was the case, it would be prudent to dispatch the creature before its backup arrived. He was about to launch an attack when soft clicks on the floorboards tingled his warning senses. He glanced at the floor where the sounds came from. There was nothing there. They came from beneath.

He refocused on the Scarred Skull. It had made no attempt to attack when he had been distracted, but strangely backed away a few steps. Concerned by the clicks that moved towards his position, Kwanza glanced at his pistol on the floor across the room. The creature snarled a warning. Kwanza shrugged. His damaged wrist would have made it difficult to use. The clicks stopped. Kwanza stared at the floorboards around his feet. Something was about to happen. It was time he killed the creature and got out of the house before it did.

The Queen drew her limb back and stabbed it through the wood.

Kwanza almost screamed when something pierced his foot. He glanced at the pointed tip sticking from the top of his boot and grimaced when he slid it off. Claws scraped on wood when Scarred Skull attacked. Kwanza rushed at it. They met in a clash of claws and blade before parting. Both had suffered fresh wounds.

Blinking away the unexpected drowsiness that threatened to incapacitate him, Kwanza wielded the knife at Scarred Skull but found he was unable to hold it steady. He staggered back when floorboards erupted in a splintered explosion of wood and dust. Strange limbs appeared through the hole and started ripping up floorboards. Supporting joists were snapped as if they were made of balsa wood. The weakened floor sagged towards the hole when something Kwanza found hard to believe climbed through. He stared into the eyes of the creature that approached him, its pretty human, almost innocent face, at odds with its terrifying spider body.

Kwanza experienced something that had been absent his emotions for a long time—acute fear. Assuming he would soon become fully paralyzed by the spider venom coursing through his bloodstream and nothing pleasant would follow, he coaxed his uncooperative hand to grip the knife tighter, rushed at the spider creature and leapt onto her back.

Caught off guard by the human's attack, the Queen staggered back. Her rear legs groped air as the human landed on her back. The clashing force sent both toppling through the hole. Kwanza wrapped his legs around her human waist and held on.

Some of the spiders on her body were crushed when the Queen struck the floor. Precious eggs burst open, spilling out her helpless malformed offspring. She screeched in anger and sorrow for their loss.

Jolted forward when they landed, Kwanza smashed his nose on the back of her head. Large spiders crawled over him, plunging in their fangs. Her hair attacked, poking his eyes, jabbing his face. One tendril wrapped around his throat, strangling him. Ignoring the many sources of agony inflicted upon his body—he was beyond pain now—Kwanza grabbed the throat tendril with his damaged hand and sliced through the thick hair limb with his knife. Dark purple pus-like blood sprayed his face. He spat out the foul substance and glanced at the cut tendril wriggling in his grasp when teeth formed around the cut. Before he could throw it clear, it slithered from his grasp, dived at his face and latched teeth onto his neck. His skin tore when he yanked the biting tendril free and threw it at the wall.

Growing weaker every second, Kwanza stabbed at the spider creature's back. The Queen bucked when the knife entered her flesh. Kwanza slipped. He grabbed at the human torso and slid around the front. Face to face with the monstrosity, he drove the knife at her face. The protective hair tendrils grabbed his knife hand before the blade connected with the Queen's skin and drew his wrist towards her mouth. She clamped teeth around his arm, severing blood vessels when she bit off a chunk of his flesh. A tendril snatched the knife from Kwanza's weakening grasp, plunged it into his shoulder and twisted savagely. Kwanza slithered to the floor when the tendrils loosened their grip.

Drowsy, wounded, and in agony, Kwanza crab-walked backwards to the wall and rested against it. He swiped away the spider on his leg and watched it scuttle back to its mother, who rose on its eight legs and snarled at him. Kwanza turned his weary head when something thumped to the floor a short distance away. He grinned at Scarred Skull when it snarled at him. He forced his hand to move to the knife sticking from his shoulder but lacked the strength to pull it free. His arm flopped limply to the floor when the creepy arachnid approached.

The Queen halted in front of the human who had slain her Ravagers and grabbed him when he started sliding to the side. She drew him close to her face, lifted a front limb and waved the pointed tip before his glazed over eyes. She wanted him to know what was coming. When she pressed the sharp tip in his ear, his drooping eyes shot open. He screamed as she slowly pressed the tip deeper. The Queen pulled her bloodied limb free and let the human's corpse collapse to the floor. Scarred-Skull rushed forward and began feeding.

CHAPTER 12

Graveyard and Crypt

The team received further hints of Ezra's imaginative mind when they rounded a bend in the path. Two stone pillars adorned with carvings of serpents and human skulls supported wrought iron gates. Perched on top of each, menacing gargoyles stared down at them. Through the gates, gravestones and mausoleums of varying designs and sizes poked above the ground-hugging mist swirling around them.

Shaw passed through the partly open gate and gazed around the cemetery. Its eclectic assortment of ornate gravestones reminded him of Highgate Cemetery. Rumoured to be haunted, it was infamous for the many sightings of ghouls, ghosts, spirits and had even inspired stake-wielding vampire hunters to descend on the site to hunt down the Highgate Vampire many claimed to have seen roaming the graves at night. "Ryker, Gunner, scout it out."

As the two men moved between the tombstones, Shaw addressed the group. "Keep together as we move forward."

Though Baloc thought Shaw was being overly cautious, he said nothing as their actions seemed to put the group at ease. Accompanied by clicks from Wendy's camera, they entered the graveyard and followed Shaw along the winding stone path.

"It has the appearance of a creepy film set," commented Winslow.

"That's exactly what it is," stated Baloc. "Or rather, the reconstruction of one. I recognized the entrance from Ezra's second movie, *The Dead Arose*."

"How many films did he make?" asked Mannix.

"Only three," answered Baloc. "His final offering—and apparently his most gruesome—was never released and was the final nail in his career coffin as a movie director. You must remember this was the early days of cinema. Though colour film in various forms had been around since 1902, and the first colour film, *Cupid's Arrow*, was shot in 1918, it was expensive and didn't become widely used until the late-thirties when the *Wizard of Oz* and *Gone with the Wind* were filmed in Technicolor. Even then, the majority of films were still black and white and would remain so for many years. Ezra, always one to embrace new technology, paid out of his own pocket to film *The Dead Arose* in colour, so for the first-time moviegoers could see the colour of blood and gory death on the big screen, something mostly avoided by other directors at that time, and Ezra's films were full of it. So advanced were the groundbreaking techniques Ezra created to portray the death of his characters in his final movie, the executives of the film studio he worked for were shocked by the gruesome killings they had just witnessed in the viewing room. So lifelike were the deaths they believed he had actually murdered some of his actors and actresses, as they couldn't see how else the effects could have been achieved. Ezra, as stubborn as he was talented, pleaded his case but refused to reveal the techniques involved because they were his trade secret. The police were informed, and when they viewed the film, they were also shocked by the movie deaths. With foul play suspected, Ezra was questioned. Even when Ezra produced those who were seen dying in the film and the investigation was dropped, the bad publicity saw him fired from the studio. Because Ezra's last film was thought to be too gory and realistic to ever see the light of day, it was promptly destroyed. Infuriated by the big studios lack of vision, Ezra turned his back on them and vowed to make a series of films that would see him become the driving force in the movie business. That's when he purchased this island and the rest, as they say, is history."

Baloc pointed at a few of the tombstones. "In *The Dead Arose*, reanimated corpses arose from the graves when the heroine of the story entered the graveyard looking for her missing fiancé."

"According to the blueprints I'm still studying," added Wendy, "the reanimated corpses from Ezra's movie were also recreated here, but simple clockwork animatronic dummies and sound effects replaced live actors. They didn't walk, only sat up or poked their skeletal arms out of the graves."

"It all seems a bit Disneylandish to me," said Mannix, his disappointment obvious. After witnessing the giant skeleton guarding the entrance, he had expected to see something much more impressive on the island.

Baloc smiled. “Don’t worry, Mannix, I’m certain it will get better.”

They found Ryker and Gunner waiting for them at the far end of the graveyard.

Shaw reached them first and nodded at the dark entrance of the large crypt to which the cobbled path had led them. “What’s through there?”

“It’s best you come see it for yourself, as you ain’t gonna believe it,” replied Ryker.

“We did a quick recce around the immediate area and all seems clear,” added Gunner.

Though Shaw would normally call the men out for not answering with the requested information, he had known when he accepted the contract this wasn’t going to be a normal job, so he was willing to give them some leeway as long as it didn’t interfere with their mission. He turned to the approaching group.

“Wait here while I check it out.”

Shaw followed Ryker and Gunner into the crypt.

Ryker appeared at the entrance a few moments later. “It’s clear.”

The group entered.

Sunlight entered through the high arched window on the far wall and highlighted much of the crypt’s interior. Thick cobwebs, whether spun by spiders or set dressing was difficult to tell, stretched from ceiling to walls and from the two stone columns supporting the roof. Though the realistic webs were in abundance, except for a few wispy strands wavering in the breeze blowing through the crypt, they didn’t encroach across the path that led to the far opening. Except for the open stone sarcophagus displayed atop a stone plinth, the room was bare.

The group approached the coffin and glanced inside at the dusty, smartly attired corpse, the wooden stake that pierced its heart and its vampire teeth protruding over its dry, stretched lips that would have groaned when visitors passed by. A sign fixed to the side of the coffin read, *'Under no circumstance remove the stake.'*

Though all present knew it wasn't real, it was hard to shake off the feeling that it hadn't once been a living, breathing person, or vampire. When they headed for the far exit, the bright flash of Wendy's camera lit up the crypt.

Surprise greeted the group when they exited the crypt and stepped onto the cobbled surface of a medieval street lined with timber-framed buildings. It was if they had stepped back in time to a bygone era.

Though Baloc was aware of the village from the blueprints, he was still pleasantly surprised by how authentic the street and houses appeared in real life. Terraced timber-framed buildings of varying sizes and designs stretched along the street either side of the sunken waterway that flowed out of a tunnel beneath the crypt they had passed through. Stone steps led down to a path slightly higher than the water level and followed its course along the street. Rotted crates, barrels and a wagon collapsed on a broken wheel were dotted along the street. Brick bridges arching over the water at intervals connected the two sides.

Mannix, a little taken aback by the authentic details of everything around him, approached the nearest house, wiped a clear patch on a grimy window and peered inside. He saw armchairs, wooden furniture and pictures hanging on the walls; all were covered in dust and none dated from the period prescribed by the dwelling's medieval architecture.

Winslow gazed up at steeply pitched tiled roofs projecting out from some of the two- and three-story dwellings, the small balconies on some of the houses and jutting overhangs of upper floors. He couldn't begin to imagine how much all this had cost Ezra, and they hadn't even started exploring the island's major features yet.

Wendy was so surprised her eyes wandered over everything without taking a single photograph, something she soon remedied when she recovered from the pleasant surprise.

They wandered along the street in silence as they marveled at everything Ezra had created. The water in the channel flowed through a tunnel under the square where the helicopter had dropped the supplies Baloc had arranged.

Baloc walked to the far side of the square where the watercourse reappeared. Ezra's movie industrial buildings lay beyond. A mishmash of different sized medieval warehouses with rendered walls of grey towered above both sides of the canal. A half-submerged barge lay at an angle across the water, causing waterlogged barrels, pieces of timber, leaves and flotsam to build up against it.

Quincy joined him by the low brick wall built around the edge of the square. "Wow, look at that." His camera went to his eye and started filming.

The group followed the direction of Quincy's camera and gazed at the dark, imposing building set at the top of a slight rise. The jumble of turrets and towers filled with dark uninviting openings extruded an ominous aura they all sensed.

Mannix smiled. "Now that's more like it. That mansion is going to make a fantastic film set."

"Which is exactly what it is," reminded Baloc.

Wendy cast her professional gaze over the distant, dark, spooky building. Spindly trees, tall and leafless growing around the building, seemed to sprout from the rooftops like malignant growths. "I'd advise you against adding it to the script until I've checked it out. From this distance it seems a strong wind might send it crashing to the ground."

"It's called Dreadmore Mansion," Baloc informed them as he turned to Shaw. "Though I'm sure we'd all like to get a closer look, I think it's best left for later as we have our accommodations to sort out."

He glanced back at the two pallets of supplies and then at the dark clouds rolling towards the island.

"We also need to unload that lot before the storm arrives and soaks everything. There is food, water, bedding, including mattresses, cooking stoves, gas bottles, flashlights, two portable generators—in fact, everything we need to ensure our time spent on the island is as comfortable as possible."

The excited group spent the next couple of hours setting up their accommodations in some of the quaint houses. They stripped the beds of their musty blankets and mattresses and remade them with the fresh ones Baloc had arranged to be ferried to the island. One of the larger dwellings was set up as a meeting room and communal kitchen, where all the meals would be prepared with everyone pitching in. On the wall beside the tables and chairs gathered from the surrounding houses and pushed together, Baloc had pinned the large blueprint overview of the island, showing the layout of the buildings Ezra had seen fit to record on the plans. He had circled the mansion as their first point of exploration.

Wendy and Quincy, with Harvey on watch, volunteered to prepare a meal while the others returned to the jetty to collect the remaining supplies.

After they had eaten a hot meal, Vince gathered up the tools and equipment he might need to get the generator running, and they set off to explore the island.

CHAPTER 13

Reunion

Ray paused at the doorway, poked his head around the frame and looked around the room he was certain the shots had come from. His eyes rested on the hole in the floor where guttural grunts came from. Avoiding the splintered debris littering the floor, he edged nearer the hole and trod softly when the floor sagged. When he was as near as he dared, he cautiously peered below. An orange glow coming from an unknown source shed light on the large creature he recognized from the swamp. Fortunately, its back was to him, and it seemed to be feeding on something. Dread gripped him when he imagined his wife was its food.

When Scarred Skull ripped off a lump of meat and raised its head to chew the bloody morsel, Ray saw the lifeless, lolling head of the body it fed upon, Kwanza. This had to be the creature that chased the hunter into the horror house. Ray grasped the opportunity and raised his rifle to shoot the creature but froze when something far more dangerous moved into view. Eerily lit by the lamp it held, Ray found it difficult to believe what he looked at was real. If he were anywhere else he wouldn't have believed such a giant spider, let alone it was part human, could exist, but here, on this island, anything seemed possible.

Shock stayed his hand, and before he could aim at its human head, it had moved from his sight. It was too risky to kill the other creature with the spider monster in attendance, so careful not to make a sound, he backed away from the hole. His anxious glance around the room spied Kwanza's pistol. It seemed the man had battled with the creature below, and possibly the monster arachnid, before losing his life.

The Queen communicated with her Ravager and gave it instructions to search the building for any other humans and kill them without endangering its own life. These humans had proved more resourceful and harder to kill than those who had visited the island previously. Her brood of expert killers had been depleted, but if she could get off the island and reach a larger landmass she was certain existed, she could replenish her brood. She left the room and went to find out what the humans elsewhere on the island were up to.

Ray cocked an ear at the click, click of the spider creature's footsteps moving away and with it the light. He flicked his NVGs over his eyes and waited until both had faded before moving back to the hole. It was his chance to kill the predator while it fed. His green-lit gaze focused on the creature's position, but it wasn't there, only a pool of blood and Kwanza's half-eaten corpse. It must have left with the spider creature. He glanced at his feet when the sagging floor bounced slightly and stepped back from the hole in case his weight was responsible. The floor continued to vibrate, dislodging pieces of loose floorboards that crashed onto the floor below. With his senses on high alert, Ray stepped farther away from the broken floor and strained to pick out any sounds above the constant creaks and groans of the floor. Suspecting he was being hunted, he aimed his weapon at the barely discernable scrapes coming from beneath the floor he stood on. Certain the predator climbed across the ceiling below, Ray waited for a clean shot. If it was the island's sole surviving apex predator besides the human/spider hybrid, he couldn't risk wounding it while Laura was somewhere in the house.

Scarred-Skull breathed in the lingering scent of its Queen as it chewed. It felt good to have reestablished a connection with her after the loss of its brethren. It studied the human responsible for their deaths. They were weak creatures who would be defenseless without the strange weapons that spat pain and death. The humans didn't need to get close to kill, leaving them no chance to use their own weapons of teeth and claws. Its head turned slightly to breathe in the human scent drifting through the broken ceiling. It recognized the smell from the human it had encountered before, near the swamp.

Deciding on caution, it employed the same tactic as its queen and climbed the wall and headed across the ceiling towards the hole. It ignored the pieces of debris its claws dislodged from the ceiling and focused on the human's movements above that moved farther away from the opening. Scarred-Skull paused and peered through a gap between the boards. The human's weapon was aimed straight at it, indicating he was aware of its presence. It glanced at the hole two steps away. The human would shoot if it tried to reach him. When another human scent, feminine, alerted it to a second human nearby, it glanced down at the doorway and watched her enter.

Laura stepped into the room and froze when her light fell on the creature hanging from the ceiling. The scar on its head labelled it as the same one that had attacked her husband in the Dollmaker's Cabin. With a better view of its physique, the hunter in her couldn't help but admire the predator's sleek, powerful form. Its muscular limbs and savage teeth and claws designed for hunting and killing prey put it a few points ahead of any big game she was familiar with. She was left with no doubts that it would soon become top of the food chain if it ever reached the mainland. To avoid startling the creature, she slowly raised her rifle. One shot to the head should see it dead.

When the human female raised her weapon, Scarred-Skull knew against two weapons from alternate directions, it would stand little chance of survival. It released its grip on the ceiling and twisted as it dropped. As soon as its paws touched the floor it sprung for the exit.

Laura barely had time to react when the creature moved. Her hurried shot sent a bullet whizzing across its rump. The creature faltered and careened into the wall before it reestablished its footing and fled. It was gone before she could get off a second shot.

"Laura!"

Laura spun the weapon towards the unexpected voice and quickly turned it away from the relieved expression plastered on her husband's face peering down at her.

"Hi, hon." She smiled. "Did you miss me?"

He smiled back at her. "A little." He leaned into the hole and looked at the doorway the creature had fled through. "Did you hit it?"

"Grazed its rump is all."

"Another wound for its collection. They are fast buggers." He glanced at the dead hunter Laura turned her gaze away from. "That Kwanza managed to kill six of them singlehandedly is impressive."

"I didn't much like the man, but he didn't deserve that."

The edges of the floor sagged when Ray sat, dangled his feet through the hole and dropped to the floor. "I'm glad you're okay." He hugged and kissed his wife.

"As I am you. I assume our next move is to hunt the predator. I think it's the same one that attacked you in the cabin, so that's twice it's got away from us now."

"It's a formidable adversary, but I'm confident we can kill it."

"That isn't the only strange animal on the island. The thing I've seen, close-up, I still find difficult to believe it's real."

"It wasn't a giant spider with a human torso by any chance?"

Laura raised her eyebrows in surprise. "You've seen it?"

"It was here a few minutes ago. I'm not sure what it is or how it could possibly have evolved, but it's real enough."

"I know. It's like a grotesque centaur arachnid has stepped out of the pages of a mythical horror story into our world. How could something like that even exist?"

Ray shrugged. "I have no idea, but I'd like to see Darwin explain it."

"Did you notice its similarity to the creepy spider dolls we saw in the Dollmaker's place? What's that all about?"

"I did, and I have no idea, but something strange is happening on this island and there might be other things we haven't seen yet."

"You got that right, hon. Though I'd rather not be, we're stuck on this island until Zane arranges transport off, so I suggest we hunt the creatures and kill them before they kill us."

"I agree, but we'll have to be even more careful now there are two predators on the loose and maybe more."

Laura glanced at her watch. "We also have another problem. Zane and his team will have arrived by now. We need to warn them."

"Hopefully the creatures will have vacated the house, so let's do the same and contact Zane on the sat-phone once we're outside."

With Ray taking the lead, they exited the room and searched for an exit.

After climbing back out the hole in the horror house's roof, the Queen crossed the Fear Fair, climbed to the top of the Ferris wheel and scanned the landscape until she picked out the humans by the village. As she observed them with thoughtful interest, she wondered why they had come here. She assumed these latest arrivals were connected to the three humans who had arrived previously and began hunting her brood, but these seemed to have a different purpose. She had ordered those under her control to observe, but not interact with the two male and one female humans until she had learned their strengths and weaknesses, but her brood were restless. Food had grown scarce from their over-hunting, so she had allowed them to attack the dark human, which turned out to be a mistake that had seen six of her brood dead. When her thoughts wondered back to the water vessel that had brought the new arrivals here, an inkling of a plan formed as to how she might be able to leave the land she had exhausted of suitable hosts for her offspring.

She gazed out at the fog that continually blocked her view and wondered what lay beyond. The humans had to come from somewhere. Unless they lived on the floating vessels there had to be other lands out there and more creatures she could claim to spread her seed. However, for her plan to succeed, she needed a suitable human host. Though she had tried to control them in the past, their wills had been too strong, and they had fought her attempts. She had been more cautious with the four young humans who had arrived a while ago, but still it had been too much for their weak brains. The resulting damage to two of them had turned them into little more than mindless shells.

To learn the ways of the humans, she had chosen a third as her host, but their weak, fragile bodies proved too inconvenient. They were prone to injury, defenseless, useless at climbing and took forever to get anywhere. Believing that such things existed elsewhere in the human's world, she had transformed into a larger version of the tiny eight-legged human copies she had found in the building by the swamp.

She still had one human left, one she had been saving for such an event that might have just presented itself, but the young female had grown weak and perhaps was now unsuitable for the task she required of it.

The Queen climbed down the wheel when the humans headed for the large building on the hill. It was time to visit her human captive to judge its condition and receptiveness to her control.

CHAPTER 14

DREADMORE MANSION

The canal that started beneath Dracula's crypt and ran beneath the square changed into a river a short distance outside the boundary wall that surrounded the village. The small waterfall formed where the stone channel ended, cascaded into a pond that emptied into a river meandering around the hill the mansion sat upon. Clumps of dark thorny bushes absent any foliage grew along its banks. Dotted across the barren landscape were remains of wooden fencing that leaned at angles like a stockade constructed to deter an unknown enemy.

Shaw glanced at the mansion but saw no sign of the three men he had sent ahead to scout the area while the rest of the group followed at a slower pace.

As the fascinated group approached the spooky and impressive mansion, it became apparent its dilapidated state had little to do with natural deterioration but had been purposely designed to portray its haunted, neglected appearance.

Wendy walked up to one of the columns supporting the seemingly sagging porch overhanging the steps and rapped a knuckle on its apparent wood-rotted surface. “Concrete,” she stated, as she examined each side for cracks. “And in surprisingly good condition.”

“Then it’s safe to venture inside?” enquired Baloc.

Searching for any large cracks or signs of deterioration in the structure that weren’t part of Ezra’s design, Wendy’s gaze scanned the front of the building and found nothing that would indicate the building was in imminent danger of collapse.

“I won’t know for certain until I’ve seen the condition of the interior, but the building seems sound, so yes, as long as we are careful, it’s probably safe to enter.”

Baloc turned towards the approaching footsteps and waited for Ryker, Harvey and Gunner to join them.

“We’ve walked the circumference and found all the doors locked, windows intact and no sign of any other point of ingress, so if there’s no other entrance into the house, it’s probably as empty as the day it was abandoned,” Ryker reported.

Shaw glanced at Baloc. “Are there any other entrances on the blueprints?”

Baloc shook his head. “Not that that’s much of a help due to Ezra making changes as he went, so I wouldn’t rule it out.”

Harvey had moved to the door and when a turn of the handle failed to open it, he examined the large, sturdy lock. “If no one has the keys, we’ll have to force our way in.”

Baloc jangled the bunch of keys he pulled from his pocket as he climbed the steps to the large door of the main entrance and unlocked it. Hinges, stiff from years of inactivity, squealed when he pushed the door open and added another layer of creepiness to the sinister atmosphere the mansion already emitted. Musty air imprisoned for years, rushed from its confinement and allowed fresh air to enter and take its place.

The group followed Baloc through the door.

*****

Ray and Laura made their way back through the Horror House's weird and confusing levels. After two dead ends and a search of umpteen spooky rooms, they eventually discovered a hidden staircase in the large grandfather clock in the hall that led to a concealed room on the top floor, and the exit they sought.

They climbed down the outside staircase at the rear of the building and moved to the front of the horror house. They saw no sign of Scarred Skull, but they did spot the spider-human hybrid climbing over the fence that surrounded the Fear Fair and heading into the encircling forest.

Ray pulled out the sat-phone and rang Zane. He moved the phone from his ear when angry static hissed and moved away from the house into a clear area and tried again, with the same result.

He glanced up at the ominous dark clouds. "The weather must be interfering with the signal." He thrust the phone into his wife's hands. "I'm going after the spider thing to see where it goes. You make contact with Zane and tell him about the monsters and what's happened to Kwanza. As soon as I discover where the spider thing lives, I'll meet you back at the village and we can work out what to do next."

"I'm not sure we should split up with those creatures running loose," argued Laura.

Ray grabbed her hand. "It's not ideal, but if I don't follow it, it might be hard to track, and we also need to warn Zane of the danger before they are attacked." He glanced across the Fear Fair towards the exit. "Are you okay heading back to the village on your own?"

Laura nodded. "It's not far, and we now have some idea how that wolf creature hunts, so I'm sure I can handle it."

"Stay alert and you'll be fine." He kissed her and hurried away.

"Be careful, hon." Laura slipped the phone into a pocket and worriedly watched her husband race across the Fear Fair before setting off for the village.

Crouched behind one of the demon hellhounds on the merry-go-round licking the wound on its rump, Scarred-Skull observed the two humans head off in different directions. He drew his gaze away from the man and skulked after the female responsible for its latest source of pain.

*****

Baloc and his team of enthusiastic explorers gazed around at the splendor of the entrance hall that the dust and cobwebs covering every surface failed to diminish. Sunlight streamed through panels of colored glass above the entrance and highlighted the grand marble staircase that split into two smaller sets sweeping left and right to the west and east wings. Large crystal chandeliers hung from the ceiling and powerless electric wall lights were spaced around the room. Except for the obvious signs of abandonment, it had little of the spookiness or the decayed appearance of the exterior. The creepiest effect stood to one side of the hall. The tall statue of a black-cloaked figure grasped a large clock in its arms at waist level. Four skulls at its feet complimented the sinister death-like figure of Father Time.

Baloc walked over to examine the ghoulish timepiece more closely and smiled at the time frozen at one minute to twelve. Ezra's attention to his macabre details never failed to amaze him. Not for the first time, he thought Ezra should have turned his obvious talents to writing horror stories. He peered into the clock-holder's face, shrouded, it seemed, in permanent shadow that the flashlight he aimed at it failed to dissipate.

As the others spread out to explore, Wendy crossed to the nearest wood-paneled wall and tapped at intervals along its length before turning her attention to the staircase. She found no signs of any serious deterioration, cracks, settlement, rot or any of the usual evidence to indicate an unsafe structure.

Baloc approached Wendy. "I know you've only done a cursory examination, but what are your first impressions of the building?"

Wendy ran her eyes over the crack-free ceiling.

"It's obvious Ezra didn't skimp on his choice of quality materials or workmanship. Given it has been abandoned for over fifty years, on the surface it seems in remarkably good condition. However, before I commit to a decision, I'll need to examine the supporting walls in the basement, as they probably aren't covered and should give a better idea of the mansion's true structural state."

She unrolled the smaller versions of the mansion's blueprints Zane had supplied her with and laid them on the dust-covered table set against the nearby wall. After scanning plan of the floor they were currently on, she glanced across the hall. "That door opens onto a corridor that leads to the kitchen, and halfway along is the basement door."

Baloc attracted Shaw's attention, and he joined them. "Wendy needs to check out the basement."

Shaw glanced at the plan and Wendy's finger pointing out the basement entrance. "Will everyone be coming?"

"I'll find out." Baloc addressed the group, explaining what he and Wendy were about to do.

After a brief discussion amongst themselves, Mannix, Winslow and Quincy decided they would rather explore the rooms on this floor. Shaw assigned Ryker, Thane and Harvey to stay with those remaining, while he and Gunner accompanied Zane, Wendy and Vince to the basement.

Shaw crossed to the kitchen corridor door and led the others through to the basement door. When a turn of the handle revealed it unlocked, Shaw pulled it open and shone his flashlight down the steps before descending. The others followed with Gunner at the rear. Their flashlights roamed the huge space at the bottom. Sand-colored flagstones covered the floor, and arched, grey stone pillars situated along its length supported the mansion above. As they moved deeper, Wendy examined the supporting pillars and walls built from stone she understood was quarried from the island and found all to be structurally sound.

"What do you make of this?" called out Vince, who had wandered deeper into the basement.

The others joined Vince beside the large circular hole in the floor where a sinkhole might have formed. The flagstones sloped towards the hole two yards back from around the edge before overhanging the pit slightly. A metal spiral staircase circled around the sides of the shaft on its journey to the bottom. Wary of venturing too close in case the edges were unsafe, they leaned forward and aimed their flashlights into the dark pit, but they couldn't see the bottom.

Baloc turned to Wendy. "What's your opinion on the staircase?"

Wendy thrust a hand at Baloc. "Hold me."

When Baloc had gripped her hand, Wendy stepped nearer the hole and gently placed a foot on the small metal landing before transferring her whole weight on to it. She stamped a foot, vibrating the staircase slightly.

"It seems fine, but I wouldn't risk going down without a safety line attached."

She ran her eyes over the pit's side before stepping back onto solid ground. "My guess is that it was a naturally formed shaft that Ezra had smoothed out to fit the staircase."

Baloc stared into the hole and wondered what was down there. "Whatever it leads to, none of this is on the blueprints."

"As Wendy advised, if you're planning on checking it out I suggest you wait until we can gather the right equipment." Shaw nodded at the hole. "However secure that staircase might be, it's best not to trust our lives with it when we have climbing gear back at the village."

"I agree," said Baloc. "It makes no sense to take risks we can avoid. We'll check it out when we're better equipped." He looked at Wendy. "Have you seen enough for the moment?"

She glanced around the chamber. "For now, but I'd like to explore the mansion further."

"Let's head back upstairs, rejoin with the others and then some of us can head for the generator to see if Vince can get it working. If he can, we'll have lights and power."

Shaw led them back up the steps.

CHAPTER 15

Attacked

Relieved to be leaving the spooky Fear Fair, Laura passed through its exit and roamed her eyes around the mysterious forest that surrounded most of the Fear Fair, a barrier to isolate it from the rest of Ezra's movie sets. Vigilance for the creature she suspected hadn't given up its hunt guided her progress along the path that wound through the forest, whose creepiness had amplified tenfold with the dark clouds cloaking it in nocturnal light.

The increasing breeze rustled leaves and swayed branches, adding to the foreboding atmosphere that dwelled amongst the trees. Occasional loud, echoing cracks that sounded like something large and monstrous moved through the forest snapping branches in its path was unnerving. Laura forced herself to remain calm. Darkness had never worried her before, but there hadn't been a monster lurking in the shadows then.

Her tactical rifle light and nervous gaze shot to the sound of a snapping twig ahead and to the right of the stone path she followed. She halted and stared at the spot she thought the sound had originated from. An almost indiscernible shape behind the bush her light and gaze focused on set her imagination into overdrive as she formed it into the wolf creature waiting in ambush. She ignored the bead of sweat that trickled down her brow, and with her finger poised on the trigger, cautiously moved to the far edge of the path and crept forward. Her eyes never wavered from the dark shape as she drew level with the bush. A few more tentative steps carried her past. She relaxed. It was only a moss-covered tree stump with a fallen branch resting on it. She silently cursed the island that had woven its fearful strands inside her head and carried on.

The attack was as swift as it was silent.

Laura screamed as much in surprise as fear when the creature dropped from above and thudded to the ground behind her. She instinctively raised the rifle when she spun to face the threat. Scarred-Skull leapt. Laura fired, dropped to the ground and rolled beneath the creature. She re-cocked the rifle as she stood.

Scarred-Skull twisted to avoid the bullet and felt it whizz by its side. As soon as its front paws touched the ground, it turned its body and sped forward when its rear paws landed. Aware it had to reach the human before the weapon barked again, its claws scratched at the stone path for traction and found it.

Laura trembled at the snarling teeth-filled maw approaching rapidly. She would only get one shot. As her finger squeezed the trigger, an intense pain in her side sent her flying. She slammed into a tree and dropped to the ground. Snarling and deep growls turned her groggy head. There were now two monsters eager to feed on her flesh. The new arrival was no less monstrous than the wolf creature. The large dark and pointed antlers gave it a stag-like appearance, but any illusion to a stag was shattered by the sharp teeth it bared at its rival for the feast that was her.

Laura crawled for the dropped rifle and snatched it from the muddy puddle it had landed in. She shook off the mud clinging to it and glanced at the wet earth clogging the barrel and workings. She would be a fool attempting to fire it in its present condition. Ferocious snarls signaled the creature's attack.

Scarred-Skull dived for the stag's front leg and bit hard.

The stag kicked outs it powerful limb and scooped up its attacker with its antlers, piercing its shoulder in the process. When Scarred-Skull lashed a claw at the stag's face, it was tossed aside.

Laura rolled away when Scarred-Skull landed beside her.

Scarred-Skull climbed to its feet, snarled at her, but turned away when the stag's hooves thundered on the ground. It dodged the antlers that stabbed at it and slid a claw along the creature's underbelly. The stag bellowed when its guts spilled out and dropped to the ground. Scarred-Skull climbed onto the dying beast and gazed after the fleeing female running deeper into the forest. Leaving the stag to die a painful lingering death, it sprung off and raced after the human with a slight limp caused by its shoulder wound.

In fear of her life, Laura rushed through the forest and cursed her stupidity. She should have killed the monsters with her Glock while they fought. Fear, panic and Ezra's damn island were responsible. Lacking the tools to clean the rifle, she unclipped the tactical flashlight and dropped the rifle behind a fallen tree she vaulted over. She would collect it later when this nightmare had ended. The sounds of the creature in pursuit spurred her on.

CHAPTER16

Library

A large smile creased Mannix's lips when he opened one of the heavily carved wooden doors situated around the entrance hall and shone his light inside. He turned and called out to the others walking around the impressive hall. "Come and look at this, you won't believe it."

"Let me check it out before you enter," said Ryker, pushing past Mannix into the room.

Too impatient to wait, Mannix followed him through. Looks of amazement formed on everyone's features when they shadowed Mannix through the door and gazed around the room that towered four stories. Light streamed through the glass-domed roof and lit up the towering tiers of platforms and the thousands of books neatly arranged upon hundreds of shelves lining the walls of the round room. Untidy waist-high mounds of books, neater stacked book piles and single books strewn about the floor, left little clear space for them to travel through the room.

Beneath the ceiling dome was a staircase formed entirely of books that led up to what seemed to be a table top. With only the front corner resting on a stack of books, it seemed to float in midair.

Flashlights roamed the room as the group ventured nearer the impressive central feature and gazed at the incredible architecture rising around them. Wooden staircases linked each of the balconies and enabled potential readers to reach the literary works that were in such abundance a lifetime wouldn't see them all read.

While Quincy filmed every detail of the room, Mannix stood speechless in awe of Ezra Houghton's creative mind. He couldn't wait to explore the mansion's other rooms. His thoughts turned to a possible scene that would play out in this spectacular library involving ghosts or a spectral sorcerer practicing dark magic.

Winslow halted at one of the simply fashioned wrought iron candelabras dotted around the room. When he blew the dust and fine cobwebs from one of the partly burnt candle stubs, he discovered there wasn't a wick, but a small light bulb shaped like a flame with two tiny filaments inside.

While Thane remained in the doorway, Ryker and Harvey tried to ignore the spectacular room and concentrated on their jobs. Their gazes continually searched the high balconies and dark areas for anything that might harm the group.

Mannix climbed the book staircase, which was surprisingly solid. When he gazed over the suspended table he saw it was a Ouija board three foot tall and four wide. The alphabet laid out in the center and the "yes, no" above the letters were written in old style text and various demonic symbols decorated the board.

Mannix ignored the skull-shaped control pointer resting to one side and focused on the ancient book resting on the board. It was open at a page with the drawing of a demon so expertly rendered Mannix wouldn't have been surprised if it emerged from the page. He picked the book up and read the words on the cover that revealed the possible plot theme of Ezra's movie mansion. The title was *The Art of Summoning and Conversing with Ghosts, Demons, Spirits and the Deceased.* Mannix flicked through the pages covered in strange symbols and sketches of ghostly apparitions, ghouls, demons and the undead and beside each what seemed to be the incantations to summon them. They appeared too authentic for his liking. Maybe it was the general atmosphere of the house, but he realized he wouldn't be surprised if such things were possible and this book contained the necessary information to bring forth the dark entities depicted within its pages. He replaced the book on the Ouija board and gazed around the room.

"What an amazing library," stated Baloc, on entering.

Mannix climbed down the book staircase and grinned at Baloc. "I'm not sure how this room will feature in your novel, but whatever you decide, it's going to look fantastic on film."

Baloc smiled at the phrase Mannix had repeated a lot since arriving on the island. He was right. Most of Ezra's movie sets would look spectacular on the big screen, which was exactly how he had designed them. Wondering how this library would fit into the book he planned to write, he gazed around the impressive room.

"There's a Ouija board up the book staircase and an authentic looking book of incantations to contact and summon forth all manner of spectral entities that I advise you not to read out loud."

Baloc glanced at the Ouija board and made a mental note to check it out later when he had more time.

"Did you find anything interesting in the basement, Zane?" Winslow asked.

"We did, but I'll explain everything later as we need to find the generator room, so Vince can try and get the lights working. If he can, it will make exploring everything easier and perhaps we'll be able to experience some of Ezra's spooky effects."

"Where exactly is this generator?" asked Vince.

Baloc smiled. "Believe it or not, it's housed underground in an abandoned subway."

"I'd believe anything after seeing this room," said Vince. "Man, that Ezra sure had an imaginative mind."

"He certainly did," agreed Baloc. "A genius way ahead of his time in some respects. Wait until you see the power plant he designed, then you'll understand what I mean." He turned to the others. "Unless anyone wants to join us, I assume you'll carry on exploring the mansion while Vince and I go check out the generator."

"Fixing a generator doesn't sound very exciting or cinematic compared to this place," said Mannix. "Quincy and I will stay here and continue looking around."

Winslow, who was enjoying himself immensely and was glad he had come, elected to stay with Mannix.

Finished photographing the library, Wendy moved next to Zane. "I'll come with you. It might be my only chance to get a photo of the subway and power room that has you so fascinated."

"That's sorted then," said Baloc. "I'll take Vince to the generator room and meet you back here."

"Ryker, Harvey, go with them," ordered Shaw. He turned to Baloc. "While you're checking out the generator, I'll nip back to the village to collect the gear we'll need to investigate the pit in the cellar.

Shaw and Baloc's team headed outside while the others reentered the hall.

When the road from the Mansion branched into two, Shaw headed for the village and Baloc led his small group right through a small patch of spooky forest. They soon arrived at the replica of a section of the poorer areas of Whitechapel, London. The sprawling streets from the eighteen-eighties were Ezra's Jack the Ripper movie set. They discovered the subway entrance about a quarter of the way along the main street, blocked by padlocked gates. While Baloc sorted through his bunch of keys for one that would fit the padlock, Ryker and Harvey watched the street.

"I didn't realize the underground was around in the eighteen-eighties," said Wendy.

"Actually," said Vince. "I live in Whitechapel, and as a railway enthusiast, I know a bit about its history. St. Mary's underground station in Whitechapel was originally opened in 1884 as part of the Metropolitan and Metropolitan District Joint Railway and closed in1938 when it became surplus to requirements."

He stepped into the street and ran his eyes over the small single-story grey stone building. It had four arched windows, two either side of the two-arched entry and exit doors.

"It looks like Ezra did his homework as I've seen photographs of the original station that was damaged by a bomb during the World War Two blitz and later demolished, and as far as I can tell, it's a fair replica."

"Thanks for the history lesson," said Wendy, photographing the station and various views of the streets.

"Got it," uttered Baloc in triumph when the seventh key he tried sprung the padlock open. He removed the lock and slid open the gates.

Ryker led them into the damp, musty station. They ignored the old elevator that needed electricity to function and, switching on their flashlights, descended the stairs that spiraled down onto the station platform. Baloc steadied Vince's load when he bounced the sack truck down the steps.

"This is another of Ezra's horror-themed movie sets," Baloc explained as they walked past the decaying subway train parked on the platform. "If you head through the train in one direction, towards the back I think, you arrive at a maze of tunnels and underground caverns called, *The Monster's Lair.*"

Vince gazed back along the platform; it sure was creepy down here. "And in the other direction?" he asked, a little apprehensively.

"I'm not sure as the blueprint describes it as maintenance rooms and workshops that cover three or more floors, but someone, who I assume to be Ezra, has penciled in *Stalking Death*, so maybe it was another of his last-minute additions or something that was never completed."

"Let's hope it's the latter," Harvey commented.

"How did this all work?" asked Wendy. "Not as a movie set, that I understand, but if Ezra's plan to turn his island into his horror theme park had gone ahead, how would he have done it? I mean, it's not like a normal theme park where there are set paths contained within a set environment, a rollercoaster, ghost train, hall of mirrors and the like, is it?"

"It's a good question that's not all that easy to answer. But from the little information I have gathered from Winslow and the scant amount of records Ezra left, it seems that each horror setup has a certain objective that has to be reached by the person or persons facing the challenge, just as in his movies. It might be to retrieve an object, rescue someone or just a simple matter of surviving and escaping from that particular environment. Look at them as living films with the tourists as the actors. To prevent them from completing their allotted tasks, Ezra connived many different ingenious and devious ways to frighten them and make them turn back or give up."

"Then it's like the scary adventure attractions we have today, where you pass through poorly lit horror decorated corridors and rooms where people dressed up as ghosts, monsters and zombies jump out and frighten you," said Ryker.

Zane shook his head. "Similar, but vastly different. Here, in Ezra's movie worlds, you feel like you are actually living it and death seems extremely possible. Apparently, the atmosphere Ezra managed to create with sounds, lighting and even smells was so realistic some of the workers that volunteered to test it out became so frightened they screamed to be rescued. I'm hoping, if Vince can get the power running and everything still works, we will be able to experience one or more of Ezra's challenges for ourselves."

"Yeah, well, count me out on that unwelcoming invite," stated Wendy. "If I wanted to be scared I'd watch horror movies alone in the dark, but I don't, and I certainly have no inclination to star in one."

Baloc smiled at her. "You don't know what you might be missing."

"It's something I'm happy to remain ignorant of, thank you very much."

Ryker led them through an archway on the right, along an offshoot corridor and down the steps at the end. His flashlight highlighted the front of another train parked in the dark tunnel, but when they drew closer, they realized it was only a painting on the wall that blocked the tunnel. Set into the sidewall was a black metal door, which Baloc unlocked and led the others through onto a metal walkway that gave access to the mass of machinery that stretched up two stories and down three.

Ryker and Harvey roamed their lights over the machinery full of dark nooks and crannies, ideal hiding places.

"You have got to be kidding me," uttered Vince, peering over the rail that edged the raised walkway. Below were what must be miles of pipes and cables leading off in all directions and many separate but connected pieces of machinery crammed into the massive space. "I wouldn't even know where to start. The steam turbines are obvious, but what powers it all? Coal, diesel, gas, what?"

"Actually, it's powered by a never-ending heat source, a thermal vent below the earth." Zane smiled at Vince's surprise. "I told you Ezra was way ahead of his time. The man was a genius."

Vince scratched his head worryingly. "I dunno, Mr. Baloc, this isn't what I expected. Look at how big and complicated this thing is. You could probably power a large town with the electricity this power plant would produce, and I haven't had any experience with thermal vents and whatnot."

"That's okay, Vince, not many have. I've spoken to a man who was an apprentice to the engineer that once ran this monstrosity of a power plant. He's in his eighties now. He told me they put together an instruction manual on how to operate it. He also said that although it looks daunting, once it's all greased up and switched on, apart from some general ongoing maintenance, you can forget about it."

Vince, slightly less worried now, rubbed his chin. "Well, if there are instructions to follow, I suppose it might be okay."

Baloc slapped Vince on the back. "That's the spirit." He roamed his flashlight around the room and spied what he searched for on a lower level. "There's the workshop where you'll find all the tools you'll need and the operating manual in a locker. I was told the water tanks that feed the machine were drained when the island was shut down, so it's imperative they are refilled before you set things in motion."

"I'll do that before I start fathoming out how it works," reassured Vince.

"Where does the water come from?" asked Wendy, clicking off photos.

Baloc smiled "Another never-ending natural source, the sea. It passes through a desalination plant before being turned into steam."

Wendy glanced around the unfathomable, but no less impressive, machinery filling the space. "It's a shame Ezra wasted his obvious talents on making movies."

"He certainly did have a knack for bringing skilled people together to fulfill his dreams, but I disagree that he wasted his talents. Yes, I know it all came unstuck at the end, but I admire the man for sticking to his dreams. There's not many people who could have organized the construction of everything we've seen on such a remote island."

Wendy wasn't convinced. "Not everyone has millions to chuck at their folly."

"Well, yes, there is that, but I'm glad he did, and hopefully my agent and bank manager will be too when I've finished my latest masterpiece of horror and suspense."

Wendy rolled her eyes.

Baloc gripped the rail and stared down at the mass of complicated machinery. "I suppose our next step is to help Vince set up the portable generator and rig up the lights, then Wendy and I will rejoin the others while Vince gets to work."

They set about the tasks, and after the power room was flooded with light, Harvey remained with Vince while Ryker escorted Baloc and Wendy back to the mansion.

CHAPTER 17

Abandoned Mine

As Laura rushed through the trees, she sensed the forest had changed. The trees were more gnarly, ancient in appearance, sinister. Limbs with twig hands reached down with an aura of evil intention and thick twisted roots poked up from the ground like tentacles waiting to snare her if she ventured too close. Laura brushed the thought away; they were only harmless trees.

She barged through a clump of thick bushes that snagged at her and emerged into a clearing. She headed for the ramshackle group of buildings that might provide a suitable defensive position to pick off the monster she heard moving through the forest. Assuming she had arrived at the abandoned mine Ezra had marked on his blueprints, Laura glanced at each of the buildings to pick out the sturdiest. The cable wrapped around a large metal wheel on a raised platform led into a three-story wooden tower with a small hut built precariously on its side. The building stood at the end of a row of single-story shacks. Like the main tall structure, the other wooden huts dotted around the clearing had seen better days, and none seemed more solid than the others. Laura entered the first hut she came to. It was an office simply furnished with a desk, chair, shelves and a small cupboard. Ivy had crept through gaps in the wood-slatted roof and sent out tendrils of growth to cover the ceiling and most of the back wall.

Breathless from her run but not daring to rest, Laura grabbed her Glock, and after checking it was fully loaded, she took position by the open door where she had a good view of the forest she expected the creature to emerge from.

The hut she cowered in and the surrounding structures creaked in the wind. Distant chains clanked and what might be a window or door slammed intermittently against its frame. Laura focused on the forest with her pistol roaming its edge. A bush rustled in an unnatural manner that made her believe the wind wasn't responsible. She aimed at the bush's dark middle, and when the monster didn't appear, she imagined it surveilling the clearing.

After a few minutes had passed, Laura began to worry. Fearing it was coming at her from a different direction, she gazed around the clearing. A sound scarcely distinguishable from the creaking hut she sheltered in, turned her around. The monster stared at her through a gap in the back wall. Two bullets spat from her weapon and drove splintering holes through the wood. Laura gazed at the bullet holes for any sign she had hit the creature. Her uncertainty was banished when the back wall caved in with a splintering and cracking of wood. The monster lashed out a claw at her as it crashed into the front wall. The hut swayed from the force and collapsed. Laura dodged outside to avoid the falling roof and aimed her weapon at the crumbling shack that covered the monster. Unwilling to waste ammo on a lucky shot, Laura fled.

Aware in her tired condition she'd never outrun the persistent creature, even if its wounds had slowed it down, Laura entered the tall building and shone her light around its dark interior. A metal cage at the back seemed strong enough to hold it at bay. She dashed inside, pulled down the metal barred gate of the mineshaft elevator and ducked behind the wide frame out of sight. She switched off the light that would give away her position and with her gun gripped ready to end the creature's life, she waited for it to appear.

Scarred-Skull crawled out from beneath the wreckage, shook off the dust and pieces of wood and followed the female's scent.

CHAPTER 18

Dreadmore - Downstairs

Gunner remained in the hall while Thane led Mannix, Quincy and Winslow along the corridor to the kitchen. After Thane had checked it was clear, the others entered.

Mannix moved to the old butler sink in the mansion's large kitchen. Dark splashes over the sides and around the plughole could be dried blood or rusty water stains. The husks of two large spiders expired long ago hugged two corners of the square basin too smooth to climb. He lifted his gaze to the grimy, web-adorned window that looked out over the back garden. A lawn run rampant with weeds and wildflowers stretched to a brick wall surrounding the back of the mansion's grounds. Behind it, a few trees grew tall and bushy.

Mannix peered through a gap in the row of trees at something on a hill—a spooky scarecrow with a pumpkin head. The back of its head must have been missing as daylight shone through its evil, slanted eyes and cruel smiling mouth full of triangle carved teeth. Perched on its head was a top hat with straw hair poking out from beneath the brim. Gnarled branches formed limbs posed as if in the act of creeping through the field. Twigs protruding from the simple brown shawl covering its shoulders and body formed clawed hands, one of which held a hangman's noose fastened around the neck of human-like child rag doll that swung in the breeze. Its swinging legs gave the effect of dying death throes as it gasped for breaths that would never come.

Mannix turned away from the scarecrow that emitted an aura of malevolence and attracted Quincy's attention. "When we get the chance, I'd like to get a shot of the evil scarecrow on the hill out back screaming to be added to Zane's novel."

Quincy glanced out the window. "Man, that thing would scare Satan."

Mannix laughed. "Yeah, I know what you mean, damn creepy."

Except for the abundance of cobwebs covering the many pots and pans hanging on the wall and the cubbyhole pantry filled with jars and tins of preserved fruit, pickled vegetables and unappetizing substances no one would ever eat, the kitchen held none of the horror effects they had come to expect from Ezra. It was a typical kitchen of the era when it was constructed.

Thane led them back along the corridor to the next room of interest.

They entered the dining room dominated by a long table surrounded by sixteen chairs. Light penetrating the grimy panes of the four arched windows along one side of the room highlighted the dusty but extravagant place settings in front of each chair and the row of cooked food down the center. The joints of ready to carve meat, included a large roasted goose, stuffed with what looked like cranberry stuffing, a baked hogs head that seemed to be frozen in the pained expression of its brutal demise, dishes of vegetables and bread rolls. A large fireplace set in one of the long walls was stacked with logs ready to light.

Winslow approached the table and tapped a dusty joint of beef. "It's artificial, some type of pottery."

Mannix picked up one of the dinner plates, turned it over and read the Royal Daulton name. These were not cheap movie props. "I'm no expert, but these must be antiques and worth something."

"Ezra sure did throw a lot of unnecessary money at this place just to make his movies," said Quincy, panning his camera around the room.

Winslow ran his eyes over the paintings on the wall, the pair of silver candelabra on the dining table, and the three arched windows at the far end. "I wonder what movie he planned to stage in this mansion?"

"Probably something involving spooky ghosts or spirits I should imagine," offered Thane, "because it sure is creepy."

"You are probably right," said Mannix. "That Ouija board in the library and the plethora of occult books about summoning spirits does point to some sort of dark arts going on here."

Quincy continued filming the room while he talked. "It's a perfect setting for a haunted house script. Add a few anxious characters, spooky, suspenseful music and lighting, some ghostly effects and you'd have a frightening movie if done right."

"As I'm sure Ezra would have," said Winslow.

"If you're all done, shall we move on?" asked Thane. The house gave him the creeps, and he was keen to leave.

The next room they entered would have seemed more at home in a stately castle. Two rows of four full suits of armour stood either side of the long room and looked as if they might come to life at any moment. The stone block walls were covered in a plethora of weapons from bygone ages, all designed to maim, damage and brutally kill the wielder's opponent. They included maces, axes, spears, pikes, swords, knives, crossbows, archer's bows with a variety of types of arrows, matchlock pistols, muskets, flintlocks, and dueling pistols.

While Quincy filmed the room, Mannix approached the nearest suit of dusty armour and raised the visor. Though half expecting to see a face inside, it was empty.

The next room they explored was the music room. The usual layer of dust covered everything, and musty, damp air filled the room. A grand piano that wasn't so grand anymore was covered in patches of peeling veneer caused by water dripping through the ceiling. Spores of mildew crept out from the water stain on the ceiling. The blue walls and ceiling were divided into panels by ornate frames of plaster molding. Other furniture included a padded piano stool, two wingchairs, a small table and a sideboard.

Winslow crossed to the piano and pressed a yellowed ivory key. An out-of-tune note was as sad as the musical instrument that had produced it. He then played a short spooky chord to match the mood of the house.

With little of interest in the room, they moved on to the next.

CHAPTER 19

Elevator

Shrouded in darkness, Laura strained to hear the monster above the clinking chains blowing in the breeze and the creaks and groans of the old building. She would let it get close, blind it with her flashlight and empty her gun at it. As the drawn-out moments ticked by, her dread of what was coming increased. Normally, a weapon in her hand instilled her with confidence that she could kill whatever prey she hunted. This creature, though, was different, and she wasn't certain she would be able to bring it down before it reached her.

She struggled for breath as fear gripped her. It felt as if someone was choking her. Her heart raced, and all she wanted to do was curl up into a ball and wait for her husband or someone to save her. But no one would, she was on her own. She fought back the panic that threatened to overwhelm her. *I'm safe in the metal cage, aren't I?* She wasn't certain of anything anymore.

The pad of paws on the wooden floor alerted her to the monster's presence. Amplified by her fear, it was the only sound she heard now. The footsteps, slow and menacing, grew nearer and nearer and stopped. By Laura's estimation, it had reached the middle of the room. It was searching for her. The creature sniffed the air and growled deeply. Her legs trembled as she waited for it to come a little nearer. The closer it came, the better chance she had of killing it.

I'm safe here. Protected.

A minute passed, then two, and still it hadn't moved. Unable to stand the suspense any longer, Laura moved in front of the metal door that didn't seem as sturdy now and switched her light on. The creature had its monstrous face pressed against the bars. Its evil and hate-filled eyes stared at her. It snarled and grabbed through the bars at her. Claws ripped clothes but missed flesh when she dodged back. She stumbled, fell, and lost hold of the flashlight when she hit the back wall and slipped to the floor. Growling menacingly, the monster rattled the door violently. Its actions shook the elevator, slamming it against the sides of the shaft. Laura fired at the monster, but its speed saved it again when it avoided the bullets by leaping onto the top of the cage. Laura snatched her light from the floor and aimed it above. The cage swung slightly as Scarred-Skull moved along the metal girders the winch cable was attached to. Though the cage's thicker ceiling framework hid most of the monster, Laura glimpsed its thigh and fired.

Scarred-Skull yelped painfully when the bullet grazed its leg. Frustrated and angry at the female that kept thwarting its attempts to kill her, it rose up and slammed its front paws onto the roof in the hope of breaking through. Metal shrieked when it buckled. Laura waited for the cage to stop swaying and fired again. The bullet missed the creature and twanged off the rusty winch cable. Weakened strands began to unfurl. When Scarred-Skull slammed its weight onto the cage a second time, the force traveled up the cable and jerked the winch. The jolt raised the metal ratchet arm slightly from the heavy-toothed cog, a simple safety feature to prevent the cable from unwinding.

Scarred-Skull pulled at the dented roof and dodged back when another shot rang out. Frustrated and angry, it again raised its front limbs and smashed them forcefully onto the cage. The weakened metal buckled, creating a gap. It gazed at its prey within.

The ratchet flipped up from the monster's latest attack on the elevator. Free of the restraint that held back the weight of the cage pulling on it, the winch began to turn.

Elevator, Scarred-Skull and Laura plummeted down the shaft.

CHAPTER 20

POWER

During the time Vince and Harvey had been working on the machinery, Vince had glanced at least a hundred times at the neatly handwritten operating manual littered with informative diagrams. He climbed one of the metal ladders that provided access to difficult-to-reach parts of the machine. The red-painted control valve he sought was half-an-arm's length away. With one hand gripping the ladder, he poked the grease gun into the gap and lubricated the valve's thread. The scampering of small paws shot his gaze to the top of the machinery. A shadow flittered across the wall and disappeared into darkness.

"Rats."

"You say something?" asked Harvey, standing on the walkway below looking up.

Vince looked down. "Think I just heard a rat, that's all." He held the grease gun out. "Can you catch this?"

Harvey shouldered his rifle and held his hands up. “Okay.” He caught the gun and peered into the deep pit stacked with pipes and machinery when he thought he heard something. Though the bright halogen lights placed throughout the levels lit up the room, the odd-shaped equipment left many areas filled with shadow. *Must have been another rat.*

Vince gripped the valve wheel and turned. Like the others he had greased, it started stiff, but as soon as the lubricant worked its way along the thread, it loosened up and spun effortlessly. He climbed down and grinned at the security guard.

“That’s it, all finished.”

Harvey glanced around at the complicated mass of machinery that had lain dormant for so long.

“You’re sure it’s safe to switch on?”

Vince shrugged.

“I guess we’ll soon find out. I just have to lower the water pipes into the hot vent to boil the water into steam, which should, if I’ve done everything correctly and nothing is broken, turn the turbines and produce electricity.”

Vince crossed from one walkway to another, climbed down to a lower platform and halted in front of the large metal wheel with a chain attached. He gripped it with both hands and turned. The chain that disappeared deep into darkness, clanked and jangled as it unwound. When the chain ran out, Vince locked the wheel and joined Harvey on the higher walkway. Both stared at the turbine as hissing and the clink of pipes heating up rose towards them. As if it had only been switched off yesterday, the turbine began to turn slowly and gradually increased in speed.

The lights long dark around the room flickered dimly before burning brightly again. “Well, damn my eyes, it’s working,” uttered Harvey.

“Of course,” stated Vince proudly. “I’m the best damn mechanic on the island.”

The two men laughed.

Vince crossed to the bank of pressure gauges and was pleased to see everything was working properly and within safety perimeters.

“Now it’s operational, is the whole island powered up?” asked Harvey.

“Not until I activate the main power feeds, which I am about to do.”

Vince crossed to the row of levers on the wall. Each one was labeled with the building or location it fed power to. He started at one end and moved along, pulling the forked levers into their contacts. A brief crackle of sparks shot from the contacts when each was engaged. “That’s it. The whole island should now have power, so let’s go see the fruits of my labor.”

On their way out, they turned off the portable generator they had placed in the tunnel to avoid the fumes filling the generator room. On entering the abandoned station, they noticed dim lights glowing in the old train destined never to move. Though a couple flickered erratically, and a few remained dark, most were on. The equally dim lights running along the platform created an eerie atmosphere. As they approached the stairs that would take them above ground, they paused on hearing a strange pattering mingled with the occasional screech coming from above.

Vince glanced at Harvey worriedly. “I’m hoping, now everything has power, it’s one of Ezra’s scary sound effects Zane mentioned.”

Harvey pointing his raised weapon up the stairs as the noise grew nearer and louder. “I have to admit my nerves aren’t liking it.”

A mass of red-eyed, dark-brown furry things with a row of sharp spines along the ridge of their backs rounded the corner and rushed down the stairs. On spying prey, their elongated teeth chomped menacingly at the men.

Vince and Harvey knew whatever these creatures were, they weren’t any of Ezra’s movie props.

“Shoot them,” screamed Vince.

“There’s too many, run!” Before he fled, Harvey sprayed the cat-sized rodents with bullets in the hope of slowing them down. Though some abandoned the chase and started feasting on the dead, wounded and dying, the majority continued their rush towards them.

Vince glanced at the train and each way along the platform. “Which way?”

Harvey pushed him towards the train. “Head through the carriages.”

Vince leapt aboard and turned left. Harvey followed close on his heels.

The spiky rodents poured onto the platform. Some boarded the train while others climbed on it and ran along the roof. The remainder flowed along the platform and the tracks.

Accompanied by the terrifying shrieks and the pattering of the vicious rodents’ small-clawed feet echoing through the train, Vince and Harvey fled for their lives. The uneven springy floor, askew seats, theatrical corpses in various states of mutilation and partially open between-carriage doors they had to squeeze through were obstacles that hampered their progress.

Vince glanced out at the rodents rushing ahead and almost sobbed when one jumped through a broken window, bounced on a seat and leaped at him. Vince swiped a clenched fist at it. The creature smashed through a cracked window and dropped from sight.

Harvey shot a glance behind. The rodents were gaining.

“I see the end of the train,” yelled Vince. “What do we do?”

Harvey peered past him at the driver’s cab and the large windscreen. “Whatever you do, don’t stop,” he shouted. He raised the rifle. “Lean to the left.”

“What?” Vince glanced behind and saw the rifle barrel aimed over his right shoulder. “Oh, crap!” He leaned to the left.

Harvey fired a short burst. The cab’s windscreen exploded in a shower of glass as Vince entered. Without stopping, Vince placed his hands on the console and leap-frogged through. He landed awkwardly, fell, rolled, jumped to his feet and continued running.

Harvey dived out headfirst, somersaulted and twisted in midair. He landed on his feet facing the train. Rodents entered the cab, some poured out from beneath and the sides and some leapt from the roof. He sprayed shots at the closest before catching up with Vince.

“Are they still coming?” asked Vince breathlessly, knowing fear and adrenaline were all that kept his legs moving.

“Afraid so.” Harvey spotted an opening set in the right tunnel wall. It was their only hope. “Turn right,” he called out.

Doing as ordered, Vince rushed into the short passage. "There's a door up ahead."

Harvey hoped it wasn't locked. "Open it while I hold them back."

Vince almost crashed into the door in his haste to reach it. He grabbed the handle, turned it and pushed; it didn't budge. Gunfire erupted behind him, so loud his ears rung. He shoulder-barged the door. It moved slightly. When a second hard shove freed the stubborn hinges, he rushed inside.

"It's open," Vince shouted, his voice dimmed by his deafened hearing.

Harvey shot the first of rodents to appear and picked off those who followed, but there were more of them than he had bullets. When he heard Vince call out, he turned and sprinted through the door.

As soon as Harvey was through, Vince slammed the door shut.

Two rodents leaped for the rapidly closing door and crashed into it when it closed.

Breathing heavily, his throat burning, Vince slid down the door to the ground.

Panting, Harvey placed his hands on his knees. "What in hell's name are those things? They resemble rats but aren't, and did you see those spikes on their backs?"

"It must be some sort of mutation unique to this island," replied Vince, thankful they had escaped from them. He looked past Harvey. "Where are we?"

A drawn-out groan drifted from the gloom-ridden room ahead.

Harvey sighed. "Nowhere we want to be."

CHAPTER 21

Hell Hole

Satisfied the rope attached to one of the posts surrounding the hole he tugged on would hold, Shaw stepped onto the top of the metal staircase and shone his flashlight into the dark depths. The staircase spiraled down farther than the beam's reach, hiding whatever lay below. He turned to those watching him. "When I've seen what's down there, I'll let you know if it's safe to follow."

Baloc nodded. "I'm certain whatever you find, it'll be nothing we expected."

Shaw had no doubts about that. He started his descent slowly and over cautiously, but after he had descended a few spirals and detected no weakness in the staircase structure, he moved faster. He stopped a few minutes later when he felt a tug on the rope. A glance up revealed the tautly stretched rope wasn't long enough. The flashlight he aimed below picked out the bottom a short distance below. He unhitched the rope and continued his descent. When he reached the bottom, and felt dizzy from the constant circling, he rested to let his equilibrium settle. A glance around his surroundings picked out a short, rough-hewn tunnel that curved slightly to an arched opening.

Baloc's raised voice echoed down the stairwell. "Are you okay, Kurt?"

Shaw lifted his gaze to the small circle of light he judged to be about two hundred feet above, making him realize how deep he was. "I'm at the bottom and going to have a look around."

He crossed to the arched opening and gazed in fascination at what the flashlight highlighted. After realizing he had been staring for a few moments, he dragged his eyes away, crossed to the staircase and shouted, "You can come down. The staircase is solid so no need to use the rope."

While he waited for the others to join him, he lit a cigar and wondered what they would discover at the end of the long passage through the archway.

CHAPTER 22

Hell's Elevator

The screech of metal was deafening as the elevator banged against the sides of the shaft and slid down its rock walls. Laura had no idea how deep the shaft was or what she should do to prevent injury or death when it came to a sudden halt. Should she remain on the floor, stand or hang from the top of the cage. What she did know was that when the elevator struck bottom, it wouldn't be a soft landing and there was little she could do about it. She climbed to her feet and held the side of the cage to steady herself.

Scarred-Skull gazed at the walls sliding by too fast for it to jump onto and waited for the fall to stop.

The winch up above turned at a speed surpassing its limit as the weight of the cage unwound the cable fed to it from the large drum outside. The dried, caked grease on its bearings did nothing to ease the friction placed on the rapidly revolving shaft and began to smoke. The rusty drum outside feeding the winch cable also turned faster than it was designed to do. Its wooden staging vibrated and swayed violently. The two brackets securing the spindle in place worked loose and set the drum free. Spinning madly, it shot forward and smashed through the side of the three-story building. Floors collapsed, and walls buckled when the whirling drum careened madly around the interior. Debris rained down the shaft and onto the smoking winch. It seized and was torn from its mounting when the cable twanged taut.

Laura was spilled to the floor when the elevator jerked to a brief halt before falling again. Above the screeching of torturous metal, she heard crashes at the top of the shaft.

Scarred-Skull gazed up at the wooden wreckage heading straight for it, but it had nowhere to go, except down. It clawed frantically at the roof of the cage. Ripping and peeling back metal.

Laura gazed up at the new sound. Claws ripped at the roof, bending and snapping sections of the damaged wire cage. She knelt and aimed her gun. Before she could fire, the elevator smashed into the bottom of the shaft, slamming her into the floor and flinging her weapon through the door bars out of reach. When the cage buckled, Scarred-Skull shot halfway through the weakened ceiling. Fear rolled Laura to the door, and she managed to force it up enough to slither under. Scarred-Skull dropped as debris struck the cage.

Sprawled on the floor, Laura used her arms to shelter her head and face from the flying pieces of wood and metal. When it was over, she glanced up at something whipping and clanging against the sides of the shaft. The cable and winch shot down the shaft. She grabbed her gun and rolled clear as coils of whipping cable landed in the spot she had vacated. When the winch bounced off the top of the elevator with a loud crash and headed for her, Laura jumped to her feet and leapt out of its path. It thumped to the ground beside her. Laura stared at the wrecked, smoking winch, that emitted pings of heated metal as it began to cool. She turned to the elevator when more debris rained down the shaft and fired two shots at the monster concealed within the thrown-up cloud of dust before fleeing along the tunnel.

Scarred-Skull dropped to the ground when shots rang out. When no more followed, it forced its way under the door, raising it higher and emerged from the drifting dust cloud. It stared after the fleeing footsteps and bounded along the tunnel after its prey.

When Laura arrived at an intersection that led left and right, she stepped onto the small gauge rail lines and felt a breeze on her face coming from the right. It had to be another exit as the tracks had to lead somewhere. She sprinted in the direction the breeze came from.

Scarred-Skull rushed from the tunnel, skidded, and ran after the sound of fading footsteps.

Laura turned on hearing the monster's approach. Its footsteps grew closer far too quickly. She fired off a wild shot in the hope of deterring it. If she was certain she could hit and kill it she would have stopped and confronted it, but it moved so damn fast it was hard to target. She couldn't risk wasting more bullets. She turned into a passage lined with thick wooden props and beams supporting the tunnel roof. Though worried that some had bent with splintered cracks, she couldn't turn back. She jumped over those that had fallen and glanced back. Scarred-Skull was almost upon her. She aimed as best she could without stopping and fired three times.

Scarred-Skull saw the female raise her weapon and leapt onto the wall when she fired. Though the human altered her aim, it was too fast. It spurted forward and leapt at the female. Laura barely managed to escape the claws that reached out for her. She stumbled but somehow managed to keep her footing.

Scarred-Skull landed awkwardly and smashed into a wooden support. The post shifted and crashed to the ground. The roof beam it had held in place swung to the side as it fell and knocked the next support free. Rocks and timber crashed to the ground when the tunnel caved in.

Laura's adrenalin fueled spurt forward was brought to an abrupt halt when a wooden beam grazed her head and sent her spilling unconscious to the floor.

Scarred-Skull screeched in triumph when its prey fell. Eager to feast on the human that had caused it so much trouble, and mindful of the collapsing tunnel, it reached for her leg to drag her clear. A rock bouncing off its wounded shoulder drove it back. Helpless to prevent it, Scarred-Skull backed away from failing rocks and timber that showered down and blocked the tunnel to keep it from its victim. Though it had been denied a well-deserved meal, it drew satisfaction from the human's death. It turned away from the cloud of dust rolling along the passage and returned to the elevator. It leapt onto the top of the battered cage and climbed up the shaft.

CHAPTER 23

Creeping Death

The increased scratching on the door at his back from the rodents outside coaxed Vince to his feet. “They can’t get in, can they?”

Harvey glanced at the door. “It’s metal, so I wouldn’t think so, but that’s not my major concern.” He stared worriedly along the short, dark corridor the moaning drifted along; it was the only direction available to them. “Come on, we need to find another exit.”

Though reluctant to head towards whatever was making the eerie moaning, Vince thought it couldn’t be worse than the hoard of vicious creatures outside the door and nervously followed his protector.

Cautiously, the two men entered the room the corridor led them to. The first thing they noticed were the pools of dried blood on the floor, splashes of blood on the walls and the four mortuary tables. An oppressive darkness stared out at them from two partly open doors among the bank of chilled body lockers along one wall. A third door was open wide enough to reveal a pair of pale, grey-tinted feet.

"Where do you think all that blood came from?" asked Vince, his eyes sweeping the room anxiously.

"It's probably just movie blood and, like the moaning, some of Ezra's scare effects," said Harvey.

"Yeah, that's what we thought about the pattering feet earlier, and look how that turned out."

Harvey pointed his rifle at the door across the room. "Let's find out where that leads."

"Nowhere safe I should think," commented Vince, shooting worried glances at the bloodstains that trailed towards the door.

A thump against metal turned their gazes to the body storage cabinets. A second thump was followed by incessant echoing bangs coming from each, as if the corpses trapped inside were trying to get out. The men backed away and rushed through the exit when the corpse's feet twitched.

The short corridor they had entered led straight for a short distance before turning sharp right. The blood trail that led from the overturned Victorian era wheelchair and disappeared around the corner was unnerving, but since they couldn't go back, they pressed on. They paused at the old-fashioned elevator doors set in the left wall.

Panting heavily, Vince grabbed at the pain in his side as he glanced back the way they had come. Though the thumping had faded, it was still unnerving, as was the eerie moaning, closer now, that came from ahead.

Harvey pointed at the lit call button. “It could be a way out of here.”

Vince glanced at the button and then the needle of the elevator’s floor indicator above. They were on the lowest floor with two more above them. Up seemed the ideal direction to head in. “Press it.”

Harvey pressed the button.

They stared at the floor indicator arrow, but it didn’t move.

Harvey pressed the button a few more times, but if the elevator mechanism still worked, it didn’t start up. He sighed. “I guess we continue on.”

The intermittent moaning that had grown louder with each step along the corridor, originated from the room they now faced and where flashes of light seeped from the half-open door. Harvey approached the door and pushed it open. The expected squeal of protesting rusty hinges pierced the hushed, tentative atmosphere of the room the nervous duo entered.

The flashing light came from the room’s single flickering light bulb suspended above the only object in the room, a hospital trolley. A white bloodstained sheet covered the form of the human body on the trolley and draped down its sides. The moaning, which had ceased when they entered the room, could only have originated from beneath the sheet that rose and fell as something breathed.

Vince aimed his flashlight at the slosh of water coming from below his feet. Beneath the metal grating that covered the floor was a pool of red liquid that might be blood-tinged water. He glanced at the trolley, the blood-splashed walls, the metal gratings covering the floor and the door on the opposite wall. “We should leave.”

“We will, but I want to look at what’s hiding under that sheet first.” Harvey’s footsteps clanked on the metal floor when he crossed to the body.

“Why in hell’s name would you do that?” Vince argued, edging towards the far exit.

“Because this place is freaking me out and I need to reassure my nerves and my sanity that Ezra’s tricks are responsible.” Harvey grabbed the sheet and dragged it back.

Though impressive, closeup the revealed corpse was obviously a prop.

Harvey put an ear to the breathing chest. “I can hear air, probably mechanically controlled bellows.” He looked at Vince and smiled. “Smoke and mirrors, that’s all.”

“Heeelllp meeeee!”

Harvey staggered back and glanced at the floor where the unnerving voice had erupted from.

Fingers wrapped around the grating from beneath were followed by a face appearing out of the pool of red liquid. It opened its eyes. Its lips moved. “Hellllp meee.”

Vince, now positioned by the door that his senses urged him to rush through, looked over at Harvey. “I think we should go.”

Harvey dropped to his knees and stared at the face that was nothing like the one on the trolley. This one appeared real, alive. “Hold on. I’m not sure, but I think someone’s trapped under the floor.”

The sound of the moving elevator that had failed to respond to their command drifted into the room. It was followed by the clatter of the manually operated expanding doors sliding open, indicating someone, or something, had rode the lift down.

The head beneath the floor turned towards the sound, and in a panicked voice, said, “It’s too late, it’s here.” The head turned back to Harvey. “Quick, you must flee. It is coming. You will die.”

Harvey still couldn’t work out if it was a real person or another of Ezra’s showpieces. “Who are you?”

“No questions. Run or you die. I hide, you leave.” The head disappeared beneath the liquid and then reappeared. “Seek large demon to be saved.” The face slipped below the surface.

As the fingers uncurled from the grating, Harvey touched them before they slipped away. Though cold, the skin had felt like real flesh.

Pounding footsteps approached the room.

“Let’s go!” shouted Vince urgently, backing through the doorway, but reluctant to flee on his own. Harvey had the only weapon.

Harvey stood and stared at the door as the footsteps approached.

“What are you waiting for?” hissed Vince. “Come on.”

Though he was almost certain Ezra was responsible for everything he was experiencing, the footfalls vibrating the floor had to be made by something or someone, and as far as he was aware, Zane’s team were the only people on the island. Giving in to his doubts and sense of self-preservation, Harvey turned away from the approaching menace and fled through the door. Vince slammed it shut behind him, and they rushed along a narrow corridor.

“What the hell was that thing under the floor?” asked Vince.

Harvey slowed his pace. "I'm not sure, but it looked like a real person, I think. It...he, wasn't the same as that thing on the trolley. I touched its fingers, and they seemed real, but... I just don't know anymore."

"Real or not, whatever made those footsteps definitely is, so I suggest we don't stop until we've escaped from this nightmare."

"You'll get no arguments from me. The...thing under the floor said we need to find a large demon to be saved, whatever that means."

Vince shot a nervous glance behind. "With a name like that I expect we'll know it when we see it."

"I see another door up ahead," said Harvey.

Vince looked at the door anxiously. "Whatever type of room we find on the other side, we head straight through, no looking under sheets or anything, agreed?"

Harvey stopped at the door. "Agreed." He opened it and they stepped through.

Vince closed the door before roaming his eyes around their new surroundings. Both were a little surprised to see it absent any blood-splattered surfaces. Rough wooden walkways spanned the pool of water that practically filled the floor of the room and reflected the few dim lights set around the walls. They had a choice of two paths open to them: either cross to the exit on the far side of the room where chains clinked like wind chimes on a breezy day or use the small rowing boat to enter the flooded tunnel on their left.

Vince moved to the boat. It was old; sections of its wooden hull were black, water-sodden, and the puddle of water in the bottom was further indication it probably wasn't watertight. "I suggest we keep on dry land."

A brief examination of the boat convinced Harvey it was a wise suggestion.

The rickety wooden-slatted paths spanning the water creaked and swayed when they walked along them, sending out ripples in all directions.

Rising bubbles beside the walkway attracted Vince's attention. Wondering what had made them, he peered into the water. He screamed in fright when a decayed, eyeless corpse bobbed to the surface. The corpse seemed to have set a chain reaction in motion as more decomposed bodies and pieces of flesh and severed limbs floated to the surface, spreading the overpowering stench of putrefaction throughout the room. They both gagged and clutched hands over mouths and noses.

No longer sure what was real or what was a movie affect designed by Ezra, Harvey prompted Vince onward, and they hurried for the far exit. In an attempt to block out the smell, they slid the large door across the opening they passed through. Though marginally better, it didn't prevent some of the stench from seeping through.

The rifle's flashlight Harvey swept around the room glinted off the chains suspended from the ceiling. So great was their number, they blocked the view of the room. Some of the hooks attached to the ends of the chains were bloodied, and some had what looked like chunks of flesh hanging from them.

They turned to the door when heavy running footsteps approached. The large door shuddered when something struck it. As the crash echoed through the room, the men fled.

The chains set in motion by their passing, jangled and clinked against those close by. They emerged from the hanging forest of metal links into an area lined with gloom-filled cages and beyond them a set of double doors. The bashing on the door that currently held at bay whatever banged on it, was unnerving and drove the men to keep moving.

Both men glanced into the cells they passed. Their flashlights picked out the damp stone walls and floor, the toilet bucket, the manacles fixed to the back wall and the blood splashes covering everything. Though three of the six cells were empty, the remaining three were occupied by corpses in various states of decay, forcing Vince and Harvey to cover their noses again. One of the corpses sat with huddled knees against the back wall, another was stretched out on the floor as near to the cell door as the manacles around her ankles would permit. Her hands stretched for the tray of rotten food forever beyond her reach.

The occupant in the last cell had been so desperate to escape her shackle, she had scratched and bitten the flesh from her ankle and foot, which also necessitated breaking the leg bone that stuck out at an impossible angle. The two men stared at the corpse of the young female who had forced her frail body through the cell bars until she had become stuck—now fated to remain forever poised in her painful, failed escape attempt.

"Do you think she's real?" asked Vince, sadly.

Harvey glanced at the girl's gaunt, lifelike face and wouldn't have been surprised if her stretched back lips emitted a moan. "She can't be real as she would have rotted away to a skeleton by now. But really, what does it matter, we need to leave."

The door across the room out of sight behind the chains slid open loudly. The violent jangle of chains quickly followed.

The head of the young girl turned and looked at them. Her bloodless lips cracked open. "RUN!"

The men ran.

Vince slammed the door shut once they were both through the next door they arrived at. The footsteps approaching from the other side were loud enough to be heard through the door. They quickly surveilled the musty room that seemed to be a rest area. The sofa, armchairs, a table, pictures on the wall and lamps were all marked by the usual bloodstains and blood splatters.

“There’s no exit,” stated Harvey, anxiously.

Footsteps grew nearer the door.

“There has to be,” argued Vince, flicking the old Bakelite wall switch up and down, but the lamps remained dark.

“Quick, let’s block the door with the sofa,” shouted Harvey, now fully convinced someone or something was chasing them.

Together they pushed the sofa against the door and for good measure piled the two armchairs on top. As they admired their handiwork, the footsteps halted outside the door. The expected banging or forcing the door open didn’t materialize, but whatever was outside breathed nasally.

“What’s it waiting for?” Vince whispered.

Harvey shrugged.

Whispers spun them around.

They are trapped.

They are ours now.

We will feast well today.

Harvey aimed his rifle at each new voice but found no target to shoot.

Vince’s head flicked to the position of each new voice. “They’re either invisible or it’s coming from behind the walls.”

How shall we kill them?

They both glanced up when the patter of feet ran across the ceiling. It didn’t sound like rodents.

Slow, make them suffer, make them squirm.

Their eyes darted to the floor when footsteps ran across the room.

They can't see us.

Humans are too slow to catch us even if they could. The voice chuckled menacingly.

Harvey noticed something on the floor beneath the rug the table rested on, a slightly raised square. He rushed over, tipped the table on its side and tugged the dusty, mildewed rug aside.

No! They've found it.

Harvey grabbed the inset handle of the trapdoor and pulled it open. Fetid air washed over him.

They will escape.

Harvey shone his light into the dark hole. A metal ladder dropped into darkness.

Hope pushed bravely through Vince's fear. "Is it a way out?"

We must stop them.

Something banged forcefully on the door.

Harvey sat on the floor and dangled his feet in the hole. "It's a way out of this room is all I know. Are you coming?"

Small footsteps pattered speedily over the floor, ceiling and walls.

The sofa screeched across the floor a few inches when something barged the door ajar.

"You can bet your life I am." Vince followed Harvey down the ladder and pulled the trapdoor into place.

We have left it too late.

Our feast escapes.

The whispers and the banging on the door fell silent.

CHAPTER 24

GIANT DOOR

"Find anything interesting?" asked Baloc, glad to have reached the bottom of the winding staircase.

Shaw pointed his cigar at the opening. "Take a look."

When Baloc moved along the short passage and aimed his flashlight through the opening, lights flickered on along its length. He turned to the others. "We have power, so Vince must have got the generator working." He switched off his flashlight and stunned by the workmanship lit by the electric lighting, swept his eyes over the details.

The thirty-foot-high, gothic-arched corridor stretched into the distance for at least sixty feet. Though some areas remained as rough rock, most of its surfaces were carved to mimic stone blocks and pillars that suggested a cathedral-like appearance. Gargoyles of mythical and monstrous creatures, jutted out like sentinels on guard. Carved leafy barbed vines and patterned stonework adorned the stone archways set along its sides.

"I wasn't expecting this," Wendy exclaimed, taking position beside Baloc.

Baloc glanced at her as the camera lifted to her eye. "I believe the unexpected is going to be the norm on this island."

Shaw moved to the front and led them forward while Ryker stayed at the back.

Their eyes flicked over the impressive carvings and arched doorways carved in solid rock that led nowhere, only decoration for the long passage.

As they approached the end, Shaw broke their fascinated silence.

"There's something ahead."

The eyes of the giant figure sitting upon the throne at the end of the corridor eerily reflected the lights.

"Mannix is going to love that," said Baloc.

"*'It will look great on film',*" said Wendy, quoting Mannix's often used mantra.

As they approached the large seated figure, Wendy moved ahead to snap off photographs.

Shaw examined the huge metal door in the wall on the right of the seated figure, it was large enough for the giant—if it came to life and climbed to its feet—to walk through upright and noticed the door handle too high to reach. "I guess we go through there, if we can open it."

"Let's try giving it a push," Baloc suggested.

Baloc, Shaw and Ryker pushed the door, but it didn't budge.

"I think this arm moves."

The three men turned to find Wendy had climbed onto the figure's lap and was examining the arm holding a sword aloft, as if preparing to strike an enemy.

"There's a joint around one shoulder but not the other," she explained.

Baloc stepped a little closer. "Will it move?"

Wendy gripped the arm and pulled. It shifted a little and returned to its original position when she let go. After a moment's thought, she pointed at the floor a short distance back the way they had come.

"Ryker, go stand on the slab that's almost as wide as the corridor." She turned to Baloc and Shaw. "When I pull on the arm, you two put your shoulders to the door and push."

Wondering what Wendy was up to, Baloc said, "Care to explain?"

"Didn't any of you notice the large slab sink slightly when you trod on it?"

They shook their heads.

"I think we were all too fascinated by the statue to notice anything else," said Shaw.

"Well, I did, and I believe it's one of Ezra's switches that for some reason isn't working. I think placing weight on that slab activates a mechanism that would move the arm and open the door. Of course, I could be wrong, and a giant stone ball could roll along the passage and crush us, but, hey, it has to be worth a try."

Baloc smiled. "I agree."

Ryker crossed to the slab. "She's right, it sunk a bit."

Wendy gripped the arm. "Ready, boys?"

Baloc and Shaw put their shoulders against the door and nodded.

"One, two, three, go!" Wendy pulled the arm.

Baloc and Shaw shoved hard against the huge door.

The door creaked when it began to open. When it had opened a few inches, both the arm and door now set into motion moved under their own power.

"Well done, Wendy," praised Baloc.

Wendy released her hold on the arm and climbed down.

Shaw nodded at the gradually expanding opening. "Anyone want to hazard a guess at what we'll find in there?"

"Not me," said Baloc. "With Ezra's imagination I wouldn't be surprised if it was life-size Giza pyramids or a rendering of hell complete with demons and the devil himself."

The arm stopped moving with the sword tip pointed at the door now open wide enough to let someone of normal size slip through but not see what lay beyond.

Baloc noticed something in the flash from the photograph Wendy took of the statue in its new position. He moved nearer and shone his flashlight along the sword blade it held. "There's writing." He read it aloud. "*Welcome to the underworld. Enter if you dare.*"

"Cheery," said Wendy. "Let's dare."

One by one, they entered.

CHAPTER 25

Large Devil

Balking from the reek so strong and vile its foulness soiled their mouths, Vince and Harvey glanced at the stagnant sewage in the channel between the raised concrete walkways that ran along each side of the arched brick tunnel.

To pick out a route to head in, Harvey shone his light in both directions. Neither invited further exploration. The decision was made for them when the approaching scampering of numerous small feet heralded the approaching hoard of malformed rodents.

Vince briefly glanced at the frightening sounds concealed by darkness and tried to avoid brushing against the foul slime and sludge-covered walls when he copied Harvey's fear-infused dash along the narrow walkway away from the impending menace.

They rounded a bend in the tunnel to find a metal grill barring the tunnel ahead. With the rodents behind, they couldn't go back. As they neared the barriers, they arrived at a side turning that furnished them with hope of escape. They rushed through the short passage and entered a large room swamped with sewage overspill and littered with decayed wooden storage crates, a stack of faded subway station signs, rusty oil drums and beer bottles.

The hundreds of scampering claw-tipped paws growing nearer by the second were accompanied by the rodents' terrifying squeals, shrieks and clashing of sharp incisors.

Vince's and Harvey's hurried splashing through the foul ankle-deep water threw up fresh waves of stench from the thick layer of sludge covering the floor their feet slipped on. More than once they were almost spilled face down into the sewage by unseen obstacles littering the floor. When they had almost reached the goal of their dash across the room, a large metal door, the rodents entered the room. Displaying no revulsion towards the foul pool, they dived in and swam furiously towards them.

The two men climbed out onto the raised ledge at the far end and rushed for the door. Harvey pulled it open wide enough for them to slip through, and glancing fearfully at the oncoming swarm of evil glowing eyes and chomping fangs promising an agonizing death, he slammed it shut.

Vince fell against the wall and panted heavily. "When will this horror end?"

Harvey, also breathless, shook his head. "Damn soon, I hope."

After he had regained some of his breath, Vince glanced around the room dimly lit by a grimy yellow bulb hanging from the ceiling. "Is that a furnace?"

"It looks like it." Harvey approached the large metal construction with an arched door set about three feet from the floor. A couple of temperature dials and levers were positioned above and to the right of the feeding door. He opened the door, peered inside, and grimacing, quickly closed it. "Skeletons, human skeletons."

When Vince's eyes scanned the room, his face dropped. The only door was the one they had entered through, and they couldn't leave through that. "If we don't find a way out of our present predicament, we might be keeping them company."

Harvey shone his rifle light into the room's dark areas. "We found a trapdoor in that other room we thought was a dead end, so have a good look around and maybe we'll find a hidden door or something."

Though the rodent claws scratching on the door was unsettling, both men knew they couldn't get through the thick metal barrier, so they were, for the moment, safe.

A few minutes spent searching the room ended with no discovery of a cleverly concealed exit; they were trapped.

As they contemplated their situation, the door scratching stopped.

Vince glanced at the door and then at Harvey. "Do you think they've given up and gone away?"

"I doubt it." Harvey crossed to the door and put an ear against it. "I can't hear anything."

"Maybe we should wait a few minutes and then take a peek?" Vince suggested.

Harvey stared at the door and imagined the rats gathered around it, still and silent, waiting for the stupid humans to open it so they could start feasting.

"I'm not convinced that would be a wise move, but we can't stay in here forever. Let's wait a while and see if anything happens."

Vince sat with his back against the wall and closed his eyes. *It would be so nice to have a few minutes restful sleep.* A metallic rattle sprung his eyes open a few seconds later. He sighed. *Now what?* He anxiously observed Harvey moving across the room with his gaze fixed on the pipe attached to the ceiling.

Fearing something bad was about to happen, Vince climbed to his feet. "What is it?"

Harvey pointed up at the rusty twelve-inch diameter pipe. "You see that?"

Vince noticed the dust drifting below the pipe and sighed. "They are inside!"

Their eyes followed the pipe that came through the same wall the door was set in, elbowed ninety degrees after five feet, and ran the length of the room before it disappeared through the far wall. A bracket bolted to the ceiling near the bend supported the weight of the pipe.

"We're safe though, right?" said Vince. "They still can't get at us."

The rodents' muffled squeals sounded sinister to the two men gazing at the vibrating pipe the monsters scurried through.

Harvey noticed dust fall from around the pipe bracket's ceiling fixing as the vibrations worked it loose. "There's something wrong here. Rats may have a certain level of intelligence, but what they are doing here shows a level far beyond what they should be capable of."

Vince shared his frightened glance between Harvey and the shaking pipe. "How so?"

"I think they've worked out a plan to get to us and seem to be communicating to carry it out."

Both men stared at the violently vibrating pipe and the supporting bracket steadily being worked free from its mooring.

Inside the pipe, the nose-to-tail row of rats rhythmically kicked their back legs so their backs slammed against the top of the pipe and their feet jolted back on the bottom.

The pipe clanging against the bracket was joined by another sound. Harvey and Vince's head turned to the door when the scratching upon it started again.

"We need to do something, quick," stated Vince.

Harvey scanned the room. His eyes fell on the side of the furnace and peered at the dusty raised lettering on the maker's plate—GROSSMAN AND DEVILLE FURNACE MAKERS SINCE 1881. He was smiling when he looked at Vince. "What did the creepy thing under the floor say we were to look for?"

"Something about looking for a large devil that would save us, or something similar, why?"

Harvey pointed at the maker's plate. "Because I may have found it. Grossman is a large man and remove the LE from the end of DEVILLE and what do you have?"

"Devil!" Vince glanced at Harvey. "You think the furnace is the *large devil*?"

The two bolts that secured the bracket to the ceiling clanged ominously to the floor. The pipe sagged. The joint between the bend and the long, straight piece of pipe started sliding apart with a menacing metallic squeal.

Harvey moved to the front of the furnace and pulled the door open "What about the skeletons?"

Vince glanced at the sagging pipe; their time had almost run out. "I don't care if they rise up and start dancing, get inside quick!"

Harvey chucked his rifle in and tried to avoid touching the flame-seared bones when he scrambled through the opening. When he moved to give Vince room to enter, he noticed a ladder leading up the chimney above the feed door; it had to be their way out. The large devil had saved them.

When Vince crawled inside, the pipe crashed to the floor. Rodent squeals filled the room. Desperate to prevent the vicious teeth from chewing on his legs, Vince jerked them inside, scraping his shins on the frame in the process. He spun, grabbed the door, and as he pulled it shut a snarling rodent leapt through the rapidly narrowing gap. Vince dodged its path, slammed the door into its frame and heard the outside catch fall into place, trapping them inside.

Harvey dodged the monster rat that suddenly appeared. As it bared its sharp teeth at him menacingly and scrambled across the bones, Harvey snatched up a thighbone. He struck the rat so forcefully its skull exploded, and its teeth shattered when the jaws smashed together. Harvey dropped the blood and gore-stained bone, snatched up his rifle and looked at Vince.

"Any more?"

Vince shook his head and glanced around the soot-blackened interior. "We're still trapped though."

Harvey pointed at the ladder above Vince. "Oh, no, we're not."

Vince glanced at the ladder. He had never been so glad to see a rusty piece of metal.

Harvey slipped off his jacket. "Before we leave, I need to collect some evidence."

"Evidence of what?"

Harvey laid his jacket on the bones and pulled the rat carcass nearer. "Evidence of these things." He glanced at Vince. "You really think the others won't accuse us of imagining things or that we mistook some of Houghton's movie props for real life creatures when we tell them what we've just been through?"

"To tell you the truth I don't really care as long as I get out of here and off this island alive."

Harvey lifted the dead rodent onto his coat, wrapped it up and tied it tight with the sleeves. He lifted the bundle, stood and slipped the rifle strap over a shoulder. "This, Vince, is our express ticket off the island. When the others see it and we tell them how many there are, they won't want to hang around."

Vince smiled. "Good thinking."

When rats began scratching frantically on the furnace door, Vince reached for the ladder and started his ascent.

Harvey slid a hand under the knotted sleeves of the gruesome bundle and let it hang from his arm to leave his hands free. When Vince was a few rungs above, he began climbing.

The small metal door set in the base of the tall, brick tower opened with a rusty squeal and emitted the two soot-blackened men. Both collapsed on the tall grass. While they recovered from their exhausting climb, they stared at the angry clouds rolling across the sky. It was as welcome as sunshine and blue sky.

After a brief rest, Harvey sat up and glanced around to get his bearings. His gaze ended on the foreboding building protruding from a dip in the landscape, positioned as if to hide its presence. "Is that the asylum?"

Vince raised his head and glanced at the uninviting building. "I think it must be. Its appearance doesn't inspire confidence that venturing inside would be beneficial for one's health."

"Or sanity." Harvey dragged his gaze away from the asylum when shrieks filtered up the chimney. He climbed to his feet and peered down the dark shaft. Though he thought it doubtful the rats could get into the furnace, they had proven themselves resourceful and their frantic screeches and claws scraping at the metal door was evidence they were trying. It was time to warn the others. He closed the hatch, took the radio from a pocket and pressed the talk button. "Harvey to everyone else, we have a problem, a bloody big one. Return to the village immediately. Your lives may depend on it." He released the button.

Almost immediately, Baloc's voice crackled over the radio. "What's the emergency, Harvey?"

Harvey put the radio near his mouth. "It will be easier to explain when we are all back at the village, but there are monsters on this island and we have proof."

After a slight delay, Baloc answered, "We are heading back now."

Harvey was about to put the radio away when Thane spoke. "Copy that, we are also heading back to the village."

Vince groaned when he stood. Though he was exhausted and his muscles ached, he wouldn't rest until he had reached safety—if that existed on this island—or he was dead.

Harvey smiled at Vince. "You ready?"

Vince nodded.

The two weary men hurried along the road.

CHAPTER 26

Demons

When Shaw led Wendy, Baloc and Ryker through the huge door, they stepped onto a flat area of stone that led to steps hewn from the rock that wound around a tall curved tower. On the left side of the pathway was a deep drop off. Their lights searched across the wide void and picked out rough-hewn buildings with stone bridges that may or may not have linked them all together. It was impossible to say for certain due to their creator's imaginative mind. A glance up the towering side of the curved staircase wall revealed evil gargoyles jutting out.

Wendy's camera flash bathed the scene in brief bursts of light when she snapped off photographs.

Shaw moved onto the staircase and noticed the spaced-out statues lining the curved wall. Each depicted a different demon holding a metal dish above their heads. He halted by the first demon effigy and sniffed the air. “I smell some type of oil, so maybe the statues are lights.”

Baloc glanced at the nearest stone figure. “The oil might be too old now, but it’s worth a try lighting them.”

Shaw flicked his cigar lighter to flame and stretched to hold it near the oil in the basin. It ignited with a whoosh and sent out an orange glow over the surroundings. He moved along the statues lighting them.

After photographing the flaming statues, Wendy removed the camera from her eye. “Impressive. Ezra certainly knew how to create an atmosphere.”

When they followed the curved steps, they noticed faint light shining through the opening the path led to.

“Is that daylight?” asked Baloc.

“How is that possible when we are so far below ground?” Ryker asked.

“I guess we’re about to find out,” said Wendy, eager to see what new marvels lay ahead. When she had first agreed to come to the island, she wasn’t sure she had made the right decision, but it hadn’t been the Disneyland-esque theme park she had half expected and she was now glad she was here. Her photos of Ezra’s creations were going to look great in the book she planned to put together. If publicized correctly, she was certain it would sell well, and her fifteen percent could bring her a much-needed boost of funds.

When they passed through the opening, all fell to stunned silence as their minds adjusted to Ezra’s latest masterpiece of architectural magnificence. Lit by daylight flooding through the large hole in the cavern roof, their eyes roamed the unexpected scene. They stood at the top of steep stone steps that descended fifty feet to a stone platform leading to an elaborately carved stone wall. The opening in the wall accessed the stone bridge spanning a rocky gorge. The river flowing through it was fed by the small waterfall cascading from the mouth of a demon head carved high in the side of the cavern.

Baloc gazed in disbelief at Ezra's latest surprise. "This could be where Ezra quarried a lot of the stone he used to construct his buildings, and then decided to use the created space for an impromptu movie set.

Wendy shook her head in delighted amazement. "I wonder if Ezra's surprises will ever cease to astound?"

"I doubt that's likely as it's impossible to predict what comes next." Baloc roamed his eyes over the spectacular vista. "But none of what we have seen so far down here has been particularly scary."

"That's not something I'm going to complain about," said Wendy, switching her camera to movie mode and filming the vista.

Though fascinated by what he saw, Zane had no idea how he would incorporate everything down here in his book, but he did know whatever he came up with, it would be an exciting read for his faithful fans. "Shall we move on?"

Excited and intrigued to discover what other wonders Ezra had in store for them, they followed Shaw down the steps.

They crossed the bridge and stepped through the opening in the wall adorned with carvings of serpents twisted around the limbs of writhing naked men and women, their faces frozen in agony, ecstasy and fear. Other snakes, some with heads of foul demons, jabbed venomous fangs at the humans' exposed stone-carved flesh.

They were greeted by a gloomy set of stone steps leading down to a pit in the floor of the corridor that led off into darkness. Vines that once grew up the stone walls carved with hellish depictions of strange, vicious demons and monsters were now dry, brittle heaps that covered some of the steps.

Baloc aimed his flashlight at the dark hole. “Anyone want to guess at the pit’s purpose?”

“Nothing welcoming, I imagine,” said Wendy, staring at the ominous opening they would have to pass.

The white fungus thriving on the dead vines glowed briefly when Wendy snapped off photos of the carvings as she followed the others down the steps. A faint rustling that sounded like slithering snakes came from the pit, halting the group around its edge. The lights they shone into its depths failed to reach the bottom or pick out the cause of the slithering.

“It’s deep,” stated Shaw.

“And extremely uninviting,” added Wendy. When she aimed her camera into the pit and took a photograph, her flash lit up dark squirming tentacles.

“Can anyone else feel the draft coming from ahead?” asked Baloc, directing his light along the corridor.

“Now that you mention it, I can,” said Wendy.

“Might be an opening to the outside,” suggested Ryker.

They carefully circled the pit and headed along the corridor.

On turning a sharp corner, they passed beneath the large archway at the corridor’s end.

“Well, Ezra’s done it again,” said Baloc, grinning. “It’s marvelous.”

Sunlight entering the purposely positioned round holes in the cavern roof bathed Ezra's devilish creations in light. It was these four towering demon statues that first drew the attention of their astonished gazes. The two highest towered seventy feet, but still fell far short of the cavern roof. Behind the statue on the higher level were towering tiers of buildings, which seemed to be carved from the rock, and stretched high above the god effigies.

Wendy recovered from her latest bout of wonderment and started taking photographs as she moved forward. The others followed with their eyes flicking in all directions as they discovered further details with every gaze. They paused at the low wall and looked at the spectacular sights Ezra had constructed but very few had seen.

"How could something like this even be built?" said Wendy, panning her camera to take multiple shots of the view.

"From what I've learnt of the man," said Baloc, "once Ezra set his sights on something he would throw money, machines and manpower at it until it was completed. From the few records that have survived from his time here, he had a large labour force brought to the island, shiploads of building materials and the latest construction machinery available. He spared no expense to realize his dream."

"He really was that rich?" enquired Shaw.

Baloc nodded. "His family made their money in coal, copper, iron and silver mines. They also dabbled in American oil, property, and later the stock market. They were rumored to be one of the top twenty wealthiest families in the world. When they lost their lives in the Titanic disaster, Ezra was the only surviving heir. As the family businesses continued to be successful, they pumped vast amounts of money into Ezra's bank account. I doubt even his frivolous spending could exceed the amount being produced. But Ezra was young, not even thirty, and had no interest in running things. Movies had captured his attention. Content to let the board of directors run things as long as they kept his bank balance topped up, Ezra set about making his own movies."

Wendy sighed. "I wonder what it's like having that much money. Never having to worry about where your next paycheck is coming from or the never-ending bills that continually appear in my letterbox."

"If Ezra and his island is anything to go by, it seems the wealth he could never deplete sent him a little crazy," said Shaw. "Not that I'm complaining. I admire the man for what he's accomplished here and wouldn't have missed this for the world."

"You have any ideas for your next book yet, Zane?" asked Wendy.

"Too many. There's enough stuff on this island for two books, maybe three." He gazed around at the impressive sights. "Down here for instance, it's different from what we've seen above ground. Those sets demand a certain plot. We have the spooky mansion as an ideal setting for a haunted house story. The Fear Fair, maybe a serial killer or mad clown on a killing rampage, and the Dollmaker's Cabin could be where a small group of people become lost and take shelter inside and face the horrors it contains. But down here, so far, I have no idea what sort of movie Ezra planned."

"The only vibe I'm getting," said Ryker, "is maybe an archeological horror with mummies or something coming to life."

"Maybe as we explore farther, Zane, something will get your creative juices flowing," said Wendy.

Baloc laughed. "If they flow much more, I'll be physically dribbling."

"Where to next?" asked Shaw.

Ryker pointed his weapon at the steep staircase leading up to another level. "That seems to be the only way forward."

Baloc glanced at the steps. "Then let's see what new wonders await us."

At the top of the steps was a flat area with two direction choices; left took them between the two tallest demon statues, and the archway formed of human skulls directly in front of the steps led into a dimly lit curved corridor.

"I'd like to see what's inside, if everyone's in agreement," said Wendy, snapping off images of the entrance.

Baloc nodded. "I'm up for that."

Shaw led them through the archway. If he was forced to admit it, he was also interested to see what new marvels awaited. He had never had a job like this, and it made a change not to have people shooting at him.

They weren't disappointed when they arrived at the large chamber at the end of the corridor. Concealed electric lights flickered, imitating flaming torches, and lit up parts of the room's interior, but left enough dark areas to envisage unimaginable things concealed in the shadows. The smooth stone walls were in direct contrast with the rough rock of the naturally formed ceiling. Stalactites of varying thicknesses and lengths hung like teeth that waited to devour them. Fascinated by their surroundings, they crossed the stone floor of the L-shaped room.

When they turned the corner, Wendy gasped at the huge devil spookily highlighted by strategically placed lights, whose flickering gave the statue the illusion of movement. Its upper body was hunched slightly forward, and its menacing face and evil stare looked straight at them.

Baloc took in the details of the thirty-foot tall statue. One of its large feet rested on the bottom of the steps that led up to the dark, arched entrance, its other rested on the front edge of the throne-like platform it sat upon. The words carved into the rock above the opening the devil guarded, hinted at what lay beyond, WELCOME TO HELL. Baloc positively beamed. “I can’t wait to see what surprises Ezra has waiting for us in there.”

Wendy flashed off a few photos of the impressive demon. “Yeah, well, let’s just hope Ezra hasn’t dug so far into the earth he actually arrived at Hell.”

As they passed beneath the demon guardian, Baloc’s and Shaw’s radio crackled into life.

“Harvey to everyone else, we have a problem, a bloody big one. Return to the village immediately. Your lives may depend on it.”

Concern etched Baloc’s features as he put the two-way radio to his mouth and pressed the talk button. “What’s the emergency, Harvey?”

“It will be easier to explain when we are all back at the village, but there’s monsters on this island and we have proof.”

Baloc glanced at Shaw.

Shaw shrugged. “We had better go find out what’s up.”

Baloc agreed. “We are heading back now.”

Thane’s voice crackled weakly. “Copy that, we are also heading back to the village.”

Though eager to continue exploring, the puzzled group turned around and Ryker led them back above ground.

CHAPTER 27

Dreadmore - Upstairs

After a search of the mansion's downstairs had disappointedly revealed surprisingly normal rooms that included a couple of lounges, a study and a large ballroom—sets for Ezra's actors to play out their roles—Gunner led the small group up the grand staircase.

As they took the left branch to the west wing, the lights flickered into life. Though the atmospheric, dimmed lighting was bright enough to make flashlights unnecessary, it still left many dark and shadowy areas.

"Good old Vince," said Winslow, comforted by the lights.

"Should make exploring a little easier," said Mannix, putting away his flashlight.

Quincy glanced along the corridor they had arrived at. A flickering light halfway along intermittently silhouetted a dark nonhuman shape that seemed to be looking at them. He pointed at it nervously. "What do you think that is?"

Gunner aimed his rifle light along the corridor and picked out the statue of a woman holding an urn standing against the wall. Gunner grinned at Quincy. "Your overworked imagination."

When they halted outside the first door, Mannix gripped the handle, turned and pushed the door open.

The door swung open with a squeal of hinges and revealed a well-lit room.

Gunner went in first and swept the room with his eyes and weapon. Except for a large wardrobe and a large cardboard box in one corner, with the words HANDLE WITH CARE printed on a sagging flap in red, and a dark stain beside it that might be blood, the room was empty. "It's clear."

The others filed in and gazed around the room choked with damp, mildewed air. Wallpaper covered in spots of mold peeled from the walls in strips and tattered lampshades balanced on the five grimy bulbs on the branched arms of the light fitting hanging skew-whiff from the ceiling.

The old floorboards, long absent their coat of varnish, creaked when curiosity moved Mannix to investigate the box. Everyone froze when the door slammed shut and the room fell to darkness. Locks clicked loudly into place around the door as flashlights were again switched on and pierced the pitch-black cloaking the room.

When faint scratching started, all eyes focused on the sound that came from behind or inside the cardboard that had now taken on an ominous air.

"Sounds like it might be a mouse or a rat," said Thane, unconcerned. "Probably made its nest in it."

That it might be a rodent brought Winslow no comfort whatsoever. He hated mice and rats in equal measure, hedgehogs, hamsters and gerbils also; in fact anything small and furry sent shivers down his spine. He edged towards the door and twisted the handle when the scratching increased. When the door failed to open, he tugged the handle forcefully.

"It won't open." His voice was edged with worry.

Thane crossed to the door and tried, but it was stuck fast, locked. When he rapped a knuckle on the door, a metallic thud rang out. Bathed in their flashlight beams, he turned to the others. "It's metal, solid. The only way we'll get out this way is if we break it down, but without tools..."

The light and their anxious gazes focused on the large cupboard in the corner when its door creaked ajar creepily. Within the darkness their lights failed to banish completely was a hint of something less dark, an indistinct form with eyes.

Their anxious gazes moved from the scary cupboard apparition to the cardboard box when it juddered and slowly turned.

Winslow, imagining it full of hungry rodents, clamped a hand over his mouth to muffle a frightened scream when something much worse, a small pale bloodied hand, appeared around the bottom corner.

The others took a step back. Mannix, who was nearest to the box, sought strength in numbers and rejoined them.

They stared at the bloodstained hand tipped with sharp fingernails clawing its way along the floorboards, slowly turning the cardboard box. It was obvious to all the owner of the hand would shortly be revealed.

"That's one of Ezra's tricks, right?" uttered Winslow, uncertain it was.

As no one else in the room knew the answer, he received no reply.

Mannix, a firm disbeliever in the supernatural of any kind, prodded Quincy to start filming as the box gradually turned and the open side came into view.

The hunched figure inside raised its head and opened its pale glowing eyes. When its lips parted and emitted a groaning screech that made the onlookers shiver, they backed tight against the wall. Winslow kicked and shoulder-barged the door without effect.

Though Mannix found his disbelief momentarily shaken by the box creature, he knew it couldn't be real. Could it? Things like that don't exist. It was this house, this island. Its atmosphere was choked with apprehension that toyed with the senses, making the irrational seem all too possible. He stepped nearer the box and pointed at the box creature, whose head now moved from side to side and snarled.

"It has to be one of Ezra's creepy movie props, rubber and mechanics. Very well done and scary, but it can't hurt us."

The others wore expressions of doubt when the box creature screeched again.

"I'll prove it."

Mannix circled the box, but evidence of the controlling wires or mechanical apparatus he had expected to find, remained worryingly absent. His bravado began to resurface when he crouched beside the box and the creature didn't turn to look at him. Even this close it looked real, and there were no joins in its skin he could detect. He stretched a nervous hand he wasn't entirely convinced wasn't about to get bitten off towards the creature.

Winslow had watched too many horror films to not know Mannix was making a bad move, and he let out an involuntary gasp when Mannix's hand had almost reached the creature.

"Are you sure that's wise?" asked Quincy, still unsure what the thing was. Living or not, it was damn realistic.

Mannix glanced at the others gathered by the door. All seemed to be holding their breath. "I assure you, it's not real and can't hurt me."

Thane grinned when the thing screeched again, and Mannix jerked his hand away.

Mannix reached out again and prodded the creature before drawing quickly back. It had shown no reaction to his touch. Mannix's confidence in his beliefs flooded back. His fingers scrunched the loose skin covering the back of the creature's neck and pulled, ripping it. He dragged it over the head and let it dangle. Metal rods, gears and cables moved in time with the creature's movements and controlled its porcelain head, glass eyes and hinged mouth. He assumed the tube connected to its throat carried the sound of recorded screeches and snarls to its lips. Mannix stood and smiled at the group.

"See, I was right."

The others gathered around the animatronic figure as their nerves started to calm. Though it was still creepy with its mechanical innards exposed, it no longer freaked them out.

"It's amazing that Ezra was creating something so lifelike back then," said Quincy.

"I agree," stated Mannix. "Houghton was the Leonardo Da Vinci of the movie business. When he wanted something that wasn't readily available, he would design it and find someone to build it for him."

Winslow glanced at the cupboard's partly open door. "What about the thing in the cupboard?"

All eyes turned to the large piece of furniture.

Mannix stepped a little nearer and peered through the gap at its shadowy occupant. If there was something inside that wasn't created by their nervous disposition, it hadn't moved. "It will be another of Ezra's scary creations, and because our only exit is barred, the wardrobe might be another way out."

"Then let's look inside to find out." Confident Mannix was right, Thane crossed to the cupboard and placed a hand on the edge of the door. It creaked when he pulled it open. His eyes scanned the empty interior. The ghoulish phantom they had glimpsed was painted on the back of cupboard. "It's only a creepy painting."

The others moved nearer as Thane stepped into the large cupboard. As soon as he was inside, the back wall parted and revealed a narrow passage. He peered at something pale at the far end that was moving. Suddenly, the ghoulish specter depicted in the wardrobe came into view and flew along the passage. Thane screamed as he staggered back. His frightened eyes remained fixated on the fast-approaching horror when he tripped and fell.

When Thane's scream reverberated through the room, it halted the others in their tracks. Recovering first, Mannix moved to the wardrobe, and standing beside Thane sprawled on the floor, looked at the phantom that seemed all too real. When it almost reached the back of the cupboard, it rose into the air and disappeared. Certain it had to be another of Ezra's tricks Thane had inadvertently triggered, he entered the wardrobe and leaned into the passage. His flashlight picked out the rail on the ceiling and then the suspended ghoul above him.

Mannix turned back to Thane and tutted. "It's a dummy, dummy. Another of Ezra's scares."

A little embarrassed, Thane climbed to his feet. "Well, it bloody well worked, coming at me out of the darkness like it did."

With the imagined danger past, the others crowded around the wardrobe and looked along the passage Mannix lit up with his flashlight.

"I guess that's our way out," said Gunner.

"Do you think there are more of Ezra's...things, in there?" asked Winslow, anxiously. He far preferred watching horror movies than being in one. Real or not, the things they had encountered so far were still scary, and he wasn't keen on something jumping out at him.

"I should think that's a distinct possibility," answered Mannix. He turned to Thane. "As you are our protector, shouldn't you take the lead?"

Ignoring the man's smirk, Thane pushed past Mannix and stepped into the passage formed between the outside structure and the back of the mansion's internal walls.

Black dust had gathered on the hardened lumps of lime and horsehair plaster forced through the wooden laths of the internal walls. About halfway along, they arrived at a narrow door set in the wall. Thane released the catch holding it closed and pushed it open. Weak light sneaked into the passage when the door swung open with barely a groan. Thane poked his head through and looked along the corridor. Ghostly shadows of a man, a woman and two children, boy and a girl, looked at him with their holes-for-eyes gazes.

"What do you see?" asked Mannix.

Thane moved aside. "Look for yourself."

A little surprised by what he saw, Mannix looked at each of the shadows in turn. What he found unsettling is that they weren't flat on the wall, but turned to the side, as if the wall was made of glass and they were behind it. The shadow figures looked straight at the door and anyone who passed through.

Quincy sneezed. "Are we going to remain in this passage for much longer?" he moaned. "This dust is playing havoc with my sinuses."

Mannix stepped into the corridor, and as the others joined him, he took in the cracked plaster walls, the large flakes of black paint hanging from the black ceiling like hundreds of bats roosting, and the dirty green strip of threadbare carpet running down the middle of the corridor. He moved to the nearest shadow and ran a hand over the expertly painted ghostly image.

Thane pushed to the front and led them along the narrow, gloomy corridor. He stopped after only a few steps and studied the thing his light focused on at the end of the corridor.

"Why have we stopped?" called out Winslow, eager to be out of the dark passageways.

Mannix peered over Thane's shoulder. "There a creepy figure sitting in an armchair looking at us."

Winslow sighed. "Glad I asked."

"What do you reckon?" asked Thane. "Another movie prop?"

Mannix looked at the armed man. "Seriously, Thane, after what we've seen?" He shook his head. "Of course it's a movie prop." Mannix strode towards the figure.

"Just thought I'd check," said Thane, leading the others forward.

When something clicked beneath Mannix's foot, he froze and stared at the figure he expected to glide towards him on rails. When nothing happened, he aimed his light at the thing in the armchair that sat slightly to the side. It seemed to be a small girl, perhaps nine or ten years old. Her face, partly hidden by long raven hair draping over her shoulders, was directed at something on her lap. Her white, puffed-sleeved dress was yellowed from age, and like the rest of her, it was covered in a layer of fine dust. The dress hung off her thighs, leaving her knees, legs and bare feet on show. Behind on the wall, written in blood red scrawl was, ***It was more fun in Hell!***

Mannix gently lifted his foot from the worn carpet and approached the armchair and the door nearby. His flashlight picked out the drips of congealed blood that had seeped from the wound in her chest and the deep gashes on her right knee and left ankle. What he first mistook for a spiderweb of veins showing through her skin, he recognized as cracks in her porcelain skin when he drew closer, like on a glaze-cracked plate. It was a doll. Lifelike and scary.

Held in one pale hand was the focus of her gaze, a small doll. Though voodoo stylized, it was an exact copy of her creepy self. Gripped in two fingers of her other hand was a long pin with a silver skull on the end. When her pin hand moved, Mannix stepped back, bumping into Thane.

"It's a dummy, dummy," quipped Thane.

"What's happening?" enquired Winslow, standing on tiptoes to peer past the others gathered behind the two men at the front. His gaze fell on the girl in the armchair as she stabbed the sharp pin into the chest of the doll she held and moaned a pleasurable sigh as fresh blood trickled from the wound in her own chest. "Oh." He glanced at the door beside the creepy girl. "I think we should leave?"

"In a minute. I want to see what happens." Mannix glanced at Quincy, pleased to see the camera to his eye filming, and refocused on the girl.

The girl slowly turned her head, revealing her pretty face with lips formed into a knowing smirk, and held up the pin. In a sweet innocent voice, she said, "Play with me."

A loud thump behind them echoed along the corridor and aimed their gazes back along the narrow passage. The overhead lights went dark. Two new lights flickered on and off. Ghostly moans drifted towards them. Replica shadow figures peeled from their painted facsimiles and drifted apart, turned and looked at them, their holes for eyes bright and menacing. Like smoky wraiths they shimmered and began drifting slowly nearer the nervous group.

"Smoke and mirrors," stated Mannix, a little nervously, as he wondered how Ezra had managed to pull off the effects.

"That's as may be," said, Winslow, backing through the group toward the door. "But it's still as scary as hell."

"Why won't you play with me?"

Winslow spun and screamed. Lit and unlit in the flickering lights, the creepy girl was on her feet and looking straight at him. He opened the door and rushed through.

"Hold on, Winslow," called out Thane, glancing at the spooky girl as he went to catch up with the frightened lawyer.

Screams like ethereal souls being tortured seeped from the walls. The door they had entered through opened and banged shut repeatedly, revealing glimpses of a phantom form standing in the doorway watching them. Footsteps produced by nothing visible, were heavy enough to raise dust from the threadbare carpet as they moved along the corridor towards them.

As the others headed for the exit, Mannix picked out the two sources of flickering light along the hall and pictured the hidden projectors creating the ghostly shadow figures. He assumed the footsteps were caused by mechanical thumpers beneath the floor and the screams a recording. He smiled and nodded slightly. *Bravo, Ezra.*

Gunner's nervous gaze flicked from the ghostly phantoms to the scary girl. "You coming, Mannix?"

Mannix turned away from the impressive spectral show and smiled at the thin wires attached to the playmate-less girl caught in his flashlight beam when he passed and stepped through the doorway.

Gunner quickly shut the door, deadening the scary sound effects.

Worried that the dark gap beneath the large four-poster bed might be harboring something he wouldn't like to see, Winslow took a wide berth around it.

Thane shone his flashlight at Winslow, who worried what might lay on the other side, waited by the door. "Is it unlocked?"

Winslow scoffed. "Yeah, like I'm going to open it after what I've just witnessed."

While Thane headed for the door to check if it was unlocked, the others gazed around the large bedroom. Even with the musty smell and layers of dust and cobwebs covering everything, the plushness and grandeur of the furnishings, including two large wardrobes positioned in the far corners, shined through. However, no one felt curious enough to open the wardrobes' doors.

Thane turned the handle of the bedroom door and pulled; the door opened easily. His glance outside revealed they were at the far end of the corridor they had been in before, but on the opposite side to the box monster room. Without any need for encouragement or communication, the rest of the group followed him into the hall.

Winslow sighed in relief. "I don't know about the rest of you, but I've done enough exploring for one day and would like to head back to the village. I am in desperate need of a cup of tea." His desk in his London office seemed awfully inviting now.

Mannix was about to voice his keenness to continue when Thane's radio crackled.

"Harvey to everyone else, we have a problem, a bloody big one. Return to the village immediately. Your lives may depend on it."

Thane was about to ask Harvey what the problem was when Baloc beat him to it.

Baloc's voice crackled over the radio. "What's the emergency, Harvey?"

"It will be easier to explain when we are all back at the village, but there's monsters on this island and we have proof."

A slight pause, then, "We are heading back now."

Thane pressed the talk button. "Copy that, we are also heading back to the village."

Slightly concerned by the mention of monsters, Winslow asked no one in particular, “What do you suppose that’s all about?”

Thane shrugged. “You heard it. Harvey mentioned he had proof monsters were on the island.”

“Great!” moaned Winslow. “As if the ghosts and ghouls weren’t bad enough.”

Mannix scoffed. “Monsters be damned. He’s probably confused Ezra’s impressive movie props with something alive.”

“I hope you’re correct,” said Thane, “because the alternative doesn’t bode well for our safety.”

“It’s pointless speculating,” said Gunner. “Let’s return to the village and see what Harvey has to say.”

Thane led them back downstairs and out of the mansion.

CHAPTER 28

SNATCHED

Harvey grabbed Vince's arm and warning him to silence, pulled him through a break in the waist-high wall that lined the side of the road and shoved him to the ground.

Fearing the rat hoard had found a way above ground and were on their trail, Vince rubbed his elbow that had struck a rock and whispered, "What's wrong?"

Harvey dropped the wrapped-rodent on the ground and pointed across the road at something moving across the landscape. "Something devilish is coming."

Vince gazed worriedly in the direction his companion indicated. It took him a few moments to realize what he was looking at, and it was a lot worse than monstrous rodents. "What in hell's abomination is that thing?"

Harvey peered through a gap in the wall at the impossible creature heading towards the road and them. "Your guess is as good as mine, but no way is that thing a naturally evolved creature. Something weird is happening on this island."

Vince cowered behind the wall. "All the more reason to get off it as soon as possible."

Both men watched the creature agilely clamber over the rough ground and obstacles in its path.

Trembling as it approached their position, Harvey focused on the creature's human features. If it wasn't for the frightening arachnid body the female part was attached to, he would have thought her pretty. Her aged eyes were filled with menace that hinted at a life not absent savagery, and in direct contrast to the youthfulness of her face. He thought she couldn't be more than eighteen, twenty at the most. Praying it wouldn't discover them, he pressed his body to the ground when the creature stepped onto the road. Both terrified and fascinated by the strange, frightening monstrosity, Harvey was unable to drag his eyes away from the creature now only a short distance away.

The Queen stepped onto the road and was about to head for her lair when she sensed she wasn't alone. Her gaze homed in on the crumbling wall the two humans hid behind, and she rushed for it. She suddenly halted with one of her front spider limbs resting on the wall and the other poised above one of the humans.

Harvey turned his head and noticed Vince's terrified expression and his wide-eyed gaze focused on the pointed tip of the spider's leg a few inches away from his face. Harvey slowly moved his rifle to aim at the leg. As his finger hooked around the trigger, the leg was withdrawn.

The Queen's first instinct had been to kill the cowering humans, who reeked of foul substances and fear, but they could prove useful if she slightly altered her plan to get off the island. When she stepped back onto the road to ponder her new strategy, she noticed movement and gazed back the way she had come. One of the three humans who had arrived on the island in a flying machine, and whom she now assumed were hunters sent to clear the way for the arrival of the second group, was following her.

As her thoughts pondered the human's threat, she glanced at the wall the humans hid behind and then back at the hunter, a more suitable candidate for what she had in mind. Her eyes scanned the row of trees behind the wall and their thick boughs overhanging the road.

Harvey slowly raised his head and wondering what it was doing, stared fearfully at the spider creature a short distance away. His skin crawled when two large spiders scuttled creepily around her body. He shifted slightly when it moved and through a gap in the wall observed the spider monster pause beneath a tree briefly before climbing the thick trunk and disappearing amongst the leafy canopy. He had no idea what it was doing or if it lived in the tree, but they couldn't risk moving until it had gone.

Vince, still shaking from his near-death experience, whispered nervously, "Has it gone?"

Harvey shook his head. "Not yet. Remain still and don't make a sound."

Breathless from following the spider creature's erratic trail over the rough and at times steep ground, Ray climbed the slope covered in tall grasses, weeds and saplings. Though his prey had left a clear trail, he had been surprised by how swiftly it moved, preventing him from getting off a shot over the rough and hilly terrain. He paused for a breather at the top of the slope and surveilled the area. His eyes followed the road to the rooftops visible a couple of hundred yards distant. From what he remembered from the info Zane had supplied them with, it had to be the lunatic asylum movie set and seemed to be what the creature headed for.

He crossed a level area of rough ground, climbed over the low wall and stepped onto the cobbled road. His eyes focused on the strange object lying on the road a few yards away. Ray moved nearer and recognized it as one of the eggs from the spider creature's back; it must have fallen off. When he poked it inquisitively with the rifle barrel, the thing gestating inside squirmed in protest. Though he was tempted to stamp on it to kill the foul creature inside before it hatched, he refrained from doing so.

When his gaze both ways along the road and into the landscape failed to detect the spider creature, Ray decided to head for the asylum to see if he could pick up its trail. He halted after two steps when a rustling above him warned him of impending danger. His gaze shot to the bending tree branches as he dodged to the side. The rifle raised to shoot the massive spider dropping towards him was seized from his grasp by a spider limb and swung at his head when it landed on the road. The force sent Ray reeling. He crashed into the wall and collapsed. As unconsciousness crept over him, his dazed gaze fell on the frightened faces of the two men staring back at him.

Vince stifled his scream with his hand when someone crashed into the wall and stared helplessly into the man's eyes as they glazed over and closed. He glanced at Harvey hoping for instructions that would save them, but he only received a finger-on-the-lips-to-keep-silent signal. He almost screamed again when the man draped half over the wall was lifted into the air.

Harvey watched the man, who he assumed was one of the hunters Zane had hired, rise into the air. He cautiously raised his head to see what was happening.

The Spider Queen examined the weapon briefly before flinging it over the wall. She picked up the unconscious human, dumped him on her back and returned the egg she had placed on the ground to her egg-tenders and set off along the road. The spiders crawled over the human cargo and secured it in place with strands of web.

When the creature had dropped out of sight into the dip of the asylum grounds, Harvey nudged Vince. "It's gone."

Vince, who thought one of the spider monster's legs had jabbed him, jumped from the touch. He calmed on hearing Harvey's voice and sat up. "Which way did it go?"

Harvey nodded his head along the road.

"The asylum." Harvey picked up the rodent bundle and climbed to his feet. "Let's move before it comes back."

Dreading a second confrontation, Vince jumped to his feet and followed Harvey to the village.

By the time Harvey and Vince reached the meetinghouse, the others were already there, sat around the pushed-together tables eating sandwiches and drinking tea and coffee, its strong aroma filling the room. All heads turned to the two men when they burst through the door, and all noticed their disheveled, dirty appearance and the rank smell of sewage both men emitted.

"What the hell happened to you two?" exclaimed Mannix, nodding to Quincy to start filming.

Harvey thudded the bundle on the table, rattling tea and coffee cups, and unwrapped it. "That happened to us."

The others stared at the monstrous rat. Its vicious teeth-filled jaw with enlarged incisors, claws and spikey back were all at odds with its recognizable rodent features.

Vince took the steaming mug of coffee Wendy had poured for him and took a generous sip as he gazed around at the astounded faces. "And it wasn't alone. There were at least a hundred, and there could be more, a lot more."

Astonished, Shaw looked at Harvey. "They were in the generator room?"

Harvey gulped down the refreshing strong coffee and shrugged. "We heard sounds, so they might have been, but they didn't attack until we were in the subway. They came down the stairs, chased us through a train and into one of Ezra's spooky movie sets."

"We barely managed to escape," added Vince, briefly reliving the moment. "And we saw and heard other things down there, whether real or not it's impossible to say for certain."

"Well, that thing sure is real," stated Wendy, snapping off photos.

"I thought your hunters killed them all?" said Mannix.

Baloc studied the rat creature. "I'm not sure this is the same species Kwanza encountered and killed. He made no mention of rodents, and I imagined something larger."

"Great!" said Winslow. "There's more than one type of killer animal on the island."

"The rats might be the least of our problems," said Harvey ominously, turning to Baloc. "Was one of your hunters a tall white man?"

Baloc nodded. "Yes, Ray Chase. Why?"

"We saw him. He was attacked by a monster you ain't gonna believe."

"Try us," said Baloc, wondering how much worse it was about to get.

"It was a giant spider, and I don't mean hand-size giant, this thing has a body as big as a pony."

Mannix scoffed. "Impossible."

"That's as may be," said Harvey, grabbing a sandwich from the plate on the table. "But that wasn't the unbelievable bit. It was part human. Its front was female from the waist up."

Mannix refused to believe it. "It must have been one of Ezra's movie props. Some sort of mechanical monster like we encountered in the mansion."

"Believe me, I wish it wasn't, but without a doubt it was real," stated Vince.

"You said you saw Ray," pushed Baloc, finding it difficult to believe what he had just heard. "Where is he now?"

Harvey shrugged. "He was slung over the spider monster's back and heading for the asylum last time we saw him, so he might be there."

"Was he alive?" asked Wendy.

Harvey remembered the hunter's glazed eyes. "As far as I could tell, but unconscious, I think."

"But you didn't see any sign of the other two hunters, Ray's wife, Laura, or Kwanza, a large South African?" asked Baloc. His carefully laid plans to safeguard the group were gradually being ripped apart.

Harvey shook his head. "Only Ray."

Baloc looked at Shaw. "If he is still alive, we'll have to rescue him."

"I agree," said Shaw, without hesitation. Though he found the tale hard to believe, the monster rat proved there was at least one formidable new species on the island. "Whatever creature they saw, I'm certain we have enough firepower to kill it."

"That's probably what Ray thought," scoffed Vince, worried none of them would leave the island. "For all we know his wife and Kwanza are already dead, and Ray soon will be."

"That thing was crafty," said Harvey. "It set a trap, hid in a tree and ambushed Ray."

"We should contact the ship to come and pick us up and leave this island hell before we are all killed," said Winslow.

"I'm not leaving anyone behind," said Baloc adamantly. "And I doubt the captain will risk his vessel and crew by venturing back out in the storm heading this way. At the very least we are stuck here until it passes. However long that may be."

"Wave some cash at him or something," pleaded Vince. "We have to get off this damn island as soon as possible before those things find us. Because if they do, we're as good as dead."

Mannix was less worried about the spider creature he doubted was real than the monster rodent on the table that undeniably existed. "What about these things? If there's as many as Harvey and Vince said, I doubt your weapons will be of much use."

"None of us have seen them above ground—*yet*—so hopefully they don't venture out of their domain. If they do, we'll handle them one way or another," said Shaw.

"Wc also need to find out what has happened to Laura and Kwanza," said Wendy.

"I've been trying to contact them on the sat-phone without success," Baloc confessed. "I suggest we put our heads together and come up with a plan on how we rescue Ray and find Laura and Kwanza without falling foul of these creatures Vince and Harvey encountered."

"Also, how we can get off this island as soon as possible before we're all killed," added Vince.

CHAPTER 29

The Captive

The Queen entered the gloom-shrouded dungeon and approached the cell guarded by one of her vicious brood. The creature, a hideous amalgamation of fox and alien DNA, moved back subserviently when she drew near. She halted at the door and peered through the small barred window at her prisoner.

The blindfolded figure, huddled beneath a cover too thin to hold back the chill seeping from the floor and walls of the cold, dark prison, folded back the soiled blanket from her face and cocked her head at the cell door. Susan sobbed fearfully when the rusty iron door squealed open and the familiar click-clack footprints on stone announced the entry of her visitor. She sobbed. Her tears mingled with the dried blood around her eyes before soaking into the bloodstained blindfold. She shrunk in fear from the strange, familiar footsteps that halted a few steps away from her huddled form.

The thing inside her wriggled when it sensed its mother's presence, and the two communicated.

Susan knew the thing that held her captive would soon probe her brain, as it had done regularly since she had been enslaved, and more blood-tears would flow. She considered, as she had done on many previous occasions, how long ago that had been. Imprisoned in blindness she had no way of judging the passing of time. The disgusting meals her captives brought her to keep her alive were of no help in counting the days, as they were intermittent, sometimes arriving when she was on the verge of starvation. The food she was forced to eat if she wanted to live, consisted of vegetation, leaves, roots, grass and berries, or raw chunks of bloody flesh. At first, she had resisted the worst of the food, but the threat of starvation and will to survive coaxed her into consuming what she could.

She glanced at the unseen cell on her left. It was once occupied by Ryan and the one next to him was where Penny had been kept. Gary, who had been wounded during his capture, had occupied the cell on her right. When they had first been brought here, they had been able to talk, if not see one another. It was a short-lived comfort as one by one their captor had visited them, and they spoke no more. Their anguished screams still haunted Susan's sleep and often her waking thoughts as well.

After Ryan had...stopped talking, the thing that had just entered her cell hadn't returned for what seemed many days, weeks even—it was impossible to say in her isolated world of darkness. When it did, it had turned its attention on her. Until that day it never touched her physically, but when it did, it planted something inside her. Its intrusive thoughts probed her brain. It felt like fingers formed of cobwebs moved inside her head, shifting through her thoughts and memories, seeking obedience and control.

In the beginning, each session had only lasted a few seconds, but over time it had gradually increased and now lasted longer. It always communicated with the thing growing inside her before starting its telepathic mind-meld or whatever it was it did, so she knew her latest session was about to start. Her strong resistance to her captor's invasive telepathic probing had, at first, kept it from going deep, but now she had all but accepted her fate and let it get on with it. It was far less painful, and if the truth be known, the attention now brought her a little comfort after being on her own for so long. She craved companionship, and her cruel visitor was the only one that gave it to her.

Susan felt the thing inside her relax and waited for her visitor to make its connection with her. The sigh that escaped her lips when the cobweb fingers began their probing was almost pleasurable. She tensed slightly when she felt them go deeper than they had before but then relaxed and gave her will over to its control. Whatever happened, it couldn't be any worse than the life she had been living the past few months.

The Queen almost smiled when she felt her captive's final barrier dissipate and allow her free reign over the human's mind. Her patience had paid off and soon her longing to spread her seed off the island would be fulfilled. She had intended for her special offspring inside the human, also a queen, to travel to the human's world and propagate their species until all were in their control—it wouldn't be the first planet their species had colonized, and it wouldn't be the last—but lately, she had been pondering the humans' world she had glimpsed during her probing of their brains and had been experiencing a longing to visit it. At first, she dismissed it as the girl's desire to be free and back home mingling with her own thoughts, but the seed had been planted and had grown healthily. She now had the means to make it possible.

The Queen broke the connection and watched the drained human slip into a deep sleep. She glanced around the cold, filthy cell. The human was now a precious commodity, and for the Queen's plan to succeed, she must be cared for as it was important she regained her strength. If that failed, she had another, stronger host that might prove suitable.

She turned and telepathically issued a command to another of her offspring, a simple drone inside her subordinate guard, to take the human to a warmer, comfortable chamber and be fed. Though it was time for her to rest and recuperate before the final stage of her plan was put into motion, the Queen decided to pay a visit to her recently acquired captive first.

CHAPTER 30

Subterranean Horrors

Laura regained consciousness with a painful throbbing in her head and a bladder fit to burst. Disorientated, she raised a hand to the source of the throbbing pain on the side of her skull and groaned when fingers probed the swelling. Her eyes shot open when a faint growl reminded her of the monster. Her frightened gaze focused on the hand-hewn tunnel terrifying sounds drifted along. Accompanying the unnerving growls were snarls and scrapes, as if something dragged claws along the tunnel wall. She gathered some comfort from their faintness and the absence of the monster that had chased her into the mine. Wondering what had become of it and surprised she was still alive, her eyes went to the dim, but welcoming, string of lights stretching the length of the tunnel. It was evidence Baloc and his team had arrived and managed to get the island's generator working.

She sat up and looked at the pile of rubble and thick timbers blocking the passage. The cave in that had hopefully killed the monster had also blocked her only known exit, not that she could have climbed the shaft, but calls for help might have alerted her husband, who would search every inch of the island for her when he found her missing.

Laura pulled her legs out from under the small amount of rubble that covered them and, grateful to have suffered nothing more serious than a few bruises, climbed to her feet. With her eyes focused along the passage, she pulled her trousers down and squatted. A contented sigh escaped her lips as the pressure on her bladder released.

A brief search amongst the rubble united her with her Glock and flashlight. She switched off the light and stowed it in a pocket, blew the dust from the gun and reloaded. The soft breeze flowing through the tunnel and the cart rails that led along the tunnel gave Laura hope of another exit; the mined ore had to have been taken out somehow. Though apprehensive about heading towards whatever made the unnerving sounds, it was her only option if she hoped to escape from her subterranean predicament. Determined to survive and find a way out, she set off along the tunnel.

The light bulbs, large and bulbous with thick glowing filaments, were probably older than her. Though some remained dark and others flickered, Laura was thankful the majority still shed light in the dark tunnel and brought a little comfort to her perilous surroundings. After rounding a curve, the narrow tunnel widened into a space where the track split into two and branched down the twin side-by-side openings. Laura halted beside the rusty rail switch lever and turned her face to each route. Collapsed and mildewed timbers and rubble strewn along the right-hand passage didn't inspire confidence of a safe path. The left passage seemed in better condition. Though the breeze and the creature sounds came from both, which might indicate the two were joined, perhaps as a circular route for the ore carts, the breeze was slightly stronger from the left-hand passage. Unfortunately, so were the worrying sounds. With pistol held ready to fire, she headed along it.

She hadn't gone far when she encountered an obstacle. The rail ran across a bridge spanning a crack in the floor too wide to jump. The bridge was formed of wooden sleepers resting on two long iron beams supported by four rusty chains attached to either side of the two metal supports. The other ends were bolted to the overhead rock to prevent the middle of the precarious bridge from sagging. Two cables stretched across the void and through rings in the chains to form a simple handrail.

Laura peered into the dark crevasse; its bottom was too far to detect. It would be impossible to climb out if she fell and survived the fall. Some of the timbers between the rails had rotted, some were missing and those that did seem in better condition weren't screaming out to be trod on. Deciding to avoid them altogether, Laura placed a foot tentatively on a rusty rail to test its strength. It seemed sound. She slipped her weapon in its holster and cautiously placed a foot on each rail and gripped the drooping handrail cables. Little by little she slowly slid her feet forward in turn. Though the track wobbled slightly, jangling the chains, it seemed strong enough to hold her weight.

When she reached the middle, her eyes went to the ceiling brackets the chains were anchored to. Though worryingly, one corroded fixing had pulled from its mooring, the rest still seemed firmly attached. She slithered on. Avoiding looking at the dark void below through the gaps left by the missing boards, she focused ahead at the tunnel that curved shortly after the bridge ended.

When she reached two thirds of the way across, the left rail jolted. A frantic jangling of chains spun her head around. The loose bracket had pulled from the ceiling and swinging from the handrail, clanged against the beam supporting one of the rails she stood on. Her eyes focused on the remaining three brackets when one started to pull free. One of the corroded bolts sheared off. When the second bracket dropped, the clashing of chains spurred Laura across the final distance. She leapt from the bridge as it tipped to the side and winced when her knee struck the rail on landing. She glanced back at the bridge now tipped to the side. There would be no returning that way.

Laura rubbed her sore knee as she stood. Worried the collapsing bridge had alerted the creatures up ahead to her presence, she drew her gun and cocked an ear along the tunnel. Though they were louder now that she was closer, they didn't seem to be moving nearer. Laura pressed on.

The source of the drips that had grown steadily louder as she progressed was revealed when she entered a small cavern with a layer of water covering the floor. Droplets of water dripped from a few small stalactites and sent out ripples when they splashed into the shallow puddle covering most of the floor. Three linked and heavily corroded ore carts rested in the puddle on submerged rails. To one side was a short side passage where a line of empty rusty ore carts was parked.

When she waded through the ankle-deep pool, Laura shivered from the freezing water seeping into her boots. A slight rise on the far side carried her free of the pool. The sounds made by whatever menace lay ahead, louder now, caused her to grip the gun tighter. Though difficult to determine with the acoustic qualities of the tunnels, they didn't seem that far away now and increased Laura's apprehension of what she was about to face. Her only comfort was drawn from the fact they still hadn't detected her presence as they hadn't moved towards her or changed the tone of their growls and snarls.

A few minutes farther along the tunnel the walls began to change from a grey pale chiselled rock to a brown bumpy surface. Laura pressed her back to the wall as she edged towards the turn in the tunnel. She halted at the edge of the bend and peered around the corner. She gasped at the human skulls scattered about a shallow alcove in the far wall. Wondering what had happened to the rest of the skeleton bodies, she slowly moved forward and crossed to the other side when the tunnel turned in the opposite direction.

Certain the monsters were just around the corner, Laura halted while she plucked up courage to face them. She gripped the gun in both hands, stepped into the middle of the passage and roamed her gaze and weapon over the ore carts that filled the large cavern. Some were overturned, as if they had crashed into stationary ones and shot off the rails, others were full of mined ore and others stood empty. Though the sounds originated from the cavern, there was no sign of the creatures that made them.

She entered. Two exits led from the space. One branched off to the right in a curve; the other led straight ahead. Laura assumed the curved tunnel led back the way she had come to join the track intersection. That left the exit on the far side. She started across the room.

She jumped and spun towards every unnerving grunt, growl, shriek and scrape of claw, but still nothing revealed itself. A few more steps and some of the things would be behind her. *Was that their plan, to surround her before they attacked? An ambush from multiple directions would be impossible to defend against.*

Laura faced the scraping sounds coming from behind an overturned cart by the wall. Was something hiding inside it? She jumped when a low rumbling growl came from the same cart. Calming her rapidly beating heart with a few deep breaths, she moved nearer and edged along its side with her gun aimed at the gap between cart and wall ready to shoot anything that appeared. She gave the side of the cart a kick. Nothing emerged to launch an attack. When her gaze around the room revealed nothing creeping up on her, she leaned nearer and peered inside. It was empty. Confusion creased her brow. She was certain the noise had come from the cart. She screamed and stumbled back when a rumbling groan again reverberated from the cart. Something wasn't right; the cart was empty.

Curiosity overcame her fear, and she peered inside again. It was still empty. She crouched and noticed something fixed to the top. A speaker. She relaxed and almost laughed. It was one of Ezra's scary illusions. A piercing screech from a few carts away drove her towards it. She knelt and peered beneath. Between the rusty axles was another speaker. The wire hanging from it led into the ground. Laura brushed away the layer of dusty soil and revealed the wire trailing beneath.

Baloc had furnished them with as much details as he had about the island's constructions, and Laura remembered reading that the mine had once been a working silver mine, abandoned when the silver seam ran out. Though Ezra had planned to use the mine as one of his movie sets and had started adding his horror touches, he too had abandoned it when it proved too unsafe. What

Laura had come across were some of Ezra's scary additions installed before it was abandoned.

Confident the cavern was free of danger, she headed for the tunnel she hoped would lead her out of the mine.

A short way into the tunnel the walls became narrower and covered in patches of a rusty tar-like substance oozing from the rock. Thick, viscous, and uninviting to the touch. Some of the oozing, creeping glop had smothered some of the light bulbs, creating patches of gloom along its length. The breeze, stronger now, carried with it a musty, acrid stench and not the fresher air Laura had hoped for, which was a concern. She pushed on.

The next obstacle to present itself was a barrier formed of pieces of timber in a crisscross pattern stretching the height and width of the tunnel. Laura halted before it and peered through at the darkness on its other side. The snapped light cable and a short string of broken bulbs strewn on the floor, led up the wall to the dead lights that continued along the tunnel roof. There was no gate, but the rotted wood succumbed to a few kicks and Laura ducked through. She fished the flashlight from her pocket, switched it on and headed forward.

Though reassured by Ezra's previous scary sound effects that grew dimmer with every step she took, the darkness still heightened Laura's nervousness. If there was—as indicated by the draft blowing through the mine—another exit, and the creature that had chased her was still alive and knew about it, maybe it was waiting for her. It did seem persistent. Aware there was little she could do about it other than be prepared if it attacked, she carried on.

Laura frowned worriedly at the alcove in the sidewall ahead, where anything could be concealed. She cocked an ear but heard nothing to indicate anything hid there. She edged closer with her weapon and light focused on the recess and got the shock of her life when she saw what was inside. Two deafening shots echoed through the tunnel when Laura fired two panicked shots as she stumbled back against the wall.

Recovering quickly from the scare, Laura stared at the creepy figure that had barely moved when the bullets struck. Its face was a skull with two round goggle-like copper rimmed monocles covering its eyes. Corrugated tubes protruding from beneath the top brown-toothed jaw, fed into a round canister fixed around its waist and that seemed a part of the strange, frightening gas mask. Its dark, boilersuit type clothing was studded with patches of thick leather and rivets. Gripped in its skeletal hands was an old miner's lamp and a small pickaxe. It was terrifying to look at and easy to imagine it was evil, alive and staring at her.

Laura hesitatingly prodded it with the pistol barrel. It wobbled but felt hard, not flesh, but perhaps bone. Shaking from fright, she kept her eyes on it when she moved past.

Her light swept the tunnel ahead as she turned a curve and entered another smaller chamber with seven more of the skeletal, gas-mask-wearing miners. All except one faced her. The light Laura aimed at each was eerily reflected in their spooky goggles, imbuing them briefly with sight. It was all too easy to picture them coming to life and attacking her with their picks and hammers when she got too close—something she couldn't avoid if she wanted to reach the exit behind the fear-inspiring figures. Suppressing the strong desire to put a bullet in each of their heads, she shook the imagined threat away. They were just more of Ezra's scary movie props.

So tight-knitted were they, Laura had to edge sideways between them to avoid touching them and caught glimpses of her anxious face reflected in their goggles. When she approached the miner with its back to her, she noticed it held two picks and seemed to be guarding the exit she headed for. Sensing its malevolence, she cautiously edged around it. The new horror to confront her was the patchwork of what seemed to be human skin covering the skeletal miner's face. Bloodstained string stitches joined the flaps of skin together and ringed the googles. Five brown teeth jutted from the mouth flap formed in a malicious sneer.

Laura had seen enough, backing through the exit with her gaze and weapon trained on the miner monstrosities she still, irrationally, believed might cause her harm. She turned her back on them when she neared the end of the short passage and entered another cavern. Her gaze focused on the sliver of light seeping through the partly open door on the far side—daylight. Rain pounded the door and trickled underneath. Her flashlight swept the room. Racks of tools, pickaxes, large hammers, long chisels and a row of creepy gas masks lined one wall.

Lightning flashed. Thunder rumbled. Laura followed the track to the door and let the strong breeze and raindrops assault her face through the small gap. After putting away the gun and flashlight, she slipped fingers in the narrow gap and pulled. The rusty door refused to budge. She grabbed one of the arm-length metal chisels, slipped one end in the gap and pushed her weight against it. The door squealed when its hinges were forced to turn. A few more heaves and it was open enough for her to slip through.

Blasted by wind, rain and briefly lit by flashes of lightning, Laura emerged from the shelter of the tunnel entrance and stepped onto the wooden platform overhanging the steep cliff. The platform vibrated when a loud clap of thunder rumbled through the sky. Through gaps in the thick boards fixed to iron girders attached to the rock, she glimpsed the churning sea below. Laura crossed to the iron wheel set near the far edge of the platform the rails led to and looked through the hole it was set in. Ore carts attached to the bottom section of the wheel and the partly submerged cargo ship below revealed how the ore was taken out of the mine. The full carts would be pushed out onto the platform and attached to the wheel, which acted like a reverse waterwheel that would empty the ore into the waiting ship when the carts turned upside down. It was an awkward but impressive solution.

Shivering from the cold gusts, Laura gazed around the platform and spied a path formed of narrow metal steps zig-zagging up the cliffside. Apprehensive about the method of ascent, she headed for it and began climbing the precarious staircase. Though it creaked and wobbled slightly from her weight, it held fast.

When her feet trod on solid ground, Laura gazed around at the long-abandoned pieces of heavy machinery and equipment. There was a steam tractor with metal tyreless wheels, a strange crane, fuel drums, tools and other pieces of equipment too corroded or hidden in rampant vegetation to identify. Pounded by rain, she passed through the small compound and stepped out onto a track almost totally reclaimed by nature. After pushing through the windblown undergrowth, Laura brushed the wet hair from her face and glanced around the landscape to get her bearings. She was between the Fear Fair and the village. When she glanced to the left, lightning lit up the giant skull of the harbour skeleton farther along the cliff where the island jutted out to sea. The creepy asylum was east of her and the mansion about half a mile left of that. From her high vantage point, she couldn't see one redeeming feature of the island marred by the presence of the vicious monsters. Even the backdrop of mountains beneath the dark clouds seemed oppressive.

A glance at the storm clouds didn't give her hope she would get through, but she thought it was worth a try. Sheltering under a tree, she pulled out the sat-phone and tried contacting Baloc. She wasn't surprised when only static answered. Though it would offer a brief respite from the rain, Laura wasn't going to risk traveling through the forest at the bottom of the grassy slope again, so she set off at an angle that would take her to its far edge where she could connect with the road that led to the village.

*****

Pondering recent events, Baloc stood outside the meetinghouse sheltering from the downpour under a building's top story overhang. His visit to the island he had for so long yearned to explore had not turned out as expected. Because of him people were missing and might have died. The rest of them were in danger of being killed by the vicious island predators the hunters had failed to kill. He had managed to contact the helicopter pilot and Captain Santiago on the emergency radio he was now thankful he had thought to bring. Because of the bad weather, both had at first refused point blank to come to their rescue, but after haggling a steep price, both had reluctantly agreed to brave the storm before it grew worse and try to reach them. Neither of them had offered any guarantees it would be possible.

Baloc was about to try ringing the Chase's sat-phone again when he noticed a hazy figure hurrying along the street. As the rain-lashed spectre grew nearer, he recognized Laura Chase. Her sodden, dishevelled and grubby appearance indicated she had suffered recent hardships.

Laura halted beside Baloc, and after catching her breath, said, “We have to leave. Kwanza’s dead and there are monsters on your island.”

Though he had suspected Kwanza might have died, Baloc was still shocked and saddened to have it confirmed. “We know about the monsters. Harvey and Vince ran into some of them. The helicopter and ship are returning to pick us up.”

Laura gazed up the dark clouds. “In this weather?”

Baloc shrugged. “Hopefully one of them will get through. We won’t all fit in the helicopter, but at least five or six of us will be able to leave.” He looked at the rips and spots of blood on Laura’s clothes; it didn’t seem to be hers. “How did Kwanza die?”

“One of the monsters got him.” Laura glanced at the window behind Baloc and noticed people moving about inside. “Is my husband here?”

Baloc tried to hide his concern. “Let’s get you inside in the warm and dry, and I’ll explain everything that’s happened since we arrived.”

Baloc opened the door and ushered Laura inside

CHAPTER 31

Risky Pick-up

It had been all they could do to stop Laura rushing off to go find her husband when she had been informed the spider creature had taken him. She had only relented when Shaw promised he and some of his men would help her look for him once the helicopter had taken some of the others off the island. The pilot had contacted them a short while ago to say it was on its way and should be here soon.

Laura had seen the sense in strength of numbers and firepower. She also needed to rest for a few minutes and eat to regain her strength if she was going to be of any use in rescuing her husband.

The shrill tone of the emergency radio broke the silence that had descended over the group as each pondered their fate.

Baloc placed the call on speakerphone. "Zane here."

"ETA two minutes," stated Emilio, loud enough to be heard over the raucous engine in the background. "There's no way we'll be able to land in this wind, so four of you will be hoisted up on one of the supply pallets we dropped off. Hitch the cable I'll lower to a pallet and hang on tight."

Baloc frowned. "How will they get from the pallet into the helicopter, and what about the rest of us?"

"They won't. Wind's too strong, and sorry, four is all we can risk taking in this storm. And Zane, sorry, but we won't be coming back, whatever you offer. The storm's increasing, and you're lucky we made it here."

Baloc had no choice other than to accept the crew's decision. "Understood and we'll be ready." Baloc ended the call and quickly explained the situation. He glanced around at the worried and disappointed faces as he decided which four would be leaving. "Wendy, Winslow, Quincy and Vince, get ready as you four are going."

"I suggest you wrap up warm as it's going to be a chilly ride," said Shaw.

"Sounds rather dangerous to me," moaned Quincy.

"More dangerous than staying on this island?" said Winslow. "I don't think so. I'm risking it."

Baloc looked at Quincy. "If you hold on tight it will be fine, but if you want to wait for the ship, someone else can take your place."

"I didn't say I wasn't going, only that it sounded dangerous is all. Anyway, you're not certain the ship will make it, so I'll take my chances with the helicopter." Quincy zipped his coat up tight and pulled on his hood.

"There's no way I'm not going," stated Vince. "I don't want to stay on this cursed island for one more second than I have to, however risky the method of departure."

Baloc turned to Wendy. "I know it's not first-class travel, but at least you'll be off the island, which will make me feel a lot better."

"Sorry, I didn't realize I was such a burden."

Baloc smiled. "I hid it well. Blame my poker face."

Wendy rolled her eyes. "I must admit, I've had enough excitement lately and won't be sorry to see the island and its monstrous inhabitants fade into the distance, though I would have liked to photograph at least one live one for our photo book."

"Give me your camera, and if I run into one, I'll ask it to pose for a picture."

Wendy smiled. "You probably would." She fished in her pack and handed Baloc a compact camera. "It's automatic, so just frame the subject and press the large button on the top."

Baloc examined the camera. "I think I can manage that."

"Okay, everyone," said Shaw. "I suggest the four who are going, plus Harvey, Baloc and me, head for the pickup point and get the pallet ready. The rest of you remain here."

When the four passengers had slipped on the warmest clothes they had, Harvey led them outside.

While Shaw and Harvey covered the square with their weapons, Baloc and Vince tied cargo netting to the four corner cables to give the passengers some protection against falling or being blown off.

Wendy looked up at the slate grey clouds and the thrumming almost drowned out by the wind howling across the island and pointed at the object that appeared. "There's the helicopter."

The others glanced at it and noticed its struggle against the strong gusts.

"It doesn't look good for an easy pickup," said Harvey. "We'll probably only get one chance."

"I'll shimmy up the winch cable if I have to," said Vince, climbing onto the pallet.

Shaw faced the other three intrepid passengers. "Time to get aboard your transport. Sit with your backs against the netting and link your arms through, then you can't fall."

Wendy dragged the wet strands of hair from her face and drew her coat hood string tighter. "Were those the preflight safety instructions, Kurt?"

Shaw grinned. "You'll be fine if you hang on."

"Don't worry, I aim to."

Wendy, Quincy and Winslow climbed over the waist-high netting and, as instructed, sat and linked their arms through the netting.

Baloc used the radio to communicate with the helicopter. "Mathias, we are all set here. Once you are in position, lower the hook and we'll attach the pallet."

"Good, because we won't be hanging about," replied the pilot. "Tell them to hang on tight as the lift is going to be chaotic in this wind."

"Will do and good luck." Baloc looked at the helicopter that was now near enough for him to see Mathias fighting the controls to keep his vehicle on course against the buffeting winds. The crew were certainly earning their fee. "Get ready, it's here."

Baloc picked up the ring the four corner cables were attached to and waited to slip it on the hook about to be lowered.

The helicopter's fierce downdraft spun the rain in a mini cyclone when it hovered overhead. Battered by the whirlwind of draft-borne droplets that stung his face like pinpricks, Baloc forced his body to remain in position and his half-closed eyes fixed on the lowering hook.

Shaw and Harvey ignored the helicopter and focused their attention on the sides of the square under their charge. The rain, wind and now the deafening helicopter engine that rose and waned in pitch as the pilot constantly adjusted the controls to keep it in position made detecting any nearby creatures almost impossible.

Shaw shot his gaze to the roof of the nearby terraced houses when he glimpsed movement from the corner of his eye. When he saw nothing, he moved back to get a better look along the ridge. Finding it empty of any threat, he returned his attention around the pickup area.

Battered by the wind now gusting through the open rear door, Mathias cursed as he battled with the controls and regretted setting out on this foolhardy rescue mission. "How much longer, Emilio, as I can't hold it here for long?"

Leaning out of the door with his focus on the hook dangling below, Emilio replied through his helmet mic. "Hook's almost down, thirty seconds, and then we can leave."

"Let me know as soon as it's attached."

Baloc's second grab for the erratically swaying hook also missed. Though his fingers brushed the cold metal on his third try, he failed to grab it.

Noticing Baloc's difficulty and keen to leave, Winslow jumped up, grabbed the hook when it swung overhead and handed it to Baloc before promptly sitting back down.

Baloc nodded his thanks and slipped the hooking mechanism over the ring. Emilio closed the hook as soon as it was in position. Baloc moved away as the noise of the helicopter engine increased and watched the pallet of passengers rise from the ground and twist as it swung.

Jostled by the pallet's unsteady lift, Winslow smiled nervously at Wendy sitting opposite. "We're off."

Wendy winced when her bum jostled on the hard metal pallet. "I wish I'd thought to bring a cushion."

Vince smiled at Wendy. "You're welcome to sit on my lap. It'll take my mind off our perilous flight."

Wendy was about to make a witty retort when Winslow yelled.

"Look out!"

When she noticed his shocked, wide-eyed stare was aimed at something behind her, Wendy twisted her head. She screamed and pulled her arms free of the netting, jumped to her feet and dodged to the other side of the small platform.

The pallet tipped alarmingly when Scarred-Skull crashed into the side and gripped the netting to prevent its fall.

Mathias cursed when the helicopter suddenly tipped precariously. "What in the hell's happening down there?"

Those on the ground watched in horror when the monster leapt from the rooftop onto the side of the pallet. Shaw raised his rifle, but the turning swing of the pallet pulled the monster from his sight before he could get off a shot. As he moved into a better position, the helicopter tilted at an angle and shifted sideways.

Wendy grabbed one of the corner cables and spread her feet to steady herself against the frightening tilt and swing. She stared at the frightening monster that snarled hungrily at her and then glanced past it at the wall speeding towards them. "Hang on," she yelled.

The pallet struck the wall with such force the monster lost its grip, smashed through a window and rolled across the floor until it struck the far wall.

Wendy jolted forward and screamed when her hand slipped from the cable. She tumbled over the netting and through the window.

Vince grabbed at Wendy with one hand as she shot past, but he missed.

All three passengers stared through the window at the monster staggering to its feet and Wendy tumbling across the floor towards it before they were pulled into the air and carried away.

With his weapon still aimed at the ascending pallet, Shaw relaxed when he saw no sign of the monster. His gaze shifted to the broken window. It was inside the house.

"What happened?" asked Baloc. He had seen the pallet tilt precariously and crash into the house, but because he had been on the far side he was unaware of the cause.

"A monster jumped from the roof onto the pallet, and when it smashed into the house, it fell through the window."

Concern etched Baloc's face when he glanced at the window and then at the receding helicopter. "And the others, did they make it?"

Shaw shrugged. "I think so." A woman's scream inside the house changed his mind. "Or maybe not."

He rushed to the front of the house.

Wendy rolled painfully when she struck the floor and, aware the dazed creature would soon recover and be upon her, used the momentum to launch herself at it. Her shoulder crashed into its chest and slammed it against the wall. Lath and plaster cracked and splintered under the force, carrying them through and down the stairs. The spindle Wendy grabbed at to halt her tumble broke. As she somersaulted down the bone-jarring treads, she kicked her feet out at the stairs. Instead of stopping her, the force drove her forward and at the creature that had come to a sprawled halt on the half-turn landing. She held out the broken rail gripped in both hands and plunged it into the creature's chest. A backhanded swipe of the dying creature's claw sent her tumbling down the second set of short stairs. The door crashed open and struck her head.

"Ow!"

Shaw entered with his weapon ready to fire. He took in the final breaths of the creature, the wooden stake in its chest and Wendy rubbing the side of her head. "I see I needn't have rushed."

"You did more damage with the door than the creature inflicted."

Baloc poked his head through the opening and was relieved to see Wendy was okay, if a little battered. "You change your mind about leaving?"

"Yeah, it's such fun here I decided to stay." She held out a hand.

Shaw pulled her to her feet. "Sorry about the door."

"I forgive you." She brushed herself down. "Did the others get away okay?"

"Yes, thankfully," answered Baloc. "Mathias will contact me when they reach land." He nodded at the dead creature. "I guess you get your photo opportunity after all. He pulled the camera Laura had given him from a pocket and held it out.

"Keep it for now. I'll use my good one, if it hasn't been crushed. She pulled her camera out from beneath her coat, switched it on and after checking it wasn't damaged, took a few shots of the dead creature.

"Now all we have to do," said Baloc, "is rescue Ray from the spider monster, and, if it doesn't sink or turn back, rendezvous with the ship in about two hours. And not get killed by the other vicious monsters roaming the island in the meantime."

Wendy sighed as she put her camera away. "What could possibly go wrong?"

CHAPTER 32

Asylum

Lashed by rain, the rescue party approached the entrance and gazed up at the sign arched over the wrought iron gates. It simply stated the purpose of the depressing building the cobbled, weed-infested road led to: LUNATIC ASYLUM.

Shaw and Gunner moved through and roamed their weapons and eyes each side of the road for signs of anything moving through the overgrown grass, wild plants and bushes that had flourished since the previous humans had left the island. Except for the wind rustling through them, all seemed normal—whatever normal was for Ezra's island.

An involuntary shiver crept down Wendy's spine at the thought of entering the asylum building rising above the dip it had been hidden in, but it was too late to change her mind; no way was she returning to the village on her own. She gripped the unfamiliar assault rifle tightly and hoped the crash course Thane had given her on how to use it was sufficient for her to defend herself and the team against the island's horrors if she had to. She followed the others through the gate.

Baloc fell into step beside Shaw and Gunner as they reached the top of the small incline and halted when the asylum was exposed in all its rain-lashed, depressing glory. The others joined them in gazing at the dark grey stone building.

Set between the double set of steps leading up to the entrance protruding from the main building was a statue of a man.

Though too far away to see its features, Baloc was aware of the statue's likeness and informed the others. "The statue is of Ezra Houghton."

"Considering what I've witnessed of Ezra's crazed and imaginative mind, it seems fitting he chose to place his statue in an insane asylum," commented Laura.

"It's often the case that people who are ahead of their time are labeled as crazy and only later as geniuses," retorted Baloc, who admired Ezra's creativity.

"Well, I guess we each see what we want to see," said Laura.

The internal lights in the room above the entrance flickered intermittently, like staring eyes blinking. A couple of the lights in the main building dimmed occasionally, as if something within had passed between the light and the windows.

"If you weren't insane before you entered that place, I doubt it would be long before you became crazy," said Mannix. "I can't imagine a more miserable and unwelcoming building, which I assume was Ezra's intention."

"It is damn creepy," stated Harvey, unnecessarily.

"Whatever its appearance, it's only a building and can't harm us, but what might be inside can, so let's keep it together and go and find Laura's husband." Shaw led them down the road.

He halted the anxious group at Ezra's statue and glanced each way along the road that swept around to the back of the asylum, where he guessed the patients were admitted. Shaw turned to Laura. "We'll enter through the main entrance and make our way through the building, searching as we go."

Laura nodded.

"Look at this," said Wendy, who had moved nearer to the statue to take a photo.

The others gathered around as she read the inscription aloud.

"You can't hide from your mind or your fears, but you might conquer them."

"Not what I'd call inspirational," said Mannix, "but it's in keeping with what I know of the man."

"I like it," stated Baloc. "It will make a great opening quote for my book."

"If you survive long enough to write it," said Mannix.

Shaw headed up the steps. "Come on, we're wasting time."

The others followed and watched him open the unlocked door. As expected, it squealed spookily when Shaw pushed it open. After a quick peek though the opening, Shaw led them inside. All were glad to be out of the rain and wind. A short hall with a black-and-white checkered tiled floor and waist-high wooden wainscoting led to double swing doors half-paneled with glass and set in an arched glass-paneled frame. Mold spores spotted the sickly green walls.

Shaw peered through the glass panels to check nothing waited for them before pushing the door open and stepping through into the reception hall. Gunner and Thane roamed their weapons around the room as they split up and moved across to cover the two exits. Harvey and Ryker covered the rear of the group.

The long mahogany counter positioned on the far side matched the wood of the wainscoting running around the walls. The ripped and stuffing-tufted receptionist's chair behind the counter had suffered the investigations of rodents searching for edible substances or nest building materials. A numbered rack of pigeonholes against the wall behind the counter held pieces of yellow-aged paper, envelopes and rolled documents. Stairs leading to the rooms above the entrance were accessed through the open doorway to the right of the reception desk and on the left an arched opening led to the main asylum building.

The small group approached the left archway and gazed along the door-lined corridor. Two old-fashioned wheelchairs, one overturned on its side and the other occupied by a creepy doll, added to the apprehensive atmosphere emanating from the building. Loose leaves of paper littered the floor and at the far end was a metal-barred door as seen in prisons.

"I would assume these doors lead to offices for the staff and the patients' quarters are through the security door at the far end," said Shaw.

"You're forgetting this is not a real asylum," said Wendy. "No asylum staff worked here, and no crazy people ever walked through its doors."

"Not until now, that is," said Harvey. "We must be mad for coming here with that *thing* somewhere inside waiting for us."

"I suggest we head for the far door," said Laura, keen to find her husband.

"Good a place as any to start," agreed Shaw, leading them forward.

Their footsteps echoed on the red-and-cream flower-patterned tiles as they made their way along the corridor. Framed black-and-white and sepia photographs hung on the walls between the spaced-out doors. All depicted depressing images of asylum patients and staff—another of Ezra's touches. One that was particularly abhorrent showed an obviously insane woman in a slatted wooden cage with her head poking through a hole in the top. Another showed doctors and nurses gathered around a male patient strapped to a chair, observing a man in a grubby white coat about to perform a lobotomy with a metal spike and hammer.

Laura stopped looking at the pictures when children appeared in one.

Though it repelled her, Wendy took a photograph of the creepy doll in the wheelchair. It had a grey hogs head with evil eyes and a vicious sneer and wore a straitjacket. Like most of Ezra's scary movie props, it was easy to imagine it coming to life and creating evil mayhem.

The barred door was unlocked and squealed on rusty hinges when Shaw pulled it open. A few strides brought them to a wide metal door that was also unlocked and groaned in protest when Shaw forced it open.

Baloc noticed the four-inch thickness of the door. "I think it must be soundproofed to muffle the screams of the patients."

"What patients?" exclaimed Wendy. "There weren't any."

"Then it just shows Ezra's attention to detail. Some of the materials and props he used here came from an actual abandoned lunatic asylum to add to the atmosphere we are all experiencing."

"Ezra brought the crazies' ghosts to the island," stated Harvey, ominously.

Wendy also felt something. Even though she knew the building was nothing more than an extravagant movie set and had never been used as an asylum, it so encapsulated the essence of early cruel asylums she could almost hear the screams and glimpse shadowy entities of long dead patients.

They entered what seemed to be a communal room. Chairs placed around circular tables filled the center of the space and a small, metal cage fronted the nurses' room positioned to one side. Two fireplaces, one at each end of the room, were guarded by large wire fireguards to prevent the patients that were never here from burning themselves on fires never lit. Four large decaying rugs with faded patterns were spaced throughout the room on the white tiled floor and yellow-and-green flower-patterned curtains draped the six barred windows that rattled when wind gusts struck. Four simple chandeliers spaced along the center of the ceiling held five lightbulbs apiece. Those that hadn't succumbed to age gave off a dim glow that failed to bring any cheer to the dreary room or banish the gloom that seemed at home here.

Keen to seek out Ray and leave, Baloc indicated for Shaw to head for the door at the end of the room. They crossed the room in silence and stepped into a corridor whose walls were covered with yellow tiles up to shoulder height with two lines of white tiles to break up the colour. The brown tiled floor soaked up most of the light emitted from dim and dusty ceiling fixtures.

They peered into the first of the open doors along its length. It was an industrial-sized kitchen, complete with stoves, sinks, cold rooms, shelves and racks of cooking utensils. A serving counter ran the length of the hatch in one wall. Their gazes into the next room fell on a long table lined with chairs and the two rows of aluminum bowls on its top filled with long rotted gruel.

Though Shaw hurried them past the following rooms that Gunner and Thane checked as they moved ahead, they glimpsed metal-framed beds with leather straps hanging from them, a room lined with communal baths and showers, a first aid station and an operating room.

Halfway along the corridor, a side passage led off to the right.

Thane glanced back at the group. “Cobwebs.”

The group stared at the mass of uninviting strands strung from wall to wall and floor to ceiling. It was a good sign they would find the lair of the spider creature somewhere near and hopefully the missing hunter.

“I guess we had better check it out,” said Baloc.

Reluctantly, the nervous group followed Shaw, Gunner and Thane towards the spider-created filigree.

Shaw brushed aside the wispy strands with his rifle barrel and peered through the open doorway they had cloaked. His eyes swept across the small cots and beds lining both sidewalls as they followed the strands of web that stretched to the far door. As the spider creature had taken Ray, it seemed appropriate they should follow the web trail in the hope it would lead them to him. Alive or dead, for Laura’s sake they needed to find out. He bade the others to silence and prompted them to follow him through the children’s dormitory.

Laura felt sadness as she took in the sight of the cots and the small beds ensconced in wire cages to prevent the children from wandering. Even if no children had stepped foot inside Ezra's madhouse, if he had salvaged them from an actual asylum, it was probable children had occupied the beds at one time.

Susan awoke. The fresh blood that had seeped from her eyes during her last encounter with her captive had congealed, sticking her eyes to the bandage that had for too long kept her blind. Barry had taken his off once and had suffered as a result. He had been the first to...go quiet. Her throat was sore. Maybe an infection. She felt strange, empty, alone, more than usual. The parasite inside her must be sleeping. Weak and drowsy, she went to move her hands to her back to probe for its betraying bulge, but found them constricted, her arms were pinned around her chest. Her lethargic tugs to free them had no effect. Her addled thoughts recalled her last memories. Herded roughly by a beast that snapped at her legs and that she feared would attack at any moment, she had been taken from her cold, damp cell and shut in a room with soft padded floor and walls. She had been given berries, sour and juicy; she had wolfed them down. Though time had lost all meaning during her long captivity, she didn't think it had been long before her jailer, the one who seemed in charge, had visited her. Though it had communicated with the unwelcome companion inside her, Susan had felt dejected when her brain hadn't received attention. A few moments after she had felt a sharp pain in her neck and had fallen asleep, awaking a few moments ago to find herself alone and constricted with a sore throat. She had been drugged. Something had happened while she had been unconscious.

The change in routine worried Susan. She sensed things were about to change. For better or worse, she couldn't say, but anything had to be better than her prolonged captivity—except to be left alone, abandoned to die. She struggled to her feet, tripped and fell to the padded floor on her first step. Her legs were too weak to support her weight. She righted herself onto her knees and yelled, "Is anyone there?"

Her first attempt was little more than a hoarse cry. Her second try was slightly louder. "Please, someone help me."

With a raised fist, Gunner halted the group following a few steps behind and cocked his ear along the corridor to which the web trail had led them. After a few moments silence, he turned to the group. "Did anyone else hear that?"

"Sounded like a woman's voice," answered Laura.

"Couldn't have been," stated Baloc. "Ray's the only one who's missing."

"Could have been that spider thing," suggested Laura. "She, it, was part human female."

"Might be a trap," said Mannix.

"What do you think, Shaw?" asked Baloc.

"It's possible the corridors distorted the voice, or Ray might be injured, pain distorting his voice."

Laura peered along the dark corridor. "It was faint, so we can't be sure it was female. If there's a chance it is my husband, we have to go on."

"We will but stay alert, and keep back a few steps while we move ahead. That way if it's a trap and we're attacked, we'll have room to react without worrying about hitting you lot."

Aware Laura's hunting experience might save them, Shaw faced her.

"Laura, you lead them. The rest of you, if something happens don't fire in panic or you'll likely shoot us or each other. If something attacks, stay calm, aim and fire short bursts like you were shown."

He checked Harvey and Ryker had their retreat covered and moved forward with Gunner and Thane. A turn in the corridor led to a row of doors along one side. Shaw paused at the first door and peered through the small observation window set in each door. Quilted padding, torn in places and grubby, covered every reachable surface.

"It's a padded cell."

"Ezra sure did include everything," said Thane.

The three men brushed aside hanging strands of web as they moved along the passage peering into each padded room.

"Please, if anyone is there, help me."

The three men froze and stared towards the voice.

"That was female," stated Gunner.

"Yeah, we heard it, too," said Baloc, when the group caught up with them.

Shaw pointed his weapon at the second door ahead. "I think it came from that room."

"Well, let's not just stand here, someone might need our help." Wendy pushed past the others and crossed to the door. When she shone her flashlight through the view window, shock appeared on her face. "Oh, my god!"

Thane pointed his rifle at the door. "Is it the spider creature?"

Shaw pushed Wendy aside and shone his own light into the cell. Though surprised by what he saw, he remained calm. "It's a girl." He reached for the locking handle.

"Are you sure that's wise?" queried Harvey. "She could be insane, dangerous."

"She's blindfolded, in a straitjacket, and we are armed. The threat is minimal." Shaw released the locking mechanism and pulled the door open.

Susan's head swiveled towards the sound of the opening door.

Believing it would be better for the sorry looking girl to hear a woman's voice, Shaw indicated for Wendy to enter.

While Shaw's men set up a defense perimeter, the others crowded around the doorway and peered at the sorrowful sight the captive girl presented.

Wendy took in the girl's soiled and disheveled appearance, greasy hair and skin, and dried blood drips running down her cheeks from the two roundish bloodstains on the grubby bandage across her eyes. "It's okay, we are not going to hurt you," she said, softly.

Susan was shocked on hearing the woman's voice. The first human voice she had heard for a long time. *Could it be possible she was about to be saved? Or was it her mind playing a cruel trick? Had she finally gone mad?* She jerked away and toppled to the soft floor when something touched her shoulder.

Wendy drew her hand back when the frightened girl fell. "It's all right, we're here to help you."

The bloody and blindfolded eyes stared at Wendy spookily.

Wendy wondered how long this poor, obviously malnourished, girl, who seemed to be in her late teens, had been here and how did she get on the island. "My name is Wendy. I am here with some friends who want to help you. Do you understand?"

After a few moments hesitation, the girl nodded weakly, her face rubbing on the padded floor.

"That's good. If you can speak, what is your name?"

Susan parted her cracked lips. "Water."

Wendy almost cried at the weak sound. She turned to the others and held out a hand. "Water."

Baloc pulled a small plastic bottle from a pocket and handed it over.

Wendy took a step nearer the girl, who flinched when she spoke. "I have water. I need to come nearer so I can give you some, and then I will release you from the straitjacket."

Susan struggled to her knees and nodded.

Wendy approached slowly and knelt. "I am going to put the bottle to your lips. I have no idea when you last drank, so take small sips or you'll bring it up again."

Wendy unscrewed the cap, placed the bottle against the girl's lips and tipped.

Susan thirstily swallowed the water before it was snatched away.

"Slowly," reminded Wendy. She returned the bottle to the girl's lips. This time the girl took smaller sips.

When she had had her fill, Wendy replaced the cap and laid it aside. "I am going to untie the straps and get this thing off you, all right?"

Susan nodded.

As Wendy set about unbuckling the straitjacket, the girl spoke. "Susan."

Wendy stopped what she was doing on hearing the name and glanced at the others in the doorway. All had been briefed on the teenagers believed to have died on the island around six months ago, and all recognized the name. “Susan Frobisher, who went missing six months ago?”

“Oh, I thought it was longer, and yes.” answered Susan.

Unable to comprehend what the girl had suffered, Wendy looked at the back of the girl’s head as she continued releasing the straps. “What about your friends, Susan? Are they also here and need rescuing?”

Susan shook her head. “All dead.”

Wendy dragged the jacket off Susan’s arms and dropped it to the floor. “I’m sorry about your friends.”

Susan stretched out her arms to relieve the aches.

Wendy looked at the roughly tied ripped length of grubby cloth around her head. “What happened to your eyes?”

Susan’s fingers brushed the blood-crusted blindfold. “When the thing that held me captive read my mind, my eyes bled.”

“Read your mind?” Wendy queried, “Are you certain?”

Susan nodded. “Oh, yes.”

“You said a thing held you captive, not a someone. Have you seen it?”

“No. We were attacked when we came on the island by wolf monsters. I must have fainted as when I came to, I was in a cell blindfolded. Penny, Ryan and Gary were in adjoining cells until they died.”

Wendy decided not to press the matter. “I think we’ll need warm water to soak away the encrusted blood from your eyes before we can remove the blindfold, so I will lead you, okay?”

Susan nodded.

"Can you stand?"

"Legs weak."

"I'll help you." Wendy helped Susan to her feet.

Susan wavered unsteadily.

"I think it will be easier once we are on solid ground," Wendy advised, supporting Susan to the door.

Thankful for the support, Susan allowed herself to be led and stepped unsteadily onto a hard floor. She sensed others around her. "How many of you are there?"

"Six," Wendy answered.

"Why did it take you so long to come and rescue me?"

"We had no idea you were here," said Baloc. "We are looking for a friend."

Susan turned to the voice.

"The man who just spoke is Zane Baloc, the man responsible for us all being here," Wendy explained. "No one came sooner because the authorities that investigated the disappearance of you and your friends reported that you had all been killed."

"My parents think I'm dead?" exclaimed Susan.

"Everyone thought you were dead," said Shaw, "and will continue to do so until we get you off the island. I know we all have questions, but they'll have to wait until later. We need to concentrate on finding Ray, so we can leave."

"It might be better if some of us returned to the village with Susan," said Wendy. "She's in no fit state to be dragged through this place."

"I'm not keen on splitting the group, but she will slow us down if we need to make a quick retreat," surmised Shaw.

"I'll go back with Wendy," volunteered Mannix.

"Harvey, Ryker, you go with them," Shaw ordered. "The rest of us will continue searching for Ray and meet you at the village once we've found him, dead or alive."

Shaw's group waited until the others had retreated around a corner before carrying on with their search.

The two remaining padded cells were empty, as were the next few rooms they encountered. The web strands in the corridor they now followed became thicker towards the end. They pushed through the sticky strands into a once plush hallway. A faded red-and-grey patterned carpet flowed up the treads of the two identical staircases hugging the sidewalls, and down the central stairs sandwiched between them. Heavily patterned wallpaper of red and gold, still in reasonable condition, lined the walls.

Baloc moved forward and ran a hand over the stair rail supported by thick, ornately carved wooden posts, leaving a clear smear in the settled dust. "Impressive."

Shaw glanced down the stairs at the lower level. A short-carpeted hallway led to a set of doors carved to match the ornate designs on the posts. His gaze up the stairs picked out a similar set of double doors; both were wide open. The web trail they had followed led through them. "We head up," he said.

They followed Thane and Shaw up the stairs and through the doors at the top. Not for the first time, all were surprised by what they saw.

"What the hell is a theater doing in an insane asylum?" asked Laura.

"One of Ezra's whims, perhaps?" Baloc suggested. "Maybe it doubled up as a movie theater where Ezra planned to show his movies."

Their eyes roamed the rows of dust-covered plush seating that stepped down towards the balcony rail and the thick mass of spiderwebs that blocked their view of the stage they imagined below. A huge chandelier, covered with small lamp shades, had fallen from the ceiling and lay draped over the rail at the edge of the raised area.

A streak of sunlight stretching from the ceiling of the main auditorium filtered eerily through the webs and silhouetted the palm-size spiders moving through them.

"Has anyone noticed the décor?" said Laura. "Everything is in shades of grey."

Their eyes scanned the floor, seats, walls and ceiling to find she was right.

"It's like we've stepped into an old black-and-white movie," said Baloc, descending the wide steps to the rail boarding the edge of the dress circle.

Only Shaw followed him down.

Gunner focused his gaze into the hallway to check nothing crept up behind them.

Careful not to touch the webs, Baloc peered over the balcony. He glimpsed shapes of seat rows through the obscuring webs, but nothing else. "We'll have to take the lower staircase to see what's down there," he whispered.

Shaw agreed. "This has to be that spider creature's lair and hopefully where we'll find Ray alive."

When they turned to leave, Baloc's arm brushed the chandelier.

The tinkling of glass beads adorning the light fixture announced it was on the move. The men turned and, powerless to stop the large cumbersome object, watched it slither over the edge and drop from sight. The crash that rang out a few moments later echoed through the cavernous room.

Shaw glanced at Baloc. "There goes our element of surprise."

Baloc grimaced. "Sorry."

A low chittering directed their gaze at the web and at the dark shapes moving towards them.

"Time we left," said Shaw.

Gunner had already spotted the danger and was descending the staircase to check it was clear by the time the others caught up.

When the chittering rose in tempo, they glanced at the insidious wave of spiders flowing down the treads and through the door more dropping from the ceiling.

"Head down," ordered Shaw, pushing to the front.

They rushed down the stairs and into the theater's main hall.

Thane and Gunner pulled the doors shut as the front edge of spiders leapt at them. They thudded against the door and dropped to the floor. Though it delayed them from getting in, there were plenty of other entrances in the theater they could use to reach them.

"I suggest whatever we are going to do, we do it quickly," said Baloc, gazing around the room.

The walls, ceiling and most of the rows of seating were covered in thick clumps of spiderweb. The shaft of light they had glimpsed from above entered through the collapsed ceiling of the central dome and ended on the stage like a giant spotlight highlighting a performance. But in this instance, it focused on something macabre hanging on the stage. Strands of web attached to the man's hands and feet and anchored to the stage's floor and ornate fronted canopy, suspended the man in an X-formation. The tattered curtains draped either side presented the impression of demon wings.

Worry creased Laura's features. "It's Ray."

Shaw grabbed Laura's arm, bringing her to an abrupt halt as she tried to push past to go to her husband's aid.

"Not so hasty, Laura," ordered Shaw.

Laura was about to pull away when she noticed Shaw staring at something. She followed his gaze across the room at the vibrating strands of web. Something large and concealed moved along them.

Shaw removed his grip.

"I know you want to rush down there and save him, but we need to stay focused if we're going to survive this."

He pointed to the aisle between the seats at the far side of the hall.

"We'll head down the right side of the room to reach him. If he's alive, we cut him down and get the hell out of here."

"Then let's do it."

Before Shaw could argue, Laura headed across the room. The others quickly followed.

Their feet crunched on the broken glass of the chandelier that had sprayed across the floor when it smashed to the ground.

Laura turned and led them down the aisle towards the stage. She glanced into the orchestra pit as she rushed by. Dark shapes moved. Staring eyes glinted in the light. She ignored them; saving her husband was her priority. Her gaze focused on her husband's face when she reached the stage. His closed eyes worried her. She placed her rifle on the high stage, climbed up, and as she stood, grabbed her rifle. As the others climbed up after her, her weapon scanned the stage. She moved along the curtain with Shaw beside her and shone her flashlight into the darkness shrouding backstage. Finding no sign of any creatures, she rushed to her husband. His feet were level with her chest. Hoping to get a reaction to show he was alive, she shook his foot. His eyes remained closed, but his chest rose and fell shallowly.

"He's alive!" Laura thrust her rifle at Baloc and slid her knife from its sheaf.

After she had sliced through the web anchoring his feet to the stage, her attention moved to the strands he hung from. They were too high to reach. Laura turned to Shaw who concentrated on the web movements across the room. "Shaw."

Shaw glanced at her. Laura nodded at the webs attached to her husband's arms.

"I guess stealth is no longer a requirement." He aimed at the thick strands above one arm, and when Laura was ready, fired a short burst. The shots echoed through the room. Ray sagged on one arm. Laura grabbed him. Thane rushed over to help her support Ray's weight. When a second short burst sent him falling to the stage, Laura and Thane lowered him to the floor.

While Laura checked her husband, Shaw returned his attention to the increased movement of the webs. The gunshots had stirred something into action. If the human-spider hybrid was in the room, he wondered why it hadn't already attacked. The return of the chittering spun his gaze to the webs on the ceiling. What seemed to be hundreds of spiders, dropped to the floor and swarmed towards the stage.

Shaw, Gunner and Thane aimed their weapons at the insidious mass of oversized arachnids.

Aware it would be a waste of ammo trying to kill them all when only a few would be hit, Shaw ordered everyone to hold their fire. He glanced at Laura and noticed her husband's eyes were open. He looked drugged. "Laura, we have to move."

Laura glanced at the menacing creatures crawling towards the stage.

"He's weak. I'll need a hand."

"Baloc, help her." Shaw crossed to the stage curtains. They needed another escape route. His light picked out the stage wings actors would have needed to reach the stage. He turned to the others. "There has to be way out back here. Let's move."

Baloc handed Laura back her rifle, and she slipped it over her shoulder. He held his in one hand and helped Laura lift Ray to his feet. Fear appeared on his face when he saw something lower into sight behind Shaw who waited for them. It was the human-spider monster. Fighting away the terror that threatened to freeze him, he let go of Ray and raised his rifle. "Shaw, duck!"

When Shaw noticed the fright on Baloc's face, he ducked as Baloc fired and felt the slipstream from the bullets shooting over his head. He dived into a roll, jumped to his feet and turned with his weapon ready to fire, but there was nothing there. Frowning, he looked at Baloc.

"That spider creature was behind you and climbed up when I fired," explained Baloc.

When Shaw gazed at the darkness smothering the gantry above stage, he sensed something lurking there, hiding, waiting. He glanced at the approaching smaller spiders. They had almost reached the stage and would be upon them in seconds. He rushed to the front of the stage and aimed his light into the dark orchestra pit. He fired a short burst at the glinting eyes. Something screeched as it fled. It was their only option. "Follow me." He leapt from the stage. Gunner followed him down while Thane protected the others.

Baloc grabbed Ray under the arm, and he and Laura moved to the edge of the stage. Without hesitating, they jumped. They collapsed to the floor on landing but were uninjured.

Ray, drowsy from the venom the spider queen had injected into him, groaned as he tried to fathom what was happening. He felt himself being pulled to his feet. His eyes focused blearily on those around him. "Laura," he uttered weakly.

Laura smiled. "Hello, dear. I'm sorry, but we have to keep moving."

"They're here," shouted Thane, jumping into the pit.

As soon as the others had passed him, Shaw fired a few short bursts at the spiders that appeared at the top of the pit and then turned and fled.

With his flashlight lighting the way, Gunner led them along a narrow corridor. He kicked the door open at its end and stepped into the theater's back rooms. With the others in close pursuit, he rushed past dressing rooms, prop stores and doors marked with stars, private dressing rooms for elite actors and actresses. The next door he arrived at was locked. He didn't waste time waiting for Baloc to search for the correct key. A short burst of bullets shattered the lock. He barged it open and stepped though to outside. He sprung up the short flight of steps onto level ground and roamed his eyes around the area to get his bearings. They had exited at the back of the asylum. A road led around to the front. He looked down the steps when gunfire rang out. Struggling with Ray between them, Laura and Baloc emerged from the building while Shaw and Thane fired at the spiders. Gunner kept the area covered.

Thane and Shaw backed out of the building and shoved the door shut. Shaw slammed his weight against it. The broken lock meant it wouldn't stay shut when the spiders reached it. "Thane, I need something to jam it closed."

Thane sprinted up the steps to find something.

Laura glanced at Shaw. "We'll carry on."

Shaw nodded. "Gunner, go with them and we'll catch you up."

Thane noticed something in the bushes, an old patient gurney lying on its side. He tugged it free of the brambles, dragged it over to the steps and slid it down. As spiders threw their bodies against the door, the two men turned it so one end rested against the stairwell wall and the other against the door.

The gurney screeched down the door when Shaw yanked it down tighter, jamming it in place. "Unless the spiders can chew through the door, that should hold them."

They sprinted up the steps and along the road.

The spider creature climbed out through the theater's broken dome and across the roof. It halted at the edge and peered down at the four humans struggling along the road. Satisfied the plan was working, she turned away and headed across the roof.

As Shaw and Thane rushed along the side of the large building, something landed with barely a sound behind them. Thane twisted his head. His assault rifle shook in his trembling hands as he raised it towards the human part of the monster. Before he could fire, the spider creature stabbed him with a limb and lifted him into the air. Blood dribbling from his mouth muffled his agonized scream. His weapon clattered to the road when life left him and warned Shaw of the threat.

Shaw turned on hearing the weapon strike the ground. His shocked gaze took in Thane impaled on one of the spider creature's limbs as another lashed out and knocked him to the ground. The spider creature flung Thane's corpse away, rushed forward and knocked his weapon from his hands, sending it skidding across the road. As the spider creature raised the bloody limb to impale a second victim, Shaw stared into the creature's human face gazing down at him and reached for the pistol at his side. He was stunned when he recognized who it was—Susan's friend, Penny Jenkins, one of the missing girls thought dead.

"Penny," he uttered.

When a distant human memory flooded into its thoughts on hearing the name, the spider creature hesitated, halting the limb aimed at the human's chest, and looked at the man who had spoken her name. "You are...in danger."

Shaw slipped a finger around the trigger as he raised the pistol, but on hearing the sorrowful plea, he also hesitated. He had a daughter about the same age. "How are we in danger?"

"You...are being...tricked. The...Queen...has left me...she is..."

The spider creature concentrated on quashing the human part of her.

"Kill...me. Please...kill..."

The creature regained control.

Shaw noticed tears seep from the girl's sad, pleading eyes, but then it was gone, replaced by an evil and cruel smile on her soft red lips. He fired as he rolled to avoid the pointed tip that jabbed at his chest.

The creature ignored the pain from the bullet that grazed her human arm and was swiftly upon the man responsible before his roll had ended. It glared at the human and lifted its bloodied front limb. As the pointed tip drove towards the human's head, a shot rang out. Blood and bone exploded from the leg when the bullet shattered the joint. The creature glanced at the useless, sagging limb and then focused along the road on the human female. Recognizing the female as the greatest threat, it ripped the ruined limb off, threw it away and rushed along the road towards her.

When Laura stopped for a breather at the front of the building, she wondered what was taking Shaw and Thane so long to catch up. Leaving her husband by the statue with Baloc and ignoring Gunner's orders to stay together, she moved to the corner of the building and peered down the side as the spider-hybrid attacked Shaw. In a single fluid movement, she slipped the rifle from her shoulder into her hands, aimed and fired. She had quickly decided to aim for the limb about to strike Shaw and not the heart of the human part of it. The creature was so bizarre she had no idea where its vulnerabilities were—if human and spider shared the same organs or if each had their own. If the latter, there was no telling how quickly it would die if a vital organ was hit. Aiming for the leg gave Shaw a chance of survival.

When the spider creature rushed towards her, Laura calmly ratcheted another shell into the rifle and aimed for the attacking creature's head.

Shaw rolled onto his stomach, aimed his pistol and fired.

When multiple shots rang out from two directions, the spider creature sprung onto the side of the building and headed for the roof. Bullets creased her back, shattering eggs and killing one of the spiders caring for the eggs.

When the creature disappeared over the rooftop, Shaw climbed to his feet, snatched up his rifle and walked over to Thane at the side of the road. Saddened by the man's death, he gave him a nod of respect before retrieving the man's dropped weapon. He glanced towards the whistling and saw Laura beckoning to him.

"It's on the roof," stated Laura, as Shaw approached, her gaze and rifle directed skywards.

"I saw it," said Shaw. "Hopefully it will stay there. We had best keep moving." He nodded at Ray. "How's he doing?"

"Better, I think. He seems to be slowly regaining his strength."

Laura glanced down the side of the building. "Thane didn't make it."

"No." Shaw headed towards the statue where the others waited.

"What's our next move, Shaw?" asked Baloc, his eyes scanning the road ahead.

"We return to the village, link up with the others and head for the jetty. If it's possible for the ship to reach us in this storm, it can't be far away now." He studied Ray. The man had a little colour back in his cheeks. "We need to stay alert as I'm sure we haven't seen the last of that spider hybrid."

"Thane?" asked Gunner, looking at Shaw.

Shaw shook his head sadly as he checked his weapon. "It's a queen."

The others looked at him with puzzled expressions.

"The spider creature, it's a queen," Shaw explained.

"And you know this how?" asked Laura.

“I recognized her, the human part. It’s Penny Jenkins, one of the missing teenagers. She spoke to me. She called it the Queen and said it’s tricked us.”

“Pushing aside how it’s even possible that Penny is now part of that thing, how has this Spider Queen tricked us?” asked Baloc.

Shaw shrugged. “That’s all she said. I think part of Penny’s consciousness, or something, is still there, inside, and it managed to regain control for a few seconds. She wanted me to kill her.”

“If what you say is true and some part of Penny is aware of what’s happened to her, killing the monstrosity would be doing her a kindness,” said Gunner.

Baloc’s eyes flicked to the rooftop. He thought he had noticed movement. “I think it’s best we debate this later. If the captain comes, he won’t wait around for us.”

“To the village, then,” said Shaw. “Laura, as you Baloc and Ray are the slowest, you’ll set the pace and we’ll follow your speed. Everyone else keep your eyes peeled for an attack.”

Keeping in close formation, they moved along the road and away from the asylum.

Satisfied all was going to plan, the spider creature watched the humans for a few moments before turning away and disappearing over the rooftop.

CHAPTER 33

Locked In

Lightning lit up the rain-lashed survivors Shaw led through the village. Thunder, loud enough to rattle windows of the houses they rushed past, trailed the bright lightning flash that lit up the tired, bedraggled group. Shaw entered Dracula's crypt and halted to let the stragglers catch up. Sheltered from the rain, Shaw ran a hand through his hair to push wet strands away from his eyes and looked at the sodden group. All were tired and anxious. Though his gaze back along the street detected none of the island's foul creatures in pursuit, he knew they were out there. The rain masked their trail, but he doubted it would be long before they appeared.

Baloc shifted to the front to talk with Shaw. "I know we could all do with a rest, but we need to reach the jetty."

Shaw nodded as he took in Ray's exhausted appearance. Whatever the spider creature had done to him, it was taking its toll. "You okay, Ray?"

Ray pulled himself upright. "I'll be fine. I'll rest on the ship."

Shaw glanced around the tired faces. Susan's condition seemed to have improved with a good meal, quick wash and some better clothes. Wendy had removed the bandage and though it had taken a few minutes for her eyes to adjust to light again, they were undamaged. "Just a short sprint through the graveyard and we'll be at the jetty."

They followed Shaw and Gunner back into the storm.

Halfway through the graveyard, Shaw glimpsed movement, nothing more than a blurred rain-defused shape, but it was enough to put him on high alert. His gaze remained fixed on the sighting as he continued.

Wendy screamed a warning when something leapt from one of the large mausoleums.

Shots from Shaw's and Gunner's weapons rung out.

Lightning highlighted the strange creature twisting in midair to avoid the bullets. Tendrils of fine, white hair hung from the large stag-like beast's neck and back. Long, antler-like spikes splayed out from its long skeletal head and large cloven hooves tipped its four powerful legs covered in short hair.

The stag creature screeched when bullets grazed its stomach and hind leg. It crashed into Shaw and Gunner, knocking them to the ground. It twisted its head on landing and stabbed its antlers at Shaw's face. Shaw jerked his head to the side and stared into the eyeless sockets of the creature brought to an abrupt halt when its antlers struck the ground around his head. Gunner rolled away from the monster and staggered to his feet.

As Shaw gripped the beast's antlers and tried to move its head, Gunner aimed his rifle at the creature and pulled the trigger. Nothing happened. As he had recently reloaded, it must have jammed when it struck the ground during his fall. He turned the weapon and clubbed the monster with the stock, but it was difficult to get a decent blow past the long, branching antlers.

Laura barged Gunner aside, straddled the beast and grabbed an antler with one hand. She yanked its head back and stabbed her knife repeatedly into its neck until it fell limp and collapsed onto Shaw, who groaned from the dead weight of the animal on his chest.

Mannix and Gunner shoved the animal off Shaw and helped him to his feet.

Shaw nodded his thanks to Laura and looked at the formidable animal that before setting foot on this strange island would have shocked him, but now was just another of the island's impossible creatures.

Wendy studied the creature. "How many more of the island's oddities are there?"

"I'm hoping we'll be off the island before we find out," said Baloc.

As Wendy quickly flashed off another photo for her collection, Shaw's rain-hindered gaze scanned the graveyard. Though he spied vague shapes skulking at the edges of his vision, they had no choice but to continue. They were against the clock now. "Let's move," he ordered, loud enough to be heard above the driving rain and wind.

They passed through the graveyard without encountering any more creatures they all suspected weren't far away. Though thankful the creatures kept their distance, Shaw was worried more hadn't attacked. Suspecting the reason wasn't anything good, he led the bedraggled group past the reception huts.

Baloc's gaze flicked to the sign stretched between the huts that none of them had taken seriously and had turned out to be a premonition of what was to come. They should have heeded its warning, as not all of them had survived.

The jetty creaked when they rushed along it.

Worry creased Baloc's features when he saw the harbour absent the ship he expected to be waiting for them. His face dropped further when he noticed the harbour gate was closed.

Shaw ran his gaze over the closed gate, the furiously spinning weather vane on top of the gate post and turned to Baloc. "It must shut automatically when the weather's rough."

Wendy stared at their blocked escape route and the spray from the waves pounding its seaward side leaping over the top. "I'm not sure the reason matters. How do we open it?"

"Was there nothing on the plans?" asked Mannix, gazing around for a control mechanism.

Frowning, Baloc shook his head. "There was a lot Ezra saw fit not to include."

Concerned the creatures might attack now they had nowhere to go, Shaw's eyes scanned the shore. "Maybe there's an override control around here, some way to open it?"

Baloc shrugged. "It's possible."

Shrieks from the shore signaled the monsters' approach.

"I guess we've run out of time to search for it," said Ryker, his weapon roaming the tree line.

Wendy studied the barrier. "We could swim to the gate and climb over," she suggested. "The ship must be nearby by now."

"Too dangerous," stated Baloc. "The raging waves will dash us against the rocks. Even if we survived and reached the ship, how would we get aboard without being crushed by the hull?"

"We have to do something, we can't stay here," pleaded Wendy.

When Baloc gazed at the shore, a flash of lightning lit up the huge skull perched on the cliff. "The skeleton!"

"What?" asked Shaw, thinking a new monstrosity had appeared.

"We can climb down the giant skeleton's arm and drop onto the ship if it moves underneath."

Wendy looked at him in disbelief. "And that's less risky than my plan, how?"

"I know it's dicey, but if we use a rope we won't have to swim. Just climb down and drop onto the ship."

Though Ryker thought the plan was crazy, it offered a chance to escape the island. "It might work, but we don't have a rope with us."

"No problem. Ryker and I can nip back to the village to fetch one," said Gunner.

"Great," said Ryker. "Thanks for volunteering me."

Gunner grinned at his friend. "You're welcome."

Shrieks, closer now, rang out from shore again.

"Whatever you decide on, make it quick or we'll be trapped on the jetty with nowhere to go," said Laura, brushing her husband's wet hair from his eyes.

Shaw made the decision for them. "I don't see we have much choice if we want to get off this damn island. We'll go with

Baloc's idea." He pointed at the hill the skull rested on. "We'll head through the trees towards the cliffs and climb the slope." He turned to Ryker and Gunner. "Watch out for the creatures and join us at the top when you have the rope."

The two men nodded and headed back to the village.

"What about the monsters?" asked Wendy, not relishing the thought of encountering more of them.

"We've fought them off so far, so we'll have to continue doing so, but to save what little ammo we have left, only fire at any that get too close," said Shaw.

Wendy sighed. "Come on, let's do this before I act on my idea and risk my life to the sea."

With Shaw leading them on and Harvey protecting their backs, they headed back to shore and the waiting monsters.

Wendy peered into the gloom-shrouded trees they rushed alongside and slowed her pace when she glimpsed one of the fearsome stag creatures thirty yards away. It rested a front hoof on a fallen tree, staring at them, as if contemplating an attack. Unable to resist the photo opportunity of capturing the formidable beast, she stopped and hoping there was enough light to record its image, snapped off a photograph.

The stag creature turned away from the fleeing humans and bellowed.

The sound carried across the island and spurred the anxious team on.

CHAPTER 34

Skeleton

Breathless from their rush up the hill, the worried team headed for the large skull.

Baloc moved to the cliff edge and gazed at the turbulent ocean below and the ship tossed about by the waves a few hundred yards out. Relieved the ship had made it, he informed the others it had arrived.

Shaw lifted a section of the thick waxed canvas draping the shoulder and peered beneath. A tunnel formed of crisscrossed metal beams led along the arm and provided them with a relatively easy climb. Wind howled through the sleeve, billowing the material and slapping it against the framework with loud whip cracks.

Baloc pulled out the radio and contacted the ship.

"You damn well owe me big time for this, Baloc," was the captain's greeting.

"I am aware of that, Captain, and I'm thankful you made it safely."

"Don't start celebrating yet, as I'm damn certain it'll be impossible to steer into harbour in these rough seas without being smashed against the rock."

"That won't be a problem as the gates are closed, but we need you to position your ship below the skeleton's hand. Our plan is to climb down the skeleton arm, lower a rope and drop onto your ship."

A slight pause as if the captain was stunned by the proposal. "Good luck with that if you think I'll be able to hold her steady, but I'll give it a try. Though you had better be quick, because at the first sign of my ship being carried near the shore I'm leaving."

"I understand, Captain. By the time you are in position, we'll be ready." Baloc ended the call and walked back to the skull where Shaw and Harvey covered the area with their weapons. "I've informed the captain of our plan and reckon we have about ten to fifteen minutes before his ship's in position."

Shaw nodded. "The arm is filled with hand and footholds, so it shouldn't be a problem climbing down, we just have to wait for the rope. I suggest you remain here while the others start climbing down the arm, and when Gunner and Ryker arrive with the rope, you can take it down to them while we guard against any threat. When you are all safely aboard, we'll join you."

"I'll go first and tie off the rope when it arrives," volunteered Mannix.

Susan, a little numbed by her unexpected rescue and the events that had followed so quickly, finally felt hope chipping away at her acceptance that she would die on this island. Though still weak, the food she had wolfed down earlier had imbued her muscles with strength. She clambered onto a girder behind Mannix and began her climb down the arm.

Ready to help if needed, Wendy followed her through.

Laura helped her husband, whose strength had still not fully returned, inside the skeleton's shoulder. Realizing her rifle would hinder her efforts in aiding her husband's climb down the arm, she reluctantly laid it aside and followed him through.

Distant gunshots directed the gazes of those outside down the hill.

CHAPTER 35

Man Down

Ryker raised a fist to bring their sprint through the graveyard to a halt. Gunner peered through the windblown rain at the dark shapes approaching. The two men split and crouched behind a couple of the large stone burial vaults either side of the path. With rifles held ready to fire, they waited for the danger to pass them by.

Gunner gazed at the hoof that struck the wet ground beside him and tilted his head slightly to stare at the stag's dreadful skeletal head. The eyeless sockets freaked him out as much as the pointed antlers. Due to its lack of eyes, he was amazed the fearsome beast could move about without bumping into things.

Pressing his rifle tightly against his chest to stop his hands from shaking, Ryker also stared fearfully at the lead stag when it walked by, and then at the two that followed side by side. The far stag jerked its head to the side, clacking antlers with the beast next to it. The nearer stag creature jerked its head towards Ryker and snorted, exhaling two streams of misty breath. Ryker locked terrified eyes with the beast's eye sockets. *Can it see me?*

As if sensing something but unsure what it was, the beast's antlers scraped along the side of the stone vault when it moved its head closer to Ryker. Rivulets of rain channeled down the beast's skull thrummed onto Ryker's leg. Prepared to shoot the beast if it attacked, Ryker froze and waited to see what happened.

The stag behind the one that showed interest in Ryker jabbed the halted beast with its antlers to get it to move. The prodded stag raised its long head and bellowed its annoyance before moving on. Ryker let the tension drain when the rest of the monster herd had passed them by.

As soon as the rain had turned the beasts into hazy shapes, the two men continued their dash to the village.

Ryker guarded the door of their meetinghouse while Gunner nipped inside. He returned a few moments later with a rope slung across his shoulder and chewing a sandwich consisting of thick hunk of cheese between two slices of bread.

Ryker shook his head in dismay. "If you've finished making yourself a snack, shall we go?"

Gunner grinned. "I was hungry." He bit off a large bite and chewed.

"To avoid running into those stag creatures again, how about we head along the road until we're clear of the village and then cut through the forest to the hill," suggested Ryker.

Gunner nodded. "Sounds good to me," he mumbled between chews.

They headed along the road, turned right at the square, and when free of the village, they veered off into the woods.

Both men were thankful for the respite from the downpour blocked by the leafy canopy above them. The crack of a branch that spread ominously through the forest slowed their hurried dash. Both peered in the direction the sound had come from, but thick, berry-laden bushes blocked their view of whatever had caused it. Unsure if wind or monster was responsible, they focused on the rustling foliage and raised their weapons as they backed away.

Gunner dropped his slightly sodden snack when a stag creature leapt from the bushes. Its hooves thundered on the ground when it landed and rushed at them. Both fired a burst of bullets at its head. Its skull exploded, sending out fragments of bone. One bullet cut through a set of antlers that dropped to the ground and tangled the dying beast's legs. It tripped, rolled topsy-turvy in a bone-snapping flip and crashed to the ground in front of them. Twigs cracked, and hooves pounded the ground when more of the beasts homed in on the gunshot. The two men fled.

Ryker panted from the exertion. He would like nothing more than to lie on the ground and rest, but with the stag creatures closing in fast, it was a luxury he couldn't afford. They burst from the trees onto a grassy slope leading up to the skull and glimpsed some of the others waiting at the top.

Ryker knew they wouldn't get far before the pursuing beasts were upon them. He turned to Gunner. "Carry on. I'll stay here for a few moments and pick off a few. It's essential you get the rope to the others if any of us are going to survive."

Gunner glanced at the advancing herd doubtfully.

"Don't worry, I'm not on a suicide mission. I aim to claim my fee for this job. I'll try and hold them off to give you a chance to get the rope to the others, and then I'll join you."

"Don't wait too long." Gunner turned away and sprinted up the hill.

Ryker dropped to the ground behind a rotten tree trunk covered in small pale mushrooms and aimed at the nearest stag creature. A single shot to the head sent it reeling to the side. It barged into another creature and both crashed to the ground. Another stag, too close to avoid those fallen, tumbled over them, breaking its neck. The stags that couldn't veer around their dead and wounded comrades, leapt over them.

A short burst of gunfire sent another stag crashing to the ground. To try and take two out with one shot, Ryker aimed at a stag's front leg and fired. The bullet shattered bone and sent the creature toppling to its knees and crashing into the one beside it. The stag dodged away to remain on its feet and in the process tangled its antlers with another. A frantic jerking of heads ensued as they tried to free themselves. One tripped and dragged the other to the ground. Two more shots saw another stag creature fall.

When the beasts were drawing too close for comfort, Ryker climbed to his feet and sprayed the creatures with bullets before fleeing up the hill. Shrieks diverted his attention to the side. A hoard of the vicious rodent creatures rushed towards him. Too fast to outrun, Ryker shot a glance up the hill. Gunner had almost reached the top. Satisfied his unwelcomed sacrifice hadn't been in vain, he fired a few shots at the rats and then at the stags. When his gun clicked on empty he turned it and held it like a club. He brandished it at the stag thundering towards him and swung when it was near enough. The stag bowled him over before the blow made contact. A back hoof landed on his chest, breaking ribs and crushing a lung before it moved on. In agony and gasping for breath, Ryker turned his head. Snarling rodents filled his vision. He screamed when they washed over him, biting and ripping his flesh.

Gunner reached the top and collapsed breathless to the ground. Between gasps, he alerted the others to the danger. “The stag creatures are coming. Ryker’s holding them off, but…”

Shaw gazed down the hill at Ryker’s gunfire. Aware there was no helping him now and they were running out of time, he slipped the rope off Gunner’s shoulder and handed it to Baloc. “You know what to do.”

Baloc headed for the skeleton and climbed inside. The others were about halfway along. It would be tight, but they might just make it. He began his climb.

“One thing in our favour is that the stag monsters won’t be able to climb along the arm after us with their hooves and wide antlers,” said Harvey.

“I don’t think the stag creatures are going to be our biggest problem,” stated Gunner.

Shaw and Harvey followed Gunner’s pointing finger and fearful gaze. A large hoard of rodent monsters raced along the edge of the wood. While the majority veered away and headed up the hill, some rushed at Ryker when a stag knocked him to the ground. Ryker screamed when they reached him.

Gunner stared at the stag creatures that rushed out of the wood and raced up the hill and the small group of feasting rats. “Ryker’s dead,” he stated, sadly.

“Shit!” cursed Shaw. *Another man lost.* He gazed at the approaching threat. Even if they had time to pick them off one by one, they didn't have enough ammo to do so, and the rats were small and agile enough to climb through the arm after them. He turned to his men. "Before we follow them down the arm, we'll pick off as many as we can to buy some time."

When a bloodlust-stricken rat nipped at a stag's front leg, the beast lowered its head and impaled it on an antler. A shake of its head sent the writhing rat flying. Before it hit the ground, rats leapt at it and started feeding.

Reminded of the rats' voracious appetite, Harvey aimed at one of the stag creatures and fired. The stag faltered for a few steps and fell. Its momentum rolled it over the rats in its path, crushing some, wounding others. Unable to resist the scent of blood and an easy meal, the surrounding rodents pounced on the dead and dying and began feasting.

Harvey glanced at his two comrades. "Kill the stags! It will slow some of the rats down."

Both men focused on the larger beasts and began picking them off. Though it halted a fair few rats, it still left too many for them to handle.

Shaw knew it was a fight they couldn't win. They had done their best, but if they lingered any longer, they would suffer Ryker's fate.

"Go!" he shouted.

Harvey and Gunner didn't need to be told twice. They moved backwards while continuing to pick off the stags and rats until they were inside the arm.

Shaw followed but remained by the opening killing as many as he could until his bullets ran out. He dropped the weapon and climbed inside.

The rats arrived a few moments later. They surged inside and swarmed over the top of the skeleton.

Shaw turned when shrieks drifted down the arm. Desperate to be first to reach the food, the rats battled with each other, hissing, snarling and biting to claim a space on the narrow beams. Shaw practically leapt from beam to beam to keep ahead of the vicious pack surging towards him. Luckily, the rats had to move slower over the tangle of narrow ironwork. He soon caught up with Harvey and Gunner. "This is no time for caution, you two! Get a move on or feel rat's teeth ripping your flesh."

Shaw's fear-inspired pep talk worked; the two men increased their speed.

Mannix reached the skeletal wrist first. He poked his head through a ragged slit in the sleeve and studied the skeletal hand. Though there was enough room for him to climb onto the back of the grasping hand, the lashing rain and strong gusts would see him pitched off into the swirling ocean and probably to his death. His gaze picked out the approaching storm-tossed vessel. In a few minutes it would be below him. He glanced past Susan and Wendy and saw Baloc behind Laura and her husband, who had just reached the elbow. Shrieks drifting down the sleeve altered his gaze to the rats entering the arm behind Shaw. Mannix focused on the coil of rope over Baloc's shoulder. They needed to start climbing down before the rats reached them.

"Baloc, throw me the rope," he shouted.

Baloc stopped and gazed at Mannix. He slipped off the rope and threw it below.

The rope landed a bit short. Mannix dived for it before it slipped off the beam it draped. He grabbed it, released the loop that kept it coiled and tied off one end to a metal beam above him. He leaned through the rip in the sleeve, dropped the rope and glanced back up the arm when Wendy and Susan arrived beside him. The rats were pouring into the sleeve.

Wendy noticed the fear spread across Mannix's face. "Ignore what's coming and concentrate on climbing down the rope as soon as the ship's in position."

Mannix nodded and tore down a strip of cloth by the rope to make climbing out easier.

Wendy poked her head out. The bow of the ship was almost directly below them. She turned to Mannix. "You go first. We'll be right behind you."

Mannix grabbed the wind-blown rope in both hands, climbed out with his feet resting on the arm, and began his perilous descent.

The look of fear on Susan's face made Wendy reach out and grab her hand. "Are you okay?"

Susan nodded weakly. "Frightened."

"Me, too. But we can do this. As soon as Mannix is clear, we'll climb down."

CHAPTER 36

Escape

The captain peered through the pilothouse window smeared with wet streaks by the worn, inadequate wiper during its juddering back and forth arcs. He could see the form of a man climbing down the rope hanging from the skeletal arm. Whipped by fierce winds and pounded by driving rain, he was surprised he managed to cling to the swaying lifeline. If he or any of the others fell into the surging waves, rescue would be doubtful. He raised his gaze when he noticed movement on the arm and was shocked by the sight of the large rat-like creatures scurrying over it. He spoke to his second mate without turning his head.

"See if you and the crew can pick off a few of those things with the rifles."

The second mate looked at the strange creatures and grabbed the handle fixed to the wall to steady himself against the latest swell to toss the boat. Pushing aside his surprise, he cast a skeptical gaze at his captain. "In this weather, we'd be lucky to hit the shore, let alone any of those things."

"If they kill Baloc, who I suspect is inside the arm of that skeletal titan, you and the men won't get the bonuses you've been promised."

The thought of the cash loss spurred the man into action. "No harm in trying though." He disappeared through the door.

With one eye on the dangling fool and the other on the foam-sprayed rocks that threatened to rip holes in the hull, the captain battled with the controls to bring his ship below the rope.

Laura shot a glance behind and frowned at the rodents scampering down the arm and the three men moving fast to keep ahead of them. She turned back to her husband, whose face was sheened with sweat. "We need to move faster, hon," she urged.

Ray had also noticed the threat moving towards them. His stomach was in turmoil, and his head throbbed with a threatened migraine. "Go on without me, and I'll catch you up."

"You're not getting rid of me that easy. Move a little faster and we'll make it."

Ray nodded. With his hands gripping one of the overhead beams, he lowered his feet to the one below set at an angle. His feet slipped on the wet metal. Weakened by whatever the spider creature had done to him, he was unable to support his weight and fell.

Laura grabbed at him. Her fingers gripped his arm, but he was too heavy to hold. She watched helplessly as he bounced off beams. Ray's feet tore through the sleeve and he fell through. His frantic grab for the beam he wrapped an arm around halted his fall. Laura scrambled down to him, noticed the sea-lashed rocks directly below her dangling husband and grabbed his arm.

Ray smiled weakly at his wife. "Was that fast enough?"

"A good effort, but I suggest you don't try it again." Laura noticed the swelling on his head where he had struck a beam. "Are you okay?"

With his wife's help, Ray hauled his tired body onto the beams. "I think so."

Laura glanced below. Mannix was nowhere to be seen and Wendy and Susan peered out of the sleeve. She guessed Mannix was climbing down the rope, an indication the ship had arrived. Though worried her husband wouldn't be strong enough to climb down the rope, she encouraged him to keep moving.

"Only a bit farther and we'll be out of here."

With extra caution, Ray restarted his descent.

Laura glanced up at the pattering feet running across the top of the sleeve and followed the progress of their paw imprints in the material. They would soon reach Wendy and Susan. *The poor girl had been through enough.* She checked her husband was still climbing as she pulled out her gun, aimed at the lead set of imprints and fired. Blood splattered the material and dripped through the bullet hole. Three more shots resulted in three more rodent casualties. Horrific screeches indicated the delight of their brethren as they pounced on the dead.

Susan almost slipped from her perch when the shots rang out.

Wendy glanced behind at Laura firing the gun and the blood splatters on the sleeve. They were running out of time. She squeezed Susan's hand gently. "Your turn to climb down."

Susan gazed down at Mannix swaying wildly on the rope and the bobbing ship. It was a frightening sight. They really needed extra climbing gear for Susan and Ray, who weren't as fit as the others, but one rope was all they had. It would have to do.

When Wendy noticed Susan's apprehension, she placed a hand on the girl's arm. "Would you like me to go first?"

Susan nodded.

"But you must climb down directly behind me. That way, if you slip I can catch you."

Susan nodded.

Wendy gripped the rope and climbed out. After she had shimmied down a short distance, she stopped and gazed up at Susan.

Susan had a fear of heights but she feared the approaching rats more. If she could reach the ship she would be safe, free, something she thought an impossibility a few hours ago. *I can do this.* She gripped the rope and, careful of rope burns, began her climb.

Laura caught up with her husband as he reached the rope. Both peered below at Susan, Wendy and Mannix climbing down towards the boat rising and falling on the rough sea.

Mannix looked at the ship's deck and the crew gazing up at him. He had to time his drop exactly right, when the ship was at the crest of its rise. The deck grew nearer. He dropped and landed feet first on the deck. Off balance from the swaying ship, he stumbled. One of the crew lurched forward and grabbed his arm, stopping him from pitching over the rail. Mannix nodded his thanks to the man.

Wendy arrived a few moments later. She dropped and managed to keep her balance on the erratically pitching and rolling ship. Glad to finally be off the island, she tilted her head. Susan was almost at the bottom, and Laura and Ray were still in the arm looking down at them. Her gaze switched to the vicious rats scampering over the arm. Gunshots from the crew peppered the sleeve and picked off one creature. A rat, eager to grab the feast, chased the carcass sliding down the side of the arm. It pounced and dug its claws into the meat as it slipped off the arm and dropped towards the cold ocean. Seemingly unaware of its predicament, it began ripping off chunks of flesh.

Just as Susan was about to release her hold on the rope, a wave struck the ship's port side and carried it nearer the rocks and beneath the plummeting rat. Wendy dodged back when the dead rat and its passenger struck the deck. Cushioned by the corpse it rode down, the rat rolled before regaining its footing. It snarled bloody lips at her as it scampered nearer and leapt. A blow from a crewman's rifle stock abruptly changed its trajectory. Another crewman screamed when the stunned rodent crashed into his chest and staggered back as the rat dropped to the deck.

The rat climbed unsteadily to its feet and gazed around at the humans, as if deciding which one would be next on its menu. The boot of the crewman it had struck stamped on its head with enough force to crush its skull. Its blood mixed with the spray washing across the deck.

The captain cursed as he battled the wind and waves to keep the ship in position. He cursed again when a surge pushed his ship closer to the rocks that would rip the hull like paper. He wouldn't be able to remain here for much longer. He peered through the rain and spray-impacted windscreen as he coaxed his vessel back below the dangling lifeline where a young girl he failed to recognize hung on for dear life. Above her climbing out onto the rope, were a man and a woman he had never seen before. Surprisingly, two had already made it onto the ship, a man and that good-looking woman. He wondered what had spooked them to make them risk such a perilous method of departure and how many had survived. He hoped his paymaster Baloc was one of them.

Susan, drenched and battered by wind, rain and sea spray, shivered as she gazed below at the ship manoeuvring below her again and at those she relied on to let her know when to drop. When the ship rose on a wave, frantic beckons and shouts of, "Now!" released her grip.

Mannix and a crewman caught Susan and steadied her against the swell of the ship when they led her aside. The crewman took her to the galley where she could get a warm drink and some dry clothes.

Ray, barely holding his grip on the rope in his weakened state, arrived next. Like those before him, he glanced below at the ship's rising and falling deck. Unable to hold on any longer, he dropped and slammed into the deck on its upward movement. He groaned when his ankle twisted and pitched him hard to the deck. Witnessing her husband's bad landing, Laura quickly climbed down the rope and dropped the final few feet. She stumbled into Mannix's arms when the ship rolled.

"You okay?" enquired Mannix.

Laura nodded. "I am, thanks, and glad to be off that island." She knelt beside her grimacing husband. "What hurts, hon?"

Ray looked at her. "Every damn thing but especially my ankle." He glanced up the length of dangling rope. He had done it. He was free of the island.

Laura grabbed his arm. "You'll survive, dear."

Ray knew he would.

"He might, but I'm not so sure the others will," said Mannix.

Those on deck looked up at the rats swarming over the arm.

Laura wished she had her rifle. "Mannix, give me a hand here. He's hurt his ankle."

Mannix helped Laura lift Ray onto his feet.

"Let's get him below deck where he'll be more comfortable," said a crewman, offering to bear the man's weight.

Laura swopped places with the crewman and gave her husband a quick kiss. "I'll join you shortly."

Supporting Ray between them, Mannix and the crewman headed below deck. Laura glanced around at the rifles the crew held. None were even remotely a match for her hunting rifle. She crossed to the nearest man. "I need your rifle."

The man handed it to her. "You're welcome to it. I can't hit a thing with it."

Wendy gazed up at the top of the rope and then along the arm. There was no sign of Baloc or the others. She hoped they were all right.

Laura planted her feet apart and aimed the rifle at a rat near the rope. While her body rolled and pitched with the ship's erratic movements, her sight on the rat barely wavered. She pulled the trigger. The rat dropped into the ocean. She cocked the bolt action rifle, feeding a fresh bullet into the chamber and winced at its gritty stiffness, a hint that it hadn't been maintained regularly. She aimed and fired. Another rat died.

Baloc halted when a bullet shot through the sleeve, ricocheted off the beam he stood on and passed out the other side. When a second shot rang out, he glanced behind. Shaw, Gunner and Harvey had almost reached him.

When a rat lunged for Shaw's hand, he grabbed it by the scruff of its neck and slammed it into a beam, crushing its head. He glanced at Baloc as he threw the rat back along the sleeve for its comrades to eat.

“Bullets are the least of your worry, Baloc. Move!”

Flinching from the bullets that picked off rats outside, Baloc headed for the rope and, without hesitating, grabbed it and swung through the gap.

Gunner used his knife to stab at the nearest rats making indents in the cloth above him and gazed ahead. Only a few more yards, and he would be safe. A ripping sound above him tilted his head at the rat clawing at the cloth. Before he had chance to stab it, it dropped through and landed on his shoulder. Its vicious incisors tore through his ear as he plunged the knife in it. The force sent it through the rat and the tip into his shoulder. Grimacing from the pain, he slid the blade out and the rat slid off.

When another rat dropped through the hole, Harvey grabbed it by the tail before it landed on Gunner's head and slammed it into the metal framework, snapping its neck.

"If you two have finished playing with the rodents, I suggest you head for the rope and start climbing," called out Shaw, slicing at rats with his own knife.

Gunner reached the rope, grabbed it and glanced down at Baloc almost at the bottom and the ship thrown about by the waves. He climbed out, wrapped an ankle around the rope and slid down.

Two rats running along the arm leapt at the escaping food. A bullet Laura fired smashed through the incisors of one rat before passing through its brain. The other landed on Gunner's back and gripped on.

Gunner almost relinquished his grip when the rat struck and dug its claws in. Aware there was nothing he could do until he reached the boat, he gritted his teeth and looked down. Baloc dropped onto the deck and stumbled to his knees. Gunner arched his back when his unwelcome passenger dragged its incisors down his back, ripping material and flesh.

On smelling blood, the rat worked its teeth furiously against its victim's flesh, scraping backbone when it bit off a morsel.

The pain was almost too much for Gunner. He felt his hold on the rope weakening.

Laura stepped back with the rifle aimed above until she had a half decent view of the rat on Gunner's back. With the movement of the ship, it would be a risky shot, but with the rat eating the man's flesh, it wouldn't be long before he fell. She pulled the trigger. The bullet entered the rat's rump and shot it to the side.

As it dropped, the wounded rat clawed air in its eagerness to return to its feast.

Gunner felt the rat's rapid departure, but it was too late. Pain and his weakened grip sent him speeding towards the ship just as a wave slammed into the ship's hull, skewing it to the side. Adrenalin and fear stretched his arms at the ship's rail speeding by. He screamed when an arm was pulled from its socket by the sudden halt and screamed again when Baloc grabbed the arm as he slipped.

A crewman rushed forward to help Baloc and grabbed Gunner's other arm. Together they pulled the screaming man over the rail. Gunner was unconscious before he hit the deck.

Hoping his descent would go smoother, Harvey began his climb.

Shaw thrust, sliced and stabbed at the rats all around him, giving Harvey a chance to escape. Shrieks and blood filled the air. He grabbed the rat that had latched its teeth onto his leg and threw it through a rip in the sleeve. The rat that jumped onto his arm was smashed against a beam. He glanced at the wave of rats coming at him from all directions now and knew he would never have time to climb out onto the rope. He stabbed a rat in the eye, another in the belly when it leapt at his face and threw his knife at one by the rope, before diving through the sleeve.

The eyes of everyone on deck were focused on the man climbing down and the rats pouring into the sleeve by the rope.

Laura lowered the rifle. She had done all she could. Shaw couldn't have survived the rodents' final attack; there were just too many.

Baloc hadn't lost faith in his head of security and willed the man to survive. *Come on, Shaw. You can get through this.*

All on board were shocked when Shaw dived out of the sleeve, and rats leapt off the arm after him like lemmings off a cliff. Shaw's hands reached for the rope the wind kept from his grasp.

Laura rushed to Harvey when he landed on deck. "We need to grab the rope." Without explaining more, she jumped on his back and climbed up until her legs straddled his shoulders.

Harvey glanced up, saw Shaw falling and guessed Laura's attention. He rushed for the rope.

Laura stretched for the wind-whipped rope and grabbed hold. "Got it!" she shouted.

With his gaze fixed on Shaw and his hands gripping Laura's legs, Harvey dragged the rope along the ship.

Shaw stared at the rope out of reach and was cursing Mother Nature's fickle games, when miraculously, the rope drew nearer. He grabbed hold as soon as it was within reach. His skin burned when he gripped it to halt his fall. Only when he wrapped a leg around the writhing rope did his speed reduce. He almost lost his grip when rats thudded into him. Claws swiped at his face and body as they tried to latch on; most were unsuccessful and fell. One landed on his leg, leaving gouges in his skin and immediately scrambled up towards his face. Another landed on his head but slid down onto his shoulder. Shaw grabbed its neck in his teeth and tossed it away. He spat out blood and stared into the malicious eyes of the rat climbing up his chest. Its one driving force was food. Shaw was adamant he would be one meal it wouldn't be enjoying. He grabbed it around the throat and squeezed until its neck snapped. He dropped the carcass and glanced up at the rats looking down at him. One tried to climb the rope but slipped. The wind bore it away and cast it into the sea.

The crew dispatched the injured rats that had fallen to the deck with kicks that sent them flying into the waves.

When the ship was again forced to the side, Laura, who still gripped the rope, and Harvey were dragged along the deck until she had to let go or they'd be pulled over the side.

As Shaw started his descent, he looked down at the ship no longer below him. He sighed. *If I didn't have bad luck, I wouldn't have any luck at all.*

The captain tried to bring the ship back beneath the rope, so the last man could come aboard, but a change in wind direction made that impossible. He was being blown towards the rocks. He glanced at the man on the rope and the direction of the waves washing over the rocks. He had one chance to save the man. He turned the wheel hard to port and reversed the engine.

Baloc glanced at the wheelhouse when the ship suddenly changed direction. *The captain's leaving.* He returned his gaze to Shaw who had almost reached the bottom of the rope and then at the waves crashing against the ship and the rocky base of the towering cliff. Shaw wouldn't last five minutes if he fell into the sea. He felt helpless.

From Shaw's higher view of the ship, he noticed its abrupt turn, the stern swinging around and the turbulent wash emitted by the propeller. Though he wasn't certain if it was a last-ditch ploy by the captain to save him or the grumpy old sea dog was in a desperate hurry to leave, he wasn't going to waste the only opportunity he was likely to get. He wrapped an arm around the rope and hanging from sore hands, swung his legs back and forth energetically until his efforts combined with the wind, sent him in a circular motion. His eyes never wavered from the ship's stern drawing steadily closer. He would only get one chance. If he was off target either the sea would claim him or the churning propellers would chop him into fish bait. When the boat was as near as he judged it would get, he waited until he swung towards it and released the rope.

The ship rose on a wave that tilted the ship when it began to drop. Shaw crashed into the stern and grabbed hold of the rail. Coldness shocked him, almost causing him to release grip, when the dipping vessel plunged his lower half into the sea.

Baloc and Harvey rushed across the sloping deck and almost pitched over the side in their enthusiasm to save Shaw. They grabbed his arms as the ship began to tilt in the opposite direction and dragged him over the rail.

The captain turned his gaze away from Shaw's awkward boarding and thrust the power lever into full speed ahead.

The old engine vibrated, rattled and groaned in protest when it was abruptly forced to change direction. It settled to a noisy, thumping hum when it succeeded in turning the prop shaft in the opposite direction and propelled the ship forward through the rough sea.

Thankful to at last be leaving the island to which he would never return, the captain headed back to port.

Shaw—battered, bruised and grateful to be alive—was helped to his feet. He looked back at the island he was relieved to be off and noticed movement on the top of the cliff. The spider-hybrid rested atop the giant skull and watched them. Wondering why it hadn't attacked them again, he turned to Baloc. "Did everyone make it?"

"Just about. Ray's a bit battered but recovering. Gunner suffered a twisted ankle, a dislocated shoulder and a few nasty rat bites, but he'll survive." Baloc noticed Shaw's raw and blistered palms. "You had better get them seen to."

Shaw looked at his hands. "I guess so."

"I'm glad you made it, sir," said Harvey. "A temporary first aid station has been set up in the galley."

Shaw nodded. Remembering those who had been lost, he cursed the damn island and its vicious inhabitants and headed below deck to get his wounds tended to.

The rest of the survivors on the deck stared back at the island as the ship ploughed into the swirling mist, shrouding it from their sight but not their thoughts.

The spider creature watched the ship disappear into the fog. Her queen's plan, though not without casualties, had worked. Their kind would thrive in the new lands to which the humans unwittingly carried her. It turned to look at the eggs now in her care. Soon, a new batch of offspring would emerge, and new creatures would be needed to furnish them with hosts. Her gaze wandered over the island and ended on the distant mountains. Perhaps it was time to find out what lay on the far side of the inhospitable mountains. The spider creature climbed down from the skull and headed for the lair that was now hers.

CHAPTER 37

Kill my Husband

Dressed in one of the crew's spare set of clothing that hung loosely on her malnourished frame, Susan sat huddled on one of the bench seats around the long table. She found it hard to believe her long ordeal was over, and she was off the island. Sadness swept over her when she remembered her friends who had not been so lucky. Assurances had been given that as soon as they reached port, arrangements would be made for her to contact her parents. Tears seeped down her cheeks at what they had been through and the thought of their reconciliation. She took another bite of the sandwich one of the crew had made her as she watched Laura tend to her husband.

Laura glanced at the sleeping form of Gunner sprawled on the bench seat as she removed her husband's sodden jacket and dropped it to the floor. His shirt was next. He groaned from his aches and bruises when she pulled it over her head. As she grabbed a towel from the pile one of the crew had placed on the table, she noticed the look of dread on Susan's face.

Susan stared at Ray's back. Sobbing with terror, she pressed back into the seat. Slowly she raised an accusing trembling finger and shakily said, "It's inside him!"

Puzzled by the girl's strange action, Laura followed the direction of Susan's trembling arm and looked at her husband's back. When something beneath his skin squirmed, she recoiled in horror, sending a line of hanging pans clanging against each other and knocking one to the floor when she came to a halt against the serving counter. Her husband smiled at her oddly.

Susan dropped the sandwich and clasped her hands to her head when the familiar voice of her captor trespassed upon her thoughts, attempting to silence her.

Laura looked at Susan. "What in god's name is it?"

Susan pushed away the voice and looked at Laura. "The Queen—it's inside him."

"Queen, what queen?"

"Something alien. I had one of her offspring inside me, but it's gone now." Susan glanced at Ray before averting her eyes. "The Queen wanted to get her species off the island, so they could spread to other lands, and she's used your husband to do that. She's inside him now."

Unable to comprehend what had happened, Laura turned back to her husband and moved beside him. She needed to find out exactly what he had inside him. She ran a hand along the lump that wriggled under her touch. It seemed to be wrapped around his spine now. It had to be a species of parasite. She glanced along the corridor when footsteps sounded. It was Shaw.

"Sorry," said Ray.

Wondering what he was sorry for, Laura looked back at her husband. His face and eyes were absent emotion. Movement cast her eyes down at the scissors he had taken from the first aid box on the table. He thrust them at her stomach. She groaned when they entered her flesh.

Susan sobbed and hugged her knees.

Shaw entered the galley, looked at Susan sobbing and trembling, the bloodied scissors Ray pulled from his wife's stomach and then shot backwards when Ray kicked him in the gut. Laura fell to her knees, holding a hand to her wound, a shocked expression on her face that her husband could do such a thing.

Ray, his will no longer his own and oblivious of the pain from his twisted ankle, grabbed his wife's hair as he stood, pulled back her head and placed the point of the scissors against her throat. "Come…near me…and she…dies."

Confused by the unexpected events, Shaw slowly climbed to his feet. "What in hell's name is happening here? Ray, put down the scissors."

Ignoring him, Ray glanced around the room, as if deciding his next move.

"He's not Ray," stated Susan. "There's something inside, controlling him. The same thing that controlled the spider creature."

Ray pressed the point harder against Laura's neck, pricking the skin. "Quiet."

Shaw was now even more confused. He looked at Ray as he worked out if he could reach and disarm him before Laura was killed. He doubted he could. When Ray turned slightly and gazed along the corridor, he noticed two things, the bulging skin on his back that made him realize Susan had told the truth, and Laura's hand reaching for the cooking pot on the floor by her leg.

Shaw tried to distract Ray, or more specifically, the thing inside him. "What is it you want?"

Ray looked at him blankly.

Shaw continued. "I assume you want the same as us, to survive and reach the mainland safely."

"I want...that," communicated the parasite through Ray.

"Good," said Shaw. "I can help you achieve that." He swept an arm around the galley. "Only us three know about you, but if you kill Laura, the others will get suspicious. The other men here are armed and will kill your host, Ray, and throw his body into the sea. You will die."

"I...kill...all!"

Shaw noticed Laura's fingers curl around the pot handle. "No, that won't work. The ship, this vessel you are on, needs many people to keep it moving. If you kill us, the ship will never reach land. It will sink, and you will die."

"I must...not...die."

"Then let me help you."

Gunner groaned as he came to, distracting Ray.

Laura grabbed Ray's wrist, pulled the scissors away from her throat and swung the pot over her head. The base of the pot struck Ray a glancing blow on the side of his head. Laura twisted out of his grip, tugging her hair painfully from his grasp and pushed him away. Ray fell onto the seat as Shaw rushed forward to help. He yanked the scissors from the man's grasp, threw them to the floor and slammed a fist into his jaw. Ray brought up a knee into Shaw's stomach, winding him, then grabbed Shaw's head and smashed it into the table. Susan screamed. Shaw instinctively reached for his knife that wasn't there. Unable to reach her husband, Laura thrust the pot handle into Shaw's hand. Shaw grasped it and swung it hard at Ray's head. The pot struck his forehead. His eyes glazed as dizziness overcame him. A second blow to the head knocked him unconscious.

To make sure the man was incapacitated, Shaw raised the pot for a third blow.

Laura grabbed his arm. "That's enough, Shaw! He is still my husband."

Shaw climbed off and dropped the pot on the table. His hands, skinned and raw, hurt like hell and his head throbbed. "Now what do we do with him?"

Hatred towards the thing inside her husband focused Laura's thoughts when she stared at Ray. "We get my husband back."

With eyebrows raised high, Shaw looked at her. "And how do you plan to do that?"

"By getting that thing out of him and killing it."

"My question still stands," said Shaw.

"The thing needs a living host to survive, so we take that away." She looked at Shaw. "We kill my husband!"

CHAPTER 38

Parasite

Gathered in the ship's galley, the team discussed Laura's plan to remove the parasite from her husband.

"You're certain that will work?" asked Mannix, skeptically.

Laura pulled her top down over the bandage the crewman had fastened over the knife wound after cleaning and stitching the cut. Luckily the blade hadn't pierced any vital organs. She glanced at her husband on the seat opposite. His hands and feet tied to prevent the parasite controlling him from hurting anyone else.

"I'm not certain of anything anymore, but in theory it should work without causing Ray any serious injury."

Mannix rubbed a hand over his chin stubble worriedly. "So, to reiterate, we put Ray in the chest freezer, and when his core temperature drops, you believe the parasite will leave his body in search of a warmer host."

Laura nodded. "When it does, we catch it in a net, put it in the microwave and cook the queen bitch."

"Won't he freeze to death?" asked Harvey. "I mean, you put meat in a freezer to freeze it, and the human body is basically a lump of meat."

"Joints of meat you freeze aren't alive," argued Laura.

"I did some brief research on cold climate effects on the body for a book I wrote partly set in the Artic," said Baloc. "From what I can remember, hypothermia is probably our biggest concern. Normal core body temperature is 98.6 degrees Fahrenheit, and mild hypothermia sets in at about 95 degrees. After that, bad things can happen to the body. It would be safer if Ray was conscious, so we could monitor his condition and vital signs accurately. To counteract the effects of hypothermia he's bound to suffer, we'll need to warm him up slowly with blankets, warm sweet drinks and be ready to administer CPR if required. We should be able to guard against frostbite on his extremities with socks, gloves and a balaclava to protect his face, but because we need to keep his torso exposed to drop his core temperature quickly, we'll have to hope the parasite recognizes the danger quickly enough to leave before Ray suffers any severe damage."

"I'm curious as to how the thing will leave Ray's body?" asked Shaw, his bandaged hands folded across his chest.

Laura turned to Susan, who stared warily at Ray. "How did the parasite leave you?"

Susan shrugged. "I was asleep. Though I did have a sore throat when I woke up."

"You think it left through your mouth?" pushed Laura.

Susan cringed at the thought. "I can't see how else it could have."

"That's good," said Laura, turning to the crewman who had just entered.

Juan held out the piece of net he had cut from a larger one. "Will this do? It's the smallest weave we have."

Mannix took the net and examined it. His middle finger would just fit through the gaps if he pushed. "It depends how fat and supple the parasite is."

"I'm sure it will be fine," said Laura. "We can double it up to make sure, and we only need to confine it for a few seconds."

Baloc looked at Ray when he shifted in the seat. "Then I suggest we do this before he wakes up."

"Juan, do you have some warm socks, gloves and a balaclava we can borrow?" asked Wendy.

The confused crewman pointed across the galley at the corridor. "Our quarters are along there. Help yourself to anything you need."

Wendy smiled at the helpful man. "Thanks, Juan."

Everyone grabbed something to support themselves against a series of rolls that clanged saucepans against each other and shifted crockery.

"I'd better get back on deck," stated Juan. "If you need anything else, send someone to fetch me."

As Juan left, Wendy nipped along the corridor and returned with two pairs of thick socks, gloves and two balaclavas.

Just as they had finished dressing Ray in the warm accessories and retied his hands and feet, he began to stir. His eyes flicked open and roamed over the group as he struggled against his bindings.

"I guess he's ready," said Baloc.

"Then let's do this," said Shaw. He nodded at Harvey and glanced at Baloc. "Can you give Harvey a hand?"

Harvey pulled Ray into a sitting position and with Baloc's help lifted the man to his feet. Wendy stayed with Gunner, who still slept from the effects of painkillers, and Susan, while the others followed them into the storeroom where the chest freezer was located. The microwave, plugged into an extension cable, had been set up nearby. The pile of frozen provisions removed by the crew was stacked untidily to one side. The erratic, rolling movements of the ship made walking difficult, and prompted into motion by the list of the ship, a frozen pack of sausages broke free and slid across the floor.

Ray stared suspiciously at Harvey and Baloc when they gently lifted him into the freezer and stepped back. Sensing the sudden coldness on her host's skin, the Queen caused Ray to increase his efforts to free his hands and legs. Ray rolled from side to side and kicked out his legs as he tried to get free. When the Queen realized the bindings were too strong, Ray relaxed and lay still. He looked at Laura peering down at him. "Set me…free."

"Not yet, hon."

Ray raised his head as he began to shiver and glanced around the icy box he had been placed in. "What…are you…doing…to me?"

Uncertain if the parasite controlling her husband could understand the situation fully, Laura replied, "To kill the thing inside you, we have to kill you."

Ray's shivering increased, his teeth beginning to chatter. "You…must not do…this. You love…me, Laura."

"I do. That's why I must do this." Concern creased Laura's features as she closed the lid against the thin wooden wedge placed there to leave a gap to prevent Ray from suffocating.

"Now we wait," said Shaw

"How long?" asked Mannix.

Laura shrugged. "As long as it takes, I guess."

"We should check after ten minutes," said Baloc.

Shaw looked at Mannix, who held the net to catch the parasite. "If the parasite moves as fast as the island's creatures, you'll have to be quick."

Not looking forward to his role, Mannix nodded. "I'm ready. As soon as I have it in the net, I'll put it in the microwave and cook it."

"And while he's doing that," said Harvey. "Baloc and I will remove Ray from the freezer, so Laura can start warming him up."

Shaw glanced at the pile of blankets warming in front of a portable gas fire and the flask of warm hot chocolate ready to administer to Ray. He turned to the microwave, its door wide open to receive the parasite. Though all expected the creature to explode and die when its insides boiled, they were unaware of its physiology and had no idea if that would be the end of it; maybe the parasite had parasites that might survive the ordeal. His gaze around the provision laden shelves of the storeroom picked out a roll of silver duct tape. He walked over, picked it up in fingers protruding from a bandaged palm and dropped it on the microwave. "Mannix, when you've cooked the thing, seal the door with the tape and toss it overboard."

Mannix, as keen as them all to see an end to the controlling parasite, nodded.

Baloc looked at his watch. "That's ten minutes."

When the Queen experienced the rapid cooling and the weakening strength of her host, she detached her tentacles from the human's brainstem. It was imperative she find a new host or at the very least somewhere warm to rethink her strategy now the humans knew of her presence aboard their vessel.

Laura raised the freezer lid. Her husband's skin was pale, his eyes closed. He lay still and looked dead. Laura felt for a pulse, his skin icy cold, like a corpse. She detected a faint rhythm.

"What do you think?" asked Shaw. "Is he cold enough?"

Laura looked at her husband's throat for signs the parasite was making its way out but saw none. "It doesn't seem so."

Baloc place a hand on various parts of Ray's exposed skin. "His core temperature has dropped. Whether it's low enough to encourage the thing inside him to leave is impossible to say, but it's a safe bet he's suffering the early effects of hypothermia."

"Let's play it safe and assume the thing has noticed the danger and is thinking of moving on," said Shaw, turning to Mannix. "Get ready with the net."

Mannix moved into position by Ray's head and held the net ready to capture the parasite when it emerged from Ray's mouth.

While everyone focused on Ray's face, Laura worried that if they didn't get her husband out of the freezer and warmed up soon, he might never recover.

The Queen placed its round teeth-lined mouth against her host's flesh and gnawed her way through. She slithered through the hole and flopped onto the icy surface. The heat was immediately drawn from her small body. She climbed onto her ex-host's chest and gazed around at the humans. Unable to resist the opportunity of a new host to rewarm her body, she leapt at the nearest.

Laura screamed and staggered back when something landed on her shoulder. She turned her head as the bloodied parasite darted for her mouth.

Harvey reacted quickly to Laura's scream. He grabbed the parasite by the tail and flung it across the room when it curled its chomping teeth towards his hand.

Shaw took control. "Baloc, Mannix, get Ray to the galley." He looked at Laura, who looked shaken by her recent experience. "Snap out of it, Laura."

Laura nodded as she grabbed a warmed blanket from the pile ready to wrap around her husband as soon as he was out of the freezer.

Shaw took the net from Mannix. "Harvey, you're with me."

The Queen's flight ended when she smashed into tins and packets of food on the shelves. As some tins fell and rolled across the floor, she gazed at the two humans heading towards her. To survive the journey and reach other lands the humans occupied, she needed a less informed host now these were alert to her behaviors. It didn't have to be human; an animal would suffice until she was off the ship. However, first she had to escape from the room. She slunk back along the shelf.

When Baloc and Mannix lifted her husband from the freezer, Laura noticed the fresh wound in his side that would need attention. She slung a blanket over him and scooping up the rest and grabbing the flask, she followed them into the galley.

Harvey nipped back and closed the door behind them to prevent the parasite from escaping.

Food tins rolled across the floor with the listing of the ship as the men moved cautiously nearer the shelves where they had last seen the parasite. Harvey drew his knife and used it to swipe packets and tins onto the floor. There was no sign of the creature.

Shaw's eyes roamed the shelf unit when he moved closer. His gaze darted to the box of cereal that fell on to its side and spilled its contents on to the floor. He glimpsed a pale form scurrying behind a sack of coffee beans in the corner. His glance at Harvey revealed him focused on the sack. "Move the sack, and I'll be ready to catch it in the net."

Harvey moved to the sack, grabbed a corner and dragged it off the shelf.

As it fell to the floor, Shaw lunged in with the net, but the corner was clear.

A tin wobbled. A packet crunched on a higher shelf.

Shaw glanced at the air vent above the top shelf. It was trying to escape. It was so small that if it got free on the ship it would be impossible to find. He draped the net over a shoulder and winced when his bandaged hands gripped a shelf support. "Harvey, give me a hand."

Harvey grabbed hold of the shelf unit and together they yanked it free of its fixings and dodged back when it tipped to the floor. Amongst the clattering, rolling cans, burst open dry food packets and a cloud of flour that sprayed across the room, they glimpsed the squealing parasite trapped under the edge of a shelf.

In his haste to reach the creature and kill it with his knife before it pulled free, Harvey slipped on a spilt bag of spaghetti and fell. He landed with his face half an arm's length from the trapped parasite. He lashed out with the knife when it bared its teeth at him. The sharp blade sliced through the creature. Creamy pus frothed from both severed halves as they flopped to the floor and lay still. Harvey relaxed and turned his head at Shaw kicking tins aside as he moved in with the net. "It's okay, it's dead."

Shaw glimpsed movement. "Lookout!" He threw the net.

Harvey's head spun back at the parasite. It was very much alive and flying towards his face, its circle of teeth chomping back and forth savagely. Harvey jerked his head away.

The net struck the parasite and shot it to the side.

"Grab it!" shouted Shaw.

Harvey scrambled to his feet, smashing a knee painfully against the shelf unit in the process. Two awkward steps through the food clutter brought him within reach of the parasite wriggling to free itself from the net. He scooped it up and wrapped the excess around the squirming creature. He turned with the bundle held out. "I got it."

"Grab the other half, and we'll cook them in the microwave," ordered Shaw.

When Harvey reached the spot where the tail end of the creature had been trapped, it wasn't there. He jerked the arm gripping the net when pain shot through his hand. He looked at the source and was shocked to see the severed tail end had grown a head. He screamed when its razor-sharp teeth gnawed a hole through the back of his hand and exited from his palm. When the net-wrapped bundle fell to the floor, the blood-covered parasite leapt onto it and started chewing through the strands.

Shaw, who had crossed to the microwave to check it was on and ready to cook the creature, turned when Harvey screamed. He saw the net fall from Harvey's grip and the blood pouring from the hole in the man's hand. He rushed over, barged Harvey aside and focused on the second parasite chewing through the net. He raised a boot and brought it crashing down. Though both parasite halves suffered from the aggressive blow and leaked more pus, both still wriggled. Shaw scooped up the messy bundle and rushed back to the microwave. The head of the tail end parasite, paused its chewing on the net to free its other half and strained its teeth-gnashing mouth towards Shaw's bandaged hand. Its head ripped free from its squashed, pus-splattered body and squirmed along the net.

Shaw shook his head in disgust at the head wriggling awkwardly towards his hand. "You have got to be kidding me." He slammed the net and the multiple parasite parts into the microwave and slammed the door, initiating the cooking cycle.

Clutching his wounded hand, Harvey joined Shaw watching the parasites and net revolve on the turntable. The head abomination leapt at the glass door, and failing to get a grip on the smooth surface, slid down. Bubbles erupted and pulsed over its vile form before it exploded and splatted the door with pus and innards.

Shaw looked at Harvey's hand. "Go get that seen to while I finish up here."

Harvey nodded and left the room.

When the microwave pinged, ending its gruesome cooking cycle, Shaw yanked out the plug, wrapped duct tape around the door to hold it shut and carried it from the room.

"It's dead then?" said Baloc, looking at the messy door of the microwave Shaw held.

"One would hope so," Shaw replied, glancing at Harvey having his hand attended to by Wendy. "I'll throw it overboard to make sure."

He looked at Ray. He still looked pale but was conscious and wrapped in blankets sipping a warm drink. “How you doing, Ray?”

“Better, I think.” He glanced at Laura guiltily. “And still shocked I stabbed my wife.”

Laura reached out a hand and squeezed his leg reassuringly. “For the tenth time, hon, it wasn’t your fault.”

“Well, thank goodness it’s all over,” said Mannix. “We’ll soon reach port and then we can, in part, put this nightmare behind us.”

Shaw, who doubted it would be so easy, went on deck and lobbed the microwave into the sea. It bobbed on the waves for a few moments before sinking into the ocean’s cold, dark depths.

CHAPTER 39

It's Over

Quincy, Winslow and Vince, thankful to have survived their hazardous helicopter ride through the storm, had rushed to the port when they had been notified of the ship's imminent arrival. As soon as the vessel had docked, the injured were taken to hospital and patched up so they were well enough to travel back to England on the private jet Baloc had chartered.

Susan had contacted her parents to let them know she was alive. At first shocked by the unbelievable news, they soon became overjoyed and tearful that their precious daughter they thought dead was alive. Arrangements were made to meet for a no doubt tearful reunion at Heathrow airport.

When all were comfortably seated on the private jet's plush comfy seats, the aircraft taxied to the runway and took off.

"Well, Zane, I guess it's no surprise what the plot of your Horror Island book will be after what we've all been through. You've certainly got enough material," said Winslow after he, Quincy and Vince had been brought up to date with the events that had happened after they had departed on the helicopter.

Baloc nodded. "It's not the book I envisioned, but with a few embellishments to add a bit more excitement to the story, I think my fans will enjoy it."

"Add more excitement!" exclaimed Wendy. "I thought there was plenty for a couple of novels, and you want to spice it up even more?"

"I know my fans. They expect a bit of unbelievability from my stories."

"Then just write what happened," said Shaw, sipping a steaming cup of coffee. "I experienced some of it firsthand and still find it hard to believe."

"So, you are sticking to fiction," said Laura, wrapping an arm through her sleeping husband's. He was still weak, but his vital signs were good, and the Costa Rican doctors were confident he would make a full recovery.

Baloc nodded. "Who would believe what we experienced and witnessed on that island actually happened when we find it hard to believe. No, I'll stick to a novel based on true events and let my readers make up their own minds what bits are true."

"What happens to your island now?" asked Harvey, unconsciously picking at the bandage on his hand.

Baloc shrugged. "I've no idea, but I don't plan on going back any time soon, if ever."

"You could get a plane to do a fly over and spray it with some type of poison to kill the monsters," suggested Gunner, trying to resist scratching his itching skin beneath the large plasters and bandages covering his wounds.

"It's an idea, but how could we be certain all the creatures will succumb to the poison and die?" said Baloc. "The rats live below ground and might not be affected. No, I think the island is best left well alone now the gates are shut so no one can reach the shore."

"They might currently be shut," said Wendy, "but the gates closed automatically when the harsh weather arrived, so maybe they'll open when it calms, allowing access to the island again."

Baloc sighed. "Damn! Good point."

"To prevent anyone from getting on the island I'd blow up the cliffs by the harbour entrance to block it and let the monsters fend for themselves," said Mannix, all thoughts of shooting a movie there firmly banished. He'd build his own film sets somewhere a lot safer. "Surely, they'll die out eventually."

"As fun as that idea sounds, it's a bit drastic," said Shaw. "A less permanent solution would be to weld the gates shut. Then at least, if access to the island was ever needed, it would be possible."

Baloc looked at Shaw. "Now that *is* a clever solution. Is that something you can organize, Shaw? When you've recovered from this harrowing adventure, of course."

Shaw nodded. "For the right price, I can organize anything."

EPILOGUE

Four months after arriving home, Baloc's publicity machine went into overdrive when the release date of his new novel, Horror Island was announced. Baloc and other members of the team appeared on TV chat shows. The documentary Mannix had edited together from Quincy's film footage, Wendy's photographs and interviews with those who had lived through the nightmare events was shown worldwide. Short film clips of the island posted on YouTube had gone viral and Laura's photograph book had become an unexpected best seller as people craved to know more about the monsters the team had battled on Ezra Houghton's mysterious island. The movie, still in the works, was expected to be a runaway box office hit.

Susan's miraculous survival story was also to be featured in a book she was writing with publishers engaging in a furious bidding war to claim the publishing rights.

Baloc had given Ray and Laura Chase permission to air some of their GoPro island footage on their island hunt special TV show to coincide with the screening of the documentary Mannix's team had edited together. Both had received record viewers.

Though all bore scars from their encounters with the island's furious inhabitants, Ray, Shaw, Harvey and Gunner fully recovered from their ordeals.

Return to Horror Island

Hardly believing they had agreed to return, the pilot and co-pilot stared at the island that had just come into view.

Swaying on the pallet suspended below the helicopter, Shaw and Gunner gazed at the foreboding island when they passed through the mist. Both were thankful their task didn't require them to step foot ashore again.

"We're here," stated Mathias, the pilot, over the radio headsets they both wore.

Shaw glanced at Gunner sitting opposite. "You ready?"

Gunner's eyes swept the cliff top for any signs of the monsters that dwelled here, sensing they were watching them but seeing none. "Yeah, let's get this done and be gone."

Shaw spoke into the radio mic. "Position us by the gate as discussed, and we'll direct you as needed."

"Heading for the gate," confirmed Mathias.

Strapped to the sides of the specially fabricated metal pallet's steel rails was everything they needed to weld the gates closed, including a small stick welder, a compact petrol generator to power the welder, Fleetweld stick electrodes, welding helmet, gloves and lengths of one meter by twenty-centimetre steel strips.

When the helicopter slowed its approach, Gunner studied the open gates. “That’s a shame. Would have made our job easier if they were still closed.”

Shaw smiled. “So it takes us a little longer. If it was easy we wouldn’t be receiving the big bucks we’re getting.”

“At least we should be safe from the island’s critters,” said Gunner, running his eyes up the towering cliffs either side of the gap the helicopter moved through.

Shaw glanced at the assault rifle and shotgun hanging from a side rail, backup he hoped wouldn’t be required. “Not something I’m going to complain about.” He looked ahead; they were almost at the gates. “Let’s get ready.”

When they came to a swaying stop a short distance from the gates, Gunner pointed at something fixed to the top of one of the gateposts. “There’s the weather vane.”

Shaw looked at the vane while he spoke to the pilot. “Mathias, take us forward two feet and right a foot.”

The helicopter crept forward and slightly to the right.

“Perfect,” said Shaw. “Now bring us lower until I say stop.”

Gunner stared up at the co-pilot, Emilio, leaning out the door controlling the winch.

Shaw raised a fist when the weather vane was within easy reach. “Stop!”

Gunner examined the weather vane fixing and pulled a spanner from the box of tools strapped to the rail. “That should fit.”

Shaw took the offered spanner and loosened the nut at the bottom of the vane’s spindle. Though tough to get turning, it soon loosened enough for him to use his fingers. When it cleared the thread and spun around the spindle, he lifted the vane free and passed it and the spanner to Gunner.

Shaw placed the battery powered drill Gunner handed him over the spindle tip and tightened the chuck. "If this doesn't work, we're stuffed."

Shaw pressed the trigger slightly. The spindle rotated slowly. When Shaw increased pressure on the trigger, the spindle increased in speed and whizzed around as if a strong wind turned the weather vane that was no longer attached. After a few moments, the closing mechanism kicked in. The gates juddered and slowly closed. When they clanged together, Shaw removed the drill.

"That was easier than expected."

Gunner grinned. "Not something I'm going to complain about. Let's hope the next part goes as smoothly."

While Gunner sorted and connected the welding gear, Shaw directed the pilot to move the platform over to the middle of the doors. When Gunner was all set, Shaw started the generator, switched on the welder, and donning gloves, picked up one of the metal strips and placed it over the top part of the door join. He looked away from the bright arc light when Gunner welded a few beads around the edge to secure it and stepped away while he welded it in place.

Gunner lifted the welding mask to check the weld and satisfied it was okay, they repeated the process down the door join.

"How's it going?" enquired Emilio over the radio, winching them down a few feet to reach the next segment.

Shaw glanced up at the co-pilot staring down at them. "Just welding the last strip in place. Five minutes and we're done."

Concealed behind bushes on the top of the cliff, the spider creature observed the newly arrived humans. Though she had no idea what they were doing, she was concerned by their presence; her brethren had suffered from their last encounter. She altered her gaze to the roaring flying machine as she wondered if her Queen had made it safely to the human's land. She missed her comforting presence and felt a longing to leave the island and be reunited with her Queen. The barrier the humans had closed might indicate these were the last to come here. If true, this would be her only opportunity to leave. Her inexperience and lack of authority had failed to control her offspring and had seen them attacking one another. She feared they would soon turn on her as they vied for dominance. If, like her Queen had successfully done, she could claim one of these humans as a host, the flying machine would carry her to their land and she could seek out her Queen. She slunk back away from the cliff edge and headed for the humans.

Gunner raised the welding mask and looked at Shaw. "Finished."

Shaw glanced at the last remaining metal strip. "Seems a shame to waste the last one, so how about we weld it across the join on top of the gate?"

"It can only help."

Shaw spoke into his radio mic. "Raise us to the top of the gate so we can weld a strip along the top."

"Rodger that," replied Emilio, and slowly raised their working platform.

"We'll have to leave soon as fuel level is fast approaching the point of no return," warned Mathias.

"Understood," said Shaw. "A few minutes and we're done." He raised a hand to let the co-pilot know they were in position, and he halted the winch.

Shaw placed the metal strip on the top of the thick doors and stood back while Gunner began welding.

Buffeted from the wash of rotors a short distance away as she climbed down the cliff, the spider creature's eyes flicked between the two humans in the flying machine and the two below; all four were currently unaware of her presence. When she had moved below the helicopter, she waited until the human in the opening looked away before making her move.

Mathias glanced behind at his co-pilot. "How much longer?"

Emilio looked below, saw Gunner had welded about halfway around the metal strip, and turned to the pilot. "Couple of minutes." Almost flung out the door when the helicopter abruptly listed to the side and dropped, he was spilled to the floor when the drop ended. Emilio looked at Mathias. "What the hell was that?"

The pilot cursed as he frantically regained control. "Nothing good I should imagine."

Gunner's wrist struck the edge of the gate painfully when the platform suddenly dropped.

Shaw staggered against the rail when they plummeted low enough to plunge the bottom of the platform into the sea. He grabbed at Gunner careening towards the rail when the platform swung away from the gate and then struck it on the return.

Gunner pushed the welding visor off his face, pulled off his gloves and rubbed his wrist. "What happened?" He grabbed at the rail when the platform lurched to the side.

Steadying himself against the erratic swaying, Shaw raised his head to the helicopter and saw the spider creature climbing the winch cable. Overcoming his shock, he grabbed the shotgun, but security straps held it in place. Fighting the platform's swinging motion, he knelt and began freeing the ties.

Emilio almost wet himself when the monster's legs appeared and trembled in fear when the creature entered the doorway. He stared at the human face that lowered towards his own as its cruel expression turned to pain. Blood splattered his legs when something erupted from its side and flopped to the floor. Horrified by the wriggling blood-covered maggot, he crabbed backwards until the side of the helicopter brought him to a halt. The maggot monstrosity left a bloody trail when it squirmed towards him with its head raised like a snake. He screamed when it leapt onto his stomach and crawled up his chest.

With her mind now free of the controlling parasite, Penny looked at the man the alien organism attacked. Confused by what was happening, she looked at her torso and what it was attached to, the pulsating eggs with foul things moving within and the large spiders crawling over her grotesque abdomen. When the man screamed, she looked at him and lashed out a spider limb awkwardly at the alien organism crawling towards his mouth. The parasite flew towards the front of the helicopter and struck the canopy. She stared at the man gazing fearfully back at her. "Help me."

Mathias jumped when the strange worm struck the screen. "What the hell's going on back there?" asked Mathias as he again brought the helicopter back under control. He looked behind when Emilio screamed, and froze at the sight of the monster in the doorway. Recovering from the shock, he tipped the helicopter to the side to try to spill the spider creature out the door.

When the helicopter tilted sharply, Emilio shot forward and crashed into the creature. A spider limb scrambling for purchase on the metal floor knocked him back against the far side. Unable to prevent her slide, Penny slid out the door. She screamed when a shot rang out and shotgun pellets peppered her spider body and the fuselage. Some of the spiders on her back leapt into the helicopter to escape the blast. Tears appeared in Penny's eyes when she dropped over the edge.

Emilio turned his attention to the large spiders that scampered towards him. He squashed one with a squelching slap and knocked another through the door before one leapt onto his neck and dug in its fangs. The drowsy effects of the venom it pumped into his bloodstream had an immediate effect. His body went limp. His terrified gaze watched the spiders crawl over him, pumping more poison into his veins. They then began wrapping him in silky strands to feast on later. He tried to scream, but his mouth refused to comply.

Shaw freed the shotgun, stood, aimed it at the rear of the spider creature's abdomen protruding from the helicopter door and fired. Blood, flesh, eggs and small spider parts sprayed out from the blast and rained down on the men below. A second shot rang out as the spider fell.

Gunner stared at the wounded creature falling towards them as he stood. "Oh, man, this ain't good."

Shaw was thinking the same thing.

They backed to the far edges of the pallet when the spider creature struck, tilting the platform precariously. Shaw shot forward and bent over the rail stared into the sad eyes of the young girl's face. Gunner, one hand gripping the far railing, grabbed Shaw's arm and pulled him back. Holding on tightly to the raised side of the slanting, swaying platform, they watched the spider haul her bleeding body up the side.

With two limbs hooked over the rail, it looked at them. Her tear-filled eyes flicked to the shotgun Shaw held in one hand. "Kill me," she sobbed.

With thoughts of his daughter in the back of his mind, Shaw raised the shotgun at her chest but found it hard to pull the trigger. He couldn't imagine what horrors the girl had been through and was still experiencing. In an effort to bring the final moments of her short life some comfort, he said, "Susan survived and is safe."

A smile appeared within her sadness.

"I'm sorry." Shaw pulled the trigger.

A sigh escaped Penny's lips as she slid off the railing and dropped into the ocean.

Expertly manipulating the controls to compensate for the awkward weight dragging the spinning helicopter lower while trying to keep it from smashing into the cliffs that were too close for comfort on either side, Mathias fed it more power. The helicopter shot up when the weight he had compensated for suddenly vanished. His eyes flicked to the foul worm that had slid down his screen and rested on the console dash. He saw it flinch. It turned its head towards him and opened its mouth. Fine tentacles extended from around its circular teeth-lined mouth and stretched towards him. Mathias shot a glance out both sides of the canopy at the cliffs slipping by. Unable to release his hands from the controls until they were clear, he leaned nearer the side window and gazed up. The top of the cliff was only a short distance away. He turned back to the foul maggot and watched it crawl nearer.

Please, God, just a few more seconds.

God wasn't listening.

The parasite leapt at his face.

Mathias shook his head to try and free it.

The parasite moved across his cheek, forced its tentacles past his lips and slithered down his throat.

Gagging, Mathias released one hand from the controls and grabbed at the parasite's putrid tail squirming into his mouth and tried to tug it free.

The parasite latched its tentacles onto the human's throat and dragged itself deeper.

Battered by the rotors wash and with their anxious gazes fixed upon the whining helicopter, Shaw and Gunner gripped the side rails when they shot into the air. Generator, welder and tools skidded across the platform when it crashed against the cliff and was dragged up, jolting the worried men holding on tightly.

"What do we do?" shouted Gunner.

"Hang on!" replied Shaw.

Rotor tips shredded overhanging bushes when the helicopter rose above the cliff and drifted to the side. Foliage they were dragged through whipped at them until the rising helicopter lifted them free. They spun in a gradually widening circle as the spinning, tilting helicopter carried them across the island.

Pondering the merits of leaping from the platform before the helicopter crashed or they were dashed against the ground or into a tree, Shaw glanced over the side. The ground whizzing past twenty yards below didn't inspire a broken-limb-free landing.

Glimpsing movement along the edge of the forest, he picked out things running through the trees. Stag creatures and smaller tapir-fox malformed beasts bounded from the forest and followed their flight path. Even if they jumped and avoided injury, they wouldn't be able to outrun the creatures. He thrust the shotgun into Gunner's hand, and regretting they hadn't brought more ammo, untied the assault rifle.

Choking, the pilot's frantic tug slipped from the slimy parasite, leaving it free to slither down his throat. He gasped down raspy breaths when the organism slipped free of his oesophagus and entered his stomach. Ignoring his churning gut and the danger the parasite presented, he gripped the controls with both hands and deftly worked the pedals until he had the helicopter flying straight and level. When he glanced behind at Emilio, he was shocked to find spiders twice the size of tarantulas cocooning his friend in web wrappings. He turned away and gazed below for somewhere to land, which wouldn't be easy with the payload hanging below. He flew past the village on his left and steered for the level ground in front of the large mansion.

One of the spiders broke from the cocooning group and scurried towards the remaining human. Unaware of the danger its actions would place it and its brethren in, it leapt onto the back of the pilot's chair and pierced the human's neck with its fangs.

Letting out a gasp, Mathias instinctively slapped at the pain.

The spider dodged the hand, jumped onto the human's cheek and pumped more venom into his skin. The scent of assault alerted the other arachnids to the fresh victim. They surged forward and attacked.

Mathias screamed when the spiders crawled over him and dug in their fangs and pumped poison into his veins. He grabbed at their foul bodies and flung them away, but they quickly crawled back. When he squeezed one in his hand until it burst, its comrades increased their attack. His limbs went limp. His body relaxed. The unmanned controls jerked wildly as the helicopter spun along an erratic flight path. The pilot gazed out the screen at the mansion speedily filling his view. *It would soon be over.*

Shaw and Gunner looked at the out-of-control helicopter they were tethered to and then the mansion they sped towards.

Shaw shot a glance back at the following creatures. The stag monsters, large enough to cross through the stream, continued their pursuit. The smaller beasts rushed along the far bank towards the bridge that would carry them across the stream that was too deep for them to enter.

He grabbed Gunner's arm and shouted, "We have to jump."

Gunner tore his gaze away from the rapidly approaching mansion, glanced at the creatures heading their way, and nodded.

They climbed over the rail, jumped and rolled. As they climbed to their feet and aimed their weapons at the stag creatures, the helicopter crashed into the building and exploded. The whoosh of the hot blast ruffled their clothing and hair as debris rained down around them.

The stag creatures halted by the loud noise and flames, spread out in front of the men. When the fox-tapir amalgamations arrived, they joined the larger beasts staring at the humans.

Gunner roamed the shotgun over the creatures. "Now what do we do?"

Shaw locked eyes with the eyeless sockets of the larger stag that took two steps nearer. "I have no idea."

The lead stag raised its skeletal head and bellowed loudly.

The creatures rushed the men.

Shaw and Gunner started firing.

Five days later…

Strapped in a harness to prevent him from falling out, the man leaned from the helicopter rear door when it hovered over the gate. He placed binoculars to his eyes and ran his zoomed-in gaze over the welded strips of metal. Baloc looked at the back of the pilot's head when he spoke into his headset mic. "Let's head inland."

The pilot moved over the cliff, flew over the cemetery and then the village.

"You see that?" asked the co-pilot pointing through the canopy.

Baloc focused his binoculars on the partly burnt ruins of the mansion. Most of the east-wing was little more than a pile of rubble, ash and remnants of walls, and the grand staircase in the middle of the building was now open to the elements. "Let's check it out."

When Baloc had been informed the helicopter had not returned to base and they had heard nothing from Shaw or Gunner, Baloc had rushed to Costa Rica to find out what had happened and if the men needed help.

The pilot steered the helicopter over to the mansion and hovered a short distance away.

“What the…” uttered the co-pilot on seeing the large vicious rats disturbed by the helicopter’s noisy arrival fleeing from a semicircle of strange animal corpses.

Baloc didn’t need the binoculars to pick out the mangled remains of the crashed helicopter or the tilted-on-its-side work platform Shaw and Gunner had used to weld the gates closed. It didn’t bode well for their survival. He ran his gaze over the creature corpses gathered close together as if facing a single point of attack and thought it was evidence one or more of the men had survived the crash. Though he failed to pick out any human skeletons, he was certain whoever had survived to stage a last-ditch defence could not have lived through such an onslaught of savage beasts for long.

“What do you want to do, Baloc?” enquired the pilot.

Baloc gazed around below for any sign of life but found none that were human. Only the large rodents waited to resume their feasting when the noisy flying machine had gone.

“Take us back. There’s nothing we can do here.”

Baloc’s eyes continued searching the ground as the helicopter swooped around in a circle and headed back out to sea.

A man, bloodied, bruised and limping, staggered from the far side of the mansion. Breathing heavily from the exertion of rushing from his fortified position in the mansion’s basement when he had heard an engine, he gazed after the retreating helicopter. Glimpsing movement, he altered his gaze and stared at the large stag that had stepped from the forest and watched him. Shaw glanced at the village he needed to reach to access the supplies left behind when they had fled the island. He turned back to the stag creature when it crossed the stream, halted and stared at him.

Shaw altered his grip on the spear and axe he had salvaged from the armoury room and nodded at the eyeless creature. This was his island now.

Beast and human moved slowly towards each other.

When they were a short distance apart, the stag creature halted and pawed the ground with a large hoof, as if marking its domain. It let out a loud bellow and rushed at Shaw.

Shaw let out a battle cry and rushed at the stag.

Human and beast clashed.

THE END

Note from Author

Thank you for purchasing and reading my book. I hope you found it an enjoyable experience. If so, could you please spread the word and perhaps consider posting a review on your place of purchase. It is the single most powerful thing you can do for me. It raises my visibility and many more people will learn about my book.

If you would like to send feedback, drop me a line, or be added to my mailing list to receive notifications of my new books, receive limited free advance review copies, and occasional free books, send feedback or drop me a line, please contact me at:
benhammott@gmail.com

BOOKS BY AUTHOR

ICE RIFT & ICE RIFT - SALVAGE

In Antarctica everyone can hear you scream!

Something ancient dwells beneath the ice...

Humans have always looked to the stars for signs of Extraterrestrials.

They have been looking in the wrong place.

They are already here. Entombed beneath Antarctic ice for thousands of years.

The ice is melting and soon they will be free.

Sarcophagus

Their mistake wasn't finding it, it was bringing it back!

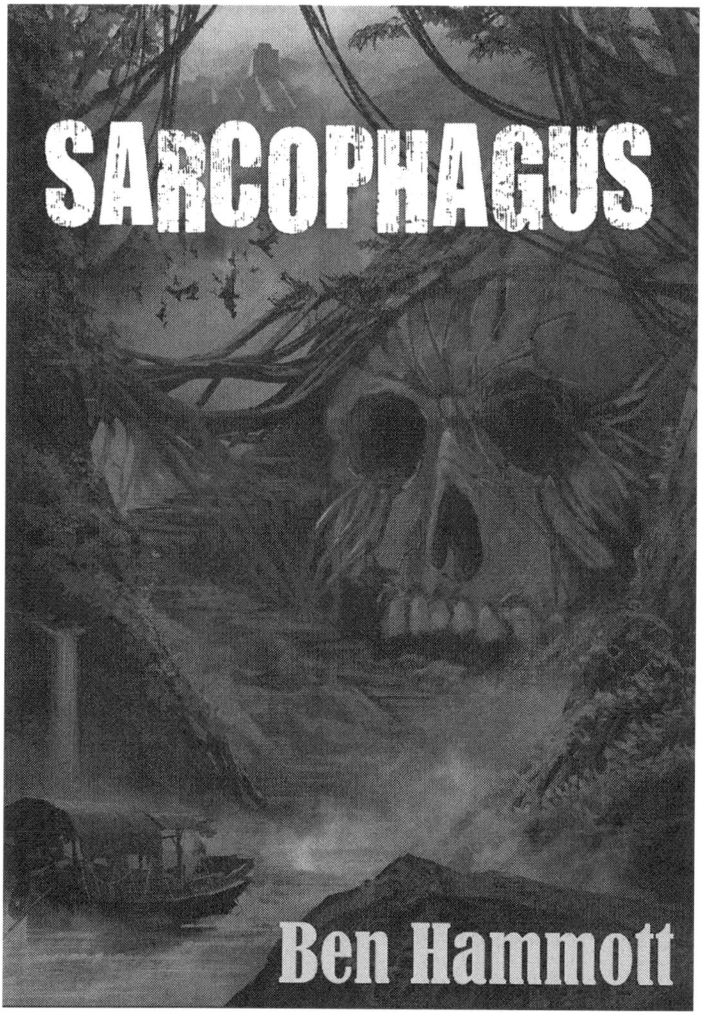

"The Mummy, meets Relic, meets Alien in this scary action driven horror thriller."

Action adventure horror set in the Amazon jungle and London, England.

Concealed in a remote area of the Amazon jungle is something the Mayans thought so dangerous they built a secret prison to entomb it. It remained undiscovered for centuries.

When a maverick archaeologist hears rumours of a mysterious lost city, he heads into the Amazon jungle, determined to find it.

He soon learns that some things are best left unfound. The dangerous past the Mayans tried so hard to bury, is about to become our terrifying future.

Extended book blurb:

When an archaeologist stumbles across a mysterious Mayan city in a remote part of the Amazon jungle, he informs the British museum funding his expedition of the discovery.

When fellow archaeologist, Greyson Bradshaw, receives news of the discovery, he jumps at the chance to travel to the Amazon jungle to collect artifacts for the forthcoming Mayan exhibition he is arranging.

The two archaeologists explore the city's subterranean levels and enter Xibalba, the Mayan underworld. In a secret chamber they discover something hidden away for centuries; a sarcophagus. Realizing its potential as a centerpiece for his exhibition, Greyson transports the sarcophagus and other artifacts back to England. The past is about to come alive.

"Hammott is fast becoming the master of monster horror. Read his Ice Rift books and you'll know what I mean. Fantastic escapism."

"The author has such a creative mind it's scary. The monsters he brings alive in his books are simply terrifying. Add atmospheric locations, characters you root for, racked up tension, a thrilling plot that forbids you to stop reading, and you have Sarcophagus."

The Lost Inheritance Mystery

A Victorian mystery adventure revolving around the search for a lost inheritance worth millions. The two rival miserly Drooge brothers, a butler, a murderous hunchback, a shadowy assassin, a fashion senseless burglar, a beast named Diablo, strange henchmen, an actor who once had a standing ovation, and many more oddball characters, all conspire in ways you couldn't possibly imagine to steal two paintings that contain clues to the long lost inheritance of Jacobus Drooge.

This is a complete standalone adventure.

Ben Hammott

SOLOMON'S TREASURE 1

BEGINNINGS: A Hunt for Treasure

and

SOLOMON'S TREASURE 2

THE PRIEST'S SECRET

(The Tomb, the Temple, the Treasure Book 1 and 2)

An ancient mystery, a lost treasure and the search for the most sought after relics in all antiquity.

The Tomb, the Temple, the Treasure series, has become an international best seller.

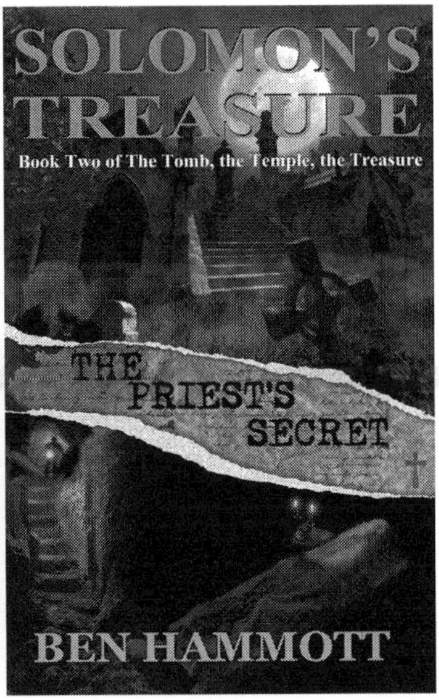

An exciting archaeological thriller spanning more than 2000 years.

Beginning with the construction of Solomon's Temple, the Fall of Jerusalem, the creation of the Copper Scrolls and the forming of the Knights Templar and their mysterious tunnelling under the Temple Mount. The story then takes us into the trap-riddled catacombs beneath Rosslyn Chapel, on to Rennes-le-Chateau, into the Tomb, Jerusalem and its secret tunnels and beyond.

The Lost City Book Series

EL DORADO Book 1: Search for the Lost City - An Unexpected Adventure

EL DORADO - Book 2: Fabled Lost Treasure - The Secret City

One of the world's most legendary and elusive treasures, sought after for centuries.

An ancient mystery

A Lost Treasure

A Hidden City

An impossible location

An unimaginable adventure

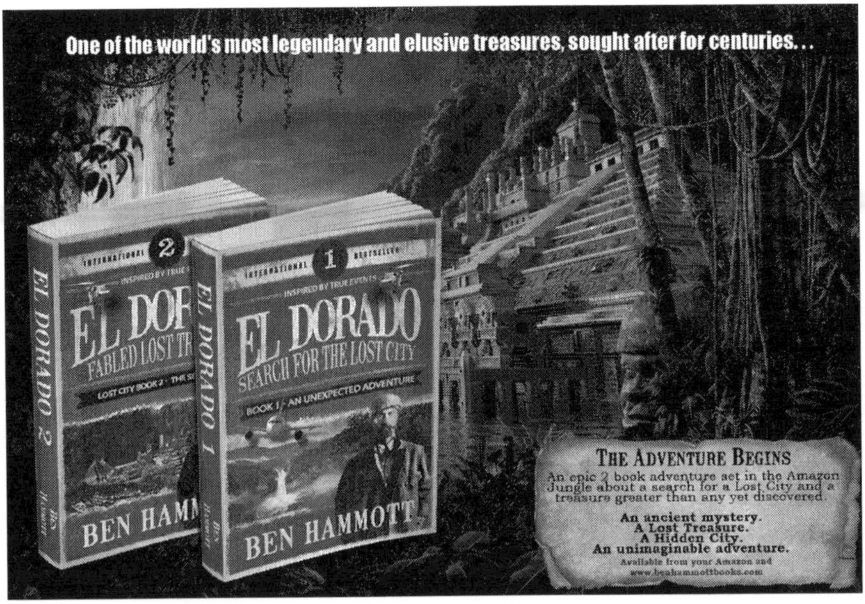

Included in Aztec and Mayan legends, Conquistadors had heard rumours of its existence when exploring the New World, but never found it.

During World War 2, Nazi inspired archaeologists were convinced they had pinpointed its location. They packed a U-Boat with supplies and set a course for the Amazon Jungle. They disappeared!

Many adventurers eager to claim the legendary gold as their own entered one of the most inhospitable places on earth, the Amazon Jungle. Most were never seen again!

And yet the exact location of El Dorado and its fantastic hoard of Mayan, Aztec and Inca treasure so many have dreamed of finding, remains a mystery. Any who may have stumbled upon it never returned to tell the tale. It was as if someone, or something, was protecting it...

An Insatiable Thirst for Murder

Serial Killer Henry Holmes

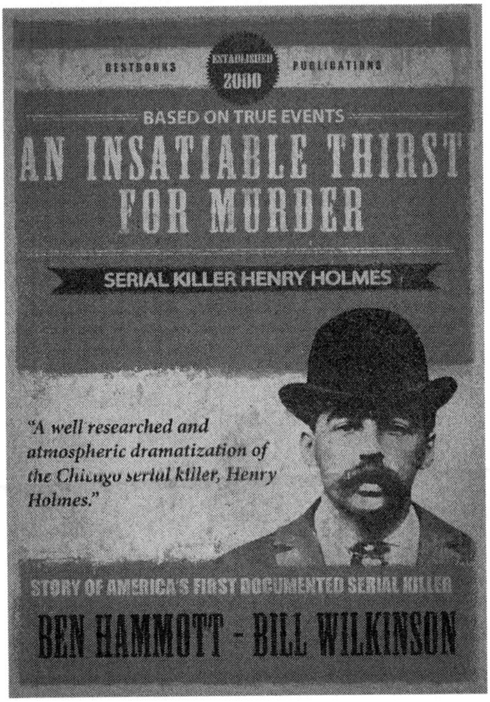

This book contains the shocking dramatization of real events carried out by the serial killer, Henry Howard Holmes.

STORY OF AMERICA'S FIRST DOCUMENTED SERIAL KILLER. (Fiction)

America's first documented serial killer, Henry Howard Holmes, holds a dubious and ghastly record that few serial killers in history have surpassed. The 19th century killer is thought to have committed over 200 murders, but, for unexplained reasons, appears to have been overlooked by many true crime enthusiasts. Set partly in the era when "Jack the Ripper" was terrorizing the foggy streets of London with his gruesome slayings in the 19th century, Holmes was committing his nefarious crimes in America, undetected.

Holmes, a handsome, well dressed gentleman with high intelligence, was a murderer and accomplished con-man. Charm and trust were his most effective weapons and he welded them as expertly as any surgeon would a scalpel.

To achieve an easy way to entrap and dispose of his intended victims, Holmes constructed a huge building that when his crimes were revealed, the newspapers of the time named the "Murder Hotel." And this is a fair description as there can be no doubt the building was constructed for the sole purpose of killing his victims and the disposal of their corpses. Though the majority of his victims were women he charmed and ensnared in his murderous grasp, he also murdered men and children.

As the trial judge said when charging the jury responsible for convicting Holmes: ***"Truth is stranger than fiction, and if Mrs. Pitezel's story is true—(and it was proven to be true)—it is the most wonderful exhibition of the power of mind over mind I have ever seen, and stranger than any novel I have ever read."***

After 2 years of research and consultation with modern day serial killer profilers, I believe this to be the most accurate dramatized account of America's first documented serial killer, H. H. Holmes.

If you hear him lock the door, you are already dead!

"Insightful thoughts of some characters during their impending death make it too easy to identify with the horror of what they experienced. By the time I got to the end of some parts, I was out of breath, literally!"

***

"Grabs your concentration by the throat with every horrific and appalling act carried out by Holmes and never lets go. The scenes are so well written that you find yourself witnessing everything as if you were there."

***

"An atmospheric dramatization of a true crime mystery using source documents and the investigations carried out by detective Frank Geyer to portray a believable and disturbing account of the heinous murders and crimes of the serial killer, Henry H. Holmes."

***

"This well researched dramatization of the Chicago serial killer, Henry Holmes, because is based on actual events, isn't something that's always easily digestible; it sits in your gut and gnaws at your insides. It becomes part of your subconscious. You think of it long after you have laid the book aside. No punches are pulled to describe the horrendous crimes carried out by this cold hearted killer."

***

"Hammott's writing is easy to read. He has a real knack for creating great descriptions of scenes, characters, and murderous action."

***

"Absorbingly horrific. As if it were a plane crash that you just can't look away from, because you're intrigued as to how and what will happen next."

"As fascinating as it is shocking."

Dead Dragons Gold - Book 1
A Gathering of Dwarfs

"This book will appeal to fans of Terry Pratchett's Discworld Sagas."

"An exciting humorous fantasy adventure which reveals what happened to the 7 dwarfs after Prince Charming had claimed Snow White as his bride."

"A dark fantasy tale interjected with humour interwoven in an original plot that will change your view of Snow White's seven dwarfs."

"If you like your fantasy stories full of originality and humour, this is the book for you and one for Pratchett fans of all ages. Highly recommended."

Not every Fairy Tale ends happily for all...

A dauntless young hero.

An impossible quest.

A Hunt for Dead Dragons Gold.

We all know Snow White lived happily ever after, but what happened to the seven dwarfs?

When their diamond mine becomes choked with the barbed roots of the thorny hedge the wicked queen erected around their land the dwarfs are forced to split up and survive using their various talents of Assassin, Thief, Bounty Hunter, Medicus, Pirate, Inventor and Priest.

After many years their lives change with the appearance of an unlikely young adventurer whose plan is to plunder the treasure hoards of the many long dead dragons. However, to achieve this he needs the foremost book on dragons containing a map depicting every location of the deceased dragons lairs. A snag in his plan is only one copy of this book exists, and it's in possession of the wicked queen who was not killed as the popular story would have everyone believe but is very much alive. Banished to the top of a lonely mountain she will only relinquish her ownership of the book if he can set her free.

All he has to do is track down thc seven dwarfs scattered across the kingdom and convince them to have the wizard lift the curse from the one they most hate. It will be a far from easy task.

For the first time, the fate of the seven dwarfs is revealed in an exciting, original story of heroic adventure, strange lands, terrifying creatures, death, dangerous deeds and dead dragons gold that takes place ten years after Snow White leaves with her not so charming prince.

A fantasy adventure about what happens when someone who isn't destined to be a hero slaps fate around the face and tries to be one anyway.

Reviews

"I enjoyed this read. It was funny, exciting action and adventurous."

***

"...had me laughing out loud, what an enjoyable read."

***

"A great twist on a well-known fairy tale."

***

"Bloody, Bawdy and Funny, it's not fairy tale for children."

Non-Fiction Books by Author

Also available is the best non-fiction account of Holmes Crimes, frauds, capture and trial:

The Hunt for H. H. Holmes and Trial of America's First Serial Killer

Holmes Pitezel Case - History of the Greatest Crime of the Century and the Search for the Missing Pitezel Children by Frank P. Geyer 1896.

(Illustrated - complete and unabridged)

4 Books in 1 Edition

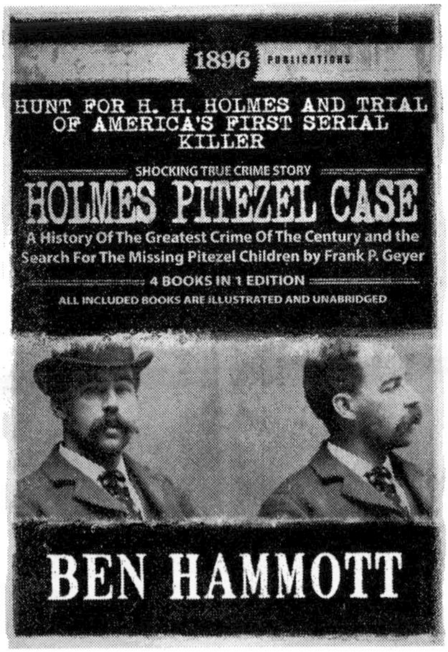

Detective Frank Geyer, the author of one of the included books, was the man responsible for bringing H. H. Holmes to justice and revealing some of his atrocious crimes.

Bonus material includes:

HOLMES CONFESSIONS With Moyamensing Prison Diary Appendix - Burk & McFetridge Co. 1895

(Illustrated - complete and unabridged)

HOLMES CONFESSES 27 MURDERS

THE MOST AWFUL STORY OF MODERN TIMES TOLD BY THE FIEND IN HUMAN SHAPE.

Every Detail of His Fearful Crimes Told by the Man Who Admits He Is Turning Into the Shape of the Devil. THE TALE OF THE GREATEST CRIMINAL IN HISTORY

Copyright, 1896 by W.R. Hearst and James Elverson, Jr. (Illustrated - complete and unabridged)

HOLMES' MURDER CASTLE

A Story of H. H. Holmes' Mysterious Work By ROBERT. L. CORBITT. COPYRIGHT, 1895 (Illustrated - complete and unabridged)

WAS HOLMES JACK THE RIPPER?

The hunt for H.H. Homes (Real Name, Herman Webster Mudgett) by Detective Frank Geyer is a fascinating read. With hardly any clues to help him, except for Holmes first confession, which Geyer believed was mostly lies, and the Pitezel's children's letters to their mother, Geyer sets off on a hunt across America on the trail of the missing children.

If it was not for Geyer's unrelenting persistence, the outcome he achieved would never have been reached.

Though it reads like a work of fiction, the Holmes murder case is real and will be enjoyed by anyone who likes a good murder mystery or detective story.

This is the complete and unabridged version of 1896 publication, **The Holmes Pitezel Case - A History Of The Greatest Crime Of The Century and the Search For The Missing Pitezel Children by Detective Geyer.**

*****